"Livy, what's going on with you?"

"Nothing." She suddenly dropped down and crawled back under her desk.

Vic, not sure how to deal with this side of Livy, walked around her desk and crouched down so he could see her.

"Do you want to go somewhere and talk?" he asked.

"Because I'm so chatty?"

"No. But I understand that after the loss of a parent—"

"We weren't close."

"As you've already said. We could still go get some coffee." He glanced at his watch. "Maybe get lunch."

"You asking me out on a date?"

Without thinking, Vic leaned back a bit. "No."

"You don't have to look so horrified."

"It's not horror. It's confusion. You're confusing me. Which," when he thought about it, "may lead to horror. But I simply don't like being confused. So the horror wasn't directed at you, so much as the confusion."

"Well, when you put it like that . . ."

Read more of Shelly Laurenston in

THE PRIDE SERIES

The Mane Event

The Beast in Him

The Mane Attraction

The Mane Squeeze

Beast Behaving Badly

Big Bad Beast

Bear Meets Girl

Howl for It

Wolf with Benefits

The Call of Crows Series

The Unleashing

The Undoing

BITE ME

THE PRIDE SERIES

SHELLY LAURENSTON

KENSINGTON PUBLISHING CORP.
http://www.kensingtonbooks.com

To the extent that the image or images on the cover of this book depict a person or persons, such person or persons are merely models, and are not intended to portray any character or characters featured in the book.

KENSINGTON BOOKS are published by

Kensington Publishing Corp.
119 West 40th Street
New York, NY 10019

All Kensington Titles, Imprints, and Distributed Lines are available at special quantity discounts for bulk purchases for sales promotions, premiums, fund-raising, and educational or institutional use. Special book excerpts or customized printings can also be created to fit specific needs. For details, write or phone the office of the Kensington special sales manager: Kensington Publishing Corp., 119 West 40th Street, New York, NY 10018, attn: Special Sales Department, Phone: 1-800-221-2647.

Kensington Books and the K logo Reg. U.S. Pat. & TM Off.

ISBN-13: 978-0-7582-6526-5
ISBN-10: 0-7582-6526-3
First Kensington Trade Edition: April 2014
First Kensington Mass Market Edition: October 2016

eISBN-13: 978-1-61773-245-4
eISBN-10: 1-61773-245-1
Kensington Electronic Edition: April 2014

10 9 8 7 6 5 4 3 2

Printed in the United States of America

Dear Reader—

As those of you who have read my books over the years know, I am against bigotry of any kind. Especially bigotry against my friends . . . the hybrid shifters.

I'm the first to say it's unfair to have prejudice against those with tusk-like fangs or snaggle-claws or excessively long legs combined with tiny paws. It's just wrong to hate those differently endowed. And, until the end of time, I will stand tall with my mutt . . . er . . . my hybrid soul siblings.

That being said, there's only so much pressure I can put on a design team. Especially the team that creates all my lovely covers. And with that in mind, I'm sure that all my loyal readers and hybrid friends will forgive the liberties taken with *Bite Me*.

Now it's true that our hero, Vic Barinov, is a grizzly-tiger hybrid, but creating a cover that can successfully get that across . . . that's a bit of a challenge. So one animal was chosen—the sexy tiger. I know some grizzlies will take this as an affront, and I'm the first to say that the Ursidae is just as sexy as the feline. But there's only so much an artist can do.

So, yes, I'm fully aware the cover has a white tiger on it, and no, it's not a mistake. It's simply the limitations of a non-shifter society, unable to conceive of the wonder that is a grizzly-Siberian tiger male with a honey fetish and introvert tendencies.

But, hopefully, in time, when the world comes to truly understand the wonders of the hybrid nation, this situation will be a thing of the past. Until then, let's all just enjoy the pretty kitty on my cover.

—Shelly Laurenston

Chapter 1

Livy Kowalski blew out a breath when the battling females landed hard on top of the casket.

Livy's father was in that casket. And it was her father's sister and Livy's mother busy fighting on top of it.

Her cousin Jake leaned in and whispered, "Like watching a somber and ancient grieving ceremony with the Windsor family, isn't it?"

Thank God Jake was here. She didn't know if she could have faced this nightmare without him.

No. Not the death of her father, but dealing with her family. Then again, this was how they mourned. Although why they all seemed so surprised by her father's death, Livy didn't know. Damon Kowalski was not exactly known for his quiet, even-tempered ways. He was a thief, a liar, a brawler, an instigator, and a drinker. Not just a drinker, but a honey badger drinker. Her father drank liquor spiked with different snake poisons. Poisons that would kill most humans unless they were treated immediately with antivenin—and sometimes not even then—but for HBs they merely caused a ridiculous high and intense hunger.

Most of Livy's kind just kept their venom intake to the rattler family, but her father had actually tried the more odious poison-spiked beers and tequila, like Black Mamba or the Puff Adder.

And, sadly, her father hadn't been right since the first time he drank that swill, going from a verbose, sometimes annoying thief to a downright bastard of a human being.

It had become so bad that, eventually, even Livy's mother refused to put up with him. She'd thrown him out of their Washington State home and eventually divorced him, but the connection between her parents had always been . . . ridiculous. Because no matter how much they argued, no matter how many times they threw things at each other, or threatened each other with the murder of whomever they might be dating at the moment, there were two things the pair did well together—sex and stealing.

Livy's parents made a great team when it came to stealing, and money was king to the honey badger shifter. Because money allowed them to pursue their off-putting lifestyle without worries as well as purchase extremely robust and necessary health insurance—plastic surgery for scarring could be costly these days.

And, it turned out, money also allowed for even more robust *life* insurance that Livy's aunt didn't think Livy's mother had a right to, considering her parents had been divorced since Livy was fifteen. Sadly, Livy's mother didn't agree with that logic since she'd been the one paying the premiums on that insurance for the last twenty years, always guessing that she'd easily outlive Damon Kowalski. Even if that meant killing him herself.

Even worse, this particular issue came to a head at Damon's graveside. Not appropriate for most people during a funeral, but honey badgers . . . well, "appropriate" was relative when it came to Livy's kind.

Livy looked around at the rest of her relatives, wondering if some of her uncles or cousins would break her mother and aunt apart—but they were too busy watching . . . and drinking . . . and bickering among themselves.

"So you're still hanging around with her, huh?"

Livy glanced over her shoulder at "her."

Toni Jean-Louis Parker, in her mourning best, gave Livy a little wave and an encouraging smile. That smile said, "You can get through this!" Livy hoped her friend was right.

But Toni wasn't here for Livy on her own. There were also Toni's parents, Jackie and Paul. Sadly, Toni's brother Cooper and Toni's sister Cherise were on tour in Europe. They were brilliant musicians who got a *lot* of money to perform for sold-out audiences. Their sixteen-year-old sister Oriana was training—and soon to perform—with the Royal Ballet in England. Twelve-year-old Kyle was studying art in Italy. Ten-year-old Troy was getting his master's in math . . . or science . . . one of those. Livy never really knew or cared. Eight-year-old Freddy was getting his bachelor's in theoretical physics and, in his off time, creating video games that were seriously fun. The youngest brother, six-year-old Dennis, was studying architecture; and the three-year-old twins, Zia and Zoe, were busy learning the many dialects of most of the world's major languages while terrorizing their nanny by just being themselves.

Oh. And there was nineteen-year-old Delilah, but no one really talked about her much. She was currently running a cult in Upstate New York that saw her as their messiah. She and her cult were also making the federal government kind of nervous, but the family liked to pretend that wasn't happening.

And no, Livy wasn't a blood relative of the Jean-Louis Parkers. They were jackals, after all. In the wild, their kind were enemies. Then again, HBs were enemies to . . . well . . . *everyone*. Lions. Hyenas. Leopards. Beekeepers. Beekeepers *really* hated their kind, but only because one didn't find grizzly bears on the African plains. Yet the fact that Livy wasn't blood had never mattered to the Jean-Louis Parkers. As far as they were concerned, she was family, which was why Toni had left her job in Manhattan and come with Livy to watch Livy's mother deck her ex-husband's younger sister while scuffing up the steel casket of her ex-husband.

Jake looked Livy over. "Where is it?"

"Where's what?"

"Your camera. I don't think I've ever seen you without it."

Livy shrugged. "Seemed wrong to bring my camera to my father's funeral," she lied.

"You brought it to our great-aunt's funeral in Poland. Won awards for the pictures you took, if I remember correctly."

"I think the novelty of it won that award. You don't see a lot of knife fights break out at the funerals of hundred-and-eight-year-old women."

Jake glanced back at Toni again. "I have to admit, she's gotten really cute."

"She's got a mate now."

"Really? Too bad."

"Why?"

"Mates complicate things."

Livy shrugged. "Never did for my parents."

"Now, now . . ." He motioned to Livy's mother and their aunt busy slapping each other like they were on an old episode of *Dynasty*. "Clearly your mom is going through her own form of mourning over her mate."

"Clearly."

Vic Barinov waited with his back to the wall. And while he waited, he thought about food. He was hungry.

Thankfully, he knew of at least two good steakhouses in this Albanian city. One catered to all shifters and the other specifically to bears. There were a lot of bears in Eastern Europe, some of the biggest in Ukraine and Siberia.

Unfortunately, Vic wouldn't be able to have something

to eat until he got this done. And he'd already been standing by this wall for the last three hours. But Vic had lots of patience. He could lie in wait for days, if necessary. Yet that sort of thing hadn't been necessary since he'd stopped working for the U.S. government. He'd left suddenly, fed up with all the politics, but at the time, he wasn't sure what he'd do with the rest of his life to ensure he could pay his bills, especially his food bill, which could be quite substantial.

Freelance work, however, had worked out better than he could have hoped. And being a crossbreed—grizzly bear and Siberian tiger—had, for once, been to his benefit. Plus his ability not only to speak eight different languages, including Russian, Polish, German, and Albanian, but to know and understand the culture of most of these nations, kept the money rolling in, and for the first time in a long time, Vic was beginning to feel his life had some stability. It was nice.

Ears twitching, Vic heard the sound of heavy panting. He lifted his head, sniffed the air. Scented the full-human running down the street toward him.

Vic waited until the panting was right beside him, then . . .

Reaching out, Vic caught hold of his target's neck and yanked him into the alley.

Feet still running, arms still pumping, his target hadn't even realized he was no longer touching the ground.

Vic held him like that until the local police charged past. Once he was sure they were gone, he lowered his target to the ground but kept hold of the man's neck. By now, the target had realized he was no longer running from the police. He briefly seemed relieved by that, until he was forced to drop his head back in order to see Vic's face.

"Oh . . . Victor. Hello."

"There are people looking for you, Bohdan."

"Don't hand me over to them, Victor," Bohdan begged while trying to twist out of Vic's grasp. "You know what they'll do to me."

"I don't know anything. Except that people are looking for you."

Vic pushed away from the wall, Bohdan still in his hand.

"Wait! Wait! I have information. Information you'll want."

"I don't need any information."

"What about Whitlan?"

Vic stopped moving, eyes narrowing on Bohdan's desperate face. "Lying to me won't help you, little man," Vic growled in Russian.

"I'm not lying."

"No?"

Bohdan pointed at Vic's hand, which was still around Bohdan's neck. "Little tight."

"And it can get much tighter. Don't make me show you how much."

Bohdan's eyes widened in panic, which was kind of sad, because Vic really wasn't putting any effort into what he was doing. If he did, he could pulverize the bones in Bohdan's neck. These full-humans . . . so breakable.

"Talk, little man."

"Packages sent in and out of country from Whitlan."

Vic frowned. "How do you know they were from Whitlan? They could have been from anybody."

"I saw him. I saw Frankie Whitlan."

Now Vic smirked. "You? You saw Frankie Whitlan? A man no one has seen in more than two years?"

"No one has seen him in America, maybe. But he is friend to many in Russia, Poland, Romania, Bulgaria . . ."

"Is he a friend of yours?"

"No. But I was in warehouse that day. Big boxes he sent out. He wanted to make sure everything perfect. He sent them on boat."

"Going where?"

"All over. But I know that at least one went to Miami."

"And who helped him ship these boxes?"

Now Bohdan smirked. "I like my throat without big slash across it, Victor Barinov."

That was fair enough. Most likely Whitlan had gotten himself involved with mobsters who'd tear someone like Bohdan apart for no other reason than they were bored.

Vic opened his hand and Bohdan dropped to the ground, landing on his knees with a grunt.

"You won't regret this, Victor Barinov," Bohdan said, grinning widely and rubbing his throat. "I knew I could help!"

Vic stepped over Bohdan and walked out of the alley. He stopped at the curb, pulling his phone out of his pocket. While he speed-dialed a number, he saw a few of the local police running back toward the alley, still searching for Bohdan.

Vic pointed into the alley and the officers nodded their thanks before charging in and taking Bohdan down. It was a loss of some easy cash for Vic, but the information he'd received about Whitlan was much more important.

"Yeah?" he heard on the other end of the phone. Dee-Ann Smith of the Smith Pack was not what one would call a chatty She-wolf. Or friendly.

"I've got information," he said cryptically, not willing to put too much detail out over the air. But he didn't need to say Whitlan's name to Dee-Ann. Frankie Whitlan was the most wanted full-human in shifter history. All three major organizations were trying to track him down and execute him for participating in and running expeditions to hunt shifters. But the man had the uncanny ability to disappear. Or he had some very powerful people protecting him. Whatever it was, the Group—the American shifter protection agency; Katzenhaus Securities—the feline protection organization—also called KZS; and the Bear Preservation Council—the worldwide bear protection organization—also called BPC, simply could *not* track the man down. All they needed was a location so they could send in either Dee-Ann Smith or KZS's sharpshooter Cella Malone to take him out. But after several years, they'd been unable to lock on the guy.

"When can you get back here?" she asked.

"I'll get the first plane out."

"Good."

The call disconnected and Vic continued moving down the Albanian street toward his rental car.

"Where are we going?" a voice said behind Vic.

"Back to the States."

"Cool."

Vic stopped walking, faced the shifter behind him. Shen Li smiled at Vic around the short bamboo stalk he had in his mouth.

"I don't need you to come with me."

"Were you planning on leaving me in Albania?"

Shen, a giant panda born and raised in San Francisco, had a specific set of skills that Vic used for some jobs. They were longtime colleagues who'd worked for the government together. Now that both were doing freelance work, Vic brought Shen in as needed. But Vic didn't think Shen was needed for this.

"You can get back on your own, can't you?"

"Don't speak Albanian. You do."

"Oh. Right. Okay. Well then, sure. You can come with me."

"Great."

The pair started off again in silence, except for the seemingly never-ending sound of Shen chewing on his bamboo stalks.

"So what's our next job?" Shen asked and Vic stopped again.

He faced Shen. "You do understand we're not partners, right?"

"We're not?"

"No."

"Why not?"

"It's easier for me to work alone and call you in when I need you."

Shen chewed and chewed while his dark brown eyes gazed at Vic.

And this was the problem with being a hybrid. Vic's bear side had no issue with the staring and the silence and the bamboo-munching. The feline side of him, however . . . wanted to tear Shen's face off. Just for that damn munching sound alone.

Working extremely hard, Vic reined in his feline tendencies and suggested, "Why don't we talk about this at another time? We need to get our stuff from the hotel and find the first plane out of here."

"Okie-dokie!" Shen walked off, and in an attempt to get control, Vic shook his head a bit, the feline snarl out of the back of his throat before he could stop it. The few full-humans walking by quickly gave him a wide berth . . . and he couldn't remotely blame them for it.

Calm and controlled again, Vic followed Shen to the rental car and, eventually, back to the States.

"How's it going?" Toni asked as she handed Livy a dark German beer.

Livy had insisted Toni's parents *not* attend the after-funeral get-together at her parents' house. The Jean-Louis Parkers were such nice people, it wouldn't be fair. But nothing would deter Antonella. She was determined to be part of the entire, horrifying ride.

Livy took the cap off her beer with her hand, yawned, took a drink, shrugged. "Fine."

"That bad, huh?"

"It could be worse."

"You're at your father's funeral—"

"I'm sure he was killed for a very good reason."

"—your mother is fighting with his entire family over money—"

"In her mind, the fact that she didn't kill him herself means she *earned* that money."

"—someone unleashed poisonous snakes in the backyard—"

"For the kids to have something to play with."

"—and your father's mistress just showed up."

Livy turned and watched the tall Serbian supermodel strut through the hallway toward Livy's mother. She wore all black, including a black fur stole, and black six-inch Louboutin shoes. Livy's mother spotted her instantly, and without saying a word, she was suddenly surrounded by her sisters and female cousins.

"Cool," Livy muttered. "Fight."

"You can't let your mother fight her."

"She probably won't. But my aunt Teddy will definitely take her on. Because I'm pretty sure before she started dating my dad, that model was dating one of Teddy's sons. And you know how Teddy is about"—Livy dropped her voice and put on her best Polish accent—" 'my beautiful, beautiful boys. They are from God, no?' "

Toni shook her head. "I swear, your entire family is like an episode of *Dallas*."

"I was thinking more like *Dynasty,* but without the shoulder pads. My people do not need shoulder pads."

Livy watched her mother—birth name Chuntao Yang; American name she'd chosen when she was nine and just moved to the States, Joan—stand her ground as the last woman Livy's father had been sleeping with walked up to her.

Toni rubbed her nose and stated very quietly, "She's full-human."

"That was his kink."

"I mean, Livy, she's *full-human*."

Livy shrugged, watching as her mother leaned in and whispered something to the woman. "Then I suggest we not let her in the backyard."

"Livy—"

Whatever her mother said, it must have been a doozy, because the woman leaned back, then hauled off and slapped Joan across the face, snapping the She-badger's head to one side.

Slowly Joan looked at the much younger woman. Her head tilted to the side, cold black eyes examining, judging. Then she head-butted the model, causing the full-human to scream and stumble back. Joan followed that up with a left hook to the jaw, a right to the gut, and another left directly to the face. And she did it all without an ounce of anger. If she were angry, that supermodel would have been missing her eyes.

Joan held her hand out and one of her sisters placed a switchblade in her palm.

Before Toni could say a word—and Livy knew she would because all this was beyond the understanding of the much more controlled and polite Jean-Louis Parkers—Livy strode across the room.

"Let's see how many *Vogue* covers that face of yours gets now," Joan calmly stated, her hand with the blade pulling back.

She was just swinging it down when Livy caught hold of her mother's wrist, held it.

"No, Ma."

Lips pursed, her mother looked at her with that disappointment Livy had gotten used to seeing years ago. Ever since Livy had told the man at the candy store he'd given her back too much change. Something her mother had *never* forgiven.

"No," Livy insisted.

"You and that weakness of yours." That weakness being Livy's conscience. She didn't use it often, but the fact Livy used it at all disappointed her family greatly.

Joan yanked her arm back. "I know you didn't get that nature of yours from *my* family."

"So you blame *us*?" Aunt Teddy demanded. "Any weakness this girl has is *your* fault, *Joan*. Definitely not my handsome brother's."

As if the bleeding, sobbing mistress no longer existed, Joan and her sisters faced off against the Kowalskis.

Livy walked back to Toni's side. "I'm in the mood for waffles. You want waffles?"

Eyes wide, the jackal said, "But your family—"

"They've got snakes in the backyard." She grabbed Toni's wrist and led her toward the hallway. "So they don't need waffles."

"Yes, but what about—"

Knowing exactly where this was going, Livy stopped by her father's mistress. "If I were you," she warned the foolish woman, "I'd get out of here. And feel free to go to the cops at your own risk."

Figuring she'd done all that she was morally responsible to do, Livy continued out the front door, down the steps, and toward the limo.

"Wait!" a voice yelled from behind them. "Wait!"

Livy stopped, turned around, her hand still tight around Toni's wrist.

Jake ran up to her. "Going for waffles without me, cousin?"

"I figured you'd be braving the snakes in the backyard."

"With those vicious little bastard pups? Don't let their age fool you. They're mean. But more importantly . . ." He held up a set of car keys. "We can take Dad's Bentley."

Livy snorted and released Toni's wrist so she could snatch the keys out of her cousin's hand. "Let's go."

The pair began to walk off, and Toni emphatically stated, "I'm not going anywhere with either of you two driving!"

Livy looked at her cousin and, smirking, the pair walked back, grabbed Toni by the arms, and dragged her behind them.

"You can't do this!" Toni protested. "This is kidnapping! A brutal, senseless kidnapping!"

"Stop bragging," Livy teased.

"I know," Jake joked. "Like she's so important she just has to be kidnapped in a two-hundred-thousand-dollar car."

"God, how much?" Toni demanded. "Your father is going to have your ass if anything happens to this car!"

"Your lack of faith in my driving skills hurts me." Livy stopped next to the beautiful car, its bright yellow paint job nearly burning her retinas. Yeah. Kowalskis weren't exactly known for their subtle sense of style.

"Just so we're clear," Toni informed both Kowalski cousins, "if I die because of your insane driving . . . I will never forgive you."

"Noted. Now get your skinny ass and narrow shoulders in the car."

"She does have freakishly small shoulders," Jake noted once they'd forced Toni in the backseat.

"I know. But I don't hate her because of it."

"That is really big of you, cousin."

"I think so."

Jake opened the passenger door while Livy walked around the beautiful car. "What do you wanna do after we eat?" he asked.

Livy looked back at the house she'd lived in during her high school years. You know, when she wasn't crashing at Toni's place or finding some house that was left untended for a few days.

"What do you think?" she asked her cousin.

Jake grinned. "Take you to the airport?"

"See? You're not nearly as stupid as your father says you are."

Jake's grin never faded. "Ahhh, yes. The love of a family. See what you're missing by living in Manhattan?"

Livy snorted and opened the driver's side door. "No. No, I don't see."

Chapter 2

As always, Livy's plans did not turn out as she'd hoped. Although she'd intended to be back in Manhattan the night of her father's funeral or, at the very least, early morning after, she'd ended up staying another full day in Washington, helping her mother contact the *many* life insurance companies. Not so that the woman could lay claim to Damon's money, but because it meant her mother most likely wouldn't bother Livy for the next few . . . years.

Her mother often forgot how annoying she found Livy until she had to spend some "quality" time with her only child. Then all those memories came flooding back and Livy didn't have to worry about seeing her mother—or putting up with her—for ages.

And despite Livy's suggestions that she leave, Toni insisted on staying. Which, in the end, was good. Because the woman knew how to get people through an airport as quickly as possible.

"Sit here," Toni said, pushing Livy down by her shoulders so that she sat on the one piece of luggage she'd brought with her. "I'll get a taxi and we'll be out of here."

Toni went off and Livy rested her elbow on her knee, her chin on her fist, and gazed off across the busy streets surrounding JFK Airport. As she waited, obscenely long legs and massive bodies began to march by her.

She didn't move or anything, but she did notice the squealing girls and the crowd of people following the full-human males walking by. It was around that time she heard a low male voice bark, "I am *not* a football player. Now get out of my face."

For the first time in days, Livy smiled. She couldn't help it. What exactly did the man expect? He was seven feet and two inches tall. Nearly four hundred pounds. And even with that handsome face, wickedly sharp cheekbones, and dark brown and gold hair that hung in ragged layers almost to his shoulders—he was terrifying-looking. Of *course* people thought he was on a national sports team. Their other option was murdering serial killer from a "Friday the 13th" movie.

Livy waited until Vic was a few steps from her before sweetly asking, "Hey, mister. Can I have your autograph?"

Snarling, Vic replied, "I am *not* a—Livy?" Vic stopped right in front of her, his expression of annoyance fading away and replaced by one of curiosity. "What are you doing?"

"Selling my ass on the streets for a few bucks."

"Times that tough?"

Thankfully, Vic had learned how to deal with what very few called Livy's sense of "humor" not long after they'd met. Which was good because Livy really didn't know how to *not* ask people strange, disorienting questions. As an artist, she found their confusion fascinating.

"Tough enough," she replied. "Hi, Shen."

"Hey, Livy. Like your hair."

Livy smirked at Shen's running joke. As a honey badger, she had black hair with a white streak off to the side while Shen, as a giant panda, had white hair with big swipes of black through it. He was also munching on that damn bamboo crap. With his fangs, he was clearly a predator. But for whatever reason, although they had the digestive system of carnivores, giant pandas ate bamboo. The problem was that pandas needed a lot of bamboo in order to survive. *A lot*. So every time Livy saw the man . . . he was eating.

Still, it was fun to watch him hang around poor Vic Barinov. Although Livy saw the grizzly side of Vic more than she ever saw the tiger, it seemed neither side of the hybrid knew what to do with the sweet, but sometimes chatty, six-foot panda who was nearly as wide as he was tall. Something else Livy and Shen had in common. Massive shoulders on relatively smaller human bodies than most shifters were used to. Oh. And they were both Asian. Well, as Jake liked to say, "Livy is half-Asian, half-Polish and allllll honey badger!"

Livy, however, had much less in common with Vic, but they'd worked together once when helping Toni rescue her baby brother from Delilah's cult.

"Before we go any further," Vic said to Livy, "my house?"

"What about it?"

Vic raised an eyebrow.

Livy rolled her eyes. "I haven't been back since the last time you threw me out."

"I didn't throw you out. I asked you nicely to leave so I could call the contractor to fix all the holes you'd put into it."

"I had to get inside, didn't I?"

"But you have your own place."

"I ran out of honey."

"So you came all the way out to Westchester for honey?"

"You have really good honey."

Vic blew out a breath. "Just tell me if I'll be facing holes when I get home."

"No holes."

"Do I have any honey left?"

"Yes. You have honey left."

"I don't know why I'm getting the tone. You're the one who keeps eating all my honey."

Livy smirked. "When you have rum-infused honey in your cabinets—you're asking for it."

That made Vic smile, something he didn't do very often. Then again . . . neither did she.

Using his bamboo stalk to point at them, Shen admitted, "I don't get the thing you two have for honey."

They stared at him while he chomped on his bamboo until Vic turned back to Livy and asked, "You need a ride home?"

"Toni went to get a cab. She should be back soon." She studied Vic a moment. She hadn't seen him in months; his work took him out of the country very often. "What are you doing back in the States? Or are below-freezing East Coast temperatures where you come to get a break from those balmy Russian winters?"

"I have information on our old friend."

"That Whitlan guy? Are they still looking for him?"

Vic nodded. "Yeah."

"You'd think they'd have gotten him by now. How hard is it to find someone in this day and age?"

"The man knows how to disappear."

Livy shrugged, not really caring. Honey badgers didn't concern themselves with the problems of other shifters. They saw themselves as honey badgers, not as part of a bigger shifter universe. A good thing, since most of the other breeds didn't really like them and some didn't even know honey badgers existed.

"What about you?" Vic asked. "What are you doing here?"

"Just coming in from Washington."

"Visiting family?"

"Dead family." Livy chuckled at her own joke, but when Vic and Shen just stared at her, she said, "Sorry. Bad joke. I was at a funeral."

Vic frowned, which made him look even *more* terrifying,

but Livy knew that was just his face. His handsome but terrifying face. *God, those cheekbones are amazing.*

"I'm sorry, Livy. Who died?"

"My father."

Both men blinked and she realized she'd surprised them.

"Livy . . ." Vic looked at Shen, back at her. "My God, I'm so sorry."

"It's okay."

"It is?"

Livy shrugged. "We weren't close."

"Still. It's your father."

"I threw a baseball bat at him once," she admitted to the two men. "Clocked him right in the head. He was out for, like, a good thirty minutes."

Shen blew out a breath. "Oh. Okay."

But Vic refused to be put off. "He's still your father. I know this must be hard for you."

"Not as hard as when he woke up and came after me with that baseball bat. Didn't catch me, though. I'm superfast when running . . . away."

Vic stared at her a moment before finally stating, "I want to awkwardly hug you."

Livy looked up at him. "Awkwardly?"

"Neither of us is very good with affection, so I pretty much assume that any physical encounters between us will be awkward."

That made Livy laugh, and without thinking about it too much, she stood up and wrapped her arms around Vic's waist, giving him a hug she hadn't given her mother when she'd left for the airport to return to New York.

Vic hugged her back and, if Livy wasn't mistaken, kissed the top of her head.

"If you need anything," Vic said, "you just let me know."

"Thanks, Vic."

Livy pulled away. Not because she was tired of that

hug—it was surprisingly nice—but because she sensed someone grabbing the rolling case she'd brought with her for the trip.

Using her foot, Livy rammed the case down, spun around, and nearly had her hands around the man's throat when Toni came running up, screaming, "He's the cabbie! He's the cabbie!"

Livy immediately pulled her hands back. "Oh. Sorry."

"He's just helping with the luggage," Toni explained. She patted Livy's leg, trying to get her to remove her foot from the bag. When Livy didn't move fast enough, the patting became a hard slap.

Livy moved her foot and the driver quickly took her bag and headed to the waiting cab.

Toni glared at her, which just made Livy chuckle. Then Toni smiled up at Vic. "Hello, Victor."

"Hi, Toni. How are you?"

"Fine." Toni patted Vic's arm, waved at Shen, since she didn't know him well at all, and headed to the cab.

"I gotta go." Livy smiled at Vic. "Maybe I'll see you around."

"You still working at the Sports Center?" he asked.

Livy sighed. "Of course. Where else would I be? In Paris? Milan? Perhaps in the middle of some great war? Why would I be there when I can take pictures of giant guys who balance on thin skates and charge around an ice rink, chasing after a little black puck? Because *that's* fascinating."

"So work's going well?" Vic asked with a straight face.

Livy smirked. *The bastard*. "See ya."

Livy got into the taxi beside Toni and closed the door.

"Huh," Toni said.

"What?"

"Nothing."

"Explain to me at what point in our friendship where I ever expressed having any tolerance of girls who play *that* particular game?"

"Fine," Toni said. "I just noticed that Vic watched you until you got into the cab."

"So?"

"His friend was busy staring at the football cheerleaders or dancers or whatever they are who'd just passed by. But Vic watched *you*."

"And? Your point?"

Toni shrugged and looked out the window. "Just sayin'."

"Again," Livy felt the need to make clear, "little tolerance for those kinds of girls."

"I feel bad," Vic told Shen as they headed toward the car he kept in long-term parking at the airport for when he came into town.

"About what?"

"Livy. I had no idea her dad passed away."

"Doesn't seem like they were close."

"So? He's still her father."

"Not everyone is as close to their family as you are."

"What does that mean?"

"It means you and me are close to our families. My father dies? I'm sitting alone in my house for a few weeks, sobbing and eating bamboo stalks in his honor. But not everybody deals with death the way I do."

"Still . . . I feel like I should do something."

"Like what?"

"I don't know. I was hoping you had some ideas."

"You know what helps me have great ideas?"

Vic sighed. "A free dinner?"

"At a steakhouse that's not afraid to include raw bamboo on the menu."

"You want me to pay for us to go to the Van Holtz Steak House?" A shifter-run establishment that catered to all species and breeds and was the only restaurant Vic could think of that offered raw bamboo as a side dish.

Shen raised and lowered his hands in the air before digging another short bamboo stalk out of the pack he kept in his denim jacket pocket. "You want ideas, don't you? My ideas ain't free."

Livy walked into her apartment, leaving her bag by the door. She didn't bother to turn the lights on. Not much to see. Some crappy furniture she'd bought on sale. A TV she left on when home as background noise. And piles of books. She liked to read. Something her parents adored about her when she was only three, but became less a fan of when she'd rather spend time reading than taking the family's fun and informative "How to remove wallets from back pockets without getting caught" tutorials, held every couple of weeks for the youngest kids.

But the reality of Livy's apartment couldn't be avoided. It was set up to make it easy to abandon at the first sign of trouble. And she only had this place because Toni kept insisting, "You have to have your own place. You have to live like a normal person." Apparently Toni didn't think a series of "safe houses" set up all over the world by Livy's family was living like a normal person.

So Livy had plunked down money on this one bedroom that didn't actually have a bed. On the rare times she stayed here, she slept on the couch and used the bedroom as an office slash art studio.

Yet as soon as Livy stepped inside that particular room, she had to walk out again. The reality was that although Livy had been doing photography, she hadn't been doing any real "art."

She didn't know when it happened. When that font of constant creativity dried up. Creativity had been with her since she was six, when she began to play with a camera that her father had brought home from a small home burglary he'd done one night when he needed a little extra cash.

There'd been film inside and once she'd used it all, she'd insisted her father have the film developed. Even her parents had been shocked at how good some of the pictures were. And not one had been a simple family photo or picture of a flower. Far from it. The images included shots of some homeless in the downtown area, teenage children smoking pot, and a full-blood bear that had been caught wandering around town. That had really freaked out her mother when it was obvious from the pics that Livy had spent time in the bear's lap, and her parents finally realized that their six-year-old daughter was wandering around the town alone when they were out of the house, working on their next heist, or arguing about something ridiculous.

Of course their attempts to curb their daughter's wandering ways lasted about . . . a week until their next heist came up. Then Livy was free to start down the photography path. She'd read every book she could get her hands on. From straight technical to those big coffee table books from the likes of Ansel Adams and Dorothea Lange. She studied all magazines, including fashion, teaching herself to understand lighting and shadow. When she was older, she purchased old cameras and camera equipment, took them apart, and then taught herself to put them back together again, so she understood her equipment inside and out.

Honestly, as far back as Livy could remember, she was never without her camera. Whether it was around her neck, hanging off her shoulder, or in easy reach inside her bag, Livy always had it because she never knew when some image was going to catch her attention.

But for the last year . . . that hadn't been the case. She'd kept her camera on her but she'd found herself using it less and less. Until eventually it got buried at the bottom of her backpack right along with the lipstick she never used and the gum she'd forgotten had been in there.

What people didn't understand, though, was losing that desire, losing her interest in photography and in art, hurt

Livy. Physically. Right in her chest. And forcing herself to come up with something interesting for her day job at the Sports Center hurt just as much. It was like pulling teeth without anesthesia. Every shot she took was like torture. She didn't know why, though. She'd done regular photography to pay the bills for years. She'd been an assistant—a sometimes thankless job depending on whom you worked for—a set dresser on fashion shoots. She'd even worked in a mall portrait studio that involved interacting with annoying families. She'd done every menial task necessary because it was all about photography, and every additional dime she got went toward her art.

So then what the hell was going on? Why was it such a struggle for her now?

Livy didn't know. What she did know was that she had a gallery show coming up in the next few weeks and absolutely *nothing* new. She kept promising the curator that she would have something new. Something new, powerful, and amazing. But she was lying her ass off. She had nothing. Absolutely nothing.

Livy walked back to her living room and sat down on the edge of her couch.

There were some artists who used the pain of loss—like losing her father—to really explore the powerful demons that drove them.

Livy, however, picked up the remote for her TV and turned it on.

As she stretched out on the couch, her cell phone vibrated. She reached down and pulled it out of her back pocket. It was Vic.

> Again, if you need anything . . . or if you want to talk. I'm here.

Livy smiled a little. Vic wasn't nearly as terrifying as he looked. He was just a nice guy. She sent him a "thanks" back and tossed her phone onto the coffee table.

* * *

"What did you say?" Shen asked while enjoying his steak with a side of garlic-infused raw bamboo.

"Just told her I'm here if she needs me." Vic put his phone on the table.

"That was nice."

"Yeah."

Shen stared at him a moment before asking, "You don't think it's enough, do you?"

"Her father died! That's huge. Don't you think that's huge?"

"It would be huge for me. Huge for you. She seemed to be just rolling along. I saw her once with that same expression when she was eating a chocolate fudge sundae at a restaurant in the Sports Center. Which is pretty much *no* expression. How can a person not have an expression while eating a chocolate fudge sundae?"

"That's how you judge people? By their expression when they're eating chocolate fudge sundaes?"

"Or because the only time I've seen her expression change is when she attacked that lion male football player."

"He was asking for it. He patted her ass."

"True. He did. But I still think tearing off part of his scalp was an overreaction. Especially when we both know how calculated that was. You know how lion males are about their hair."

Vic looked down at his meal. A seventy-two-ounce prime rib with a pepper-honey glaze. Perfect for both his tiger and grizzly sides.

"I just think I should do something for her," Vic admitted.

"Send her flowers."

Vic and Shen looked up from their meals at the same time, stared at each other, and finally said together, "Nah."

CHAPTER 3

Livy stepped out of the elevator and headed toward her office. As she walked, she heard her name. People calling out a greeting of some kind, but she didn't reply. She wasn't big on greetings. She found them irritating.

Moving down the hall, Livy didn't look into the other offices. She didn't look up at the people walking by. She just kept her head down and traveled on. That was how Livy mostly traveled . . . unless she had her camera out.

Livy pushed open the door to her office and stepped inside. She didn't have a giant office on the underground floors of the Sports Center, where shifters of all kinds came to play their dangerous shifter games, but it was still a good size for what was essentially a staff photographer position.

Two or three years ago, Livy never would have come to the Sports Center. She'd never have had a reason. But financially things had changed. At one time, Livy had been on her way up. She'd traveled to many parts of the world and taken the kind of photographs that she knew future artists would study. But then, well . . . she'd had some . . . issues. A few editors she'd argued with. A few countries she'd pissed off. And her family's reputation always haunted her.

Her cousin Jake had, on more than one occasion, kindly

offered to give her a whole new identity. He could have, too. That was his specialty. But Livy didn't believe in running. Whether it was running from who she was or running from a pissed-off hyena, it went against everything she'd been taught by her parents.

Honey badgers don't run. They fight.

Of course, it was kind of hard to fight when a country revoked one's visa to get their dislike of you across.

Although, at first, none of that mattered. Sure, they could take away her visas, deny her access to the Louvre without armed guards shadowing her, and keep forcing her to go to goddamn anger management classes. But the one thing they could never do was take her art from her.

Unfortunately, though, it seemed she'd done that to herself.

After a year of taking pictures of guys who considered sports an actual career, Livy no longer thought of herself as an artist. She was once considered a prodigy, but now she was just some chick who took pretty pictures of physically perfect people. It was not a challenge.

It was a job.

Livy dropped her backpack on the floor and plopped into the chair behind her desk. There were stacks of proofs for her to review. Pictures of shifters from tristate teams that played football, hockey, soccer, basketball, and whatever else that she didn't give a shit about.

These were the pro teams. Or as Livy liked to call them, the "teams with all the penises."

Okay. True. That wasn't fair. Unlike full-human sports, there were many females on the pro shifter teams. But most of them were She-bears and big-armed tigresses. So Livy wasn't sure that counted.

Livy sat at her desk, staring straight ahead, her phone vibrating in her back pocket, her PC pinging away, telling her that e-mail was arriving.

Livy ignored it all.

But she couldn't really ignore the tall, beautiful woman who suddenly filled her doorway. Well, she could ignore her, but she'd tried that before and got hit in the face for her trouble. The reasoning? "I was worried you were dead. . . . I was just checking that you weren't. Aren't you glad someone cares?" Cella Malone had asked at the time with no sense of irony.

"Hey, Livy." And here came the requisite sad face. The expression everyone used when someone they knew had a death in the family, but they didn't actually know the person who'd died. Toni had burst into tears at the news. But she'd known Damon Kowalski well, once even managing to get Livy's father to pay for art school by using an extreme level of guilt.

More sad face from the She-tiger who coached the New York Carnivores hockey team. "How ya doin', hon?"

Livy briefly debated not answering and seeing if the female would just leave, but . . . she wasn't in the mood to be hit. Again.

"I'm fine."

Cella gave her the "Be brave, little one. Be brave" expression.

Unable to keep up the façade anymore—and for Livy, five seconds of keeping up the façade was damn near a record—she asked, "Need something, Cella?"

"I know it's your first day back . . ." And Livy watched the She-tiger actually struggle with the mere idea of giving Livy work "at this difficult time."

Putting it down to Irish-Catholic guilt, something even Catholic honey badgers never worried about, Livy decided to let the woman off the hook.

"It's all right," Livy soothed. "I, uh, need something to do to get my mind off things." That was what people said when they were going through mourning, right? It sounded right. Like something she heard on one of those made-for-TV movies she'd had on in the background last night while she was up playing computer games.

"If you're sure," Cella hedged.

"I'm sure. What do you need?"

Malone held up an eight-by-ten picture of one of her players. "Is it possible we can make him look less . . . serial killer-y?"

Livy stared at the picture. "The man is seven-five, he weighs nearly five hundred pounds, and he's missing part of his face."

"Not missing it." Malone looked at the picture. "Those are just claw marks . . . from his wife. A lovely She-lion." She leaned in a bit and whispered, "Given during the throes of passion, I've heard."

"So I don't need to put 'How to Stop Domestic Violence' pamphlets in his locker?"

The She-tiger gazed at Livy, not getting the tacky joke at all. Before this job, Livy had spent most of her time with full-humans. Like most HBs, who either hung around other HBs or full-humans. It was rare for a honey badger to be around so many other breeds and species of shifters, and Livy often had to remind herself that life among shifters was . . . different. Shifter males often respected their mates because if they didn't they knew the repercussions would be swift and long-term. Cops were rarely involved. Shelters never used. So those tacky jokes she heard around full-humans—that she, tragically, was not above using—most shifters never got.

Livy's father once pushed Livy's mother during a fight, around the time his drinking had just begun to get bad. Joan Kowalski retaliated by pinning his hand to the kitchen table with a steak knife. The move, of course, didn't kill him . . . but it reminded Damon how far he could go with a fellow shifter. Especially a female one.

"Do you want me to take the scars out? Or rebuild his

jaw?" Livy finally asked when the She-tiger continued to just stare at her.

"I don't know if his fans would like that." Cella continued to study the pictures. "Maybe we could put a hat on him."

Livy scratched her cheek. "A hat? You want me to take the picture with him wearing a hat?"

"Uh-huh. Just cover his face a bit."

A couple of years ago, this would be where Livy would jump up, snarl she couldn't work under these conditions, and storm out. Unless the photo editor was rude about his feedback; then Livy would just go for his face. This time, though, the fight completely out of her, Livy just shrugged and said, "Sure. Let's use a hat."

Malone blinked and now studied Livy. "Really? You don't mind?"

"Nope."

"Okay." Malone placed the photo on Livy's desk and walked to the doorway. She stopped, looked back at Livy, nodded, and walked out.

Once she was alone, Livy spun her chair away from the door so that she faced the wall behind her. She had some proofs of shots she was planning to use for her gallery show but she didn't even see them. She didn't see anything. She just stared straight ahead and waited. For what? Livy had no idea.

"How do you tolerate that noise?" Dee-Ann Smith asked, her cold, dead, dog-like eyes glaring. She sat behind a desk with absolutely nothing on it. No computer. No paper. No phone. Not even a little lamp. There was just a chair on one side, two chairs on the other, and a metal desk in between. And there was just something so damn disturbing about that. The woman had missed her true calling as a Soviet agent during the Cold War. The Communists might have actually won with her on their side.

Vic shrugged. "What noise?"

"*That* noise." She pointed at Shen, who sat next to him, munching on his bamboo.

"What about it?" Vic asked her.

"That doesn't annoy you?"

"Not as much as it's obviously annoying you." Vic raised his hands, then lowered them. "Did you hear anything I just told you?"

Before Dee-Ann could answer, Cella Malone suddenly slid into the doorway, her shoulder hitting the defenseless wood there.

"Sorry I'm late," Cella said, smiling at Vic and Shen. "What are we talking about?"

"Was wondering if that bamboo eatin' gets on ol' Vic's nerves."

Vic's mouth dropped open at Dee's words. *That* was her main concern?

Cella, now standing beside Dee on the other side of the desk, placed her hands on her hips and stared down at Shen. "I think I could get used to it. Besides, as a male, there are definitely worse things he could be doing."

Dee grunted. "You have a point."

"And let's face it, you canines have a very low tolerance for sounds."

"All shifters are sensitive to sound."

"We are, but you guys get weirded out by the most minor noises. And when I'm traveling with the team and we all hear a siren, only the canines start all that goddamn howling."

"Ain't nothin' wrong with a good howl, feline. Better than hissin' like a slowly deflating air bag."

"I'm getting cranky," Vic announced and he watched the two females slowly turn their attention directly on him. "Cranky," he growled out between clenched teeth.

"Problem?" Dee-Ann asked him.

"Why did I come all this way if it was a waste of time?"

"Don't worry. You'll get paid for your information."

Out of the corner of his eye, Vic saw Shen wince. And with good reason. He wasn't some rat like Bohdan, running around, passing out info for coins or to get out of trouble. And it annoyed him when people acted like he was.

Vic stood and stepped around Shen's legs.

"Hold up, hoss."

"We're done, Dee-Ann."

"Wait."

Vic stopped.

"Close the door, hoss."

Vic glanced back at Dee-Ann. After a moment, he stepped back and closed the door.

Dee-Ann moved from the chair to her desk, resting her ass against the metal. She motioned to Cella and the She-tiger leaned in. They whispered back and forth to each other for nearly a minute before they focused on him again.

Finally, Vic couldn't take it anymore. "What's going on?"

"Management," Cella said, "has been backing off finding Whitlan."

"How long has this been going on?"

"Few months."

"Why?"

"We're not sure. But they're definitely not putting the resources to it that they had been."

"But we ain't giving up," Dee-Ann said flatly.

"We've been given different assignments, but we just can't let this go," Cella explained.

"You can't work on it openly, though," Vic guessed.

"We have other assignments. But if *you* have some free time . . ."

"You want me to do what *three* major organizations haven't been able to do in more than two years."

Dee-Ann grinned. "Yup."

* * *

"Hi, Livy!"

Livy, working hard not to sigh, swiveled her desk chair around and gazed at the wolfdog standing in her doorway. *How painful is* this *particular conversation going to be?* Most days she could easily tolerate Blayne Thorpe. It was fun to torment the long-legged wolfdog. Cruel, but fun.

But today . . . today was not a good day.

"What's up, Blayne?"

"You busy?"

No, but she lied. "A little."

"I'll keep it really short then," she promised as she moved into the office.

"Okay."

Once Blayne was in, she immediately held up her hands and said, "First off, I'm *so* sorry to hear about your father." She put her hands on her chest. "My heart just broke for you."

"Thank you."

"Are you okay?"

Livy knew that saying she was "fine" would just lead to Blayne making it her mission in life to prove how far from fine Livy was, so she said instead, "As well as can be expected."

"I understand. And I promise not to keep you. I just desperately need your help."

"With what?"

"Well, you know my and Gwen's wedding is coming up."

"I'm sure you two will be really happy together."

Blayne frowned, head tilting to the side like a confused Labrador. Then her eyes grew wide and she laughed. "No, no! We're having a double wedding. I'm marrying Bo and Gwen's marrying Lock."

"Uh-huh."

"And I let Gwen handle a few things, which initially was working really well. But she had a little fight with one of our vendors and did that thing she does with her neck."

Livy frowned. "What thing she does with her neck?"

"Trust me . . . if you ever see it . . . you'll know what I mean. Anyway, we're kind of in a bad way and I'm hoping you can help us out."

"I don't understand."

"Well, I was wondering if you'd be our photographer!" She grinned that big Blayne grin, but Livy couldn't even really see it.

"I'm sorry . . . what?"

"You do such nice work and Gwen doesn't scare you at all. So it would be *perfect*."

"Are you asking me to be your . . ." Livy swallowed down the bile in her throat. "Your *wedding* photographer?"

"I know it's a lot of work. I do. But it would *really* help me out. And we don't want video or anything. Just those lovely pictures you do."

Livy would later realize that although she heard and knew the words coming out of Blayne Thorpe's mouth, she didn't really understand anything at the moment except one thing . . . she was being offered a wedding photography job.

Wedding photography.

Wedding. Photography.

Livy Kowalski. A *wedding* photographer.

"You don't have to answer now," Blayne went on, oblivious. "But we have every intention of paying you very well. I won't ask for a friend discount or anything." She laughed. "So just let me know!"

Blayne started to walk out, stopped, faced Livy. "And again, I'm really sorry about your dad."

Then she walked away.

Leaving Livy unable to do anything else but stare at that doorway and wonder when exactly her life had completely fallen into the very pits of hell.

• • •

Vic didn't know what was wrong with him. Why did he agree to things he didn't want to do? But he had agreed.

You're an idiot.

"I don't do wet work," Vic reminded the two females.

"Don't worry," Cella said with a smile. "You find him, Smith and I will take care of the rest."

"Any idea who these packages your contact told you about were going to?" Dee-Ann asked.

"No. They were routed through several countries. It won't be easy to track, but at least one of them was headed to Miami, Florida. I think we'll start there. We'll head out tonight."

Dee thought a moment. "What about Whitlan's kid?"

"Allison?" Cella asked. "We checked her apartment. Remember? Livy went in for us last year. She didn't find anything that pointed to Allison Whitlan knowing where her father is. Or that she has contact with him at all."

"He abandoned her and her mother before she was even five," Vic told them. "She may not want to be in touch with him."

"It's been a year. Things might have changed." Dee-Ann scratched her arm. "Think Livy would help us again?"

Vic shrugged. "I can ask."

"Ask." Dee-Ann slid off her desk and Vic knew she was done with them. "Barinov, you don't discuss what you find with anyone but either me or Cella."

"All right." Vic opened the office door.

"And let us know if you have to leave the country again."

"I will."

He walked out, Shen right behind him.

While they waited for the elevator, Shen asked, "Are we doing this for free?"

"I don't know."

"Isn't that something we should find out ahead of time?"

"They asked me to do them a favor."

"You could have said no." Vic looked at Shen. Still eating bamboo, the giant panda shrugged and added, "Just sayin'."

The elevator doors opened and both men stepped in.

"So where to now?" Shen asked.

"Get something for Livy. You know . . . to cheer her up."

"Flowers?"

Vic stared at the panda. "I thought we agreed last night she wouldn't want flowers?"

"Yeah, but when I thought about it again . . ."

Sighing, Vic admitted, "Some days you make me want to tear your arms off."

Shen nodded. "Surprisingly, I understand that."

Unable to resolve how her life had come to this, Livy ended up where she felt most comfortable in her office—under her desk. It was a small space under there because of the desk drawers, so it gave her the illusion of being in a nice burrow.

And that's where Livy stayed until the smell of roses, lilies, and some other annoying flowers filled her sensitive nostrils.

She tried to ignore the smell but it kept getting more potent as someone moved in and out of her office. Repeatedly.

She sniffed the air, trying to ignore the flowers and center on the person.

Vic. It was Vic in her office. With flowers.

Confused and curious, Livy quietly crawled out from under the desk and peeked around the corner of it to see Vic Barinov bringing in another giant flower display as well as a large fruit basket.

Getting to her knees, Livy asked, "What are you doing?"

Vic stopped and looked at her. "Were you under the desk?"

"Yes."

"Are you always under the desk?"

"Not always."

He shrugged, walked out, came back with another basket. This time filled with an array of cookies.

"Vic?"

"We couldn't agree."

"Who couldn't agree . . . what?"

"It's Shen's fault," he complained, which really didn't answer her question.

"Okay."

"First he said you wouldn't want flowers. Then today, he thought you might, although he had no empirical proof regarding the veracity of that belief."

"Empirical proof?"

"Right. So I brought you flowers. And cookies." He walked out of her office. "I also," he said from the hallway, "got you a plant." And he came in with a five-foot-tall standing plant that he put in a corner. Christ, Livy was only five-one.

"And," he said, gesturing at two other baskets, "food." He pointed at one basket. "Nuts and fruits, nuts being the emphasis of the overall basket." He pointed at the other. "Fruits and nuts, with fruits being the emphasis." Went back into the hallway and came in with another basket. "And meats and fish."

He placed the baskets in front of her desk.

"And"—he walked out again and quickly returned with one more basket—"honey. European and American. They didn't have any African or Israeli bee honey."

Glancing around the room, he finally settled on placing that basket beside the standing plant.

Resting back on her heels, Livy asked, "Why?"

"Why what?"

"Why are you bringing me anything?"

"It's what people do when a friend suffers a loss."

"We're friends?"

"I just bought you all these baskets, so we better be."

Vic had always found Livy . . . unusual. Cute. Really hot, when she wasn't ripping a lion's scalp off. But definitely unusual. Still, why was she hiding under her desk? That seemed weird. Even for her.

Even worse, when he suggested they were friends, she just stared blankly at him. It kind of hurt his feelings.

"I brought you honey. You could at least pretend we're friends."

"Yeah. We're friends. Just don't know why you felt the need to buy me baskets of . . . stuff."

"Because that's what people do, Livy. It's called empathy."

"I've heard the word."

Vic rolled his eyes. "Look, Livy, I know you're this great photographer but—"

"Oh yeah," she suddenly cut in. "Great *wedding* photographer, maybe."

"What?"

Livy shook her head. "Forget it."

"Livy, what's going on with you?"

"Nothing." She suddenly dropped down and crawled back under her desk.

Vic, not sure how to deal with this side of Livy, walked around her desk and crouched down so he could see her.

"Do you want to go somewhere and talk?" he asked.

"Because I'm so chatty?"

"No. But I understand that after the loss of a parent—"

"We weren't close."

"As you've already said. We could still go get some coffee." He glanced at his watch. "Maybe get lunch."

"You asking me out on a date?"

Without thinking, Vic leaned back a bit. "No."

"You don't have to look so horrified."

"It's not horror. It's confusion. You're confusing me. Which," when he thought about it, "may lead to horror. But I simply don't like being confused. So the horror wasn't directed at you, so much as the confusion."

"Well, when you put it like that . . ."

Glad she understood what he'd been trying to say, Vic asked again, "Sure you don't want some lunch?"

"I'm not really hungry. But thanks anyway."

"Okay." He started to stand up, but stopped, remembering his conversation with Dee-Ann. "One other thing . . ."

"Yeah?"

"You up for a job?"

Livy closed her eyes. "Let me guess . . . you need a photographer for your nephew's birthday party?"

"His birthday's in June." Vic scratched his head, again confused. "You do that kind of photography, too?"

"What job?" Livy asked and something told Vic not to push her.

"Remember that woman's apartment you . . . uh . . . went into last year?" He hated saying "breaking and entering." That was a felony.

"Whitlan's daughter? Yes. I remember."

"Would you do it again if I need you to?"

"Yeah, sure," she said dismissively, her shoulders slumping.

"You don't have to."

"It's the best job I've had offered to me in a long while. So I'll do it."

"You'll be working with me and Shen this time."

"Why?"

"I'll explain that later. But after I get back."

"You're leaving already?"

"Yeah. But staying in the States." Vic studied Livy a little longer. He didn't like the way she was acting. But, again, people mourned differently. "So if you need me, Livy . . . you call me. Understand?"

She looked up at him, gave a very small smile. "I do. Thanks."

He headed out. "I'll call you about the job when I get back."

"Okay."

Vic walked down the hall and met up with Shen.

"I booked our flights," Shen said, closing up his laptop and slipping it into its case.

"Good."

"So what did she like?" Shen asked as they headed toward the elevators.

Vic stopped, thought a moment, and admitted, "You know . . . I still have no idea."

Chapter 4

Eventually Livy decided she wasn't going to get anything worthwhile done, so she crawled out from under her desk, picked up her backpack, grabbed a jar of European honey from the basket Vic had given her, and left her office.

Livy walked home. She didn't look around like she usually did. Didn't seek out those images that gave her ideas or had her scrambling for her digital SLR camera. Instead she just walked with her head down and feeling pretty damn sorry for herself.

Livy never had before. She knew a lot of artists who did. Who, no matter how successful or not they were, always felt sorry for themselves. Complained about anything and everything. Made everyone around them miserable. Livy had always prided herself on not being like that. She was too focused on her work. Too lost in her photographs to bother with any of that unnecessary bullshit.

But these days . . .

Still, Livy knew she had to get over herself. Everybody kept trying to say it was the loss of her father, but she knew better.

More like the loss of her career. Her soul.

Dragging now, Livy reached her apartment building. She

went up the stoop, opened the door, and walked to the elevator. A few minutes there and down the hallway until she reached her place. She put the key in the lock and walked inside.

That's when she stopped. She had to. That python had slid right over her feet before disappearing behind a large pile of books she'd placed against the wall a few weeks before and hadn't bothered to do anything else with since.

Because Livy lived in a building filled with full-humans, she didn't have snakes in her house. Ever. They could disappear into your walls and set up a nest and the next thing you knew, you'd have snakes all over the damn place.

Livy headed down the hallway until she reached her kitchen. But she stopped right at the doorway . . . and gawked.

"Livy!"

Misleadingly skinny arms wrapped around Livy's neck and she was hugged tightly. Something that anyone who knew her knew she hated. She was not a hugger. Nor did she like to be hugged. By anyone. Even her mother didn't hug her.

"What are you doing here?" Livy demanded.

"Don't worry." The skinny arms slipped off and went back behind a narrow back. As always, her visitor looked like a little girl. But she wasn't. "I didn't break out. I'm here legally."

"Prove it."

"Livy—"

"Prove it or I'm calling the cops."

Feet stomped over to the kitchen table and an already rumpled document was pulled out from the front of a backpack and held out for Livy.

Livy looked at it. A Certificate of Release from New York prisons. Where her cousin Melanie "Melly" Kowalski had been living for the last ten months. She'd been given eighteen months, and why she was out early, Livy didn't know. But she had a bigger issue.

"Why are you here, Melly?" Livy asked, handing the certificate back to her cousin.

"I need a place to stay. Your mom said you wouldn't mind."

"Oh," Livy said. "Okay."

Then Livy turned and headed toward the front door.

"Hey," Melly called after her. "If you're running out, pick me up some vodka, would ya?"

Livy reached the sidewalk outside her building and stopped. She looked around. Didn't see anything right away, so started walking.

Maybe she could stay over at Toni's. Because she couldn't stay at her apartment. She refused to stay at her apartment.

"What is happening to my life?" Livy asked the air. "What is happening?"

As they walked down the full-human airline ramp toward the plane, Shen announced, "We'll need a good company name."

Vic sighed. "We're still not partners."

"Why not? We make a good team."

"Do I actually have to state that I work alone? Because I work alone."

"You work with me all the time. You worked with me just yesterday. You're working with me *now*."

"See? The fact that you argue everything with me makes it impossible for us to be partners."

They reached the entrance to the plane, but before Vic could bend down to get through the opening, Shen gave him a quick shove from behind. Vic stumbled forward, his head banging into the body of the plane.

"Ow!" Vic barked. "What the holy hell—"

"Are you okay?" Shen asked, his arm around Vic's shoulders. "You poor guy."

Shen pressed his hand to the back of Vic's head, lowering it enough so he could get into the cabin.

The two flight attendants helping passengers rushed forward.

"Sir, are you all right?"

"He's fine," Shen said. "But a little ice pack for his head would be great."

"Of course," one attendant agreed as she rushed off.

"Come on, buddy," Shen said, patting Vic's shoulder. "Let's go force those long legs of yours into that economy middle seat."

"Oh." The remaining attendant leaned in. "You know, we have some seats available in first class."

"That would be really nice. He gets so uncomfortable in those small seats."

Smiling at Shen, the attendant led the pair to seats in first class. Once they were settled, the attendant went back to her work.

"See?" Shen asked Vic.

"See what?"

"See how helpful I was. I got us in first class."

"Unless the plane is booked completely, I *always* get first class. All they have to do is look at me. But I've never had to ram my head into a plane to get first-class seats."

"You know, you're very unappreciative of what I bring to the table."

Vic leaned over, searching the aisle for a flight attendant. "I wonder if I have to wait for takeoff before I can get a vodka . . ."

Sitting at the kitchen table in the apartment Toni shared with her mate, Livy rested her head on her crossed arms. "Maybe I should go to Europe."

"Are you allowed in Europe?" Toni asked as she put away dishes in the overhead cabinets.

"Parts. They seem to like me in Germany."

"You could also throw your cousin out of your apartment so you don't have to leave the country."

"That sounds disturbingly like work."

"Olivia—"

"Uh-oh," Livy sighed, knowing she was about to get a Toni Lecture.

"—I know you're going through a rough time. This isn't what you wanted for your life. But every artist goes through struggles." Toni placed her hand on Livy's shoulder. "But every struggle you endure will only make you better at what you do."

"You gave that speech to Kyle when he refused to wear his diapers anymore."

Toni glanced off. "Are you sure?"

"Yes. I clearly remember because he'd torn off the diaper you'd made him put on and threw it at your head. But before throwing it, he'd filled it."

"Little bastard." Toni shuddered. "Look, the point I'm making is . . . suck it up! You're a great artist. I know it. You know it. You're just having a bad time of it. Add in the death of your father and I'm not exactly surprised you're a little depressed."

Toni's phone went off and she glanced at the caller ID. "It's Russia."

"Now the entire country is contacting you?"

"It's the Russian hockey team. The game went so well last year they want to have one here. I'm in charge of making the arrangements." She smiled with pride at doing the job she loved so much, which made Livy snarl a little. "Well, if you're going to get such an attitude, I guess I'll answer the phone."

She did, walking out of the room for her conversation.

Livy thought about getting something to eat, but before she could move, she suddenly realized she was surrounded. By wolves.

Lifting her head off her arms, Livy looked around at the Smith Pack females now sitting at the kitchen table with her or standing behind her.

"What?" she asked the females.

"You all right, darlin'?" one of them asked. "You look mighty sad."

Ronnie Lee Reed, second-in-command of the Smith females, held her baby out. "Wanna hold him?"

Livy glared at the lion-wolf hybrid—and he glared right back, all that hair nearly covering bright blue distrustful eyes.

"You're kidding, right?" Livy asked.

"What in the world does that mean?"

"Your baby's evil." When she saw the mother's distressed expression, Livy quickly added, "Not like unholy evil, if you believe in a standard god."

"A *standard* god?" Sissy Mae Smith, Alpha Female of the New York Smith Pack, asked as she sat down catty-corner from Livy.

"Personally, I'm a fan of the Nordic and East Asian gods. They have quite an edge to them."

Sissy Mae laughed. "An edge? Darlin', have you actually *read* the Bible?"

"Yes," Livy replied, ending the laughter instantly.

Sissy Mae stared at her. "You read the Bible? The entire Bible?"

"Yes. I've also read the Torah, the Koran, the Vedas, Norse mythology, Roman and Greek mythology, and *The Tao of Pooh*." When the She-wolves continued to gaze silently at her, Livy added, "As an artist, I have to be open to everything."

"Artist?" one of the She-wolves asked.

"Our Livy here," Sissy Mae said, "is a photographer." She pointed at Livy. "That's right. You're doing Blayne's wedding."

With rage and panic welling up inside her, Livy asked, "I am?"

"Aren't you?"

"I never agreed—" Livy's phone vibrated and she pulled it out of her back pocket and quickly glanced at the screen. "Excuse me," she said, pushing away from the table. She walked across the kitchen and answered her phone.

"Hello?"

"Hey, cousin."

"Hey, Jocelyn. How's it going?"

"Not bad. Sorry I couldn't make the funeral."

"No problem." Jocelyn was Livy's first cousin on her father's side and she'd been knee-deep in the middle of a job when news came in about Livy's father. Kowalskis had been known to walk out in the middle of jobs when family issues came up, but from what Livy could tell from Jake, Jocelyn had been driving a getaway car through Rome at the time of the funeral and then immediately lying low for a bit until the dust settled. Something Livy didn't expect her cousin to walk away from until it was safe. Even for a funeral.

Three wolves walked into the kitchen while Livy was on the phone with her cousin. The Reed Boys, they were called. Laid-back Ricky Lee was mated to Toni. Rory Lee was the oldest and the crankiest of the three brothers. He rarely spoke to Livy unless he felt he had to out of politeness. And then there was Reece Lee, one of the Carnivore hockey players. Livy found Reece the most entertaining and had used him more than once as a model for her portrait work.

When he walked in, he spotted Livy right away and waved at her. She nodded back as her cousin asked, "So how did it go?"

"Fistfight on the casket. Poisonous snakes in the backyard. My father's ex-girlfriend head-butted by my mother." Livy shrugged. "The usual, really."

"Sounds it."

Ronnie Lee, seeing her brothers, stood with her son in her arms. "Take Reggie, I need to go to the bathroom."

At their sister's request, Ricky Lee immediately changed direction and walked over to Livy by the sink, Reece dropped to one knee so he could tie a boot that didn't need it, which left poor Rory unprepared. His sister shoved the baby in Rory's arms and the stoic wolf suddenly appeared terrified. If the females of the Pack noticed, none of them said anything. Instead, they kept chatting among themselves.

Livy asked her cousin, "So what's up?"

"Well, I'm going to be in Manhattan in the next couple of days for a job. Thought you'd like to sign on."

Livy frowned at the statement. "Huh?"

"Your mother called me . . . said you needed work."

Rubbing her forehead, Livy asked, "She said what?"

"Uh . . . oh."

While her cousin was stammering on the other end, Livy watched Rory Lee carry his nephew through the open door and into the dining room. He began pacing back and forth, gently patting the child's back.

"Shit," her cousin muttered. "I knew I should have talked to Jake first. But your mother sounded so—"

"Casual?" Livy asked.

"Yeah. Exactly. So I guess she's still not a big supporter of your photography career, huh?"

"Apparently not."

Rory suddenly stumbled past the open doorway, Ronnie Lee's baby now attached to his uncle's throat by his little baby teeth, his little baby claws dug into his uncle's shoulders.

"Hey," Jocelyn asked, "are you okay?"

"Yeah. I'm fine," Livy lied, watching in concern as poor Rory stumbled back the other way, desperately trying to pry his nephew off his neck.

"Maybe we could meet when I get into the city."

"Sure."

"Okay. I'll talk to you later."

"Yeah. Thanks, Joce." Livy disconnected the call and glanced over at Ricky. "Are you going to help him?"

"I find it's better not to get involved."

Ronnie walked back into the kitchen just as her baby was finally yanked off Rory's neck and sent flying right into her arms. She easily caught her child and then all the She-wolves turned on Rory, gawking at the poor wolf in horror.

"Good Lord, Rory Lee!" Ronnie snarled. "You don't throw babies! Especially mine!"

"Look what he did to me!" Rory pointed at his unmarred neck.

"What am I looking at?" Sissy Mae asked. "'Cause I don't see nothin'."

"Just wait until the little bastard grows into his fangs," Rory promised. "Then you'll see!"

"I don't know what's been wrong with you lately," Ronnie said, sitting back at the kitchen table. "It's like you've lost your dang mind!"

"Where's Toni?" Ricky asked Livy.

"Taking a call from the Russian team."

Ricky sighed. "I'm sensing another trip to Siberia coming up."

"Now?" Livy snorted a little. "It's freezing over there."

"It's a winter nightmare, but they do take good care of us when we come over." He moved a little closer. "Just so you know," Ricky said low, motioning to his Packmates, "they're probably going to crash here for the night."

"All night?"

"Yeah. There's a game on. We'll watch it on our big flat screen, which we all love, and then, before you know it, they're asleep on our living room floor. Toni doesn't mind, but you—"

"Yeah. Tell Toni I'll check in with her later."

Chuckling, Ricky nodded. "Will do. Have a good night."

Livy made it out of the apartment and down to the street before Reece caught up with her.

"Hey," he said, catching her arm. "You're not staying?"

"Can't. Your friends get on my nerves."

Reece laughed. "You're not a subtle gal, are ya, Livy?"

"Nope." Heading down the street, she waved back at him.

Once she hit the corner, Livy stood there for a second, wondering where she'd go now. Without her raising her hand, a taxi stopped in front of her. Livy opened the door and got in.

"Where to?" the cabbie asked.

Livy thought a moment, then smirked. "Westchester."

Vic watched over Shen's shoulder as the panda did what he did best and hacked into the delivery company's computer system. They'd found a security guard willing to let them in, but they didn't have a lot of time.

It didn't take long to figure out that this company was, truly, a delivery business. They delivered cars and other heavy items for their rich clients to and from foreign countries. But they also moved illegal products like elephant tusks and stolen paintings and protected-animal meat and furs. Also for their rich clients.

But that still didn't explain the circuitous route the package from Russia took to get to Miami. Once Shen was into the system, he discovered that the package had gone from Russia through Japan down to Australia to South Africa into Argentina up through Peru through Columbia and into Cuba before hitting Miami.

The question that Vic needed answered, though, was where had it gone from there.

"It was a pickup," Shen finally said. "Someone came and picked up the box and took it. No name provided, though."

"All right." Vic patted Shen's shoulder. "Let's go."

"Give me a minute."

Vic waited while Shen erased evidence that he'd been tooling around the company's system. Once done, they headed out, Vic handing the rest of the cash he'd promised to the security guard.

They walked away from the port toward where they'd left the rental SUV.

"So now what?" Shen asked.

"Every time we think we're close, there's another dead end with this guy."

"There's got to be something we can try."

Vic stopped, hands in pockets, his gaze locked on the clear sky. "We can check the daughter's place again," he said, resigned.

"That could have been where the package was going."

"Doubtful."

"Maybe. Or maybe a father making a desperate attempt to know his daughter after missing out on the last thirty years. He wouldn't be the first. And whoever picked up the package and brought it to her . . ."

"Might know where we can start looking." Vic nodded. "It's better than nothing."

They walked on, reaching the vehicle quickly.

"And when we're done with this," Shen said as he opened the passenger's side. "We need to shut that place down." He gestured in the direction of the company they'd just left.

"Absolutely," Vic said, immediately thinking about the animals that had suffered for the most ridiculous reasons.

Shen glanced at his watch as Vic opened his door and got into the SUV. "I think we can make the red-eye if traffic is good."

"Great," Vic said, starting the SUV. "I'm so ready to go home."

Chapter 5

They'd taken the red-eye back to LaGuardia and now Vic was tired and cranky. Plus, he couldn't seem to shake Shen. The panda had gotten in the cab with him and was now getting out as Vic paid the driver.

"Why aren't you going to your hotel?" Vic asked as they headed toward his Westchester house.

"I wanted to make sure you got home safe and sound."

Vic stopped outside the chain-link gate surrounding his home. "You want me to make you something to eat, don't you?"

"I'm a guest," Shen said, easing the gate open and stepping onto Vic's property. "It's the polite thing to do."

"You are such a—"

"Hello, Victor!"

Vic gritted his teeth. He was *not* in the mood for this. For her. At least with Shen, Vic could be as cranky and rude as he deemed it necessary this early in the morning. But Shen was a panda. Tolerant as most bears were. It was the reason his father could put up with Vic's beautiful but high-maintenance mother. He was a tolerant grizzly. Sure, you startled a grizzly, you risked getting your face ripped off.

But otherwise, they put up with a lot as long as you kept the sounds low and the food supply substantial.

But this female wasn't a bear. She was a feline. And a pushy one at that.

"Good morning, good morning," she practically sang from behind him. And Vic wanted so badly to shut his gate and walk into his house without answering, but damn his Russian parents with their insistence on polite behavior. Polite behavior that didn't allow him just to ignore a lady, no matter how annoying the lady might be.

Hand gripping the strap of his travel bag, Vic slowly turned and faced the pretty She-tiger standing behind him.

"Hi, Brittany."

"I'm so glad you're here." She held up a perfectly baked coffee cake on a crystal plate with a crystal dome top.

Sure. She could have bought it at the bakery like most women would have. But not Brittany, local tigress, mom of two, and female in search of a long-term mate. Nope. She'd made that perfectly designed and probably incredible-tasting cake all by herself while raising her two perfect cubs and running a rather successful party planning company out of her house.

What exactly was he supposed to do with Brittany? Vic was far from perfect. In fact, he enjoyed the imperfection of himself and his family. And he could just imagine how poorly his mother and Brittany would get along. He shuddered at the thought.

"I made this just for you. My famous lemon honey coffee cake with buttercream glaze."

"Sounds—"

"Why don't I cut you a slice myself?" She walked around him, past Shen like he didn't exist, and up the path to his house.

Vic watched her move. He knew if she were in her shifted form, her tail would be calling his name, swinging from side to side, twitching at the tip.

"That is quite the ass," Shen muttered.

"Yes. It's perfect."

Shen chuckled, rolled his eyes. "You and your antiperfection agenda."

Vic was about to reiterate—yet again—why he felt the way he did about anyone who tried so hard to be constantly perfect, but he was too busy watching Brittany walk into his house . . . unobstructed.

"You never leave your door unlocked," Shen told him.

"I know."

"Then how—"

A few seconds later, they heard a female's startled scream turn into an angry roar.

Running now, Vic and Shen charged up the path to the house. Vic yanked the metal security door open and ran inside, down the hall, and into his kitchen with Shen right behind him.

That's where they found Brittany with a blood-covered hand over her face, roaring at the cabinets over his refrigerator. Confused, Vic grabbed a towel and pressed it to her wounds.

"My God, Brittany, what happened?"

"She attacked me!"

Vic and Shen looked around the room, but didn't see anyone else.

"Who attacked you?"

She yanked the towel from his hand and pointed at the cabinets. "Her!"

Now *really* confused, Vic walked to the cabinets over his stainless-steel refrigerator and opened one of the wood doors. Opened it and stared.

A naked Livy Kowalski, comfortably curled up inside his cabinet, held out an open jar and softly asked, "African honey?"

Vic wanted to be angry. She'd broken into his home, eaten his honey, and attacked his neighbor. And yet . . .

Closing the cabinet door, Vic faced a raging Brittany.

"Brittany," he began, "I am so sorry. This is all my fault."

"Your fault?"

"Well, I don't allow her out of that cabinet without my permission." Vic forced himself to keep his focus on a now-horrified Brittany because of Shen and what he was sure was his reaction, but Shen was smart enough to turn away from them all.

"Your permission?" Brittany growled. "You keep a woman in your *food* cabinets?"

"It would be cruel to make her stay under the sink. She's not *that* small."

"Do you really expect me to believe that, Victor Barinov?"

Uh-oh. She was seeing through his lie, which meant he'd never get rid of her. Yeah, yeah, Brittany was really pretty and probably gave a guy a wild ride in bed. But Vic wasn't nineteen anymore. He really hated waking up in the morning with a woman he had nothing to say to. And he had absolutely *nothing* to say to Brittany.

But before Vic could either spill his guts—"I have no idea why a honey badger is in my cabinet!"—or lie more—"And she's my cousin! That's double wrong!"—his older sister suddenly stormed into his kitchen, Vic's six-year-old nephew hanging off her hip.

"Well, I've left him!" Irina, called Ira by the family, announced to the room.

"Again?" Shen asked.

Which got him the quick Ira-response of, "Shut it, Shen."

Vic focused on his sister. "She doesn't believe me."

Ira blinked. "Who doesn't believe you?"

"Brittany."

Ira and Brittany sized each other up as only She-predators could. Like Vic, Ira was half bear, but the Siberian tigress side of her didn't much like this other cat in territory Ira felt the need to protect, at least until Vic found a mate of his own.

"Doesn't believe you about what?" Ira asked.

"About *my* little Livy."

His sister glanced around, her eyes settling on the cabinet. The first time Vic had found out that Livy was breaking into his house was when his sister had opened a cabinet and found the honey badger sound asleep, her fingers and face still sticky from the honey she'd devoured. Although Ira hadn't reacted nearly as violently as Brittany. Instead, she'd quietly closed the cabinet, tiptoed out of the room, and told Vic, "There's a naked woman in your cabinet . . . and she's eaten all the honey."

After a moment of silence, Ira suddenly announced, "Well, not everyone is comfortable with that sort of relationship in this society." She smiled at Brittany. "But Livy does have her benefits. When he's out of town, she comes over to do my laundry and clean my house. But I *insist* she put on clothes first! I have a child to think of."

Brittany threw up her hands. "I'm leaving!" she announced, her expression disgusted. "And I'm taking my cake with—"

When her words abruptly ended, Vic and his sister looked down. Shen was sitting at the kitchen table and had a handful of cake, his mouth covered in the buttercream frosting.

He swallowed and said, "Really good cake. And I'm not even a lemon guy."

Maybe if Shen had cut the cake, Brittany would have still taken it. But seeing that his hands had been in it . . .

Definitely something bears could overlook, but not a feline. And Brittany was all feline.

Spinning on her heel, she stormed out, slamming the front door behind her.

After a moment of silence, Ira asked, "So Livy's naked in your cabinets again?"

Vic shrugged. "Yeah."

* * *

Livy was reaching for another jar of honey when the cabinet doors opened. She winced at the bright light from the kitchen windows.

"What are you doing?" Vic demanded. "Why do you keep breaking into my house?"

"As much as I protect you from these pathetic females, you'd think you'd appreciate my presence."

"I don't." He frowned. "And why are you always naked when I find you?" Vic folded his arms over his chest. "Tell me you didn't eat your way into my house again."

"Of course not." Livy licked honey off her thumb. "I *burrowed* my way into your house. There's a difference."

"Dammit, Livy!"

Vic went in search of the hole Livy had created as his sister placed her son on the ground and tapped his butt. "Go watch TV, Igor."

"But I want to see naked Livy!"

"Igor . . ."

The little boy ran off before his mother could get really terse, and Ira Barinov walked over to the cabinet. She was shorter than her brother by nearly a foot but that still made her over six feet tall. Ira held her arms up. "Come on, cranky badger."

"But I'm comfortable."

"You already have him freaking out about holes. You don't want him to think too much about your naked ass rubbing against the cabinets storing his food."

Livy knew Ira was right. Vic was quite mellow most of the time, but sometimes he could get surprisingly obsessive over the strangest things. And once he locked on, he just never let go. She really didn't want to be on the receiving end of that, so Livy waved Ira's arms away. "I can get down on my own."

"Not without your claws, and you already left scratches in the wood where you climbed in. Let's not make it worse."

Deciding not to argue, Livy placed her hands on Ira's massive shoulders and let the hybrid lower her to the floor. She ignored the pat on her head that followed.

"So what brings you to my brother's territory?" Ira asked.

Livy walked around the kitchen island and grabbed the clothes she'd left there the night before.

"I thought he was out of town."

Ira chuckled. "Not why did you choose his house. I just assumed you couldn't find an open window anywhere in the City. I'm talking about why did you feel the need to burrow into his honey cabinets."

"Oh, nothing. Just my entire life is falling apart."

"It couldn't fall apart at your own place?"

Livy heard no vicious tone in her words. It was just a question. So she answered while grabbing her clothes, "I couldn't stay at the apartment. Not with her there."

Ira leaned against the counter, and pulled a bowl of fruit close. "Who?" she asked after choosing a few grapes and popping them into her mouth.

"My cousin."

"If you didn't want her there, why did you invite her?"

Livy pulled her head through her sweatshirt. "I didn't invite her."

"Oh." Ira shrugged. "Then throw her out."

"It won't matter. She'll just come back." Livy finger-combed her hair off her face. "We always come back."

"Like a chronic illness," Shen offered around a mouthful of cake. And when Livy and Ira stared at him, he shrugged and added, "It felt like you needed an analogy there. At the end." The women kept staring, so he suddenly dug his laptop out of the bag resting against his chair. "Forget it."

Livy pulled the straps of her backpack over her shoulders. "Well, I'm out of here."

"You're leaving?" Ira asked.

"Since your brother's home now—"

"Oh, come on. Stay. We have cake." She glared at Shen. "Stop eating the cake!"

"I'm hungry!"

"I appreciate the invite, but once your brother finds that hole—"

"Dammit, Livy!"

Livy pointed at where the yelling had just come from. "Yup. I'm out." She went to walk around the island, but Ira reached across and grabbed Livy's arm.

"Stay. Please. We can chat!"

Livy couldn't help but frown. "Chat?"

"She's looking for a girlfriend," Shen explained, his gaze locked on his laptop screen. Two big fingers quickly moved across the keyboard.

"I'm not really girlfriend material."

"Have you ever thought a pair of shoes were cute?"

Livy shrugged. "Yeah. I guess, but—"

"Good enough!"

Ira yanked Livy over to the table, removed her backpack, and forced her into a chair. "I'll make breakfast!"

Vic walked back into the kitchen. "You keep putting holes in my house," he rightfully accused.

"I don't want criminals to see any broken windows when I'm not here. The holes are harder to spot."

"Now isn't that nice of her?" Ira asked, her head in the refrigerator. "Oooh. There's bacon."

"Stop siding with her." Vic sat down opposite Livy.

"If you don't want her breaking into your house, then give her a key."

"I offered."

"I don't like keys. It implies . . ." Livy thought a moment. "Permanence."

"I'm not asking you to marry me. I'm asking you not to break into my home."

"Yeah," Livy replied. "I know."

* * *

Vic did not understand this woman because *she* didn't seem to understand the most basic things. Like how it made more sense to take the keys he'd had specially made for her rather than burrowing expensive and not easily repaired holes into his house so that she had a place to crash for the night. Vic had finally had to hire a shifter contractor to take care of the hole problem because he'd run out of lies to tell the full-human one he normally used. And the shifter contractors? They overcharged! Thieves! All of them! Especially the bears.

Yet the strangest thing about it all? Vic strongly felt that if he'd asked Livy very seriously not to come back into his home, she wouldn't. Out of some Livy-only-understands-it sense of honor. But he couldn't bring himself to do that—he just didn't know why.

Livy's phone went off and she pulled the device from her back pocket. But one look at the screen had her dropping her head to his thick wood table—hard. The sound was so loud, Ira turned away from the stove, where she was busy putting bacon in one of the pans he never had time to use.

The phone stopped ringing, but then started up again a few seconds later. Livy lifted her head, took several deep breaths, and answered.

"Yeah?" Livy's mouth set in a hard line. Strange. It wasn't like she smiled much, but her mouth was usually quite relaxed . . . wait. Why did he know that? How often was he staring at this woman's mouth? "Yeah. She's there. Yeah, I did leave her alone. She's not a child." Livy paused, dark eyes narrowing. "Because the little twat is *not* my problem," she snapped into the phone.

Livy winced and the yelling from the other end of the phone reached Vic. Most of it at this point was in Mandarin, but Vic could tell by the tone and what he knew of the language—which was enough to successfully get around

China when necessary—that Livy was getting her ass reamed . . . by her mother.

"You are a spoiled child! Undeserving of the Yang or Kowalski name if you can't do one thing for your family!"

"Melly is—"

"Your cousin! And an important part of this family! You are so selfish!"

"Fine! I'll—"

"No, no! I wouldn't think of asking the *princess* to lower herself to help her family. I would never dare to tread on her oh-so-important artistic life! I sent your cousins over to watch out for Melly. And they went. Because they understand family! *Unlike you!*"

Livy sighed and said in English, "Whatever, Ma."

There was a long pause. Dangerously long. Then Vic heard her mother scream, *"I no longer have a daughter! My daughter's dead to me!"*

But at the hysterical words, Livy only crossed her eyes. Vic sensed this was not the first time those two sentences had been hurled at her.

The screaming on the other end stopped and Livy lowered the phone. Vic assumed her mother had hung up.

"I have to say, I didn't understand the words," Shen observed, "but the tone I recognize from when my grandmother and mother go at it."

Bringing eggs and milk over to the island, Ira asked Shen, "You don't know Mandarin?"

"As I've been telling you since I was in college with your brother . . . I am *sixth*-generation Chinese American. The most Mandarin I know is from the Chinese restaurant down the street. So you can keep your Russian racism to yourself."

"Excuse me," Ira snapped back. "That was not *Russian* racism. That was good ol' American racism, thank you very much. And we're damn proud of it."

"It took her years to hone," Vic muttered.

"Sure did!" She grinned. "I'm gettin' pretty good at it, too."

Ira placed the eggs and milk on the counter, but quickly noticed her brother's frown. "What's wrong?"

"Is any of that fresh?" Because Vic hadn't bought groceries in months.

"I brought them last night," Livy admitted.

Stunned, Vic gazed at Livy. "You did?"

"I didn't think you'd be home for a while. I wanted to make sure I had enough to eat."

Vic studied Livy for a moment.

"What?" she pushed, when he didn't say anything.

"You never crash for more than a night. You're really avoiding this cousin of yours, aren't you?" he guessed.

"I get around her . . . and all hell breaks loose. She's crazy. I don't mean cute, endearing crazy or even annoying, pain-in-the-ass crazy. She's just nuts."

"Is that why your mother is insisting she stay with you? So you can take care of her?"

Livy snorted. "Hell, no. My mother hates Melly," Livy said flatly. "The whole family hates Melly."

Eggs forgotten, Ira walked around the island and rested her butt on it, arms crossed over her chest. "They do?"

Livy dropped her phone on the table, which explained why her phone wasn't in a sexy or cutesy case like most women had for their smartphones, but was in some sturdy rubber that could take a real beating. Because she probably beat the hell out of the thing.

"Melly," she began, "is . . ." Livy thought a moment before announcing, "Crazy. I don't mean shifter crazy. I mean motherfucking crazy. She was in jail . . . no." Livy shook her head. "She was just paroled from *prison*. No one in the damn family wants to deal with her, but we all do."

Vic said, "I don't understand . . . if your family can't stand her . . . why is your mother forcing you to take care of her?"

"Because . . . she's got skills. And my family will always exploit skills. No matter how annoying you may be."

"Skills? What skills?"

"Well . . . Melly can look at a painting, like a Monet or a Renoir or a Bernardo Zenale—'cause she really liked him—for, like, two hours—and in three days give you a perfect replica. Aged perfectly and everything. There are at least two of her Monets, and a François Clouet in the Louvre." She paused. "But you don't know that because we could all go to jail, yada yada yada, blah blah blah."

The silence after that was long and painful, until Vic's sister pushed the plate of nearly finished dessert across the table to Livy and asked, "Cake?"

Livy stood. "Thanks for breakfast," she told Ira after she'd finished eating. "It was good."

"It was bacon," Ira joked. "Who can ever go wrong with bacon?"

"You going home?" Vic asked.

"Guess I should. At least to make sure my apartment's still there."

"Maybe it won't be that bad." And Livy appreciated him trying to make her feel better. It actually gave her a brief moment of hope—until it was dashed by Shen.

"Uh . . . Livy?" He glanced up from the laptop he'd been working on even while they ate breakfast.

"What?"

"I was searching around . . . about your cousin . . . because, ya know . . ." The panda shrugged. "Crazy girls usually mean hot sex and I wanted to see what she looked like."

Ira sneered. "All these years, Shen, and you *still* disgust me."

Shen ignored his friend's sister and pointed at his computer screen. "Is this her?"

Livy walked around until she stood behind Shen and the

Barinov siblings stood behind her. Then, together, they all watched the horror unfold.

It was especially horrifying when Melly, while guzzling back another glass of vodka and orange juice, admitted to the PC camera Livy used for online meetings, "You know what? I totally am not supposed to be drinking right now. I think the judge said that." Melly thought for a moment, her eyes gazing up at the ceiling. "Yep! Totally not supposed to be drinking. I think it's part of my probation or whatever." She shrugged. "Well, like, who's going to find out? Am I right, girls?" That's when Melly leaned back and Livy could see her other female cousins that Livy's mother had sent over to "take care of Melly" in the background, including Jocelyn—who Livy thought knew better! And the whole group of them were already drunk and out of control.

Fists in the air, the She-badgers began chanting, "Chug, Melly! Chug! Chug! Chug!" And Melly did.

"Is this live?" Livy asked.

"No. It was posted a few hours ago."

"Right." Livy nodded, knew what she had to do. "Okay. Thanks for breakfast."

"Where are you going?" Vic asked.

"Back to the apartment. I've got people to kill."

Vic shook his head. "Anyone else, Livy, and I'd assume they were just being overly dramatic. But you . . . I'm pretty sure you're going to kill them."

"Yeah. I'll get away with it, too. By the time I'm done, it'll be like they never existed."

"That's an option," Vic told her, trying to be reasonable. He was always trying to be reasonable, which made her think he was much more bear than cat. "But I have a job for you. It's very important."

"Whitlan's daughter again? Seriously? Can we not just leave that girl alone?"

"We need you to check her apartment, which would be much safer than dealing with your cousin right now."

"Breaking and entering could still put me in jail, though, Barinov. If I get caught."

"But much less time than first-degree murder."

He had a point.

"It's not like your cousins are going anywhere," Vic added.

Not until they'd slept off whatever they'd drunk. And if they'd added some snake poison for that little extra kick, they could be out for days.

"We'll do this together," Vic offered.

And Livy couldn't help but snort. "You? You're going to break in with me? 'Cause I don't exactly see you blendin' into the walls."

"Shen and I will be your backup."

Shen finally looked away from the tits Melly had decided to bare on camera. "Wait. How did *I* get in the middle of this?"

"You're the one who keeps wanting to be my partner," Vic snapped at his friend.

"Yeah, but—"

"Just do what I tell you, panda." Vic smiled at Livy. "Okay, Livy?"

Livy took a breath. "It's probably a good idea. That way I can more carefully arrange the murders."

Vic nodded at her statement. "See? That sounds like a good plan."

But Ira gawked at her brother. "That really sounds like a good plan to you?"

"Better than the first one," he shot back.

CHAPTER 6

Once Vic had Livy's solemn promise not to suddenly run off so she could eviscerate her cousin, he slept most of the day. Not even bothering to change, but dropping facedown over his bed, fully clothed. He woke up when the scent of his sister's garlic chicken snaked up the stairs to his bedroom. But he waited until his nephew climbed up on his back and tugged at his hair before he actually opened his eyes.

"Uncle Vic, Mommy says dinner is ready." Vic didn't move, so his nephew tugged harder. "Uncle Vic! Uncle Vic! Dinner!"

When Vic still didn't move, his nephew leaned over to see Vic's face. That's when Vic unleashed his fangs and gave a low-volume roar.

Igor squealed and laughed, trying to quickly get off Vic so he could make a run for it.

Flipping onto his back, Vic caught his nephew around the waist and tossed him up in the air.

Igor laughed while kicking his legs and swinging his arms until his mother yelled up the stairs, "Would you two stop fooling around and get down here for dinner? Now!"

Grinning, Vic stood, tossing the boy over his shoulder and taking him downstairs to the kitchen. He plopped Igor in a chair, adding a few phone books so the boy could feel as tall as he would likely be one day, and looked around.

"Where's Livy?"

"Outside," his sister said, putting big bowls of food out for them. "Staring off into the distance like she's analyzing all the ills of the world." Ira shook her head. "These artists. So moody."

Vic stared at his sister a moment before asking, "So how's your husband?"

Ira, eyes narrowing, put her hand over her son's face so she could give Vic the finger without guilt.

Chuckling, Vic headed outside to the backyard, but stopped when he saw Shen walk into his kitchen.

"Are you staying?" Vic asked.

"You're not going to cruelly send me off to a hotel now are you? All alone?"

Then Shen fluttered his eyes in a way that Vic was entirely not comfortable with.

"Don't do that," Vic muttered before walking out the back door to find Livy.

As his sister had said, she was sitting on one of the benches in his backyard, her body almost lost in one of his leather jackets—and staring up at the sky.

Vic sat down next to her, grimacing when the bench creaked ominously.

Slowly, eyes wide, Livy looked over at him.

"It's not my fault. It's this weak full-human furniture."

"Why do you have full-human furniture when you are far from full-human?"

A little embarrassed, Vic shrugged. "It came with the place."

"Did all the furniture come with the place?"

"No."

"Did you choose the furniture?" When Vic didn't answer, Livy said, "Your sister. That's what I thought."

"What? It's too girly?"

"No. Not at all. It's big and comfortable and damn sturdy. But it was carefully purchased and placed, and I don't see you doing that with furniture. You're a 'whatever is lying around is what I'll use' kind of guy."

"And you know this because . . . ?"

"I'm the same way. If I ever invest in a house, Toni will probably design it for me." Livy thought a moment and added, "Or Kyle. He's very choosy about home decoration. Pretty much redesigned his parents' place when he was ten. He did a fabulous job."

"He's just a *kid*."

"He's brilliant. And a little evil. But I think that's what I like about him."

"So what's going on?" Vic asked when she went silent again. "You seem moodier than normal. Is it your father?"

"No."

"Your cousin?"

Livy rolled her eyes and gave a snort of disgust, but she didn't say anything else and Vic had a feeling that wasn't it either.

"Work?"

And that's when Livy gave a long—rather dramatic, for Livy—sigh, and looked back up at the sky.

Vic noticed that Livy didn't have her camera. She always had some camera on her, from a small, silent Leica to her big, digital, SLR Nikon rig that made her look like a hardcore photojournalist. But lately, Livy didn't seem to have anything but the camera on her phone—which she never used for photography for "very specific moral reasons."

Vic didn't know what that meant, but what he did know was that the work he'd seen from her was amazing. And disturbing. And kind of freaky. Then again, so was Mapplethorpe . . . but honestly, Vic was more an Ansel Adams man.

Shots of beautiful vistas in dramatic black-and-white were more his speed. Odd things done with whips . . . not so much.

Still, Vic knew how much Livy's work meant to her.

"Don't you have a show coming up?" he asked.

Livy, her legs pulled up on the bench, used her arms to turn her body toward him. "How do you know about my show?"

"You sent me an invitation."

"I did?" Livy looked off, then nodded. "Toni. She probably sent out the invitations." Suddenly, Livy shook her head. "I've got nothing."

"What do you mean?"

"I mean . . . I've got nothin'. I am creatively drained. I'm dead inside."

"You always seem dead inside."

"I'm not. I'm just quiet."

"Maybe you need to do something different. Get away from everything. Do you get a paid vacation from the team?"

"I never needed a break before. Creativity just poured from me like sweat from a long-distance runner. But now there's nothing. It's over."

"Or," Vic reasoned, "you can stop being a drama queen and just take a break to see if that helps."

"Yeah. That's an option, too."

"See?"

"Then again . . ."

Vic sighed. "Then again what?"

"When will I have the time? Now that I'm doing a goddamn wedding."

"You're doing a wedding?"

"Looks like it."

"Why, if you don't want to? Unless it's family."

"Not family. Just a pathetic weakness for cash."

"What *are* you talking about?"

"Blayne asked me to shoot her wedding. To get her off my back, I texted her an outrageous sum that no one in their right mind would pay."

"I don't think Blayne's been in her right mind since birth."

"I didn't even include a price breakdown *and* I demanded half in advance."

"And she still said yes."

"Of course she said yes!" an exasperated Livy exploded. "Because she's Blayne and is marrying a man who clearly has no control over her."

"You could still say no."

"And then you know what will happen?"

"She'll make you sad with her tears of pain?"

"More like I'll rip her face off because of her goddamn tears of pain."

"That will cause awkward times on your derby team."

"Don't care. But Toni *will* care because the Smith Pack *loves* Blayne. And that matters now that Toni is with Ricky Lee."

"Your life is very complex."

Livy burrowed deeper into Vic's jacket, looking way more adorable than she had a right to. "I know."

"So you're feeling like a sellout?" Vic asked.

Livy briefly wondered if she could permanently live in this jacket. It smelled good and made her feel surprisingly warm in the bracing East Coast cold. "Yes. Besides, what idiot would turn down that kind of cash?" She peeked over the collar of the jacket to look directly at Vic. "It's an *ungodly* amount of money. Un. God. Ly."

"But didn't Da Vinci work for royals? And the Church?"

"Huh?"

"Renaissance painters, the good ones, were commissioned to paint royals all the time. Bach and Mozart wrote music for royals."

"Your point?"

"You do what you have to during the day, so you can do what you love at night. Money, sadly, gives you freedom. Unless of course you plan to go off the grid, set up house in the middle of nowhere, and live off the land completely. I call that the Full Ted Kaczynski."

"Because I love being compared to a paranoid schizophrenic."

"We both know you're not a schizophrenic."

Livy smirked. "Thanks for that."

"All I'm saying is if you can get top dollar doing work that'll take you a few hours, thereby freeing you up to work on your real stuff . . . who cares? Unless, of course, you believe this is as good as you'll ever be—a wedding photographer for rich shifters who aren't intimidated by honey badgers."

When Livy scrunched herself deeper into Vic's coat, the hybrid smiled.

"You've gotta know that's not the case here."

"Do I? I've got nothing new to show for my gallery opening—"

"Then do limited prints of your early work."

Livy let the silence stretch for a bit before she asked, "May I finish?"

"Sure. But you know I'm right."

Livy sighed. "Yes. I know you're right. I guess I just wanted to—"

"Prove you haven't lost your creative genius?"

"*Would you stop doing that?*" Livy snarled, annoyed and surprised Vic understood her so well. Even Toni hadn't been fully grasping Livy's concerns lately, but the jackal also had a billion more things to worry about these days than just her family's performance schedules.

"Sorry. Feel free to go on."

But Livy had nothing else to say.

"Livy?"

"What?"

"It's okay to be afraid sometimes."

"I'm a honey badger. I'm fearless."

"In a fight? Yeah. Around snakes? Definitely. But this isn't a fight or snakes. It's something intensely personal that the average person would never understand."

"Then how come you do?"

Vic looked at her, his painfully bright gold eyes glinting in the darkness from the light seeping out of the kitchen windows.

"So you're calling me average?" he asked.

Startled, Livy said, "No. I'm not calling you average."

"So you think I'm astounding?"

"Astounding? How did we get to astounding? You didn't even *pause* at above average. Just leapt to astounding."

Vic stood, grinned. "I notice you didn't actually dispute astounding, though."

"Well—"

"No, no," he said quickly, reaching down and lifting her, then carrying her toward the back door. "Let's not ruin the moment."

After dinner and a few hours of TV watching, Ira went out to the backyard so she could inform her husband of "why I'm not coming home tonight, you bonehead," and Vic carried his sleeping nephew up to bed. He changed him into his favorite Captain America pajamas and tucked him in for the night. Then he went to his room and closed the door behind him.

Vic took off his clothes, pulled on a pair of black sweatpants, and crawled into bed. This time *under* the covers.

Happy to be home—even if there was a giant panda sleeping on his couch—Vic let out a relieved breath and settled in for the night.

As Vic began to drift off, he thought about dinner. The food had been delicious and the company more than tolerable, which for Vic was a big thing. He might put up with a lot on any given day, but that didn't mean he found those things tolerable. And yet, he'd truly enjoyed Livy's company. She wasn't painfully chatty, so when she did speak, her words had meaning and were often direct. He also discovered she was extremely well-read, but not a snob about it, and she had a vast amount of knowledge about really bad TV. It turned out she would flip on a channel and just leave it for the night while she worked—no matter what came on. She told them it was background noise that helped her focus, but she seemed to be fully aware of every storyline of every show she'd seen, from bad romantic comedies to bad biographies about the latest "story of survival" headline to the names and history of common reality TV superstars. Yet she retold those overblown shows with such a jaundiced eye that Vic knew he'd gladly have her over for dinner again. Because nothing had as high a meaning to someone with his Russian heritage as excellent dinner company.

Vic was nearly asleep when he realized that thinking about Livy made him feel surrounded by her scent. He was surprised how much he liked it, and how well it mingled with his own.

Vic's eyes popped open and he used his elbow to prop himself up. He sniffed the air, letting his nose lead him until he was halfway off his mattress so he could look under his bed. And that's where he found Livy.

"Olivia?"

"Yeah?"

"Was there a problem with your room?"

"No."

"Then why are you under my bed?"

"It's higher than the other beds."

"It's . . . what?"

"The other beds are lower to the floor and harder for me to get under. This one had more room. It's almost a little *too* roomy."

"And being in an actual bed—on the bed, I mean—just doesn't work for you?"

"Do you have an issue with me being under your bed?"

"Yeah. Kinda. It makes me feel like a bad host."

"You shouldn't. It's nice under here. And whoever cleans your house while you're away does a great job. It's clean as hell. I get under some beds and come out the next morning covered in dust bunnies."

"And you're sure you're comfortable?"

"Very."

"Well . . . okay then."

Vic stretched back out on his bed and stared up at his ceiling. It was really strange having someone *under* his bed who wasn't lying in wait to kill him. Something he had to be more wary of when he worked for the government. Now, though, he just had to tolerate a honey badger under his bed . . . snoring.

Vic blinked. She was asleep? Already?

"Lucky her," he muttered, because Vic didn't see himself going to sleep anytime soon while he had a woman asleep under his bed. Especially a woman with such smooth skin, dark eyes, and hair that always smelled like honey . . .

Wait. What was he doing? This was Livy he was thinking about. Livy. Honey badger and occasionally whiny artist. Livy. Who was like a sister to him? No. He never thought about Ira's smooth skin. Did she even have smooth skin? He didn't know, but Livy sure did. Really pretty, smooth skin . . .

Confusing himself even more with this internal dialogue,

Vic turned on his side and covered his head with his pillow. If nothing else, maybe the pillow would block out the honey scent coming from Livy's hair. What did she do? Bathe in honey?

Wait. Did she bathe in honey?

Vic growled. *What the hell am I doing?*

CHAPTER 7

Livy woke up the next morning still under Vic's bed, but now with a six-year-old cub staring at her.

"Yes?" she asked, keeping her voice low so as not to wake up Vic.

"Why are you under my uncle's bed?"

"It's comfortable."

"It is, isn't it?"

Livy and Igor continued to stare at each other for a few more minutes before Livy asked, "Hungry?"

"Yes."

"Pancakes work?"

"Is there honey?"

"I think I left at least a jar or two in the cabinets."

"African?"

"Don't push your luck."

"Okay."

Livy followed the little boy out from under the bed and out of the room, carefully closing the door behind her so she didn't wake up Vic.

Together, the pair moved through the house full of sleeping hybrids and a panda until they reached the kitchen.

Livy split the work with Igor, letting him carry things from the refrigerator and pour things she'd measured out into the bowl. Once Livy added the eggs herself—she couldn't risk shells getting into the batter—she placed Igor on the kitchen table and put the bowl in his lap. She gave him a wooden spoon and taught him how to stir the batter without getting it all over himself and her.

She didn't really think much about what she was doing because she'd seen Toni's mom do it with her own kids so often over the years. At the time, it had just seemed logical to get the kids to help because it cut down on their fighting. But now, as Livy looked into Igor's glowing face, she realized it had more to do with letting the kids feel involved and less with creating baby slave labor.

When the batter was pretty well mixed, Livy released Igor's hand so he could continue on for a little bit longer. As he did, a wide grin on his cute face, he glanced over his shoulder and crowed, "Look, Uncle Vic! I'm cooking!"

"I can see that."

Vic stood in the doorway, arms crossed over his chest, as he leaned against the frame and watched them. How long he'd been standing there, Livy didn't know. Nor did she ask.

Still wearing his black sweatpants, Vic had also pulled on a plain white T-shirt that appeared kind of old and worn. It was also a little tight, so that Livy could make out Vic's muscular arms and chest pretty well. And she had to admit . . . those muscles were damn impressive.

"You ready for tonight?" he asked Livy.

"Yes."

"What's tonight?" Igor asked.

"None of your bus—"

Livy cut Vic off with, "I get to do what I learned when I was your age."

"Make batter?"

"Pick locks."

Vic immediately pushed himself away from the door frame and clapped his hands together. "Okay! Let's get you in the shower, kid."

As Vic was reaching for his nephew, Livy heard keys in the back door and a few seconds later, an enormous grizzly came storming into the kitchen.

Vic stared at the bear for a moment before saying, "Hi, Dan."

"I'm here for my wife," the grizzly announced . . . loudly. He pointed at Igor. "Go get your mother, son. I'm taking her home!"

"Okay, Dad!"

Livy removed the bowl from Igor's lap, and the boy jumped off the table and ran off to find his mother.

Once the boy was gone, Dan whispered, "How did that sound, Vic? Pretty tough?"

Gawking at his brother-in-law, Vic slowly nodded his head. "Uh . . . yeah. Sure. Tough."

"Great." He looked at Livy. "Hey, Livy."

"Hi, Dan."

"Were you in the cabinets again?"

"Pretty much."

The bear leaned over a bit. "Are you making pancakes?"

"And bacon. Plus my honey–maple syrup mix. The ultimate in delicious decadence."

"Oh man. That sounds really good."

"You're welcome to stay," Vic offered.

"Yeah, but I should really drag your sister home by her hair." He blew out a breath, glanced up at the ceiling. "But I really want pancakes with that syrup."

"Then tell her she has to stay," Livy suggested. "Until you're done eating."

"Oh. Good idea. Thanks, Livy!" The bear grinned at her and walked off to order his wife to stay until he finished his breakfast.

Livy looked at Vic. "Are they happy like that?" she asked.

"Very."

She shrugged and walked to the stove. "Then that's all that matters."

Shen parked the windowless black van two blocks away from their target and turned off the engine. He looked back at them and announced, "I'll go recon the area."

The driver's door closed behind him and Livy asked, "He's going to recon the area?"

Vic shrugged. "He never really left the geek room, as I called it. He and his geek coworkers used technology and their obsessive natures to track down targets, and the rest of us took it from there. It's a relationship that's worked well for me in the past."

Livy, dressed in skintight black clothes, replied, "Huh."

Vic watched her slip on black gloves and cover her black-and-white hair with a black knit cap.

"You got everything you need?" he asked.

"What do I need?"

"Livy . . ."

She chuckled. "I've got everything."

"Good. Now she's supposed to be out of the apartment the entire night, but—"

"Would you stop worrying? I know what I'm doing. I learned to do this while I was in the womb."

"And it's my job to worry. That's what *I* do."

Livy tucked her hair under the cap. "And you're surprisingly good at it."

"I'm just asking that you be careful."

"I will. Promise."

The van door opened and Shen said, "It's clear, Livy."

"Thanks."

Livy slipped a tiny black backpack on and stepped out of the van. "I'll be back," she said, before she disappeared into the darkness.

Shen got into the van, closed the door, and sat down on the floor. He pulled out his laptop and began accessing their target's security system.

Smiling, Shen pulled out one of his cut bamboo stalks and began his infernal chewing while he worked.

"So," he said around the stalk, his eyes locked on his computer screen, "she looks mighty good in that little outfit, doesn't she?"

"Shut up." And Vic forced himself not to throttle the panda laughing at him.

Livy slipped into the alley beside the building. As soon as she did, she felt . . . at home. In the darkness, moving through the shadows. It was in her blood. Both sides of her family, for centuries, were thieves. Honey badger thieves. Their targets ranged from art to silver, gold, banks, and crown jewels. What the family didn't tolerate were tacky home invasions of any kind, targeting the poor, or stealing from their own family. A Kowalski never stole from another Kowalski. A Yang never stole from another Yang. Not without repercussions. And honey badger repercussions could be . . . painful.

The funny thing was, Livy had done all she could to pull herself away from this part of her life. She was an artist, a phrase that offended her mother on a visceral level. "We're not artists," she'd drunkenly snarled during a Thanksgiving dinner many years ago, "we *steal* from artists. You never get that right."

But her mother's constant pushing and her father's indifference just made Livy more resolute. She was an artist, a photographer. At least that was what she'd always thought . . . until she'd run out of ideas, creativity . . . desire. When it came to art, desire was a big part of it. Not sexual desire, but the desire to create, to produce, to explore the world around oneself. Without the desire . . . an artist had nothing.

And right now, Livy had nothing.

So she fell back on what she knew: breaking and entering.

Although, for Livy, breaking and entering wasn't the challenge it was for most. She didn't need fancy equipment to get at a target. All she needed was an idea of a building's layout and the cover of darkness, both of which she currently had.

So, using her claws, Livy began climbing the building's wall, sure that Shen had already dealt with the security cameras surrounding the area.

She moved quietly and quickly as she was trained to do. It wasn't an easy climb, but at least she didn't have to go all the way up to the penthouse floor this way. She could do it, but it would be a drag and an excessive amount of work.

Finally, Livy reached the air duct near the twenty-third floor. Holding on with one claw and the balls of her feet, she used her free hand and a small screwdriver to remove the bottom screws from the metal screen. Once done, she lifted it and pulled her body inside. The space was small but Livy could maneuver her way through almost any space. Yes. Even with her broad shoulders. Of course, sometimes she was forced to dislocate her shoulder, which she hated doing. It was not pleasant and just because she was a honey badger didn't mean she was into pain. Because she wasn't.

Dislocation unnecessary, Livy quickly made her way down the air ducts and into the back stairwell until she was at the emergency door that led up one flight of stairs to Allison Whitlan's apartment. Livy eased that door open and crept up the stairs until she reached another emergency door. She checked for alarm wires, found them, and disabled them. Then she went in, through a small hallway until she reached a service entrance.

According to Vic's contacts, tonight was the staff's night

off, and the mistress of the house was at some charity event with other rich people like herself. But Livy still listened at the door for a moment before getting out her tools and picking the lock.

She waited another breath before opening the door and taking a step inside the dark hallway. She waited again, heard nothing; so she slowly closed the door, and began moving through the apartment.

The place was enormous. Had to cost several million. A place where Livy would love to crash some night when she needed a new temporary burrow.

Livy checked her watch. She had time, so she moved through the apartment carefully, looking for any signs that the woman was in touch with her father. With the infamous Frankie "The Rat" Whitlan. A man Livy could not care less about. But how could she turn Barinov down when he'd filled her office with all those baskets?

Livy stopped in front of a Picasso. She leaned in, studied the signature. Nodded. It was a real one. Not a Kowalski replica that most art experts would be hard pressed to prove wasn't a real Picasso.

Livy checked the bedrooms first. The apartment had nine. She took the most time in the woman's office. She found tons of information about Allison Whitlan's finances and her charity work, plus lots of handwritten notes on Post-its, but nothing that screamed, "My daddy, Frankie Whitlan, is at the corner of Fifth and Broadway!"

Checking her watch again, Livy realized she was running out of time, so she did a quick sweep of all the bathrooms, and then the giant kitchen.

Livy's last stop was the TV room and the living room. She did the living room first, sweeping through quickly, before walking toward the exit to head to the TV room.

Livy stepped into the hallway, but stopped, blinking slowly, her mind processing.

After nearly a minute, she slowly backed up into the living room, stopped again. Waited another moment, took a breath, and turned.

Livy stared, studied what she saw, her mouth slowly dropping open, her heart racing hard.

Then, after several minutes of studying the stuffed animal carcass standing hideously beside Allison Whitlan's fireplace, Livy said a word she hadn't said since she was a toddler . . .

"Daddy?"

CHAPTER 8

Vic checked his watch again. Now he was getting worried. "Where the hell is she?"

"We should have wired her," Shen said, his focus still on his laptop.

"I tried. She said no."

"Your girlfriend is not big on communication, is she?"

"We both know Livy is not my girlfriend."

"She's constantly in your house, making you breakfast, and eating honey while naked. And you don't slap said honey out of her hand like you do with me. What else would you call her?"

"My friend whom I find considerably less annoying than you. And you don't eat honey."

Vic opened the van door and stepped out. "I'm not liking this."

"We'd hear sirens if she'd been caught. Just relax. Your girlfriend knows what she's doing."

Vic glared at Shen. He thought about knocking that bamboo stalk out of his mouth but knew it wouldn't really help the situation.

Glancing at his watch, Vic debated his next move . . . but that was when he realized he didn't have a next move. He had nothing. This was all Livy. All she'd wanted from them, all she'd allowed, was Shen handling the security cameras, getting her the intelligence on the building, and the two men accompanying her to the target site. Other than that . . . she'd had no use for them.

And, Vic realized as he saw a limo he was guessing had Allison Whitlan in it turn the corner to park at the front of the building, he was now going to pay for this stupidity when Livy was busted and ended up doing hard time for . . .

His increasingly panicked thoughts faded off when he saw Livy come out of the dark alley and head toward him.

Sighing in relief, Vic smiled and stepped farther out on the sidewalk. But as Livy neared him, Vic's smile faded. It wasn't just the expression on her face, which was . . . disturbing. It was her entire body. He'd never seen her so stiff before. Normally, Livy moved like a very loose lumberjack. She didn't amble like Dee-Ann. It was a street-savvy walk. Like she could handle anything that came her way.

Yet now . . . now she looked like she'd kill the first person who said anything to her. Man, woman, or child. Like she was just waiting for that one thing to set her off.

When she was close enough so that he didn't need to yell, Vic asked, "Livy? What happened?"

"Later," she said, walking right by him and to the van. She grabbed the big backpack she brought everywhere.

"Livy?"

"*Later.*"

Then she and her backpack were gone, and Vic had absolutely no idea what the hell had just happened.

"What's going on?" Shen asked from the van.

He looked at the panda and threw his hands up. "I have no idea."

Chuntao Yang, who'd renamed herself Joan when her family first moved to America, woke up early. Her sisters and an aunt needed to catch a flight to Belgium in the afternoon. They had to prep for a job in Italy. It was always risky when they worked that close to the Vatican, but the payoff would be outstanding.

Still, they had to plan carefully no matter what country they were working in. Joan had no desire to go to prison. Her kind, honey badgers, filled prisons all over the world, which meant she'd end up spending most of her time fighting. So she'd rather stay out of prison and enjoy her life.

Joan put on her favorite red dress—she looked wonderful in red—matching Jimmy Choo red heels, just enough gold jewelry to highlight her attributes, and her red cashmere coat.

Satisfied with what she saw in the mirror—and when wasn't she satisfied?—Joan headed down the stairs toward the kitchen, where her sisters and aunt were making breakfast and preparing for their afternoon trip.

Once she got to the bottom step, Joan placed her travel cases on the floor and dropped her coat over the banister. Fluffing her hair, she walked down the hallway, her mind turning, planning for this next job.

Joan loved her work. Loved how it took her out of her problems. Everything in her life narrowed into planning and executing The Job. So much so that when The Job was complete, her problems had usually gone with it. Or at least the worst was over.

And the way things had been going lately . . . well, Joan was really looking forward to this particular job. More than she could say.

As she neared the kitchen, Joan could hear her sisters and aunt chatting in English and Mandarin. For years, Joan refused to speak her native language because she wanted to be able to blend in as much as any Asian woman could blend in America. It had worked to some degree. She could speak English, French, Russian, German, Italian, and Spanish flawlessly, her accent in all those languages near perfect. But when she got angry enough, the Mandarin came out of her with or without her consent. Of course, only her family and her ex-husband ever seemed to get her that angry. No one else was worth the trouble.

Joan was about to step into the kitchen when she stopped, her daughter's scent surprising her.

Slowly, Joan turned, and yes, her daughter stood behind her, just a few feet away. Unsure what she was doing at their safe house in Chicago, Joan was about to ask. But Olivia cut her off.

"Who did we bury, Ma?" she asked.

Joan blinked. "What?"

"Who did we bury in Dad's grave?"

Without looking behind her, Joan knew from the sudden silence that her sisters and aunt were listening to every word. Not that she blamed them.

"Who did we bury?" Joan asked. "Well . . . your father, of course."

Livy shook her head. And Joan now realized that her daughter was angry. Not just angry . . . livid. And because her daughter was a lot like Joan herself, that was a very rare sight.

"It can't be Dad."

"It can't?" Joan asked, trying to sound bored. "Why not?"

"Because I just saw him."

Joan felt her heart pound in her chest while she fought her anger at him for not contacting her in all this time. "He's alive?"

Her daughter stared at her for a moment. A long moment that told Joan something was very wrong.

"Livy?"

"No. He's not alive. He was stuffed and placed next to some bitch's fireplace for all her friends to gawk at while eating hors d'oeuvres and drinking champagne."

Livy's words tore through Joan, her heart no longer pounding from excitement but despair and anger.

"So it can't be Dad in that grave. Now I'll ask you again, and then I'm going to start flipping the fuck out . . . who did we bury in that Washington graveyard?"

As soon as Livy cursed, she knew she'd hear it from her aunts and great-aunt. They might be honey badgers but the whole respecting-the-elders thing was big among her brethren. So as soon as that "fuck" left her mouth, her aunts were on her, yelling at her in Mandarin and shaking fingers at her while her great-aunt Li-Li helped her mother into the kitchen to sit at the large table and held her hand.

Livy, in no mood for any of this, pushed past her finger-wagging, yelling aunts and stalked into the kitchen after her mother.

"Answer me."

Livy's aunts followed, but before they could get in the middle of this, she spun on them, bared her fangs, and hissed a warning.

"Stop it," Joan said. "All of you."

"I'll get you some tea," Li-Li said before going to the stove, briefly stopping to give Livy a hard "Li-Li glare," as it was called among the Yangs. Then she scratched the big, brutal scar on her old neck and continued on to make the tea.

Livy ignored her relatives and pulled out a chair, catty-corner from her mother, and dropped into it.

"Sit down," her mother ordered her sisters.

They did as they were told, but Livy's aunt Kew stopped to poke Livy in the shoulder while snarling, "You were always a horrible daughter."

"Touch me with that finger again," Livy warned, "and I'm eating it."

"Kew, please," Joan pushed, and for the first time, Livy heard her mother sound very tired.

Aunt Kew stomped over to her chair and dropped into it, arms crossed over her chest, legs crossed at the knee, one foot shaking dangerously.

Yeah. Livy knew she'd be hearing about this little episode until the end of time. But she really didn't care.

"I want to know what's going on," Livy told her mother. "And I want to know now."

"Your father and I," Joan began, "may have divorced when you were eighteen—"

"You divorced when I was fifteen."

"The *first* time."

And that's when Livy began to get a headache.

"Anyway," her mother went on, "we never stopped—"

"Messing with each other's heads?"

Her mother paused, lips pursed, before she admitted, "It's what we always did well. Long before you ever came along.

"But no matter how much we argued," her mother continued, "no matter how much we threw things at each other and cursed at each other . . . we still loved each other."

"And were business partners."

"Yes," Joan hissed. "That, too. We had an agreement. No matter where we were; whom we were seeing at the time; or what jobs we might be working on, we always—*always*—met on certain dates at this little hotel we loved by the Baltic Sea. Dates and a location that only we knew."

Livy frowned, wondering how only she managed to have parents who would pick the goddamn Baltic Sea for their romantic getaways.

"And?"

"And your father didn't show up for *two* of our set meetings. We'd been meeting each other like this for more than ten years and he'd never *not* shown up once, let alone twice. Even when he was dating that porn star. Even *she* couldn't keep him away from me." She shook her head, started to rub her eyes, but quickly remembered the amount of makeup she used on her face, so she stopped, and pulled back any tears that might threaten to ruin all that careful work.

"I checked with his brothers and sister," Joan went on. "Checked with the police and morgues in several countries. I did everything, but he never made contact with anyone. I spoke to Baltazar and he agreed with me."

"Ma, Uncle Balt would agree with anything you asked him, because he's had the hots for his brother's woman since the day Dad brought you home."

Joan slapped her hand against her knee. "Stop acting like I killed Damon myself!"

"I never said you killed him . . . you just *lied* to me. About my own father. And I have no idea what you did to the body that's actually in that casket."

"That one was already dead and not by me. And I didn't tell you because I knew you'd make a big deal about it."

"And you had to make sure you got that life insurance before his girlfriend or Aunt Teddy did. Right?"

And that's when they all started yelling at her. Aunts, great-aunt, mother. Standing over Livy and yelling at her in English, Mandarin, and for some unknown reason, a little bit of Italian.

All of which proved that Livy was right. Because when her family started yelling, it was usually because they were lying their collective asses off.

"She must have found something," Shen said, busy on his laptop.

"But what could she have found? I mean, the woman was once poisoned by a cult member whom she did really horrible things to once she woke up from a brief coma, and I can still say . . . I've never seen her look that angry before."

"Yeah. I know."

"Have you found her yet?" Vic asked, looking over Shen's shoulder.

"I think so. Yes. Here it is. She took a flight into O'Hare. No bags checked. She arrived this morning. She didn't rent a car, and it looks like she paid cash for the flight."

"O'Hare? She goes into Whitlan's daughter's apartment, comes out, and immediately goes to Chicago?" Vic stared at an equally confused Shen. "Dude . . . what the fuck?"

Livy had nearly made it out the front door when she heard, "So what are you going to do about all this?"

Livy stopped and faced her family. Her mother, aunts, and great-aunt were all staring at her, arms crossed over their chests.

"What do you think I'm going to do?"

"You can't tell your uncles."

"You want me to say *nothing*?"

"What would telling the Kowalskis about this do for anyone?"

"They already know he's dead," one of her aunts said. "What would telling them about *how* he died change anything or make anything better?"

"So we let these full-humans get away with what they did to my father?"

"A father," Great-Aunt Li-Li felt the intense need to remind her, "that you said you were disowning."

"What does that have to do with anything?"

"We just don't think you should upset things," Joan said, stepping closer to Livy and running her hand softly down Livy's arm. "Let's just leave things as they are."

"I don't think—"

Her mother's soft hand was now a fist, one forefinger pressing against Livy's nose, pushing it hard. "You don't have to think." And her mother's voice was low, dangerous. "Just keep your mouth shut and be smart. Understand me?"

Livy stared at her mother. Hard black eyes stared back. Eyes just like Livy's.

Without saying a word, Livy turned and walked out.

The four women sat down in the kitchen table and stared at each other.

"She's going to make this ugly," Kew finally informed them.

As if Joan didn't already know that.

Joan would be the first to admit she'd never really understood her daughter. Nor had she bothered to try. All that art talk that had nothing to do with what things cost, or how they could be taken, sold, and the cash received and split up equally among all those involved. That was what art meant to Joan and to Damon and to both sides of their families. Yet Livy believed herself to be an actual artist. She took pictures and expected people to pay to hang them in their homes. And some did. Joan clearly remembered that nosy bitch Jackie Jean-Louis coming to her house, more than once, to "discuss Livy's future."

Livy's future? Joan had always thought her future would be the same as Joan's and her sisters and her brothers and their mothers and aunts and uncles and on and on. But Jean-Louis and that ridiculous family of hers kept pushing the art thing again and again until Livy actually believed it. And she was as stubborn as . . . well, as stubborn as Joan. So Joan knew there was no point in fighting her. Instead, she'd let her go off and do whatever she wanted. Art school? Sure. Why not? Jobs taking pictures for fancy magazines? Whatever.

There was simply no point in getting a bug up her ass about it because Livy was going to be Livy.

"Well," Joan snarled, "I'm not giving any of those Kowalskis the life insurance money. He was *my* husband."

"Ex-husband," Kew reminded her.

Joan scowled at her sister.

Li-Li tapped her long, manicured nails against the table. "Stop this. We need to know what that girl is going to *do*."

Joan laughed. "I'll tell you what she's going to do." She looked at each of her sisters and her aunt. "She's going to tear this world apart to get at whoever did that to her father."

Aunt Li-Li nodded her head. "Then we should cancel the job." When her nieces just stared at her, thinking of all that money slipping through their fingers, she added, "If you want to keep some control of this situation, Chuntao, then we stay. It's what a caring family would do . . . and we pretend, very well, to be a caring family."

Joan looked at her sisters. "She's right. We do very well at pretending to be a caring family."

CHAPTER 9

Livy stepped off the plane and headed through the airport. She didn't have any luggage. Just her trusty backpack and a whole lot of bitterness.

But the thought of going back to her apartment and facing whatever nightmare was there had Livy dropping into an empty seat in the middle of busy JFK.

She had no idea how long she sat there, staring at absolutely nothing. But, eventually, a text came in on her cell phone. At first, she was going to ignore it, assuming it was Vic again, who'd been trying to get in touch with her ever since she'd left him standing by that van. But then she decided to look anyway.

> Hi. It's Blayne. Can you come to a meeting about the wedding?

Although Livy knew this was probably a bad idea, she realized going to a meeting about a wedding she wanted nothing to do with was way better than going home.

Livy stood and headed toward the exit and, hopefully, a cab. But after less than a minute, she stopped and looked behind her. That was when she realized that airport security was following her.

She didn't know why. She hadn't done anything. Then again . . . Toni had mentioned that when she was in a bad mood, Livy had a tendency to growl under her breath and glare a lot.

If she was doing that at the moment, Livy didn't know. Still, she did jerk her body toward the security team, smirking when they backed up and instinctively placed their hands on their weapons.

Livy turned and walked out of the airport and grabbed the first cab that could take her back to Manhattan.

Vic snapped awake as soon as Shen walked into his room.

"She got a plane back from Chicago," Shen said. He'd been monitoring her movements as much as he could from his computer. But Livy, unlike the rest of the universe, wasn't much for revealing her whereabouts through her cell phone or social media. So Shen had to use more unsavory means in order to locate her.

Vic was surprised that Livy had gone to Chicago. As far as he knew, she had no connections there. No family. But after a little digging, he found out that the Kowalskis and Yangs had safe houses all over the States and a lot of other countries. Where those safe houses were specifically located, though, Vic couldn't find out.

Yet he still found it strange that Livy had sought out her family. For as long as he'd known her, she never went to her family for anything. If she needed help of any kind, she went to Toni or Toni's parents. No one else seemed to be of use to her. Including Vic.

He'd tried calling her, texting her, e-mailing her . . . everything. And Livy never once called him back. He had no idea what she'd seen in that apartment or why she wasn't talking to him. But hearing from Shen that she was back did make him feel a little better.

Vic got out of bed and headed to the bathroom for a quick shower.

"Do you even know where she's going?" Shen asked.

Vic stopped and faced the panda. "I have no idea."

"I checked your cabinets before I came up here . . . no Livy."

Disappointed to hear that, Vic said, "I'll try the Sports Center first."

"Good plan. You also going to give Dee-Ann a heads-up about what's going on?"

Vic thought on that a moment before deciding, "Probably not."

"Probably also a good plan. That woman terrifies me."

Livy walked into the private dining room of the Van Holtz Steak House in Midtown and dropped into one of the chairs around the big table.

There were already six people in attendance. Blayne, Gwen, two older felines, plus the future grooms, Lock MacRyrie and Bo Novikov, whom Livy knew through her work with the Carnivores hockey team.

Blayne waved at Livy from across the table but before she could speak, the wedding planner, a She-tiger whom Livy had heard was the mother of Cella Malone, leveled bright gold eyes on Livy.

"Well, well. If it isn't the overpriced wedding photographer. Glad you could join us."

"Barb," Blayne said to the feline. "You promised to be nice."

"I don't like it when my clients are taken advantage of."

"Livy would never take advantage of me! She's one of my closest friends!"

Barb shook her head. "Blayne, you say that about everybody."

"Because it's true." She grinned. "People love me."

"I can't believe you're okay with this female's outrageous cost, Bo."

"I know she'll be on time," Novikov said flatly. "That makes her worth every cent. Now if I could just get the rest of this wedding on some kind of schedule—"

"This is going to be fun, Bo," Blayne argued. "I'm not turning it into some kind of nightmare event so you can feel we're on time."

"I don't think I'm asking for a lot for this thing to at least start at a certain time."

"This *thing* is our wedding."

"It sounds like it's going to be complete chaos. Chaos!"

Livy didn't really pay attention to the bickering. Instead, she was busy staring down the She-tiger across the table. The lioness beside her—Gwen's mother, whom Livy had met at one of the derby bouts—watched silently, but Livy could tell she was happily anticipating a good fight.

"You're being unreasonable!" Blayne yelled at her mate.

"*I'm* being unreasonable? By expecting some order out of what's quickly turning into an insane event?"

The She-tiger, still staring at Livy, suddenly raised an eyebrow. A move that Livy found . . . offensive.

So, in a calm, reasonable way, Livy scrambled across the table, her fangs out, her claws leaving gouges in the shiny wood.

She nearly had all those fangs and claws embedded in the roaring She-tiger's face when big grizzly bear arms wrapped around Livy and yanked her off the table. Lock, like most grizzlies, was surprisingly fast and smart, pinning her arms to her sides so that she couldn't claw at him or anyone else.

As Livy hissed at the She-tiger, and everyone stared at her, Bo Novikov nodded his head. "Livy's right. This meeting is taking too long."

Now everyone looked at Novikov, watching as the seven-one hockey player stood up. "I've got training."

He walked out and Livy decided that was a good idea,

too. She pulled away from MacRyrie. Picked up her backpack and slung it over her shoulder.

"Send me a schedule of when you'll need me there," she told Blayne and Gwen. Then she walked out of the restaurant.

Once outside, Livy debated where she should go next. The fact that she hadn't been able to get into it with that She-tiger left her feeling . . . empty.

So Livy did the most unreasonable thing she'd done in a very long time . . . she went home.

Chapter 10

Livy pushed on her apartment door. She had to push hard . . . because there was a body in front of it.

Using her shoulder, she shoved and one of her cousins finally rolled away, allowing Livy to walk in.

She stepped over bottles of beer, wine, vodka, and whiskey; nearly empty bags of junk food; and puddles of vomit and blood. Yet Livy didn't understand just how bad this party had gotten until the king cobra slithered across her feet.

They'd brought in poisonous snakes. A honey badger–shifter delicacy, which Livy wasn't against now and then. Yet she was relatively certain her neighbors didn't want to go to their bathrooms to find king cobras slithering out of their toilets.

Livy walked through her living room and down the short hallway to her kitchen. She stopped in the doorway. Melly was passed out on the floor, a half-eaten puff adder lying across her stomach.

Crouching down beside her cousin, Livy gently pushed the hair out of Melly's face. "Melly? Honey? Can you hear me?"

Slowly, Melly opened her eyes, looked up at Livy. She smiled.

That was when Livy punched her in the face.

Melly came up swinging, dragging Livy to the floor with her. The rest of Livy's cousins roused themselves from their drunken stupor to try to separate them.

Completely sober, however, Livy was able to push her cousins off and grab hold of Melly by the front of her dress. She lifted her cousin up and dragged her, kicking and screaming, to the bathroom.

By the time Livy had the toilet seat up and Melly's head shoved under the water, the rest of her cousins had Livy by the arms and hair and were pulling her back.

Melly jumped away from the toilet, black-and-white hair dripping wet, gasping for air. Then she came at Livy.

Yanking her arms away from the hands holding her, Livy rammed into her cousin. Snarling and hissing, they battled their way out of the bathroom and into the bedroom, across the bedroom, next to the bedroom window . . . and eventually *out* of the bedroom window.

Still fighting, the pair fell the sixteen flights until they landed hard onto the roof of a black-and-white sedan. Livy landed on her back, but she quickly flipped over, pinning Melly underneath her by holding her cousin's arms down with her knees.

Far away, Livy heard raised voices yelling at her as she pummeled her cousin repeatedly on the face and neck, but she chose to ignore all that.

Finally, hands grasped Livy and yanked her back.

Someone leaned in and tried to help Melly. It took a second for Livy to realize it was a cop. Whether Melly even realized that, Livy didn't know. She just knew her cousin started swinging at him while screeching, *"Let me at that cunt! Let me at that cunt!"*

"You little *weak* bitch," Livy hissed, a greater insult not known to the honey badgers.

"You ungrateful whore!"

"*I'm* ungrateful?"

"A *weak,* ungrateful whore!"

Livy yanked her arms away from whoever was holding her and dove at her cousin. She took her, and the cop holding Melly, down hard.

Far away, Livy heard raised voices yelling at her again as she pummeled her cousin repeatedly but, also again, she chose to ignore it.

"Vic! Vic!"

Vic turned around, but all he saw were the oversized, tree-like sports guys walking toward him. But amid all that bulk was a raised arm waving.

He waited until the guys moved past him, a few stopping in front of him, expecting Vic to move instead, but he wasn't about to move for anyone. Especially not hockey players, a sport he simply did *not* understand on any logical level.

Once the players cleared, Vic was able to see Toni rushing up to him. And ambling behind her, Ricky Lee.

"I'm so glad I found you," Toni said when she reached Vic, her hand resting on his arm.

"What's wrong?"

"I need your help."

"Sure."

"I need to go to Russia. Now."

"Well—" he began, quickly searching for an excuse that would get him out of making a trip back to Russia as part of Toni's security team. He still hadn't found Livy, and until he knew what had happened to her, he wasn't about to go anywhere. But he also didn't want to alarm Toni by telling her that Livy had gone missing.

"But I just got a call," Toni went on, a bit of panic in her voice. "Livy's in jail."

Shocked, Vic demanded, "What? What the hell happened? *When* did that happen?"

"It doesn't matter. I just need to get her out."

"No problem. I'll post bail."

Toni frowned, confused. "No, no. I need *you* to go to Russia. *I'll* get Livy out of jail."

Vic studied Toni a moment before turning his gaze to the wolf standing behind her.

Reed gave that annoying grin of his, which told Vic the woman was serious.

"You want *me* to handle negotiations with those Russian bears for a sport I don't even respect?"

"Of course not," she said, exasperated. And they'd only just started this goddamn conversation. "Just stall them until I get there."

"I see. And that makes sense . . . how?"

"I don't understand what you mean."

"You want me to go to Russia to *stall* bears while you bail Livy out of jail rather than you going ahead to Russia and letting *me* pay her bail? How is that remotely logical?"

"Because I manage Livy when she gets into trouble."

"No. You manage those ridiculous meatheads who fight while skating. You also manage your terrifying siblings. Livy you do *not* manage. Nor should you, since she's a grown woman."

"You say that, but where is she? Jail!"

"I didn't say she was a grown woman who made good decisions. But I'm not about to take a seventeen-hour flight just so I can stall a bunch of cranky Russian bears while you bail your friend out of jail so you can then lecture her about how bad it is for her to go to jail."

"I can't believe you're being so unfeeling!"

"Unfeeling because I'm simply not giving you what you want?"

"That's exactly what I mean!"

Chuckling, Reed put his arm around Toni's shoulders. "I know you don't wanna hear it, darlin'—"

"No!" Toni snapped. "I don't."

"But Vic here is right. This deal is too big for you to walk away. You're about to sign the most important deal this team has ever had. You don't want to risk that."

"But I'm *not* walking away. I'm just asking Vic to—"

"No," Vic said calmly. "I'm not going to Russia. Not for this. Zubachev is expecting you, but if *I* show up?" Vic shook his head, thinking of the Russian shifter team owner's reaction to that little change in his schedule. Ivan Zubachev, like most grizzlies—Russian or otherwise—was just not good with change. Any change. Ever. "I'd rather set myself on fire, Antonella."

Toni stomped her foot, most likely ready to argue the point until she "accidentally" missed her plane. At least Vic was sure that was her subconscious plan.

"Vic—"

"Forget it, Toni," Vic cut in, unwilling to continue this argument. Instead, he patted Toni's head. His hand was big, so he pretty much covered her entire head and a good portion of her face. "It's all right, little canine. I'll take care of your friend for you."

Toni slapped off Vic's hand. "It's not that easy, you know."

"I'm sure it's not," Vic said as he walked away, choosing to ignore what he secretly called her "dog yapping." He had to; the feline in him wanted to start clawing at things when her voice got so unbearably yippy. And absolutely no one wanted him to unleash his claws.

Toni continued to yell at him as he walked away, but he still refused to listen. He'd take care of the problem. What more could the damn woman want?

But once he was in the elevator, Toni's hand slammed

against the open door to keep it from closing. "You can't just walk away," she told him.

Vic pulled out a box of bamboo sticks that he always kept on him in case Shen ran out. The container resembled a pack of cigarettes but the marketing read "Bamboo for the Giant Panda on the GO!"

"Now," Toni went on. "What you'll need to do is—"

Vic tossed the box a few feet away. Toni stopped talking, looked at the box, and back at Vic, her eyes narrowing in warning. "I'm a jackal, Barinov," she snarled. "I'm not some stupid Labrador retriev—"

A blur dashed by them, dove at the box, rolled a few feet away, bounced back to relatively small feet, and held the box up, triumphant.

"You dropped this!" said the pretty wolfdog as she bounced over to them. She held the box out to Vic and he took it, raising his brows at Toni.

The jackal closed her eyes, let out a breath.

"Hi, Toni!" the wolfdog chirped.

After a moment, Toni replied, "Hi, Blonde."

Blayne's smile vanished and her lip curled. "It's *Blayne*!"

"Whatever."

Blayne focused on Vic, her smile quickly returning. "So what's going on?" she asked.

"Livy got picked up by the cops," Vic told her, hoping one of Blayne's overreactions to any situation that had nothing to do with her would distract Toni long enough for Vic to get away.

"Oh no!" Blayne's hands briefly covered her mouth, her eyes wide. "I was afraid that would happen after the way she reacted this morning at the meeting."

"What are you talking about?" Toni asked.

"She came to our meeting about the wedding and she went after Mrs. Malone like a rabid squirrel. And in case you weren't aware, squirrels are way meaner than any predator I've ever met."

"Why would Livy be at a meeting about your wedding?" Toni briefly closed her eyes before asking, "You didn't ask her to be one of your bridesmaids again, did you?"

"Not after she threw that locker at me."

Vic raised his hand. "I'm sorry. I need clarification on that one. Livy threw a locker at you? A *locker*?"

"Yeah. We were in the locker room after a derby bout. I asked her to be one of my bridesmaids—assuming she'd take it as the compliment it was—but she didn't say anything. Instead she just walked over to the lockers, pried one off, and *wham!* Next thing I knew, I was dodging a locker." She grinned. "Good thing I'm spry!"

Vic nodded. "Good thing."

"So I didn't ask her to be a bridesmaid."

"Good," Toni said.

"Instead, I asked her to be my wedding photographer!"

Vic stepped out of the elevator and grabbed hold of Toni before she could get her hands around Blayne's throat, sweeping her up in his arms and holding the snarling, snapping jackal against his body.

Blayne stumbled back. "What the hell?"

"You," Toni spit out. "*You* asked one of the great photographers of our time to be your *wedding* photographer?"

"I intend to pay her!"

"That's not the point! Would you ask Ansel Adams to photograph your baby shower? Or Renoir to paint your bedroom?"

"Well . . . if they were alive today and available for that sort of—" Blayne leaned back as jackal claws nearly slashed her face off. *"You're being unreasonable!"*

Vic moved back to pull Toni farther out of claw range, and he nearly walked into Ricky Lee.

"What'cha doin' with my woman, hoss?" the wolf asked calmly.

"Keeping her from killing Blayne."

"Who'd wanna kill Blayne?"

"Blayne asked Livy to be her wedding photographer."

Ricky Lee shook his head. "My Toni gets real protective of her family's talents. And she considers Livy family. Blayne's lucky you were around. I'm not nearly as speedy as you. Now, why don't I take her." Ricky Lee put his arms out and Vic transferred the jackal over. "And I'll get us both on that plane to Russia. You handle Livy."

"Will do."

Now safely in Ricky Lee's arms, Toni pursed her lips and glared at both men. "This is ridiculous. Put me down, Ricky."

"Nah." He leaned in, kissed her cheek. "Let's get you to the airport, darlin'."

"Wait—"

"I'll take care of Livy," Vic promised, knowing that was what was bothering her.

"You can't just take care of Livy. You have to get her *and* her cousins out. Trust me when I say, you can't leave Kowalski cousins in lockup. They don't like being trapped together. They'll tear each other apart and end up in actual prison."

"Don't worry. I've got this all covered."

"And," she went on, "you'll need to keep Livy away from Melly once you get them out. She's really cranky when she's been in jail for a while, and Melly knows every button to push to make Livy snap."

"I'll deal with it. Now go before you miss your plane."

"Vic—"

"Go."

"She's erratic when she's upset," Toni warned as Ricky Lee walked off with her. "And being asked to be some heifer's wedding photographer is bound to make her upset!"

Blayne stamped her foot. *"You're still being unreasonable!"*

* * *

"This is what you wanted, isn't it?" Melly accused, her eyes locked on Livy across the cell they were sharing with their cousins and several other full-human women Livy didn't know. "To see me back here. Where you think I belong."

"Where I think you belong is in rehab or a maximum-security mental hospital."

"You are such an evil bitch, Livy!"

"*I'm* evil? You trashed my apartment."

"I had a little party with family and a few friends. Why are you so uptight?"

"A little party does not involve cobras and puff adders."

"And black mambas," Livy's cousin Jocelyn muttered.

Livy closed her eyes in horror at the thought of one of the deadliest snakes in the world skittering through her defenseless neighbors' plumbing. "You have to be," she growled at Melly, "the dumbest twat this side of the *universe*."

"I was hungry!" Melly screamed back.

Livy held up her hands. "I can't with you, right now. I've got a lot on my mind and—"

"Boo-hoo," Melly singsonged, her voice a nasty sneer. "My father died so everybody must pity me."

Jocelyn's eyes grew wide. "Wow. She went there," she said to the other cousins. "I mean . . . she actually *went* there."

"Shut up," Melly snapped at Jocelyn.

"But who the fuck says that to someone who just lost their father?" Joce demanded. "Who?"

"Livy's always been a bitch. Uncle Damon dying doesn't change shit about that."

Livy didn't say anything. She didn't move. She didn't growl, snarl, or hiss. But a true honey badger never actually needed those warning signs to know when a fellow HB was about to go off like a bomb. Quickly, Jocelyn knelt in front of Livy, placing her hands on Livy's knees. "Don't."

"Don't what?"

"Livy." Jocelyn cocked her head to the side. "I can't let you."

Studying her cousin, Livy asked, "Because you care if Melly continues breathing? Or because of her talents?"

"Don't be silly, Liv." Jocelyn, the oldest and most mature of the Kowalski cousins, reached up and gently petted Livy's cheek. "If she didn't have talents, I would have killed her myself before she graduated kindergarten. But this goes beyond our instinctual need to destroy the weakest of our kind. So I can't let you. Understand?"

Livy let out a breath, nodded. Besides. If she was going to kill her own cousin, she should do it without surveillance cameras and so many witnesses.

Jocelyn, satisfied by Livy's nonverbal response, smiled and stood. When she turned, Melly was standing there.

"You would have killed me in kindergarten?" When Jocelyn didn't reply, Melly began to sob.

Jocelyn, disgusted, glanced back at Livy, eyes crossed.

"I can't believe we share blood," Jocelyn whispered at Melly before she walked off.

Livy heard someone sniffing, and she looked at the bars she was trapped behind. She recognized the face of the polar bear standing there, sniffing the air. Slowly, dark brown eyes focused on her.

"Olivia."

"Crushek."

He gestured to a uniformed cop. The door was opened and Livy stood. "I've gotta bring them," she said, motioning to her cousins.

"Then bring them."

The bear turned and walked off. With a shrug, Livy and

her cousins followed. They were near the elevators when another plainclothes cop ran up to them.

"Hey! Crushek! You can't just—"

Crushek faced the man, stared down at him.

"I can't what?" Crushek asked.

The full-human swallowed. "These . . . women . . ."

Crushek blinked. "What about them?"

"They put two of our officers in the hospital."

Crushek looked down at Livy. "What did you do?"

"They got between me and my cousin, but it wasn't that big a deal. Couple of busted noses, a few broken fingers, and some bruised egos . . . but everybody's alive."

"Don't do that anymore," he told her, pointing one, big, blunt finger. "Understand?"

"Yes."

Crushek looked back at the other cop. "They won't do that anymore."

"Look, Crushek, you can't just take people out of here . . ." He cleared his throat, tried again. "Take people out of here . . ." Another throat clear. "Whenever you feel like . . ." He gawked up into that unrelenting polar bear stare and, after a few moments, threw up his hands. "Do whatever you want," he snapped before walking off.

Frowning, Crushek asked Livy, "What was that about?"

"I'm sure it's nothing," Livy offered.

"Yeah. You're probably right. Let's go." The polar walked toward the elevators.

"He has no idea, does he?" Jocelyn asked.

"Like most bears . . . he's completely oblivious." Livy shrugged. "That's kind of what makes him cute."

Her cousins moved off and Livy was about to follow when she looked over her shoulder at Melly. The little idiot was talking to a cop. She had her butt on his desk and was leaning down so that her top was probably giving him a very nice shot of her braless tits.

Livy briefly entertained the thought of leaving the bitch here, but she didn't want to hear about it later from her mother. So she walked up to her, grabbed Melly by the back of her head, and yanked her off the desk by her hair.

Instead of fighting while Livy dragged her ass across the floor toward the elevators, Melly waved at the detective and called out with a giggle, "Call me!"

CHAPTER 11

Vic, leaning back against his SUV, glanced over at the full-human female standing next to him.

"I really appreciate you guys helping me with this," he said.

Dez MacDermot smiled up at him, squinting one eye closed against the midday sun. "It's no problem. Things are pretty quiet right now for me and Crushek anyway."

"You know, I heard from Dee-Ann that her bosses and Cella's have had them back off the Whitlan case. Any idea why?"

"Nope. But our department hasn't been pushing us, either. Which is weird, because for a while there, that's *all* they had me and Crush working on. But Dee-Ann quietly mentioned that you were looking into it for us."

"Yeah. Just seeing if I can find out anything on my own."

"Well, just let me know if me and Crush can help you. It bothers me that Whitlan might be able to get away with all this bullshit. I've heard rumors there are a lot of fellow law officers who don't want Whitlan caught. Some high-level guys whose careers will be very hurt if Whitlan's brought in."

Frankie "The Rat" Whitlan had turned out to be quite a

piece of work, using cops to protect his illegal business by turning rat on fellow criminals who were in his way.

Yet none of that was why shifters of every breed and species had been after the son of a bitch. It was because he'd run one of the most successful shifter-hunting businesses in the world. For an exorbitant fee, Whitlan could arrange a hunt involving anything from lions, bears, tigers, wolves . . . *any* type of shifter. And for hard-core hunters, shifters were the ultimate prey. The power and strength of the predator combined with the intelligence of thumb-possessing humans.

The fact that an untold number of shifters were stuffed and on display in rich people's homes was what made Whitlan "most wanted" among their kind. So for any of the protection agencies to be backing off this guy was strange.

"You don't think that's what's happening here, do you? That someone from our side is trying to protect Whitlan?"

Dez jerked a bit in surprise at Vic's question. "No. I wasn't thinking that at all. Are you?"

"No. But I do feel something's going on."

She snorted. "There's always *something* going on. You guys are always involved in such complicated politics."

"True."

Crushek walked out the side door, Livy and six other honey badger females behind him.

Vic studied Livy as she caught sight of him and began to move his way. Despite some already healing bruises on her face, she appeared to be just fine.

Until one of the other badger females said something to Livy. Something only Livy could hear. But whatever was said, it was enough.

Livy turned wickedly fast, her open hand flying out and slapping the other female right across the face. Hard. So hard, the blow had the other female stumbling, briefly dropping her to her knees. She was up fast, though, charging Livy.

"Crush!" Dez called to the polar.

"What?"

She motioned to the women behind him, and Crush turned, eyes widening in shock. But before he could move, the other females stepped in, separating the cousins and moving them away from each other.

Vic motioned them over with a wave of his hand, now recognizing Melly as the one Livy had slapped.

Once the females were in front of him, Vic announced, "Listen up, ladies. I'm going to make this very quick. You have not been bailed out. Instead, you've been released, and any record of your arrest has been expunged."

Melly threw both fists high in the air. "Rock on!"

"Hold it," Vic cut in before she could walk off feeling invincible.

Vic pointed at Dez. "This is Detective MacDermot. She'll be accompanying you ladies back to Livy's apartment, where you will clean up whatever mess you left there."

"Fuck her," Melly snapped.

"You'll clean it up," Vic continued on, "or Dez will be dragging *your* ass"—he pointed right at Melly—"back to prison."

Dez looked at some papers she held in her hand. "Melanie Kowalski. Nice little sheet you have here, Mel." She looked up, studied Melly. "Have you been drinking, Miss Kowalski? Because according to what I've read here, the judge—"

"All right, all right!" Melly crossed her arms over her chest. "I'll clean up her apartment." Then, quite suddenly, she burst into tears. "I just don't know why you're all being so mean to me!"

It was quick, what Vic saw. But he knew he'd seen it. The

way Melly's cousins had looked at her. If they'd been full-blood honey badgers, they would have torn Melly apart, destroying her for being weak.

"Oooo . . . kay." Vic glanced at Dez. "Why don't you and Crush take the ladies to Livy's apartment?"

"You've got it."

Vic caught Livy's arm before she could follow her cousins. "Come on. You're coming with me."

"I can't," she said.

"Well, you can't stay with Melly."

"Fine. Then I'll go somewhere else."

"Is there a reason you can't go with me?"

"Because at this moment," she said flatly, "I can only think about wrapping my hands around your scrawny neck and choking you until you pass out or die."

Frowning, Vic brushed his free hand against his neck. "I don't think anyone's ever said I had a scrawny neck. Even when I was a baby. In grade school, they called me Big Neck Vic."

"It's not you," Livy admitted. "I'm just projecting my feelings for my cousin onto you, which I'll admit is hardly fair. But I'm . . . unbelievably tense."

Vic thought about that a moment. "Tense? So tense that if some tourist came up to you and asked you how to catch the J Train, you're likely to beat them to death in the street?"

Livy shrugged. "Probably."

Vic opened the passenger door. "Then you better get in."

"Yeah, but—"

"In. My 'scrawny neck' can handle you . . . but some poor full-human just visiting for the day? He or she would probably not be so lucky. So get your ass in the car."

"I guess you have a point." Livy walked toward the car. "So where are we going? Your house?" she asked.

"No. Someplace else. You'll like it."

Livy started to get in the SUV, but stopped, looked at Vic.

"I . . . appreciate all this, but I'm still not ready to talk about—"

"I'm taking you someplace where you can relax. That's it. Besides, I'm not really in the mood to fix a bunch of badger holes in my house."

Her smile was small, but there. And he was surprised how much he needed to see that smile.

CHAPTER 12

When Livy woke up, she had no idea where she was.

Blinking the sleep out of her eyes, she tried to focus on the sights out her window. After a few minutes of staring, Livy finally asked Vic, "Where the hell are we?"

"Massachusetts."

Livy's head snapped around. "We're *where*?"

"The great state of Massachusetts."

He sounded so damn cheerful about it, she wanted to deck him.

"Why are we in the great state of Massachusetts?"

"I was trying to think of where I could take you that you could relax. I thought about Lake Baikal."

"Lake Baikal?" Livy gawked at the man. "In *Siberia*?"

"Yeah. But that would be a lot of travel."

Before Livy could respond to that ridiculous statement, he pulled up to a roadblock manned by several uniformed police.

"Great," Livy muttered. "More cops."

"Deputies," Vic corrected. "And be nice."

Vic stopped his SUV and rolled down the window. One of the deputies walked over, rested his forearm against the window frame, and leaned down to look inside. Because he had to lean *way* down, and his head nearly filled the entire open window . . . Livy knew this was a bear. One of those bears who had to live out in the middle of nowhere because their ginormous head would freak out the everyday full-human schoolchild.

"You brought me to bear territory?" Livy asked.

Vic shrugged. "It's one of the few places in the world I feel completely comfortable. And I assume if I feel comfortable, you'll feel comfortable with me."

"And that logic works for you?"

"For the moment."

The deputy eyed Vic, then Livy, then back to Vic.

"What'cha got there, Barinov?" The deputy sniffed the air, his wide nose making a disturbing amount of noise. "Don't recognize the scent. And we don't let just anybody into our little town."

"This is Livy. Honey badger."

The deputy's grin was wide. "A honey badger? A *real* one?" he asked with what sounded like true enthusiasm. "Hey, guys," he said to the other deputies, "we've got a real honey badger here!"

The deputies suddenly crowded around the SUV, all of them staring into the vehicle to get a look at Livy. As if she'd suddenly turned into a carnival sideshow.

"She is just the cutest little thing," the first deputy said. Then he reached the longest arm Livy had ever seen on a human being across the cab and attempted to "coochie-coo" her face.

Livy leaned away from those giant sausage fingers and hissed, flashing her fangs as extra warning. A warning that made the bear giggle. He giggled. Like an eight-year-old. "She is just the cutest thing! I just wanna hug her! Hug her! Hug her! Hug her!"

Livy looked at Vic. "Can we go home now?"

"No. You need to relax. Plus . . . honey!"

"I can get honey at your house."

"And I can get more holes in my house. No thanks." Vic asked the deputy, "Can we go in, Mike?"

"Sure. And don't forget the festival's happening this whole weekend. It already started." Deputy Mike waved at Livy. "Bye, cutie!"

One of the other deputies hauled a heavy-looking, solid concrete block out of the way—by herself—and Vic drove on. Heading down the road to . . . somewhere.

Livy, confused, asked, "What the hell was that about?"

"What was what about?"

"Most shifters don't try to coochie-coo me."

"This is a bear-only town. They're not used to outside shifters. And few of them have seen honey badgers."

"So?"

"So . . . he thought you were cute."

"When someone says I'm cute, they usually mean I'm cute as a woman. He acted like I was as cute as a stuffed toy. I think he wanted to cuddle me," she said with disgust.

Vic shrugged. "You know, I can actually see that."

"Shut up."

Vic pulled into town and parked in one of the many empty spots along the tree-lined street.

He shut off the motor and gestured to the town outside the vehicle. "Welcome to Honeyville."

Livy's eyes rolled so far back in her head, Vic was worried she'd go permanently blind.

"I know. Pretty obvious for a bear-only town, but don't worry," he promised. "The town lives up to its name. They sell an array of honeys here. Foreign and domestic. And their home brand is—"

"Please stop talking."

Vic did, because when Livy was polite like that . . . it was because she was about to start hurting people.

He got out of the SUV and looked around. He'd always

liked this town, since the first time his parents had taken him and his sister here for vacation. Considering their mother was feline and Vic and Ira were hybrids, the bears had always been surprisingly welcoming to the family. Unlike the cat territory in the next town over.

But he had no intention of going over there. If the cats didn't want him there, then they certainly didn't want his money. Besides . . . the bears had honey.

Vic walked around his SUV, caught hold of Livy's hand, and started walking, pulling the woman behind him.

"Where are we going?" she asked.

He didn't bother to answer. Instead, he led her to his favorite store and walked inside. The woman behind the counter looked up at him and immediately smiled.

"Holy shit! Vic Barinov!" she exclaimed. Rita Thompson, a sixty-year-old hippie grizzly who smoked pot at least three times a day, threw her arms open. "Get the hell over here!" She grasped Vic in an actual bear hug, the six-ten She-bear gripping him tight. "What the hell are you doing here?"

"My friend here needed a break and I couldn't think of a better place to go."

Rita looked around, then leaned over her counter and down at Livy. "Oh! There you are!"

"I'm not *that* small."

"You're like a hobbit!" Rita leaned over a little more. "Do you have hairy feet, too?"

Rita and Vic laughed, but Vic stopped when Livy glared at him.

"*Not* relaxing!" Livy snarled.

"Sorry." He turned to Rita. "We're actually here for some of your delicious—"

"What *are* you?" Rita asked Livy, cutting Vic off. "You're clearly not a fox." She walked around the counter and sniffed, frowned. Sniffed again. Frowned again. Then Rita leaned down and took a big sniff of the top of Livy's head. Sharp, pointy, multiple fangs replaced Livy's human teeth, but instead of attacking, she said, "Lady, if you don't get the fuck away from me, I'm unleashing everything I've got packed in my anal scent glands until you're blind from the stench." Rita jerked away from Livy and Livy finished with, "And trust me when I say that no one will come into your store for *days*."

"A honey badger," Rita snapped, facing Vic. "You brought a honey badger into our town?"

"She's my friend and under my protection, and she promises not to attack anyone. Right, Livy?"

"No."

"What are you talking about?" Rita demanded. "I don't give a fat shit if she attacks anybody. They're bears!" Rita clapped her hands, pressed her forefingers together, and pointed them at Vic. "But she can*not* raid our hives."

"Of course she won't raid your hives. Right, Livy?"

"No."

Vic bared a fang at Livy, and after she rolled her eyes, she said, "Fine. I won't raid your hives."

"See, Rita? Nothing to worry about. I promise, we're here to buy. A lot. I'm trying to cheer up my friend."

"Good luck with that," Rita muttered before facing them. She put on her best fake smile and made a wide gesture with her arms. "Please. Look. We have honey from all over the world, but don't forget our local wares. And feel free to try anything we offer."

Without moving anything but her eyes, Livy examined everything Rita had to offer before announcing, "Do you have a cabinet I can use?"

Once Vic dropped a wad of cash on the She-bear, Rita let them use the kitchen in her house behind the store. With over fifty honeys to choose from, Livy sat inside the cabinet under the sink and Vic sat outside it, his unbelievably long legs stretched out in front of him.

Livy had to admit, these were the best-tasting honeys she'd ever had. Not only were there different types of honey, but there were honeys infused with all sorts of things. Chocolate, raspberry, peanut butter, cinnamon . . . the list went on and on.

Even better and much to Vic's credit, he didn't once ask what was going on with her. Didn't mention Whitlan's daughter or anything to do with that.

Instead, they just sat there in the She-grizzly's kitchen, ate honey, and chatted about the most nonsensical stuff. Like sports.

"You have no idea," Vic complained, "how hard it is to be six-five and two hundred and fifty pounds in junior high and *not* join the football or basketball teams. The principal called my parents about it. Mr. Lawrence. He was very concerned that I was not taking full advantage of the American experience—to which my father told him to go fuck himself. 'My boy,' " Vic said with a heavy Russian accent, " 'do not need your weak American sport. He is Russian! He fights bear!' Mr. Lawrence," Vic went on with his normal voice, "was full-human, so he thought that was a lot of hyperbole, but I was, in fact, outside fighting bears. My cousins were visiting from Moscow that fall and they were beating the crap out of me in the backyard."

"Aaaah, family."

"Speaking of which . . . Smelly Melly?"

Livy chuckled at the nickname. "Did you get that from Shen?"

"Of course. So what's the deal with your cousin?"

"What do you mean?"

"I mean, why was she in prison?"

Livy normally didn't answer questions like that about family members, but sitting here, in some strange bear's kitchen, in Massachusetts, in a town called Honeyville, while eating fifty different kinds of honey . . . she thought, *Why not?*

"Melly was in prison because she felt her boyfriend was ignoring her, so she hooked up with another guy. When fucking someone else didn't work, she arranged her own kidnapping."

"I'm sorry," Vic cut in, a spoonful of lemon-infused honey poised in front of his mouth. "She what?"

"Arranged her own kidnapping. It was an elaborate plan, too. The FBI became involved, there was blood at the scene, and calls from the"—she made air quotes with her fingers—" 'kidnappers' with their demands, and she was just about six miles away at some resort with the guy she'd convinced to do this with her because of the money her boyfriend *didn't* actually have. And, even after that, they were ready to let her off with most likely a wrist slap because they figured out she was crazy but not crazy enough to actually commit to Bedford Mental Hospital. But then she showed up to her sentencing drunk. So drunk she tripped over the defense table and vomited up a crapload of vodka on the baliff, which pissed off her judge. Got eighteen months, but as I found out a couple of days ago . . . she only served ten."

"Wow," he muttered, his cheeks sucked in a bit from the sourness of the lemon. "That's *mighty* crazy."

"That's Melly. Crazy Melly." Livy lifted her spoon. "These are the most *amazing* honeys I've ever tasted."

"I know."

"A few, though, I've had at your house. Now you see why I keep going there."

"Now you know why I get so cranky when you eat it all. I love my honey."

A door opened somewhere in the house, and Livy heard what sounded like clanking metal coming toward them. After a minute or two, a male polar walked into the kitchen, dressed in full armor. Like, King Arthur kind of armor.

The polar placed his helmet—complete with a vibrantly colored feather plume—on the table. He stood there for a second until his head slowly turned and he looked down at Livy and Vic.

"Victor."

"Hi, Ken."

"What'cha doin' in my kitchen?"

"Eating your wife's honey."

"Oh. Okay."

"Why are you in armor?"

"Renaissance Faire's in town this weekend. You should come. Jousting starts this evening."

"Thanks for the offer, but I'm not sure my friend would want—"

Livy crawled until she was stretched over Vic's lap. "There's jousting?" she asked the polar.

"Sure is. It's an all-weekend thing for us. First rounds start tonight."

"Can anyone join?"

"Well—"

"No, Livy," Vic said.

"Quiet." Livy quickly scrambled completely out of the cabinet. "Can you get me set up with armor and a horse?" she asked the bear.

"I think so, but we don't have a fox joust at this faire."

"I don't want to joust foxes." Livy grinned. "I want to joust bears."

CHAPTER 13

Vic shook his head, unable to believe this was happening. "Do you have any idea how insane this is?"

Livy put on another helmet, but it was so large it spun around her head like a top. "You can keep saying it, but it doesn't change anything."

"Are you *trying* to get killed? Are you suicidal?"

"As long as I protect my head . . . I should be fine."

"Should be . . . you *should* be fine? That's great, Livy."

"I need to do this."

"Why? Why would anyone in their right mind need to do this?"

All the bears preparing for the joust stopped putting on their armor and focused on Vic. He stared back. "Yeah," he challenged. "That includes you people."

"I learned this in the court-ordered anger management class I took. About how to work off your aggression. Yoga, running, boxing, Krav Maga, Muy Thai . . . nothing helps. But I've never tried jousting before. So I'm going to try jousting."

"But you're going up against bears, Livy." He pointed across the tent they were in. "I mean, look at that guy over there."

The eight-foot polar realized that Vic was talking about him. "Hey! What are you pointing me out for? Like I'm some kind of freak? That just hurts my feelings, man!"

"Oh, suck it up," Vic growled.

"Your feline is showing," Livy warned.

"Because you're not being rational and there's an eight-foot, four-hundred-pound whiny baby over there begging me to claw the holy shit out of him."

"You are rude!" the polar complained.

Vic was about to go over there and show the idiot how rude he could be when Livy caught his arm.

"Don't beat him up because *I'm* pissing you off."

"Who says he can beat me up?" the polar demanded.

"*I* could beat you up," Livy shot back. And when the polar just stared at her, she asked, "Want me to prove it?"

The polar thought on that a moment before he stalked out of the tent.

"Help me find a helmet," she ordered Vic.

Sighing, he walked over to a row of helmets. "I don't know why you're doing this," he said. He grabbed one of the helmets. "I know you're upset and I know when you're ready, you'll tell me why. But doing something this stupid—" He placed the helmet on her head. It fit perfectly.

She lifted the visor, grinned. "How do I look?"

"Like you're welcoming death."

"Your faith in me is heartening."

"Can't we just go and sit in the audience and mock people dressed in clothes from another century? You know . . . like normal shifters do?"

"Most times I'd say yes, but I need to do this. And if I survive, you'll be really proud of me."

"And if you don't?"

"Have me cremated and tell my family I left town. They don't deserve anything better than that."

"What about Toni?"

Livy blew out a breath and shook her head. "Yeah, she'll

figure things out on her own, and then . . . yeah, you're dead."

"Again . . . why is this coming down on *me*?"

Livy shrugged, picked up her sheathed sword, and walked out.

"Hey," a sloth bear said from behind Vic, "don't you play hockey?"

"No, I do not!" Vic roared.

"Wow," the sloth bear said, backing away from him. "You are one bitchy hybrid."

Livy stared up at the horse one of the faire employees held for her. She glanced over and said, "You can't be serious."

"These are horses bred for two things. Handling the weight of big guys in armor . . . and not panicking at the scent of shifters. Helping some tiny feminist trying to prove something was not on our list of things to accomplish during the breeding process," he finished.

Livy looked under the horse and asked, "Huh. What's this? It looks bad."

The faire employee bent down to see what Livy was looking at and that's when she rammed the pummel of her sword into the employee's tibia. She heard something snap, and he went down with a roar onto one knee. Before he could fall back, Livy climbed onto his shoulders and mounted the horse that was way too big for her.

She looked down at the now-sobbing bear. "Thanks for the help."

Vic walked into the prep area and stopped when he saw her.

"Have you ever ridden a horse before?" he asked.

"No. There were horses at the private school I went to. Riding lessons were mandatory and were part of our gym grade, but every time I got close to them, the horses tried to stomp me into the ground. Eventually, I had to be excused."

"But now you're going to ride one that's too big for you so that you can . . . joust?"

"That's the plan." Someone put a lance in her hand. It was heavy and too long, but Livy held on to it. "How do I look?" she asked again.

"Suicidal."

"If you're going to be negative . . ."

Livy moved around in the saddle.

"What?" Vic asked.

"I wish I didn't have to wear this armor. It's making my skin itch."

"Take that armor off, female, and still try to joust, and I'll beat you to death myself."

Livy nodded. "Subtle."

"I'm not subtle. Never said I was subtle. Worried you're about to do something stupid? Yes. *That* is accurate."

"Honey badger's up!" someone called out.

"I'm up." Livy stared at the back of the horse's head. "You can go now," she told the beast.

Vic dropped his head into his hands.

Chuckling, she tapped the sides of the horse's flanks with her heels and rode to the field. True, she might not have ridden the horses at her fancy private school, but that didn't mean the gym teacher wasn't a bitch who hated Livy so much she made the fourteen-year-old sit and watch the others for the entire period. At the time, Livy hated Mrs. Webb, but at the moment, she'd discovered a newfound appreciation.

Once Livy was led into position, she looked around at the crowd. The faire was surprisingly big and had a lot of attendees. Even the cats from the town next door came to the Honeyville Annual Renaissance Faire.

And apparently the joust was the most popular attraction;

the makeshift arena was already packed, with the audience continuing to grow.

"Honey stick?"

A seven-foot, older grizzly stood next to her, his face obscured by an enormous beard and long brown and gray hair. Another hippie, she was guessing. Like Rita.

Livy took the offered honey stick, bit off the tip, and sucked out the honey inside while the grizzly studied her a moment before asking, "I know you honey badgers are tough and all, but you do know that we're going to crush your tiny little body into the dirt, don't ya?"

"Yeah. I know that."

"You don't mind?"

"Not as much as I probably should." She shrugged. "Trying to work out some issues."

"Ahhh. I see." The grizzly leaned in. "Well, me and the guys had a thought. You see, the reason we have this first night of jousting is because we always have to work through the cats from next door before we can get to a good rousing joust with the rest of us. The felines bring a lot of money to this faire, so we put up with 'em. But it gets a bit boring."

Livy again looked around at the audience, which was still growing . . . with bears.

"You want me to take out the cats . . . don't you?" Livy asked.

"Cat humiliation and bear entertainment all rolled in one. Think you can do that?"

"What do I get out of it?" Because at the end of the day, Livy was still her mother's daughter.

"Year's supply of your favorite honey from Rita's store?"

Livy immediately thought of the cinnamon-infused honey and she sort of shuddered. A good shudder, though. A delicious, honey-filled shudder.

"I'm in."

The grizzly patted her leg. "Have fun, sweetie."

Livy planned to . . .

* * *

Vic rested his forearms against the wood barriers used to block off the jousting area from the crowd surrounding it and watched Livy.

He didn't know what the hell she was up to. Why was she doing this? What had happened when she went into that damn woman's apartment?

"Is she your girlfriend?" Rita asked him.

"Who? Livy?" He shook his head. "No. No. Just a friend. A good friend," he quickly added. "I've got her back or whatever. But just . . . um . . . we're just . . . ya know . . ."

Rita placed her hand on his shoulder and rested her head against his arm. "Breathe, sweetie. Breathe. It's going to be okay."

"Don't start, Rita."

She laughed. "You always get so flustered over the strangest things."

"Livy isn't a strange thing. She is currently, however, suicidal."

"She'll be fine. She's just going up against the cats." Vic glanced at Rita and she quickly added, "No offense."

Yeah, the bears did like to forget that he was half-feline, but that was still more than most cats were willing to do for him.

Livy hefted her lance like she was trying to get used to the weight.

"This is crazy," Vic growled. "Stupid and crazy."

"I've never heard honey badgers called stupid before."

Vic waited for Rita to say more. When she didn't, he looked at her, and she shrugged. "Really. I haven't heard them called stupid."

Sighing, Vic returned his focus to the field just as the signal was given and the joust was on. Livy lowered her lance and spurred her horse into a full gallop. At least this time she didn't try to *talk* the horse into going.

The two riders charged toward each other until their lances rammed into the other's shield. Livy fell back against her horse, but she held her seat. Her opponent, however, didn't seem to even flinch. Hard to tell, though, with that helmet on his head.

The crowd cheered as Livy and her opponent rode to the end of the barrier and turned to face each other again. Livy's helmeted head tilted to the side and Vic knew she was sizing up her opponent. She readjusted her grip on the new lance that had been handed to her and moved around a bit in her saddle. Then she nodded.

The signal was given, and the two riders charged toward each other. Livy lowered her lance just a bit seconds before it hit her opponent, sending him flipping off his horse so that he landed hard on the ground.

The bears in the crowd went wild. The cats . . . not so much. But at least they had the decency not to hiss.

Sadly, as the joust progressed into the evening, that decency didn't last. Not with Livy knocking each and every cat that came along off their horse. Leopard. Bobcat. Cheetah. Bengal tiger. Cougar. On and on it went. Finally, it was down to a massive lion male who had openly shown his dislike of Livy when he'd walked by her at the end of a break and roared in her face, baring large fangs.

Livy didn't even look at him. She just let one of the bears pick her up and put her back on her horse.

The signal was given once more. The riders charged, and their lances hit each other at the same time, knocking both off their mounts. Vic figured that meant a redo of the ride, but to his horror, this particular Renaissance Faire seemed to like the old-school rules of jousting.

Livy and the lion were given weapons. The lion swung the mace he now held, ripped off his helmet, and roared again at Livy.

Livy looked at her own mace, then back at the lion.

"Uh-oh," Vic said.

"What?" Rita asked.

But Vic didn't bother to answer. Not when Livy answered for him by throwing down the mace, jumping onto the wood barrier, and throwing her small, armored body at the surprised lion. He stumbled back as Livy wrapped herself around the lion's head, tossed off her helmet, opened her mouth wide, small but sharp fangs glinting in the torchlight seconds before she dug those fangs into the top of the lion's massive brow.

"Owwwwww!" the lion screamed. *"Get her off me! Get this crazy bitch off me!"*

Rita giggled into her hand. "Oh, I love her!"

The lion ripped Livy off his head and threw her across the field. Livy rolled a few feet, stopped, jumped up, and came at the cat again. He stumbled back, Livy tackling him. Now she was biting his face, her claws dug into his big mane of gold hair, the cheers of the crowd nearly drowning out the cat screaming, "My hair! My beautiful, beautiful hair! *Get her off me!*"

Two of the jousting judges, one a cheetah—who were never fans of lions anyway—the other a sun bear, looked at each other and the bear suggested, "Screaming like a three-year-old girl about his hair? That seems like an automatic loss to me."

The cheetah nodded. "I believe I agree with you on that."

The sun bear stepped forward and called out in ridiculous-sounding old English, "Ye Lady Honey Badger wins this challenge!"

As soon as the words were spoken, Livy pulled her fangs out of the lion's face and dropped to the ground. She spit out blood and calmly walked away, not even glancing at her opponent. It was as if he no longer existed to her.

"She is fabulous," Rita told him.

"She's insane."

"But *fabulously* insane."

Vic briefly closed his eyes. "Shut up, Rita."

Livy's next opponent turned out to be a black She-bear. And Livy did all the things she'd done before with the cats, but when the black bear's lance rammed into her, Livy flew off her horse, past the judges, and into the wood barrier surrounding the field. The portion she hit was destroyed on impact, and Livy disappeared under a pile of broken wood.

The crowd grew silent, all eyes on where Livy had gone down. For a full minute, no one moved. No one said a word. Even Vic. He was just too stunned. Too horrified.

But then the wood moved and Livy's arm suddenly shot up, one thumb raised. The crowd lost it; the cheers, roars, and stomping shook everything around him.

Vic let out a breath seconds before he ran over to her. He and several others pulled the wood and debris away until they reached her.

Crouching down, Vic lifted the nose shield of Livy's helmet. Her face was covered in blood, but her eyes were open and alert—and she smiled.

"Crazy," Vic admonished. "You're crazy."

"Yeah, but we're still gettin' free honey for a *year*. And isn't that what's important?"

"As a matter of fact, Olivia . . . *no!*" Vic finished on a healthy yell.

CHAPTER 14

Vic stood Livy in front of the couch in the house he'd gotten for the night. It was one of Rita's rental homes. A pot-smoking hippie she might be. But a capitalist one. She charged an exorbitant amount of money for the one-night use once she found out about the free honey deal her brother had made with Livy, but Vic wasn't about to drive back to New York now. The traffic alone would make him homicidal.

Moving slowly, Vic removed Livy's helmet, which he'd been unwilling to do at the joust. He grimaced when he saw her face. By now the blood had dried, and he could see the myriad other bruises and cuts she'd gotten from all the jousts.

"That bad?" she asked.

"Yes." Why beat around the bush when dealing with a crazy person? He didn't see the point in bothering.

"Then if I were you, I wouldn't take off the rest of my armor."

"I have to. I need to make sure none of your ribs are piercing something important. I'd rather not find you dead tomorrow, blood everywhere."

"Well, when you put it like that . . ."

Vic turned Livy to the side and crouched down so that he could unbuckle her breastplate. Once he had all the straps apart, he lifted the metal up and over her head. When he did that, the padded shirt she'd worn under the armor was lifted up, as well, and all Vic could do was sigh out, "Oh Livy . . ."

Vic quickly set aside the armor, then removed the shirt completely. He couldn't believe how bruised her body was. Not just in one spot, either, but all over her chest, neck, and shoulders. Even her breasts. She was just one big bruise.

"Tell me honestly," Livy whispered. "Will I ever bikini model again?"

"Not funny."

Livy chuckled. "Come on. It's a *little* funny."

"Did you lose any teeth?" Vic asked, as he worked on getting off her chain-mail leggings after making Livy sit on the couch.

"Me? My teeth are like granite."

"Granite breaks."

"Not from some cat."

"Lift your right leg," he ordered, easing the leggings down as she lifted her right leg, then the left.

"So what are we doing?" she asked.

"Crashing here for the night. After what you put me through, I'm not in the mood to drive."

"Put *you* through? What are you . . . my mother?" She held up her hand. "Check that. What are you . . . Toni?"

"I now understand that poor jackal a little better. You must have put her through hell all these years."

"She might have implied that . . . more than once." Livy drummed the fingers of one hand against her knee. "I'm hungry."

Vic tossed aside the leggings. "We can order food. Bears love free delivery. Why hunt when it can be delivered right to your door?"

He examined her legs. "At least these look pretty good."

"Why thank you."

Vic blinked. "I mean they look relatively undamaged."

"So you don't like my legs?"

Frowning, he looked at her. "I never said I don't like your legs. Why wouldn't I like your legs?"

"I see the She-bears around here. They have long legs."

"Because most of them are over six feet tall. Some are over seven and play on the WNBA. Of *course* they have long legs."

"You're very logical, aren't you?"

Vic had no idea where this conversation was going. Did she have a head injury? Well . . . more than just the obvious ones he could see?

"I guess." He shrugged. "Being logical is part of what I do."

Livy nodded. "It's very sexy."

Vic quickly stood and began to feel around Livy's head.

"What are you doing?" she asked.

"Trying to see if you have any skull damage. Did you black out at any point today?"

She slapped his hands off her head. "No."

Vic stood back. "Are you sure?"

"Yes, I'm sure."

"You're not lying to me, are you?"

"No."

He shrugged. "All right. But we should watch for signs of concussion." He looked around until he found the doorway leading to the kitchen. "I bet that's where Rita keeps the delivery menus."

Vic turned to walk to the kitchen.

"You've got a nice ass, too."

Vic froze mid-step. "Livy—"

"Don't ask me again if I have a concussion. I don't."

He faced her. "Then what the fuck are you doing?"

"I'm hungry."

"Which was why I was going to get the menus . . ."

"And a little horny."

Vic took a step back. "What?"

"I can't help it. I think it was the jousting. Beating the crap out of those cats has got me kind of . . . worked up." She gazed at him, then raised an eyebrow.

Vic pointed at himself. "And you want *me* to do something about that?"

"Well, you're here."

"Gee. Thanks. That's so romantic."

"I'm not talking romance. In fact . . . I'd like to avoid romance as much as possible. My parents had romance . . . that didn't end well for them."

"Because your dad passed away?"

"No."

Vic sighed, rubbed his eyes with his fists. "I am unsure where this is going, Livy."

"Bedroom?"

Vic quickly dropped his hands. "Livy."

"What? I'm young and healthy—"

"And battered!"

"—you're young-*ish* and healthy—"

"I'm only thirty-three," he snapped, insulted.

"—so why can't we work off some of my untapped energy?"

"Because you may be operating under some kind of temporary brain damage. You'll hate yourself in the morning . . . and I'll be forced to hate myself for taking advantage of you."

Livy snorted.

"What?"

"I like that you think you can take advantage of me." She stared at him a moment, snorted again. "*You.*"

"And I'm *out,*" Vic snarled before turning away.

* * *

Giggling, in a tremendously good mood after going toe-to-toe with those cats, Livy reached out and grabbed Vic's arm. "I'm sorry," she said quickly. "I'm being a douche."

"You are!"

"And I'm sorry. Really." Livy realized that she was making the bear in him panic. Vic, at least while human—she had yet to see his shifted form—was so very much bear. And grizzlies were easy to startle, quick to enrage, and not at all hard to panic. Livy was managing to do all three without much effort.

Then again, Vic had never seen her after she'd worked off her rage. She was probably completely freaking him out right now. And she really needed her friends.

She'd thought about telling Vic what she'd found in Allison Whitlan's apartment. That she'd found her father. But she wasn't ready to talk about it. She wasn't ready to think about it. She definitely wasn't ready to get Vic's pity over it. And although he knew something was wrong, he was still giving her space. As much as she liked tucking herself into cabinets and under beds, Livy still needed space when it came to everything else. She hated being crowded.

Livy knew she'd eventually tell Vic what was going on, but not until she knew what she wanted to do. And, at the moment, she had absolutely no idea.

"I'm starving," she told him. "I'd love some Chinese food."

Vic eyed her suspiciously. After a few seconds, he said, "There's Honey Panda Inn. They deliver. And have a really good General Tso's Honey Chicken."

Livy held her arms up and away from her body. "Now how do we say no to *that*?"

Vic paid the giant panda and took the large box filled with food. Closing the door with his foot, he walked into the kitchen.

Livy, now thankfully back in her jeans, boots, and a cub-sized Honeyville T-shirt that reached down to her thighs, was pouring two glasses of white wine after discovering the wine fridge tucked between the dishwasher and the cabinet filled with local honeys.

Placing the box down on the counter, Vic briefly studied Livy. "Are you sure you should be drinking?"

"You don't like girls who drink?"

"No, no. It's not that. It's just . . . you're healing. Liquor can mess with that. Especially if you get the fever tonight."

"What fever?"

Vic blinked, faced Livy. "The fever. The fever that every shifter gets when they heal from a traumatic injury. It allows us to heal from horrific injuries, sometimes within twenty-four hours. You know . . . the *fever*."

"Oh. Yeah. Heard about that. We don't get that. You got two options with honey badgers: kill us or get ready to keep fighting until you're too tired to fight anymore."

"You were injured during the joust. I saw the—"

Livy took a gulp from her wineglass while lifting her T-shirt at the same time. And she was right. All those horrifying-looking bruises that had made him worry she had internal bleeding and he'd either have to rush her to the local hospital or she'd be dead by morning were fading away.

He also saw that Livy's bra seemed to have faded away, as well.

Vic swiftly focused on the cabinets rather than Livy's perfect tits before he snarled, "Livy, where the hell is your bra?"

"I took it off. It was too constricting." She set down her wineglass. "That's a good Riesling. You should try some."

Thinking wine was just what he needed to take the edge off, Vic was taking a step toward the other side of the kitchen so he could get the wine she'd poured for him, when Livy suddenly held up her hand.

"Stop."

Vic did, immediately scanning the room and area for trouble. It was in his training.

"The light in this kitchen is amazing."

"The light?"

"Yeah. It really highlights your great cheekbone structure."

That made Vic laugh.

"What?"

"Just wondering if I might have missed my calling as a supermodel."

Livy smirked at Vic's remark. "You're way too big for that."

"Thank you very much."

"Not an insult. Those male models are surprisingly thin and not nearly as tall as you. I used to work for a fashion photographer one summer and I was way unimpressed with the models."

"You wanted to be a fashion photographer? You?"

"I'll just assume that you're not talking about my wonderful fashion sense and assume you mean my general distaste for people obsessed with themselves."

"I mean both."

"And I worked in almost every area of photography when I was in high school. Even things I would never consider doing long term, just so that I knew what it was like. What it was about. And if there were ways I could twist it to my purposes."

"There's the Livy Goal I'm used to hearing about."

Livy picked up the extra glass of wine and walked over to Vic. She handed it to him and continued to study his face.

"You're making me uncomfortable."

"You're always uncomfortable," Livy muttered.

"Not always."

"Huh," she finally said.

"What?"

"I'm just sorry I don't have my camera with me. Between the lighting and—"

"Hold that thought!" Vic suddenly told her before putting his wine down and rushing out of the room.

Livy shook her head and sipped her wine. "Such a strange man sometimes," she murmured.

A few seconds later, Vic returned, placing Livy's digital SLR camera on the kitchen island.

Livy stared at the camera, then looked back at Vic. "Why?" she asked as she placed her wineglass on the island.

"Because Honeyville is beautiful in the winter. So I grabbed it from your office at the Sports Center. Thought you might get inspired out here, and I wanted you to be ready. And I was right!"

Then he grinned at her. A grin so wide and beautiful and earnest, Livy didn't know what to think. Although what blew her away was how well he'd handled getting her camera to her. He didn't push it on her as soon as she got in the car or when they parked near the honey store. He didn't brag about it or gloat. He didn't order her to do it. He just brought her camera . . . in case.

In case.

Which meant that he was leaving it up to her. No pushing involved.

Her family was all about pushing. And, to be honest, so was Toni. Although for Toni it was pushing Livy to do the right thing as opposed to getting her to learn better pick-pocketing techniques.

Vic's grin faded. "You're mad. I pissed you off. I'm sorry. I wasn't trying to push—"

"I know," she cut in. "I know you weren't."

And because he wasn't pushing, Livy climbed up onto

the island, dropped her arms on Vic's shoulders, and kissed him.

She kissed him hard.

And she'd have to admit . . . she was pushing.

Vic fell back against the sink, Livy still holding on to him, her mouth still pressed against his.

Shocked and confused, he pried her off, his hands around her waist, and held her out in front of him.

"What are you doing?"

"Kissing you."

"Why?"

"Because I really want to."

"Why?"

"Why not?"

Vic placed her on the ground and began backing away from her. "Yeah, uh, I don't think this is a good idea."

"Really?" Livy watched him a moment before she began to move forward, matching him step for step.

"And why don't you think it's a good idea?" she asked.

"It's just not a good idea. We should just stay friends."

Vic kept moving, and Livy kept tracking him around the kitchen. He felt like a cobra she'd locked on.

Livy gave a very small shrug. "You don't think I'm pretty. Is that it?"

"Are you kidding? You're gorgeous."

"You think I'm gorgeous?"

"Yeah."

"Okay."

He looped around the island and she was right with him.

"You think my shoulders are too wide?" she asked. "Make me look too square?"

"Your shoulders work fine because you've got that long, sloping neck, and surprisingly long legs for your height."

"Tits too small?"

"Perfect for your size."

"Think it's tacky I used *tits* instead of *breasts*?"

"Actually, I thought it was kind of sexy."

Vic's back suddenly collided with a corner and before he could maneuver out of it, Livy slapped her hands on the counter on either side of him.

Livy gazed up at him. "Can I ask you a question, Vic?"

"If you really have to."

"Do I make you nervous?"

"Not exactly . . . unless I made you mad and have no way to protect my eyes and major arteries."

"You know," she went on, "Toni thinks you're shy. But I don't."

"You don't?"

"No. I don't think you're comfortable around people, but that's not the same as shy. You're not desperate to be around people but emotionally unable to connect. You just want people to leave you alone most of the time."

"Okay."

"Just like most bears. And the longer I've gotten to know you, the more I realize that you *live* bear."

"I live bear?"

"Yeah. You live like a bear, which makes me wonder about the feline in you. I mean, Novikov has that weird suddenly growing mane thing he does when he's angry. But I haven't seen that with you. I haven't seen a true, outward sign of your feline side."

"What is your point, Olivia?"

"I just want you to tell me."

"Tell you what?"

"Is the problem that you live like a bear"—she leaned in, lowered her voice even more—"but fuck like a cat? And is that what has you completely freaked out right now? Because the cat in you is the side you can't control?"

Vic worked hard not to take his eyes off Livy, not to look

away. Not to show her any weakness or that there was any truth to her words at all. But she did look away . . . and down at his crotch.

When she finally looked back at his face, she didn't smirk. She grinned.

"Yeah," she sighed out, her voice triumphant. "That's what I thought."

CHAPTER 15

Vic grabbed Livy by her upper arms and Livy wondered if he was going to pull her close to kiss her or slam her face-down on the kitchen island so he could fuck her raw. She was definitely up for either.

Sadly, Vic did neither. He simply moved Livy out of his way and practically ran out of the kitchen.

Yep. You spooked him, she thought as she followed after him.

True. It wasn't the first time she'd freaked out a man. In fact, in the past, freaking out men had been something she'd often done for fun. But she'd thought she had a better connection with Vic. Had always thought he'd understood her and liked her despite that understanding.

She guessed she was wrong.

Livy made it into the hallway leading to the front door. Vic was already at the door, but seemed suddenly confused with basic lock operation.

"Vic," she called out, walking toward him, "you don't have to leave. I promise to—"

Livy stopped talking, her face too busy grimacing at seeing Vic Barinov finally manage to open the front door but also slam it into his head.

He snarled in pain and stumbled back, and Livy walked quickly to his side. But by the time she reached him, blood was already dripping down his face from where he'd split his forehead open.

She took hold of his forearm with one hand and closed the door with the other.

"I'm fine," he kept saying. "I'm fine. I'm fine."

"You're not fine. And I'm not about to send you out into the Massachusetts cold while you're bleeding from the head. I'm not that big a bitch."

Vic gazed down at her, his left eye blinking excessively because of the blood that was dripping into it. "You're not a bitch. Who told you that you're a bitch?"

"Really, Barinov? That's what you're worried about?"

Livy pulled Vic down the hall and into the living room. She pushed him onto the couch and studied the wound. "Stay here," she ordered.

In the first-floor bathroom, Livy dug up a first-aid kit, clearly created for both human and shifter since she found muzzles of several sizes as well as bandages and pain ointment.

Shaking her head, Livy ignored the muzzles, grabbed several large towels, and returned to the living room.

"Get up," she ordered Vic. He stood and she placed one of the bigger towels under him. "That way we won't get blood on it," she explained as she pushed him back onto the couch.

Livy silently cleaned up the wound and Vic's face. Although his skin had split where the door had hit him, it hadn't done any major damage from what she could see. He would, however, have to suffer through a lump on his head for a little bit.

And while Livy worked, Vic watched her. Closely.

Finally, when Livy was nearly done, Vic said, "Well . . . this is awkward, huh?"

"No."

"You don't think this is awkward?"

"No."

She opened up an oversized adhesive bandage. She stepped in close so that she could place it perfectly over his wound. She rested the palms of her hands on either side of his head and carefully lowered the bandage with the tips of her fingers. She'd nearly placed the adhesive part against Vic's skin when he snapped, "How can you not think this is awkward?"

Livy jerked back. "Do you want me to lie and say I feel awkward? I can do that."

"I never want you to lie to me," he muttered.

"Okay." Livy moved back, her legs straddling one of Vic's so that she could get in close.

And again, she'd nearly placed the bandage, when he snarled, "I just don't understand how you cannot think this is strange after what just happened."

Livy closed her eyes. She'd placed the bandage but now it was crooked, part of his wound exposed. And, even if his wound had been covered, the obsessive photographer in her could never have let that stand.

So, Livy ripped the bandage off Vic's head and reached for another one.

"Ow!"

She slapped the fingers he was about to use to touch his swollen head. "Don't touch."

After removing a new bandage from the packaging and peeling off the paper that protected the adhesive, she looked directly at Vic and said, "Don't say a word until I'm done. Understand me?"

"Yes."

Livy again took up her position straddling Vic's leg and carefully placed the bandage. Once it was on and it was perfect, she let out a sigh and began to back away from the big idiot. But before she'd pulled more than an inch away from him, Vic's arm wrapped around her waist. He didn't say anything, though. He just kept her there.

"We're okay, Vic," she told him, assuming he was still bothered about what this would do to their friendship.

"I panicked," he admitted, still not releasing her.

"You're not the first guy I've ever made bolt from the room. I doubt you'll be my last."

Vic wrapped his other arm around Livy's waist and pulled her in between his legs. He rested his head against her chest and then just stayed that way. Without saying a word.

Confused, Livy stood there, with her hands kept at her sides.

"Livy?"

"Yeah?"

Vic leaned his head back, his chin still resting on her chest. "Some days . . ."

"Yeah?"

"Some days you make me want to drive a railroad spike through my head."

"I have to admit . . . I did not see the conversation going that way."

"Do you even like me? Or am I just . . . convenient? Like an open window at someone's empty house? Because I have to tell you, at the moment . . . I'm feeling more like an open window."

Livy rubbed her eyes with the palms of her hands. "What the fuck are you talking about?"

Vic suddenly stood, forcing Livy to step back, but he still kept her encircled in his arms as he towered over her. "What I'm asking you," he said, his voice rising with each word, "is have you secretly wanted me all this time, *or would Shen be getting this same offer to fuck you like a tiger if* he'd *picked you up at the precinct?*"

In that moment Livy realized that honey badgers truly *were* fearless, because Vic Barinov had bellowed the last half of that sentence only a few inches from her face and she hadn't flinched. Although she could have sworn the windows behind the couch shook a little. Nah. Probably her imagination.

Livy thought about Vic's question, and replied, "I never would have said that to Shen . . . he's not half-cat."

"See?" he yelled. "That is *not* an answer! At least not one I'm willing to—"

Livy went up on the coffee table behind her, slapped her hands hard against Vic's face to hold him there, and kissed him. Again.

Vic again tried to pull her off. "Livy," he growled against her mouth. "Just—"

"No," she said, tightening her grip on his face and wrapping her legs around his waist so she now clung to him. "No talking. Just kiss me, Vic." She pulled back a bit so she could look him in the eye, but she kept her grip tight. "Kiss me now and I promise we'll talk tomorrow. We'll talk all you want about anything you want. Tomorrow."

Vic's eyes narrowed on her, the gold lighter than usual. Lighter and brighter and untrusting. "You better not be lying to me," he warned, his low voice nothing more at this point than an angry growl. "You know I hate it when you lie to me."

Livy leaned in, placed a soft kiss on Vic's mouth. A small one. Then another. And another. Moving from one spot to another. Teasing him. Sometimes nibbling his lip here, then there.

She had no idea how long she kept it up. Livy simply lost herself in it. Enjoying the feel of her mouth against Vic's.

But suddenly, Vic made a chuffing sound, and he gripped Livy's head between his hands, holding her in place. That's when he took her mouth. His lips pressed hard against hers. Livy opened to him and Vic's tongue was immediately there. Seeking, exploring. Taking over as felines like to do.

It felt . . . perfect.

Like the perfect picture. Maybe you didn't know it was perfect when you shot it, but then you saw it on a print or on your screen and you knew. You knew. And this time, with Vic, it was the same thing. Weird . . . then perfect.

Vic pulled away, both of them gasping for air. He set her down, not gently, either.

"Get naked," he barked at her. "And get upstairs." Then he walked off.

Kind of confused about which she should do first—shouldn't she go upstairs and then get naked? If she got naked down here, then she'd have to get dressed down here tomorrow—Livy just stood there.

A few seconds later, Vic stalked back into the living room.

"Too long," he barked, picking her up around the waist, and securing her under his arm like so much laundry.

It would be humiliating if it was anyone else. Anyone else in the entire *world*. But it was Vic. Polite, sweetly charming, socially inept Vic.

Livy was just so entertained by this new side of him that she really didn't give a shit where he carried her.

As long as he fucked her once he got there.

Vic took Livy to the master bedroom. His careful, practical bear side had gone into hibernation a good ten minutes ago. Now, all that was left was the cranky feline that had made Vic give up dating full-human girls when he was seventeen. They couldn't handle the cranky feline when it came out. Few could.

And yet, when he threw Livy on the bed, she laughed. Hard.

Deciding that Livy's laughter meant she was still taking too long to get naked, Vic reached down and yanked off her boots. He didn't even bother to untie them. Couldn't wait. Didn't want to.

Once he'd done that, Livy had only managed to get her jeans unzipped, which, again . . . not fast enough!

Honestly, how hard was it for a woman not wearing many clothes in the first place to get said clothes off in a timely manner?

Vic caught hold of the waistband of Livy's jeans and yanked them down. They were kind of tight, though, so he had to lift her legs up and drag them off. Livy's legs flipped over her head and she ended up rolling backward until she rested on her knees. Now she only wore the T-shirt. He must have taken off her panties along with her jeans.

Startled black eyes blinked up at him, her hands resting on her bare knees.

"You all right?" Vic asked.

"Yep."

Taking Livy at her word, he took a step toward her.

"Condoms?" Livy asked.

"What?"

"Con. *Doms*. Remember those?" She pointed at her crotch. "No one gets in here without one."

Annoyed he hadn't thought about that before now, Vic growled and looked around the room. He didn't think Rita kept any in her houses unless you specified an "adult weekend" when the reservations were made. But the thought of leaving a nearly naked Livy to go hunt some down through Honeyville was bringing his fangs out.

"Get my backpack," Livy suddenly ordered him.

"What?"

"My backpack. You brought it in the house, didn't—"

Vic didn't wait for her to finish. He just stalked out of the room and went to search out her backpack.

He found it in the kitchen, grabbed it, and returned to the bedroom.

Livy was still kneeling on the bed, appearing completely calm. "Open the back pocket and go into the zippered compartment."

Vic did as ordered. Without looking, he located the zippered pocket with his fingers and opened it. He reached in and pulled out a long strip of condoms. Eyes narrowing, he focused on Livy.

"What?" she asked.

"You just carry around piles of condoms?"

"In case I feel like taking on the hockey team one night. You know, when I'm bored."

"Can you ever give me a straight answer?"

"Maybe when you ask me a question that suggests one of the photographers I trained with told me exactly what to include in my backpack and travel bags so that I was always prepared for any situation rather than strongly suggesting I'm a whore."

Vic blew out a breath. "You're right."

"I know."

"Sorry."

"Feeling a little possessive there, Barinov?"

"Kind of."

"Don't feel bad. One might suggest I've been feeling a little possessive about you lately."

Shocked at that admission, Vic gawked at Livy. "Really?"

"Did you see me haul off and slap Melly outside the precinct?"

"*Everyone* saw you slap Melly."

"Well, although there are many reasons I should slap the shit out of Melly Kowalski, in this particular instance I did it because she suggested that she wouldn't mind 'nailing that,' when pointing you out to me. Her words. And I wanted to make it clear to her that I was not okay with her nailing anything. Especially you."

"Really?" Vic asked again.

"Really."

"I like that."

"I can tell. Now come here."

Vic dropped Livy's backpack and walked toward her. As he did, she stood on the bed and walked to the edge. They met there, but Livy snorted.

"What?"

"I expected us to meet eye to eye. Instead, I'm looking at your throat. So tall."

"Does that bother you?"

"No." Livy nuzzled his neck. "Do you want it to bother me?" she murmured.

Vic briefly closed his eyes, worked to keep control. "Not at the moment."

She looked up into his face. "Then shut up, Barinov. Shut up and kiss me."

Vic did. His mouth moving over hers, his hands pulling her close until she was tight against his body.

Livy pulled her arms away from his grasp so she could wrap them around his neck, her tongue sliding between Vic's lips and stroking.

Vic lowered her to the bed. He felt desperate, bordering on fully out of control. He knew he couldn't risk that. Knew he wasn't ready to reveal that side of himself yet. Hell, he might never be ready to reveal *everything* about himself to anyone, much less Livy.

Vic pulled out of their kiss and began moving down Livy's body, pushing up her T-shirt until he'd exposed her breasts. His tongue was rough as it dragged along the skin, teasing the nipple. Livy was sure such a rough tongue would have annoyed most women. But Livy's skin was tough and not only easily tolerated the feel of it, but loved it.

But Livy had always been impatient. She couldn't stand to wait for anything, but especially getting off. So she placed her hand on Vic's head and pushed. Hard.

Thankfully, Vic laughed. Laughed and moved down her body until he was crouching by the bed. His hands gripped her thighs and yanked her down a bit until her pussy was right at the edge of the bed. He held her legs wide open and buried his face between her thighs. His rough tongue lapped at her, tickling and exciting her clit in the process. She didn't know whether to giggle or scream. Then he slid that tongue deep inside her, tormenting her by using it like a slow-moving cock. Vic eased it in and out, taking his time.

Livy began to writhe on the bed, her hands gripping the comforter under her so that she didn't unleash her claws and dig them into Vic's scalp.

But then, with his tongue still inside her, Vic pressed his thumb to her clit and began to move it in small circles.

It was all Livy needed, her back arching off the bed, her claws ripping into the bedding. She cried out, her body nearly coming off the bed, but Vic held her down, kept her pinned. She liked that.

Hell, she liked everything. Until Vic was gone. Why was he gone? Where did he go?

Livy opened her eyes, but Vic hadn't gone away. He hadn't left the room. He'd just stepped away to push down his jeans and put the condom on.

Then he was gripping Livy's legs again and yanking her lower half up, his cock pressing against her. He paused. Just long enough to make sure he had Livy's attention. Then he pulled Livy closer and thrust hard. So hard, so mercilessly, that Livy started coming again. And at this rate, Livy wasn't sure she'd ever stop.

Vic had only so much control, and he had to really concentrate not to lose himself in Livy. He wasn't ready to let that happen. Wasn't ready to forget that there were some things he had to keep to himself. But while trying to keep control of one part of himself, he was losing control in another way.

Vic was never this rude and demanding in bed. Never. He wasn't Mr. Sensitive, but he wasn't this . . . brutal.

But what didn't help was that Livy really seemed to like it. She liked him just fucking her like they were two animals who'd met on the African plains or something.

Even worse . . . Vic liked it, too. Perhaps too much. It would be hard to go back to women expecting a more polite first ride. Because at the moment, his cock was as happy as it had ever been.

Only Livy's shoulders were on the bed as she gasped and groaned. Her hands suddenly gripped her breasts, her fingers tugging at her nipples since Vic couldn't with his own hands busy.

"Oh God!" she panted, her fingers tugging harder, gripping tighter, and Vic knew she was coming again. "Oh . . . oh . . . God!"

It was like her pussy had turned into a vise, all that wet heat gripping his cock hard and pulsating until Vic bit back a roar that might have destroyed every window in the damn rental house if he hadn't stopped it.

Gasping, Vic pulled out of Livy and fell on the bed beside her.

Lying on their backs, they looked at each other, then back at the ceiling.

After a few minutes, Livy said, "Vic?"

"Yeah?"

"Now I'm starving."

"Good," he sighed, the feline in him sated and curling up for a little sleep, leaving his bear side awake. "I'm hungry, too."

CHAPTER 16

The food was ice-cold but remarkably delicious.

They ate while naked on the living room floor. Vic tried to set some nice mood lighting, but the automatic fireplace didn't work and he ended up covering one lamp with a linen napkin and turning on the TV, but muting the sound. It worked out surprisingly well.

Vic didn't find out, though, until they were in the middle of their meal that Livy hadn't eaten anything since hours before she'd gone into Whitlan's apartment. How she'd lasted through two plane trips, that entire joust, and their amazing sex fascinated Vic. And watching her heal before his eyes, the bruises on her body and face all but gone, blew his mind. Shifters healed fast, there was no doubt about it. Yet it seemed honey badgers were even more resilient. Instead, the more food Livy put into her mouth, the stronger she became.

"This is a really nice place," Livy remarked as she devoured more of the General Tso's Honey Chicken. "A lot of times these rental vacation homes are . . ."

"Tacky," Vic filled in for her.

"The pictures they have online never look the same as what you actually get. And sometimes they smell weird."

"Rita's smart. She keeps updating the homes she rents

out so that they don't just look like you're renting out Grandma's house while she's in a nursing home."

"So you've been coming out here for a while."

"Since I was a kid. My parents brought me and my sister here at least once a year. They also took us to an all-bear town in Siberia every other year, and Moscow every Christmas to see the relatives."

"Seems like you spent more time with bears than tigers growing up."

"I did. My mother's family pretty much cut her off when she married, then bred with a bear. They wouldn't have been so hard on her if she'd had a couple of cubs with a tiger first, and then got married. The Cat Nation, in general, is pretty tolerant of that, but step outside that breeding plan of theirs, and you get the big family shunning." He grabbed another egg roll. "What about your parents?"

"What about them?"

"I'm sorry. Was that out of line? Asking about your dad?"

"No," she replied easily. "I just don't understand the question."

"Well, your dad's white and your mom's Chinese so . . ."

"Race, religion, politics . . . none of those mean a thing to honey badgers." Using chopsticks, she popped another piece of chicken in her mouth, chewed, swallowed, and added, "Unless they're in the mood to start a fight."

"Pardon?"

"Badgers love starting fights, and we'll use anything available to us to do it. Bigotry of any kind is fair game, whether we believe in the philosophy or not. Religion, no matter what you were raised as or believed in, is also a great fight starter. And then there's politics, which is the best for when you really just want to see people beating the shit out of each other for a ridiculous reason. Badgers will go from one extreme opinion to another, whether they believe in it or not, as long as it gets that ugly fight rolling."

"I always thought of foxes as the troublemakers."

Livy snorted. "Foxes are lightweights. Cute little con artists and gold diggers. But honey badgers . . . we've been changing history since before a Roman honey badger told Julius Caesar that he doubted Pompey would have a problem with him crossing the Rubicon. And, of course, everyone knows about Rasputin—although he was kind of tall for one of us. But I think his mother was full-human."

Vic had been about to put the last bit of egg roll in his mouth but he stopped and stared at Livy.

"And the rumor still holds that the Hundred Years' War was started by badgers," she went on. "And who can forget that the Borgias were all honey badgers?" Livy nodded. "Yep. My kind can start a knife fight at a sit-in peace rally using nothing more than overly expressive eyebrows. I'd call it a curse if we didn't really, *really* enjoy starting shit for shit's sake."

"Even you?"

"Are you kidding? My parents sent me to private schools from preschool through high school for one simple reason. Private schools are a veritable shit-starting paradise. and they wanted me trained to be the best. But I met Toni when I was fourteen and she got me to focus on my photography instead of starting fights in the teachers' lounge. She convinced me to make it the most important thing in my life. Once I did that, I stopped caring about making everyone else miserable. I don't think my parents ever forgave Toni for that, either."

"Why would they want you trained in shit starting?"

"If you don't desensitize yourself to fucking with people's lives, it's impossible to rob them. It's impossible to break into their homes and take things that are invaluable to them if you don't enjoy tormenting rich people just a little bit. And the Kowalskis and Yangs do not steal from the poor. So it's private school for all of us."

"They don't steal from the poor? Because stealing from the rich gives them a sense of higher moral ground??"

"That and they just don't like rich people."

"And sending you to private school had nothing to do with getting you a better education?"

"As far as my parents were concerned, I was getting my education from them. I knew the basics and multiple dialects of four languages by the time I was nine. But all the kids in the family went to private school because that's where the wealthy are. The people we're trained to size up from the first 'hello.' In fact, when I met Toni's mother, she was carrying around her Stradivarius violin while she was trying to rein in her kids. And my first thought was, 'I could get at least fourteen million for that on the open market.'" Livy shook her head. "It's a beautiful instrument. My parents could never believe I didn't bring it home with me."

Finished eating, Vic folded his arms and rested his chin on them. "Why didn't you?" Vic asked her. "Why didn't you bring that violin home to your parents?"

Livy took a sip of her wine and replied, "Because I liked the Jean-Louis Parkers. A lot. They treated me like family from the very beginning. Still do. It never occurred to Jackie and Paul *not* to attend my father's funeral. Even though they knew there would be fighting and snakes and supermodel mistresses."

"They were there for *you*. That's why it never occurred to them not to go."

Livy pushed her empty plate away and sipped more of her wine.

"Oh," Vic said, "I should warn you . . . Toni found out that Blayne asked you to photograph her wedding."

Livy winced a little. "Did Blayne duck in time?"

"No, but thankfully I was standing there, so I managed to get hold of Toni before her claws made contact."

"You're fast."

"Speed's important for my line of work."

* * *

Livy watched Vic roll to his back, his hands behind his head, his gaze on the ceiling. She reached back and grabbed her camera off the couch. She adjusted the shutter for the low light in the room and raised the camera so she could look through the viewfinder.

Without moving his position, Vic asked, "Are you taking my picture?"

"Yes. But you'll have to hold your position. It's dark in here."

Livy lifted one knee and balanced her camera on it. She checked the composition. Adjusted her body so that the camera moved the tiniest bit. Happy with that, she pushed the release, her heart racing a bit when she heard the slow-because-of-the-low-light *click* of the shutter.

"That better not end up on the Net," Vic teasingly warned.

Livy took a few more before crawling over to Vic's side, the camera held in her hand. She straddled his chest and looked through the viewfinder. "I wish the fireplace worked," she murmured. "The firelight would look great on your face."

"My cheekbones again?"

"They are fabulous." Livy reached down and tipped Vic's head slightly to the side. "Thanks for bringing me here," she said. "I really needed this."

"Toni said to get you away from Melly. This seemed like the best option. Not sure what you'll do, though, when we head back."

"My cousin Jocelyn is going to take Melly to one of our New York safe houses, which I appreciate."

"One of your New York safe houses? You mean your *family's* safe houses?"

Livy snapped Vic's picture. "You can find Kowalski or Yang safe houses all over the world. In some cities, we have several."

"Have you ever used them?"

"No. You never know when a relative is going to be

there. Sometimes several, if there was a very big recent job and they're lying low. And then you must deal with family, which I try to avoid. Besides," she reminded him, placing her camera aside, "I have your house if I need to crash somewhere."

"Anytime you want . . . just no more holes. It's costing me a fortune to get those fixed."

"What if I fix them?"

"No holes."

"Fine."

Livy stretched down, her arms sliding around his neck. She nibbled his jaw, then bit hard into his neck. Vic's body jerked beneath her and he snarled a little.

"You play rough," he grumbled, his arms still behind his head.

"I can stop if you want me to."

"No need to be hasty. Just pointing things out."

Livy licked her way back to his mouth, teasing his lips with her tongue. She twisted his hair around her fingers and massaged his scalp with her knuckles.

It was funny, Livy didn't usually "play" with men. She was kind of a get-in-get-out girl. But this was Vic, and she actually enjoyed his company in and out of bed.

Vic finally pulled his hands out from behind his head and stroked them up Livy's sides and around to her back, smiling as soon as he unleashed his claws, the tips dragging along her spine.

Sighing, Livy kissed Vic, burying her hands deep into his hair, and holding his head tight while she took his mouth.

But then he suddenly pushed her away. "Here," he growled, pushing a condom packet into her hand.

"The cat awake again?" she asked, moving down his body until she straddled his knees and had easy access to his cock.

"What do you think?"

Livy removed the condom from the packaging, but she held

on to it while she took Vic's cock into her mouth. She deep-throated him, sucked, deep-throated him again. She pulled back, ran her tongue around the tip, then sucked him deep again.

That's when Vic snarled, "Unless you want a mouth full of—"

She pulled his cock out of her mouth before he could finish that lovely description and put the condom on it. Livy took her time lowering her pussy onto it, but Vic suddenly gripped her waist and yanked her down.

Vic gasped but Livy laughed. "So impatient."

"You take too long." He ground his hips up and Livy wondered if he was trying to reach the back of her throat that way. And wondered if he possibly could.

Livy pressed her hand against his chest. "Are you going to let me do this, or are you going to try and rule from below?"

Vic studied her for a long moment, gold eyes squinting at her.

"No," he finally stated. "You can take control later."

Vic lifted Livy off his cock and before she knew it, she was on her knees in front of the couch, her head and arms resting on the cushions. Vic settled in right behind her, a knee pushing her legs apart. Then he was inside her, buried deep. Big, long arms stretched past Livy, his hands taking hold of the couch back. It was like being mounted by a giant, which she found shockingly arousing.

"What's so funny?" he panted against her ear.

"As a matter of fact . . . nothing." Livy turned her head and rested her cheek against the couch cushion. She allowed her whole body to relax. "I'm just sitting here, waiting for you to fuck the hell out of me."

What was this woman doing? Vic had known that taking a honey badger into his bed was a dangerous proposition.

How could it not be? But he just figured that would mean he'd end up covered in lacerations and feeling used. Something most shifter males learned to get over very quickly.

But this was worse. Because every time Livy let him know how much she was enjoying his rude and demanding bedroom antics, he knew he was becoming more attached to her. Attached to a woman who had an apartment she never lived in because she kept ending up in other people's cabinets instead. Or under their beds.

Vic knew that getting attached to Livy Kowalski would only lead to trouble. Yet here she was . . . accepting the multiple sides of his nature.

How dare she?

"You know, you're making me nuts!" Vic accused.

"I know." Livy chuckled. "And I'm not even trying!"

Livy looked back at him and leaned up a bit, kissing him on his jaw. It was a sweet, simple kiss. Again, just accepting Vic as he was.

He fought his intense desire to say something really stupid. Something he wouldn't be able to take back that would have Livy Kowalski running for the nearest exit.

Vic knew he couldn't say anything. He couldn't.

So he fucked Livy instead.

Who knew a little kiss would get Livy nailed to the couch? Not that she minded, because again, she didn't.

She liked the way Vic fucked. That huge cock, reaming her from behind, filling her up. His big body over her. Some might feel overpowered by such a big man, but the position reminded Livy of being in the cabinets in Vic's kitchen. All that was missing was the honey.

Then again, maybe the "honey" here was the multiple orgasms Vic was pounding out of her. Orgasms so powerful, she had to bury her face in the couch cushion and scream them out.

Livy finally collapsed to the couch, Vic thrusting a few more times until he came seconds later.

His arms wrapped around her, Vic pulled her back and up until he could kiss her.

They stayed like that for a bit, Vic holding her in his arms while they slowly kissed and waited for their hearts to stop racing.

That was when Livy said, "Vic?"

"Yeah?"

"I'm still hungry."

He nodded. "Yeah. Me, too."

Together, they looked at what was left of the food across the room.

"It sure is far away," Livy sighed.

"We can make it," he said, back to his kind, sweet, and extremely goofy bear self. "How can we not?" he asked. "You're a knight of the realm."

And Livy laughed. Because seriously . . . how could she not?

CHAPTER 17

Vic woke up in a very good mood. But as soon as he turned over and saw that Livy wasn't lying in bed beside him, his mood quickly soured.

Had she left? Had she already bailed on him? He wouldn't put it past her.

"Well, I'm not chasing after her," he muttered, sitting up. "If she wants to go, that's up to her. It's not my problem."

He swung his legs over the side of the bed. "I do need coffee, though." Vic stood. "And I'm not sure where that is."

Dragging on his boxers, Vic walked barefoot and bare-chested down the stairs and into the living room. He headed into the kitchen and quickly located the coffee beans. He ground them up, put them in the European coffeemaker, and patiently waited with his back against the counter and his arms crossed over his chest.

Vic looked around the kitchen. He knew there was no food in the refrigerator but he wasn't in the mood to cook anyway. He decided to check the cabinets and, to his surprise, he didn't find Livy in any of them. But he did find several cans of honey-covered peanuts.

As he walked back toward the coffeepot, he noticed that the shadows outside the French doors leading to the yard abruptly changed. Vic stopped and leaned over so he could look around the large marble counter, and that's where he found . . . not Livy.

Wondering whom Livy had pissed off now, Vic put the peanuts down on the counter and walked outside.

"Hey, Mike," Vic greeted, gearing himself for a statement that started off something like, "We put that honey badger friend of yours in jail . . ."

"Barinov."

"What's going on?"

"Thought you'd want to know about your girl."

"What about her?"

"John Leary saw her going through his territory not too long ago—"

"I'm sure she didn't mean anything by it, and if she attacked any of Mr. Leary's beehives, I'll replace—"

"Nah. That ain't it."

"It's not?"

"Ya see, she kept walkin', didn't she? Right past all those beehives. Seemed strange, especially since she was in her honey badger form and all, so Leary followed her for a bit. See if she was up to anything."

"And?"

"Well . . . she kept walkin', didn't she? Right over county lines."

Vic stared at the deputy. "What?"

Mike shoved his hands into the back pockets of his jeans and looked down at the ground, but didn't repeat what he'd just told Vic.

"Are you telling me that Livy went into cat territory? And no one stopped her?"

"Well, Leary's never been a chatty black bear."

As if that excused the man somehow. Because it wasn't just about Livy going into cat territory that was the problem. It was that she was going into cat territory after she'd just kicked their asses at yesterday's joust.

Vic's boxers began to rip apart as he shifted to his hybrid form. Mike backed away from him, hands raised. "Now come on, Barinov. We don't need a whole heap of problems from those cats, now do we? And you . . . going over there looking like . . . like . . . *that* . . ."

But how this turned out was up to the felines. And what those felines were currently doing to Livy.

Livy had been climbing up a tree, trying to get to the hive of Africanized bees, when she was yanked down by a leopard.

She landed hard on her back, but quickly flipped over. There were about twelve of them. All big cats. Two leopards, a cougar, three She-lions, two cheetahs, a jaguar, a Bengal tiger, and two male lions.

And at least four of these cats were ones that Livy had defeated at yesterday's joust, which was probably making them pretty cranky about Livy being here.

She'd known exactly when she'd crossed over into cat territory, but she hadn't cared. She'd spotted some Africanized bees and had followed them back to their hive because African honey was one of her favorite raw honeys.

In retrospect, though, this was probably not one of her better ideas. But here she was. On her own. Facing down a bunch of angry cats.

So Livy charged the biggest one. One of the male lions, who was a few pounds heavier than the tiger. And much bigger than a honey badger,

Livy was able to launch herself at the lion's face, attaching herself to his skull with her claws and fangs.

Roaring, the lion swung his head and tried to use his paw to knock her off. Livy held on, digging in deeper with her fangs while tearing at the cat's flesh with her front paws.

One of the She-lions grabbed Livy from behind with her mouth and yanked her off. She swung Livy around, shaking her. She tossed Livy in the air and managed to catch her on the way down. But Livy's body had flipped around in midair so that she was able to clamp her front claws onto the She-lion's muzzle, lacerating the fur and flesh on both sides. The She-lion began her own attempt to shake Livy off, but she was smarter than the male, waiting until Livy lifted her paws so she could start raking them again through the cat's muzzle.

A good shake and Livy was again flying. She hit a tree, bounced forward, and landed on her paws. She hissed and moved away from the tree so she didn't have anything blocking her back. She sized up her opponents, deciding to go for that tiger next. But the cougar charged first, coming right at her. That's when Livy saw a shadow fall over her. She looked up but all she could see was a mass of shaggy, black-striped brown and orange fur.

A paw the size of two platters swung out, and the cougar went flipping off into the trees. Livy didn't even see where he landed.

All that fur over her head moved forward, the body so tall, she didn't even have to scrunch down for it to pass. It just walked right over her like she wasn't there.

The cats backed up, and Livy scrambled around so she could get a good look at what she now scented was Vic.

She'd never seen him in his shifted form and she understood why. He kind of resembled a woolly mammoth in a way, but that could have been all the fur. There was just so much of it! He didn't have tusks like a woolly, but his front fangs extended past his lower jaw a bit. Still, that was nothing compared to the size of Vic's paws. They were just so . . . big. Giant paws attached to giant legs, which were attached to a giant . . . beast.

One of the lion males charged and Vic turned slightly so the cat ran right into his side. Vic didn't budge from the force, but the lion flew back and landed unconscious a few feet away. It was as if he'd run into a brick building. The other lion male roared and charged; Vic brought the cat down with one blow against the shoulder. Livy heard a crack as Vic and the cat made contact, and screaming, the lion went down. But it wasn't just his shoulder. It was his shoulder and chest. They appeared . . . concave. He was even having trouble breathing.

Vic looked over the other cats, waiting to see if they would challenge him.

For some unknown reason, the tiger raised his front paw, suggesting he was about to walk toward Vic. In response to the tentative move, Vic took in a breath. When he released it, the breath came out as a roar. A roar that shook the ground beneath Livy's paws, tossed the smaller cats back, and had the tiger carefully putting his paw back down on the ground.

When the roar finally ended, everything was silent. The birds. The Africanized bees in the hive above Livy's head. Everything was silent. Except Livy. Who gave out a hissing laugh that her full-human friends often called "Livy's evil laugh." And it was even more evil-sounding when she laughed like that in her honey badger form.

Vic chuffed at her and Livy walked around to his back leg. Using her claws, she climbed up onto his back until she realized that her paw was tangled in his mass of fur. She tried to get it free, but she was getting to the point where she was afraid she'd have to cut her way out.

That was when Vic's tail swung around. Compared to the rest of him, it was a very unimpressive tail. Barely any fur on it and extremely thin considering his overall size. But long like a tiger's tail. So, yeah, unimpressive. At least that was how Livy felt until that unimpressive tail dug into the fur around her paw and untangled the mess. That was when she realized that Vic had a prehensile tail.

How cool was that!

She'd always heard that shifter grizzlies, polars, and black bears had prehensile lips just like the full-bloods, but because Vic was a hybrid, it seemed that prehensile addition had landed elsewhere.

When Livy was comfortably secure on Vic's back, he turned his nearly fifteen-foot-long body around and slowly made his way back into bear territory. He didn't seem to have much speed at what was nearly two thousand pounds, but then, he didn't really need it.

They made it back to the rental property without any problems and Livy quickly shifted to human.

"Don't shift," she ordered Vic. "Not yet."

She jumped off his back, shocked at how long it took her feet to touch the ground. She walked around until she faced Barinov. She studied him closely, then walked up to him and pushed a mass of stringy fur off his face. That was when she finally saw his eyes. And they were human eyes staring back at her. The one physical part of him that didn't change.

Livy grinned and stepped back. She walked all the way around him, and when she was right in front of him again, she finally announced, "You look . . . so . . . *cool*!"

No. That wasn't what he'd expected her to say. Not that he minded. It was nice to hear someone say something other than, "Uh . . . oh . . . my . . . um . . ." upon seeing Vic's shifted form. Or screaming and running away at the sight of him.

Livy didn't do that or react as anyone else had when he was in this form. Instead, Livy stepped close and ran her hands down the fur on his muzzle. Vic lowered his head and she pressed her face against his snout. He felt the sigh she let out to his very bones.

When she moved away from him, Vic knew something was very wrong. Something that had absolutely nothing to do with the bitter cats in the next county or his shifted form.

Vic shifted back to human and waited. After nearly a minute, Livy said, "I'm hungry. Are you hungry?"

"Yeah. I'm hungry."

Livy nodded and walked into the house through the back door. Vic followed and found her looking into the refrigerator. There was a little Chinese food left, but neither of them wanted that. So they called in an order to the local diner and had it delivered.

Vic had showered and put his jeans on by the time the food arrived. He was setting it out on the table when Livy came downstairs.

She carried a cell phone and wore a bathrobe that was several sizes too big for her. She finger-combed her wet hair off her face and sat down at the kitchen table.

"Looks good," she stated.

With all the food out, Vic sat catty-cornered from Livy and reached for the bacon.

"My father's dead," she suddenly announced.

Vic pulled his hand back, focused on Livy. "I know. And I am sorry."

"No," she said softly. "You don't know." She rested her arms on the table, hands clasped together over the plate he'd put out for her. "I just assumed his funeral was probably one of my parents' schemes. Another way for them to somehow make money. That in four or five years Damon Kowalski would suddenly pop up and say, 'Why do you get so upset, *trochę rage*. Always sensitive . . . like your mother.' "

" '*Trochę rage*'?" Vic repeated, with a small laugh. "Your father called you Little Rage?"

"Since I smacked him right across the mouth when I was six months old."

Vic leaned down a bit so he could look in her eyes. "But now you're sure your father's gone. Why?"

Livy let out a big breath before looking directly at him and replying, "Because I found his stuffed carcass in Allison Whitlan's apartment."

* * *

Vic blinked those gold eyes at her, his entire body jolting in surprise. "Wait . . . what?"

"She had him by her fireplace. Someone went to a good taxidermist. You could barely tell he'd been shot in the back of the head."

"Livy . . . I . . . um . . ."

"Please don't say you're sorry. I don't want to hear sorry."

"What do you need from me?"

"You gave me what I needed. Time. I needed time to figure out what I should do."

"You don't have to do anything. Now we know that Allison Whitlan must be in some kind of contact with her father. Dee and Cella can take it from there."

"It's not that easy, Vic."

"It's not?"

"Not for me. It'll never be that easy for me."

Vic placed his hand over her forearm, his fingers warm and dry. Comforting. "I can't even imagine how hard all this must be for you. I really can't. But what I do know is that you need to let the people paid to protect our kind do their jobs."

"They may be paid to protect your kind but not mine. The honey badgers have always been on our own. We always will be."

Vic leaned back in his chair. "What's your plan, Livy? Track down Whitlan by yourself? Take him down by yourself?"

"Honey badgers are a lot of things. We're mean. We're rough. We're mostly felons. We take shit from no one. But the one thing we're not . . . is stupid. I have no intention of going after Whitlan by myself."

"Then what are you planning?"

"The only thing I can." Livy picked up her cell phone, pulled up an important number she'd never used before, and sent out a quick text before she focused back on Vic and said, "Vengeance."

Baltazar Kowalski pulled his cell phone out of his back pocket and looked at the text he'd just gotten.

One of the men breaking into the reinforced safe in the basement of the bank—a safe that held millions in diamonds—glared at Balt over the ski mask he wore.

"Do we really have time for you to chat with your pretty girlfriend?" the man whispered in French.

Balt ignored the man and studied the text.

"What is it, brother?" Kamil asked, his gaze straying from the guards they'd secured and drugged so that they were out cold during the job.

"It's from Damon's girl." Damon. Their brother was supposed to have been with them on this job. They all did their own individual jobs, of course, but several times a year, the Kowalski brothers worked together. Especially on these kinds of jobs where a lot of money and risk were at stake. And Damon had been the best at organizing and pulling these jobs off without a hitch. So his loss was felt most at this time.

"What does she say?" Edmund asked.

"She wants us to meet her in New York. Now."

The five brothers stared at each other. Olivia wasn't like any of their children. She never contacted them for anything. Had never involved herself in the family business. Before Damon's funeral, they hadn't seen her for a good seven years or so. When they did see her, she did no more than wave at them before disappearing with Balt's boy, Jake. For waffles, Balt had been told later. Although he could never understand why anyone would go out and get waffles when they had perfectly delicious cobras slithering around the backyard of Damon's old house.

No. The Kowalski men had never understood Damon's girl . . . including Damon. But Olivia was still family. She was a Kowalski. A strange Kowalski, but still one of them. Which meant only one thing to Balt, Edmund, Kamil, Gustav, Otto, and David.

The brothers locked gazes and, without another word between them, stopped what they were doing and packed up.

The full-humans they were working with looked up at the brothers. "Where the hell are you going?" one of them asked.

Balt zipped up his black bag, and slung it over his shoulder. He didn't answer the man; there was no point.

Another full-human pulled his .45 and aimed it at Otto. Baltazar stepped in front of his brother and walked up to the man until the gun pressed against Balt's chest. He gazed at the full-human and waited. After several seconds, the man looked away. Balt reached over and took the gun from the full-human's grasp.

"Nice Glock," Balt said in French. "I have one at my house." Then he used the weapon to beat the man who'd pointed it at Otto until he was bleeding and sobbing on the ground.

Balt tossed the gun to the ground and motioned to his brothers. "Come," he said in English, trying to get used to the difficult language again since they were going to America. "We have plane to catch."

CHAPTER 18

Toni stepped away from the Russian bargaining table and walked out into the hallway before answering her phone. It was Livy, which was strange. Livy wasn't really a fan of talking on phones. She'd been known to text when necessary, but that was about it.

"Hey, Livy."

"Hey."

"Everything okay?"

"Yeah. I need to ask a favor, though."

"A favor?" Toni frowned. "You?"

"I've asked for favors before."

"Yeah. I guess. Can't really remember one, though."

"Can I ask a favor or not?"

"Okay, okay. No need to get testy. What do you need?"

There was a pause, then Livy asked, "I need to borrow the brownstone."

"The brownstone?" Toni wasn't quite sure what Livy was talking about. "What brownstone?"

"The one your parents rent from the wild dogs."

"Oh! You mean the wild dog house." At least that's what Toni's family called it. It was a beautiful piece of real estate that the wild dogs could sell for a fortune but instead chose to rent out for an insane amount of money. Of course, Toni had thought her family was only renting it for that one summer when Toni's mother was "stalking" the Alpha Female's adopted son, Johnny. Not literal stalking. Her mother, thankfully, was not interested in Johnny as anything but a music student. A prodigy training a prodigy. But the wild dogs were as protective of their pups as jackals, so it had required a lot more work. Still, Toni thought her parents would stop renting the house once that summer was over and they'd returned to their lives on the West Coast. But her parents were still renting the place, whether they were in it or not, with the logic that they could crash there anytime they were in Manhattan. The wild dogs loved this plan, as well, because they still received their rental payments without having to worry about out-of-control neighbors or squatters.

"Yeah. Sure. But are you sure there's nothing wrong?"

"Nothing you have to worry about. A family thing. But I swear, any damage done to the place, I'll make sure it's fixed and perfect before you get back to the States. Okay?"

Toni was annoyed Livy had even felt she had to say that to her. Livy had always watched out for Toni's stuff like she was protecting her own. Even more so.

But that was the least of Toni's worries from what Livy had said. "A family thing? What family thing?"

"My family thing. Nothing you have to worry about."

"I know which family you meant, Olivia. But you only *deal* with my family. So I'm sorry if I'm questioning—"

"Antonella?"

"What?"

"Can I have the place or not?"

"Of course you can. It'll be completely empty. Coop and Cherise are still in Europe on tour. But make sure you use the keys! No breaking and entering and no damn holes, Olivia. I mean it. But, look, that's not the real issue—"

"Have a good time with the bears!" Livy cheered. "Love you more than soap!"

The call ended and Toni stamped her foot and wondered how long it would take her to get to New York if she left right now.

"Hey, little doggie," an excessively thick Russian accent barked from inside the room. "You have work! Or did you forget?"

Toni pushed the door open and stared at the table filled with Russian bears. She'd long ago stopped feeling any fear at being around so many bears once she realized that the only bear she had to worry about at the moment was Ivan Zubachev, the Russian hockey team owner, who ruled with an iron paw.

She hated that he still insisted on calling her "little doggie" although everyone and their mother knew he adored her. Why? Because she had made him lots of money. The game between the Carnivores and Zubachev's team had been a huge event, bringing in a lot of money not only to the two teams but to the Siberian shifter-run towns that had played host.

Now, it was time to bring the Russians to America, and Toni was on deck to make it happen. That was when she realized she couldn't walk away from this. She couldn't tell Zubachev that she had to go check on her friend but she'd be back in a week or two to finalize the deal. The Russians had hard and fast rules for negotiations, and Toni's need to protect her friends and family from themselves wasn't really part of that.

Toni looked down at her phone. No. She'd have to trust that Livy could take care of herself. Even if her family was involved, Toni was sure that it was probably just an issue with Melly or something. An issue that could easily be handled by violating that woman's parole and putting her right back in a cell.

"She'll call me if she needs me," Toni reminded herself. "She'll call."

Clinging to that belief, Toni walked back into the room, closing the door behind her. "All right, gentlemen, let's get back to work. And *no,* we will not force Bo Novikov to shift to his animal form and put him on display in a gilded cage at the Sports Center so that the world can see what a true freak he is. And stop asking if you can!"

With keys in hand, Livy walked up the stairs to the front door. She looked at the keys and back at the door. No. She had to do this. She had no choice.

Livy had the key in the lock when she stopped. "Are you going to keep shadowing me?"

"Yes."

Sighing, Livy turned but ended up with her face buried in his stomach. She pushed and pointed at the street. "Down," she ordered. *"Down."*

Vic went down the stairs, and now she could almost look him directly in the eyes.

With space between them, Livy could be clear and concise and inform Vic that she would be doing this on her own. She didn't need him or his help. She appreciated it and all, but she didn't need it.

Livy started to speak, but thought she was *too* far from him. So she walked down a couple of steps, bringing her closer, but now he was taller again. She hated the thought of yelling up to him that she didn't need him or his help. That seemed tacky.

She motioned him closer with her hand. Vic leaned down. "What, Livy?"

"Well, what I don't . . ."

"What you don't . . . what?" Vic frowned when she didn't answer. "Livy?"

That's when Livy grabbed the back of Vic's neck, pulled him closer, and kissed him. She didn't know *why* she kissed the man. She had no idea. Maybe it was those damn lips. He had the nicest lips. And such a handsome face.

Even worse . . . Vic kissed her back. His arms going around her waist, he lifted Livy up and walked forward until Livy was pressed against the front door. Their kiss was desperate and demanding and completely unreasonable. Unreasonable because this hadn't been Livy's plan. She was supposed to send him off, for no other reason than to keep him safe. Getting involved with her family was dangerous. Unbelievably dangerous. And she didn't want to be the reason anything happened to Vic.

But when he pulled away from her, his eyes locked on her mouth, his breathing hard, Livy knew she wouldn't be able to "shoo" him away.

"I'll get us some clothes," he said, slowly removing his hands from her waist. "And Shen. He'll be good help for this. Okay?"

Livy nodded, instinctively licking her lips, which she immediately stopped doing when Vic started growling at her.

With a hearty snort, Vic turned and started off toward his SUV. But he abruptly stopped, glared at Livy over his shoulder. "Don't make me come look for you," he ordered.

"What if I do?"

"Olivia."

"Kidding. I'm kidding. I'll be here."

"Good."

Livy watched Vic until he reached his SUV and drove off. She blew out a confused breath. Her heart had raced from that kiss. Her heart didn't race from much of anything. Maybe good sex but just a kiss? What exactly was happening to her? Because she didn't like it.

Deciding not to worry about this on top of everything else, Livy went back to the door, unlocked it, and stepped into the house.

Surprised to find the lights on, Livy walked down the

marble-floored hallway, which reminded her of a very small Versailles, and past the living room by the stairs, where she heard what sounded like an episode of *Dr. Phil* coming from the large-screen TV . . .

Livy stopped walking, freezing right in the middle of the arched entrance, her gaze locked onto the twelve-year-old boy watching that large-screened TV from the couch.

"Kyle?" she snarled.

Eyes wide, Kyle Jean-Louis Parker slowly looked over at Livy. "Uh . . . Livy? Wow. Uh . . . hi?"

"Why aren't you in Italy?" Livy demanded.

Kyle was an artistic prodigy, sculpting and painting his greatest strengths. He was so amazing, he'd been accepted into a prestigious Italian art school at the age of eleven while getting tutored in the basics like math and science so he wasn't left behind scholastically.

Yet he was supposed to be in Italy receiving all that great education, not *here* in the middle of his parents' rental home. And he especially wasn't supposed to be in his parents' rental home without his parents.

"Does Toni know you're here?"

Kyle stared at Livy a moment before replying, "Sure."

"You are the worst liar, Kyle Jean-Louis Parker," Livy complained as she pulled out her cell phone to call Toni. There were just some lines Livy never crossed when it came to Antonella, and all those lines involved Toni's siblings. And the kids knew that. So Livy had no qualms about ratting out Kyle to Toni, even if that meant Toni would be flying back from Russia on the wings of her rage.

But before Livy could complete the call, an arm reached around her and took the phone. Startled, she spun around, fangs unleashed, which had Cooper Jean-Louis Parker immediately crossing his arms over his chest, tucking his hands under his armpits, and barking, *"Not my hands! Not my hands!"*

Livy retracted her fangs and gazed at the eldest male sibling of the Jean-Louis Parkers. "Not your hands? Most people tell me not to touch their face."

"I can play without my eyes," he said, now grinning. "Can't play without my hands." He held those hands up. "These babies are insured for a reason."

Cooper was a pianist who'd been playing for massive audiences since he was five or so. Of all Toni's siblings, he was the most normal. At least as normal as any child prodigy could be, she guessed.

"What's going on?" Livy asked.

"We're giving Kyle and all of Italy a break."

Livy's head tipped down as she studied the handsome jackal she thought of as her own brother. "Really?"

"They're trying to control me!" Kyle yelled from the couch. "Control my brilliance! They have yet to realize they can't control me! Their narrow, noncreative minds simply don't understand what I'm trying to do! They can't *conceive*—"

"Stop it, Kyle," Livy cut in calmly.

"Whatever," the boy muttered. "They don't deserve me."

Coop shook his head. "How do you do that?"

Livy was one of the few people Kyle ever listened to, but Livy had no idea why. Although if she had to guess . . . "He may have seen what I did to that squirrel who got between me and that beehive in your parents' backyard. You know how cranky I get when the squirrels fight back."

Coop chuckled and handed the phone back to Livy. Together they slowly walked down the hallway toward the kitchen. When they were out of earshot of Kyle, Coop said softly, "Don't call Toni."

"I don't get between you guys and Toni, Coop. You know that."

"I do know. But there's no reason for her to come back right now. Cherise and I have control of the situation, and my parents know what's going on."

"What is going on?"

Coop smirked, shrugged. "He's been fighting with all the teachers, making the other students homicidal *and* suicidal."

"Aren't these all *adult* students?"

"Oh yeah, they are."

"Then why doesn't the school just get rid of him?"

"The school doesn't want to lose him. You should see the piece he made for his midterm project." Shaking his head, mouth open a bit, Coop searched for the right words. "It was . . . breathtaking."

If Coop thought it was breathtaking and he was willing to admit it out loud . . . Livy couldn't wait to see it.

"So it was decided to give everyone involved a break. And since Cherise and I have a concert coming up in Manhattan, Mom and Dad thought a little winter break here would help Kyle."

"Why not send him to Washington to be with your parents?"

"I think they were hoping a little Kyle-only time would be to his benefit. It's a bit harder to make that happen when you've got five other kids to manage."

Livy understood that. In all honesty, she'd never figured out how the family managed to do as well as they did. Eleven pups, ten of them prodigies, one of those prodigies a definite sociopath—it shocked many to find out that *wasn't* Kyle—how could the family *not* fall apart? Yet they never did. Instead each of the children thrived in their own way.

The problem with Kyle, though, was that he wasn't just an artist. He was also kind of a twisted psychologist-in-training. With a few choice words, he could destroy a person's self-confidence and will to live. And although most of his siblings were so used to Kyle and so certain of their own brilliance, they could handle him, it still made for lots of fights. Fights that could get on anyone's nerves eventually.

So letting Cooper and Cherise—the two oldest when

Toni wasn't around—manage him for a little while was most likely a good idea.

Unfortunately, it changed everything for Livy.

"Well, as long as you make sure Toni doesn't get mad at me when she comes back," she said to Coop.

"Don't worry. I've got you covered."

"Good. Thanks." Livy walked around Coop to leave through the front door, but Coop caught hold of her arm, held her.

"Wait. Why are *you* here?" He raised a brow. "And why are you coming through the front door? You know . . . I don't think I've seen you do that in a decade. Maybe longer."

"It's nothing." She tried to walk away, but Coop gently tugged her back.

"Livy?"

"What?"

"Do you think only Toni can read you? What's wrong? Why are you here?"

Livy lifted her free hand and dropped it. "It's . . . it's been a long week."

Coop frowned. "And I've been tasked with taking care of *Kyle*. We all have problems, so just tell me."

"It's complicated. And I don't have time to really tell you. I need to find a place to—"

"You can stay here."

"It's not just me, Coop. It's my family. And with Kyle and Cherise here, I can't bring them—"

"*Your* family is coming here?" a voice from the doorway eagerly asked.

Livy snarled. "Kyle—"

"Honey badgers? Honey badgers are coming to stay with us?"

"Kyle—"

Kyle clapped his hands together and turned in a goofy circle. "I'm so excited!" he cheered. "Honey badgers! Honey badgers! Honey badgers!"

Livy looked at Coop, but he could only shrug in confusion.

"Kyle, what are you going on about?" Livy demanded.

"Tell me your mother's coming. Please! You think this time she'll sit for me? I promise not to ask her to do it naked this time. But she has to wear red. She looks so amazing in red. She has those razor-sharp cheekbones." Kyle stopped crowing long enough to look Livy over and add, "Guess you get your looks from your father, huh?"

Coop grabbed Livy's arm again before she could go over there and throttle the kid.

"Honey badgers are coming!" Kyle yelled again. "Honey badgers!" He charged down the hallway and to the stairs. "I need to get my pencils and pad! Because honey badgers are coming!"

Livy and Coop stared at each other for several long seconds until Coop admitted what they were both thinking. "I really never saw that coming."

Jessica Ann Ward-Smith, Alpha Female of the Kuznetsov wild dog Pack and wife and mate of the Alpha Male of the New York Smith Pack Bobby Ray Smith, was trying to get her daughter into the little T-shirt she'd purchased for her, but somehow that attempt had turned into a tugging match. A tugging match the little wolfdog was winning.

"Give it to me, Lissy!"

Laughing hysterically, her daughter dug her little feet into the kitchen table and kept pulling.

"Lissy, come on. Mommy has to go."

But her daughter was in what Blayne called the "wolfdog zone," where she became hyper-obsessed with just one thing. And that one thing, at the moment, seemed to be playing tug with her goddamn T-shirt.

"Auntie Jessie?" one of the other pups asked as he walked into the kitchen.

"Yes?" she growled out, still trying to snatch the T-shirt back.

He climbed up on a chair and reached across the table to grab an apple. "There's a bunch of limos outside the house across the street."

"Yes. Some of the Jean-Louis Parkers are coming to stay."

"I remember them. But the ones outside don't look like Jean-Louis Parkers." He bit into the apple, chewed. "They're . . . wider."

"Tall and wide?"

"No. Just wide. Like short linebackers."

Confused, Jess stared at the boy. The Jean-Louis Parkers were jackals, a lean breed of canine like the wild dogs. Actually, all the smaller breeds were relatively lean. The foxes, the cougars. She could only think of one small shifter breed that one would consider wide and that was connected with the Jean-Louis Parkers, and that breed was . . .

Jess gasped, her hands going to her mouth—which meant her daughter, who was still desperately pulling on the T-shirt, went flying back.

"Lissy!" Jess ran around the kitchen table. "Are you okay?"

Lissy got to her feet, threw the T-shirt at Jess. "Tug!"

Sighing, Jess turned away from her daughter and quickly walked to the front of the house. By the time she was stepping outside, the majority of her wild dog Pack was already out on the stoop.

A few of the pups came outside, as well, but Jess snarled and the children ran right back inside.

"I do not like," Sabina growled beside Jess, her Russian accent always getting thicker the more uncomfortable she became.

"Is Cherise still with Johnny?" Jess's adopted son, a brilliant young violinist, always found time to perform with the musical Jean-Louis Parkers.

Sabina nodded and ran into the house. A few minutes later, she returned with Cherise and Johnny.

"What's going on?" Johnny asked.

"Back in the house."

Johnny, now nineteen, sighed. "I think we both have to admit I'm a little too old to—"

"Inside!"

Johnny threw up his hands. "I hate when you get like this." But at least he said it while going back into the house.

"Do you know them?" Jess asked Cherise.

She studied the good number of shifters getting out of luxury cars and limos—double-parking on the street like it was somehow legal—and entering the wild dogs' rental home across the street.

At first, Cherise shook her head. "No, I don't . . . oh. Oh." She pointed at four Asian women stepping out of a red, late-model Mercedes-Benz. "That's Livy's mom and aunts." She lowered her voice to barely a whisper. "Her mom can be a little . . . strong-willed."

"Is that nice way of saying 'bitch'?" Sabina asked.

Cherise thought on that a moment before admitting, "I wouldn't challenge her."

"You would not challenge bug."

"Sabina," Jess warned. "Be nice." Thinking a moment, Jess turned to Cherise and said, "I hate saying this, Cherise, but when I rented our place to your parents, I didn't think I'd have to specify no massive honey badger meetings. We have pups to think about."

"But I doubt my parents would have meetings that involve any honey badgers other than Livy. I mean, my mom was always very nice to Livy's mother, but only because it annoyed Livy's mother so much." She snapped her fingers and reached into the back of her jeans pocket to pull out her phone. "Let me check with Coop."

She dialed and was silent for a moment. "Hey," she finally said into the phone. "I'm over at the Kuznetsov Pack house . . . what's going on? Why are there honey badgers . . . what?" Cherise suddenly blinked, her hand briefly covering her mouth. "What?" she asked again, her eyes beginning to tear up. "How is she? Is she okay?" Cherise shook her head. "Of course, I won't cry in front of Livy." But she was crying now. "It's just . . . yes, I know she hates that! Fine! I'll tell them. Okay."

Cherise disconnected the call and wiped her eyes with the back of her hand.

"Cherise? What's going on?"

"That's all of Livy's family going into the house. Your pups will be safe, and the Jean-Louis Parkers will take full responsibility for the house."

Jess glanced at Sabina, but her friend was as confused as she.

"Is Livy okay?"

"She's fine. It's just . . . her dad."

"Yeah. I heard he passed away."

"Yes. We'd heard it was some kind of car accident or something. But . . ." She wiped her eyes again. "Livy found his body stuffed and on display in some woman's apartment. I guess her family's here to figure out what to do about it."

Stunned, Jess stared at Cherise. Of all the things she'd expected the jackal to say . . . that was not even a thousand miles close.

"Why don't you stay here for lunch, Cherise?" Jess asked as more limos showed up across the street. "Maybe even dinner?"

"Shouldn't I be with Livy?" Cherise choked a bit, seconds before full-on sobbing exploded out of her. *"She's family!"*

Jess smirked. "And will you be able to not cry around Livy if we send you back now?"

"Nooooo!"

"Then it's for the best that you stay here until you can. We'll let Livy handle this in her own way."

She hiccupped. "I just feel so bad for her!"

"I know. But the best you can do for her now is let her deal with this herself."

"But I don't want you to worry about the house—"

"We're not worried." Why would she worry? Honey badgers with a mission had bigger things on their agenda than destroying a house during a drunken spree.

One of Jess's Pack took a still-sobbing Cherise back into the Pack house and the others followed. Only Sabina stayed behind, the two women staring across the street at the honey badgers entering it.

Jess folded her arms over her chest. "I hope they tear apart whoever did such a thing to Livy's father."

"They are Slavs, like me," Sabina replied. "And the world will bleed for the wrong done to them, my friend. The world will bleed."

Jess nodded in agreement at her friend's ominous words and was about to go inside their house when something soft hit her in the back of the head. She looked down and saw a T-shirt, then looked up and saw her daughter standing in the doorway. One chubby little arm pressed against the doorway kept her standing on her stout little legs. With her free hand she pointed at Jess and screeched, *"Tuuuuuuuuuuuuuuuuuuuug!"*

Jess's fangs were out, but before she could move, Johnny appeared behind her daughter. Still holding his violin and bow, he picked the girl up in his other arm and said, "I'll play with her. I'll play with her. No reason for anyone to get hysterical!" And with that he disappeared into the house.

Sabina smirked. "Don't know why you look like that. You could have nice, boring wild dog with science degree and breed nice, boring wild dog pups. *You* picked hillbilly wolf with unstable family. Now you have unstable pup. Yet so much shock. Sometimes you make no sense."

Jess watched her friend go inside and thought about how much she hated it when Sabina was right.

CHAPTER 19

Livy hugged her cousin Jake. She was so glad to see him. Last she'd heard, he'd been in Belgium. But here he was.

And so was nearly everyone else.

The only ones who hadn't made the trip so far were the family cubs and a parent to watch out for them, as well as older family members who were too tired or sick to travel. Except great aunt Li-Li, of course. She may be old, but not too old to find out what was going on with her family. Livy also guessed those currently in prison wouldn't be showing, nor would the ones who were currently on the run from law enforcement so they wouldn't go to prison.

Yet even without all those Kowalskis, the living room of her friends' rental house was packed with Livy's family, all waiting to hear what she had to say.

It was a strange moment for Livy. When she'd sent out the vague text to the Kowalskis ordering them to New York, she'd expected only a few to show up. But within twenty-four hours . . . here they all were. For her.

"You all right?" Jake asked her.

"Yeah."

He leaned in and whispered, "I see Auntie Joan and the Sisters Grimm with her. She does not look happy. Oooh.

And your great-aunt Li-Li with her big, disturbing throat scar that freaks me out. I keep expecting it to start talking to me."

"Stop."

"Good luck with that, cuz. Unless, of course, you will need me to protect you from them with my overt manliness?"

Livy snorted and playfully pushed her cousin's head away.

"You should see your place now, Livy," Jocelyn told her, offering a bite of the Danish she'd picked up from the spread that Kyle had put out. Yes, Kyle. It seemed that like most torturers, Kyle was also a wonderful host.

Livy waved the pastry away. "Did Melly come with you?"

"Yeah. She's out in the back, though. On the phone."

"On the phone with who?" When Jocelyn raised an eyebrow, Livy sighed. "Tell me she's not on the phone with anyone who has a restraining order on her."

"Does her ex-boyfriend have a restraining order on her?"

"Several."

"Oh. Then I can't tell you that."

Livy, unwilling to deal with more than one tragedy at a time, focused instead on Kyle. He was talking to her mother, and based on the expression on Joan's face, he was trying to convince her to pose for him. With as little clothing as possible.

"Coop?" she said, and pointed.

Cooper, busy catching up with Jake, followed where Livy was pointing. His eyes crossed and he promised, "I'll handle it."

"Thanks."

Coop walked over to Kyle and grabbed his brother by the scruff of his T-shirt, dragging him out of the room.

"Don't give me an answer yet!" Kyle begged Joan. "Think on it! Your beauty must be captured for all time!"

Jocelyn laughed. "I love that kid."

"You would."

"Olivia," her uncle Otto called out. "One of those hockey players you take pictures of is here to see you."

Livy looked over at the living room archway to see Vic and Shen standing there with large duffel bags and computer cases. She'd guess there was more equipment out in Vic's SUV.

"I am not," Vic growled at Otto, "a hockey player."

"American football then?" Otto asked.

"Uncle Otto," Livy cut in before Vic could start roaring, "these are my friends Vic and Shen. They're going to be helping me."

"Helping you with what, Olivia?" her uncle Balt asked. "You have us here. Now tell us what you need."

Livy looked at Vic and he motioned to the stairs with a nod of his head. He and Shen headed upstairs to get situated while Livy faced her family.

She walked to the front of the room and looked over all their faces. Livy had silently rehearsed how she planned to discuss this. Starting off by thanking those who'd made the trip before carefully explaining everything she'd learned since she'd discovered her father's body.

Yet after all that rehearsing what came out was, "My father's dead."

The honey badgers stared at her for several long seconds until Jake gently said, "We know, hon. We were at his funeral."

Livy shook her head. "No. That wasn't him in the casket. My mother put some other guy in there. Right, Ma?"

All heads turned toward Livy's mother, and Joan threw up her hands. "Can't even trust my own daughter to keep her mouth shut!"

"You whore!" Aunt Teddy accused, one finger pointing at Joan. "What did you do to my dear brother?"

"I didn't do anything to him. I didn't kill him. I was just sure he was dead."

"But you couldn't get his insurance without the body. So who did you kill? One of the many lovers you cheated on my dear brother with? You disgust me," Teddy sneered.

"I don't care."

"Stop it," Livy calmly cut in, not in the mood to fight or watch others fight. "This isn't about my mother. This isn't about insurance. This is about who killed my father."

"I loved my brother," Balt said, his eyes sad, "but he probably died in some bar. Or over woman."

"No," Livy said. "My father was hunted down. For entertainment. For sport."

The room became silent as her family tried to understand what she was telling them.

"How do you know this, little Olivia?" Balt asked. "How do you know this is true?"

"Because I found my father's honey badger form stuffed and on display in a woman's apartment. My father's death wasn't over a woman. It didn't happen during a bar fight. My father was murdered. Not because he was an asshole—as we all know he was—but because he was a shifter. Because he made good sport. And, as Damon Kowalski's daughter, I'm not letting that go. I'll never let that go."

The family remained silent. There was no rallying cry. Nor was there dismissal of what she'd said. Instead, Livy saw sly glances passed between siblings, cousins, spouses.

Balt studied Livy a moment before he asked, "What do you need from us, Olivia?"

That was simple. "I plan to rain down vengeance on the man who did this to my father and anyone protecting or helping him. And you trifling band of miscreant felons are going to help me."

Balt slowly stood and stalked over to where Livy was standing. They stared at each other for several seconds before Balt threw open his arms and wrapped them around Livy.

"My little Olivia! You make us all so proud!"

Livy looked over at Jake and Jocelyn, but both quickly turned away before they started laughing hysterically.

"We will make the ones who did this to our brother pay and pay and pay until there is nothing left." He finally released her from the hug, but he still kept one arm around her as he faced the rest of the family. "Now the world bleeds—"

"*Or,*" Livy emphatically cut in, "we can just go after the ones who did this. Rather than taking it out on the *entire* world. That seems excessive."

"If you're sure."

"Yes, Uncle Balt." She patted his ridiculously broad shoulder. "I'm sure."

Vic helped Shen plug in all his equipment. They'd found a room in the enormous house with a desk and chair, so they made the executive decision that it would be their office.

When Vic had gone back to his house to pick up his stuff, he'd found Shen still there, watching the History Channel while sitting on Vic's couch and munching away on long stalks of bamboo.

At first, Vic had been really annoyed. He didn't want a roommate. He especially didn't want Shen as a roommate. But as soon as Vic told Shen what Livy had found in Allison Whitlan's apartment, the giant panda's whole attitude had changed. Vic didn't even have to ask Shen for help, Shen just assumed he would be helping. He'd gotten off the couch and packed his equipment. And while packing, he'd asked, several times, how Livy was holding up, true concern in his voice.

That had meant a lot to Vic because Livy meant a lot to him. And getting her through this wouldn't be easy.

"How tall are you?"

Crouching beside the desk, Vic had to lift his head to see who'd spoken to him. It was Kyle Jean-Louis Parker, which was strange. Why was he here? Weren't most kids in school?

Deciding it was none of his business—and he didn't really care one way or the other—Vic went back to his work and replied, "Seven-one."

"Really?"

Vic realized he was missing one of the cables, and he again raised his head to ask Shen to hand it to him, but he found that Kyle was now leaning over the desk and right next to Vic's face.

Jerking back, Vic snapped, "What are you doing?"

"You have amazing bone structure. Such dramatic lines. Are you of Slavic descent?"

Vic frowned. "You don't recognize me, do you, Kyle?"

"Should I?"

"I helped save your brother from a cult last year."

"Which brother?"

"You've had more than one brother kidnapped by a cult?"

He shrugged. "I don't know. I don't really pay attention to what the rest of my siblings do. Their lives bore me."

Shen, who'd been wiring the other side of the room, suddenly stood so he could get a good look at the person Vic was talking to. And as soon as he saw twelve-year-old Kyle, he widened his eyes at Vic.

"So," Kyle went on, "have you ever modeled before?"

"No. And I don't plan to start now."

"You'd be foolish to throw away this opportunity."

"What opportunity?"

"To be immortalized by *me*."

Vic had no idea how to respond to that. He'd never met a child with so much arrogance.

"You don't mind being naked, do you?"

"Livy!" Vic yelled out, not willing to continue this conversation. It could only end badly for him. Very, very badly.

"Believe it or not," Kyle said, "Livy understands me better than most. She's an artist. At least as much an artist as anyone who uses a *camera*. But she has an excellent grasp of my sensibilities. My needs. Which is considerably more than the rest of my family understands."

Kyle's older brother appeared in the doorway and Vic was so relieved to see the man.

"Did he ask you to pose naked?" Cooper demanded.

"Unlike you," Kyle sneered, "I'm not constrained by society's ridiculous norms. Nor have I sold my soul for record deals and an easy career. I believe that *challenge* is what brings out true artistic genius!"

Cooper stepped up behind his brother, dropping his hands on the boy's shoulders. "Take your brilliance and wait in your room until Livy is done."

Turning the boy around, Cooper shoved Kyle, but he missed the open doorway and rammed the boy into the wall next to it.

"Sorry, little brother. Total accident."

Hands over his nose and mouth, the boy glared at his brother. "Liar," he snarled before walking out of the room.

Cooper faced Vic. "Sorry about my brother."

"No problem."

"You guys here to help Livy?"

"Yeah. Cooper, this is Shen Li."

"His business partner," Shen volunteered.

"You are not my business partner."

"Well, not until the contracts are signed."

Vic decided not to argue with the man now. It was too much trouble.

Cooper closed the office door and asked, "How's Livy holding up? Really?"

With a shrug, Vic admitted, "At first, she just took off, and the next thing I know, she's in jail for hitting a cop."

Cooper grinned. "You could call that Livy's five stages of grief. Avoidance, followed by indescribable rage, followed by three more stages of avoidance."

"Not this time," Vic replied, grabbing one of the duffel bags and pulling out the needed cables. "Now she's running right into the fray."

"Look"—Cooper stepped closer, lowered his voice—"we'll have to watch out for her. Livy's family doesn't always have her best interests at heart. Especially when it comes to getting even with people."

"Don't worry. I won't let anything happen to her."

The jackal stared up at him. He looked just like Toni—except for the hair. Hers was kind of a wild curly mess, but Cooper's was just slightly wavy.

"I'm glad she has someone like you watching her back," Cooper said. "Livy needs that. She can get in over her head sometimes, hurt innocent people while getting out of that trouble, and although she'd never admit it, end up feeling a little guilty about it all." Cooper opened the door and stepped into the hallway. "And I'm sure none of us wants to deal with a feeling-guilty Livy, now do we?"

Vic stared at the doorway long after Cooper had walked off, until Shen came up beside him and asked, "Problem with the kid?"

"Which one?"

"The one you're still scowling after."

"No. No problem."

"Uh-huh."

"You think they ever dated?" Vic asked.

"Who?"

"Cooper and Livy? He seems awfully . . . familiar."

"Doesn't she consider Toni's family *her* family?"

"Yeah. I guess."

Shen pulled out a short bamboo stalk from his back

pocket. "He is good-looking, though," he said as he chomped. "For a dude. The kind of good-looking that girls like."

Vic glared at the panda. "You're just pissed that Kyle didn't ask you to pose for him."

"I may not have your cheekbones, but I do have these adorable dimples!"

Livy sat down at the smaller wooden table in the kitchen, right by the window that looked out over the large—for a city—backyard. Melly was still out there and still on the phone.

Her uncle Bart walked in. "Yes," he said to Livy. "You need to sit. I get us drinks."

"I don't need a drink, Uncle Bart."

"You need drink. We drink in your father's honor."

"You know," Livy had to admit, "his death doesn't make him less of a bastard."

Bart chuckled. "Yes. He was that. Just like our father. Another bastard."

Bart placed two glasses on the table and poured vodka into both. He dropped his substantial bulk into the chair across from Livy. He was not a fat man. Like most honey badgers, his power was in his shoulders and chest. If he were taller, he'd appear less cumbersome, but because of his height, he lumbered when human.

Tapping one knuckle on the table, Bart said, "I know he never say . . . but your father was very proud of you."

"He thought my being a photographer was stupid."

"True. You have brains to manage this family. And the ones who manage the family get a cut of the jobs even when they risk nothing. But you, little Olivia, were always . . ."

"Difficult?"

"We are *all* difficult. We are badger. But you were different. Always went your own way. As a baby, you used to watch everyone. Everything. Even then . . . always plotting." He chuckled again. "Plotting to get out. Get away. Which is okay."

"It is?"

"Not everyone can live this life. Not everyone should. Some of us have no choice. This . . . it is all we know. All we want to know. And some of us . . ." He gestured out the window and Livy watched Melly hysterically scream, *"Why won't you love me, you son of a bitch?"* into her cell phone. "Some of us have exactly what we deserve."

"I didn't get far away, though. I'm right back with all of you."

"Do not be foolish, girl. You are not back. You will never be back. But we are still family. And when you need us, you call. Understand?"

"Yes."

"Good. Now"—he reached into his jacket and pulled out a pack of cigarettes—"what happened to your father—"

"There's no smoking in this house, Uncle Bart."

The cigarette now dangling from his lips, Bart glared at Livy. "A little smoke does not harm *us*. We are badger."

"It isn't about us. No smoking. I also don't want any snakes in this house, either. Absolutely *nothing* poisonous, and nothing bigger than a garter snake, for snack purposes only. And only if that garter snake is dead before it hits the front door."

"But—"

"I'm just borrowing this house from friends. So please don't ruin their home."

"Do not worry. We treat this house like we treat your grandma's house."

"You only treat Grandma Kowalski's house well because she'd shoot her own children in the back with her crossbow."

"Yes. She would. And we still think she's more tolerant than you, little Olivia."

Livy snorted at that—since her uncle was right—and

reached for the glass of vodka he'd poured for her. She didn't drink, just held it in her hand.

Her uncle Bart, however, downed his in one gulp, and poured himself another. "Now, this is what we have planned so far . . . me and your uncles, we stay here. So will Jake and Jocelyn, since you like them."

"Aunt Teddy?"

"She likes Ritz Hotel, so she will stay there."

"The Ritz is letting her back in?"

"Jake has given her new identity so that will not be problem."

"Unless the staff remembers her . . . and something tells me they will."

"Not our problem."

Livy agreed. It wasn't as if her aunt didn't know how to take care of herself.

"You know," Livy felt the need to point out, "it won't be easy finding Frankie Whitlan. The BPC, KZS, and The Group have all tried and failed."

Bart stared at her. "Who?"

"The bears, the cats, and the rest of 'em."

"Oh, them. That is because they all have their rules. Honey badgers . . . we have no rules. We will find this Whitlan . . . and we will find anyone who helped him." He finished off another shot of vodka and poured one more. "You do know, little Olivia, that your father never trusted full-humans. Ever."

"I know."

"He only met with them face-to-face when one or all of us, his brothers, could go with him. He said full-humans were traitors to their own, so how could they not be traitors to us?"

"He used to tell me that when I was still in the high chair."

"And he was right, which is why I know truth."

"Truth? What truth?"

"Shot in drive-by, thrown out window, found castrated behind strip joint . . ." Bart shrugged. "We would bury Damon's body again and go about our day. But killed like this . . . hunted . . . like *this*? That would never have happened to your father."

Livy leaned back in her chair. "What are you saying?"

"I think it was shifter. Shifter lured your father . . . then human killed him."

"We don't know that, Uncle Bart. And I don't want us distracted."

"Distracted?"

"We are out for Whitlan. And only Whitlan."

"Someone is hiding him. Helping him."

"And they'll suffer. But this isn't an excuse for the Kowalskis to go on a killing spree. You guys get the information, and we get Whitlan. If, and only if, someone tries to stop us from getting Whitlan, then they pay the price. Understand me?"

Bart smirked, nodded. "Strong-willed. Like your father. You would have made great boss."

Livy didn't reply to the compliment. Instead, she looked out the window in time to see Melly screaming, "*I will track you down! I will track you down and* make *you love me!*"

"Don't worry, little Olivia," Bart said, patting her hand. "I make sure your aunt Teddy takes little Melly with her."

Livy smiled at her uncle Bart. "Thank you."

CHAPTER 20

It was decided over many more glasses of vodka that Livy would go back to work. She would continue on with her daily routine because her uncles didn't think it was a good idea to involve her in the hell-making of other people's lives. Although what it really came down to was her family wasn't sure that Livy's artistic sensibilities wouldn't suddenly come into play at the worst time possible. They insisted it wasn't a lack of trust so much as her not understanding how the Kowalskis liked to do things. Livy, however, understood better than most. It was hard not to when one had grown up with her father.

Still, she didn't argue the point. Arm twisting wasn't really her thing. She didn't enjoy hearing people in pain. She didn't enjoy making people cry . . . usually. So Livy would happily go back to her day job and let her family do what they had to do.

But what her uncles needed right now was someplace to start. So she led them upstairs and searched the multiple rooms for Vic or Shen.

She found Shen first. Asleep faceup on a bare mattress in one of the small rooms, the giant panda's body was stretched out across a twin bed, his head and arms hanging over the side, And there was snoring.

"Like giant stuffed toy," Otto muttered.

Deciding not to wake him up, Livy continued searching. She finally found Vic in one of the bigger rooms, making up the bed.

Livy watched him for a moment. Hospital corners. He was making hospital corners with the sheet. Livy, a known sleep-twister, didn't bother going to all that trouble with her own sheets.

Shaking her head, she said, "Hey, Vic—"

"Hey." He was busy smoothing out the sheets, so he didn't turn around immediately. "I was going to put us in the master bedroom, but Kyle already had it and he's already turned it into some kind of terrifying art studio. Just FYI, that kid has bones in there. I didn't look too closely so I don't know if they're human or not, but you may want to have Cooper look into that. Anyway, I grabbed this room since it had a king and a bathroom attached, but if there's another room you want us in, just let me know and"—Vic finally stood and turned—"I'll make sure to put . . . *you* in there all by *yourself*," he finished, spotting her uncles standing around Livy. "Because you sleep alone. Yes, you do. Alone is how you sleep."

Vic cleared his throat, nodded at her uncles. "Gentlemen."

"Vic, these are my uncles." She pointed at each one. "Baltazar, Kamil, Gustav, Edmund, Otto, and David. Uncles, this is Victor Barinov."

"Barinov?" Otto asked, frowning a little.

"Yes."

"You have information for us?" Balt asked Vic.

"Uh, yes." He grabbed a folder off the nightstand. "Here's what we've pulled together so far. Do you want me to go over it with you?" Vic asked as he handed the info to Balt.

"I can read," Balt snarled, snatching the folder.

"I wasn't suggesting—"

"We will talk later, Olivia," Balt said before he and the rest of her uncles walked away.

Once they were gone, Vic sat down on the bed and dropped his head into his hands.

"What's wrong?"

"They hate me," Vic said. "Couldn't you tell how much they hate me?"

"They don't hate you," Livy told him, closing the door and walking over to the bed. "They hate your father. And I think they all have a thing for your mother."

Vic's head slowly came up. "My father?"

"He's helped INTERPOL prevent several Kowalski jobs over the years. And helped to put away a few of my uncles' cousins."

"Oh." Vic thought about it a moment, then said, "Yeah. That does make it awkward, doesn't it?"

Livy chuckled. "I wouldn't worry about it. Besides, your parents are badass if they've got my uncles worried."

Vic grinned. "My parents are kind of badass. Of course, they both come from two families of badasses. Stalin actively avoided my great-grandfather. And my mother's mother was one of the most feared snipers in the Red Army. The Germans called her *der Schrecken*."

And together they said, "The Nightmare."

"Was she really that bad?" Livy asked.

"Oh yeah. She was a Siberian She-tiger with amazing aim. As soon as those guys turned around, they'd get picked off from behind. Then at night, she'd shift to her tiger form and . . ."

"Get a little snack?"

Vic grimaced. "It was a long Russian winter, and food was scarce. She did what she had to do, I guess." Vic shrugged. "I liked her, though. She made the best cookies."

He let out a breath. "I hope I didn't make things weird for you and your uncles."

"Weird how?"

"Accidentally suggesting we're sleeping together."

"We are sleeping together."

"I know. But no uncle wants to hear that about his niece. Especially when he still calls his niece *Little* Olivia."

"They couldn't care less about that. They're more worried I'm bedding down with someone as dangerously close to a cop as they're willing to allow."

They were silent for a few minutes until Vic asked, "So, what's next?"

"I go back to work tomorrow. Like everything is normal. You should know, though, they think a shifter might be involved. But I made it clear we're not playing that game. We are out for Whitlan. That's it."

"They could be right, though. Keep in mind all three organizations had backed off this case . . . that suggests someone with the power to make that happen."

"Or the money." When Vic frowned a bit, Livy added, "Even shifters have bills to pay. But we'll wait and see. If a shifter or shifter*s* are involved, we'll talk about it then."

"If you're telling me that because you want me to be prepared for the fallout . . . don't worry about it. You betray your own . . . you get whatever's coming to you."

"I'm fine with that. But I'm more worried about my family using this opportunity to fuck with shifters they've always hated. And that isn't what this is about. Not for me."

Again they sat in silence for several minutes. Then, Livy stretched out on the bed and placed her head in Vic's lap.

Vic gently stroked her head, big fingers easing through her hair, stopping briefly to massage her scalp.

He didn't speak, seeming to understand that Livy didn't want a lot of conversation. She just wanted to lie here, quietly, and let the guy she was fucking play with her hair.

And the fact that he got that without Livy saying a word spoke volumes about the man.

Wearing her mink coat—something other shifters thought was tacky—and smoking one of her French cigarettes, Joan sat on the marble bench in the backyard and stared up at the sky.

Melly had finally been dragged off by one of her cousins so there was no more crying and screaming about how, "No one understands that I *looooooooovvvvveeee* him!"

So that was something to be grateful for.

Her sisters and Aunt Li-Li had gone off, as well, to get a hotel suite at the Kingston Arms. The Yangs didn't have the reputation that the Kowalskis did at the local Manhattan hotels, so it shouldn't be a problem. Joan had briefly entertained staying here with her daughter, but why torment herself? They'd never gotten along, and she didn't think that would change now. Especially since Joan didn't think she'd done anything wrong. But leave it to Olivia to turn this whole thing into a big deal.

Of course, any time Joan thought about what her husband must have gone through during his final moments, the indignity of being hunted like some poor animal in the wild . . . well, her rage took over. Something no one should want.

Her anger might not come out often, but when it did, the world shuddered in the face of it.

But, for once, Joan was going to let her daughter take the lead on this. To be honest, she wanted to see what her daughter would do. How she would handle it. If Olivia handled it well, then at least Joan wouldn't have to worry about her safety. Not involving herself in the family business put Olivia at risk in a way she wouldn't be if she was involved.

Then again, there was that time Olivia was snatched by full-human men who wanted her father to do a job for them.

Olivia had only been sixteen at the time, and both families had quickly gotten together, plans on how they would deal with the kidnapping already in the works, when Olivia had suddenly walked in the back door of their Washington house. Covered in blood, with a handcuff still dangling from her wrist, she'd walked barefoot through the kitchen, stopping only to point at her father and inform him that, "After what I just went through, you *better* pay for my art school." Something her father had initially refused to do—even after a painfully long plea from Antonella Jean-Louis Parker on Livy's behalf—because he'd rightfully thought it was stupid.

But when they didn't find anything but the empty van and lots of dried blood, Damon went ahead and paid for that education he didn't believe in.

So maybe Joan didn't need to worry about her ridiculous daughter with her ridiculous ideas about being a great artist.

A glass of scotch was held in front of her face and, smiling, Joan took it.

"Thank you, Baltazar."

Her husband's brother sat down next to her. It was freezing cold out, so he also wore his mink coat.

"Don't be mad at little Olivia."

"Who says I am?"

"You did. I heard you say to your sister, 'I am so mad at her.' "

Yeah. She had said that.

"Besides," he went on, "did you really expect her to do anything else once she found Damon in some full-human's house? Stuffed and on display like some deer?"

"You have a point."

Balt pressed his shoulder against Joan's and lowered his head a bit so she had to look him in the eye.

"Stop it, Balt."

"What? I said nothing."

"I'm still your brother's wife."

"My brother's *ex*-wife. Or, if you were still married . . . widow. Besides, you cannot live your life alone and miserable."

"Who says I'm miserable . . . or alone?"

Balt's back straightened. "Who? Tell me his name?"

"Balt—"

"I want to know his name."

"Stop."

Balt drank his shot of vodka in one gulp and poured himself another from the bottle he'd brought out with him.

"Let's focus on something else."

"Fine," he grumbled, sounding like the seventeen-year-old she'd met all those years ago. A seventeen-year-old who never gave up on trying to get in her pants.

Joan put her arm around Balt's giant shoulders. "Tell me the plan."

"Right now, we need name. There is someone very important who protects this Whitlan. I want their name. So tomorrow, my brothers and I go to Florida."

"What's in Florida?"

"The company that shipped Damon's body."

"Good. You deal with them. I'll deal with Allison Whitlan."

"Olivia will not like if you kill her, my beauty. Unless Whitlan girl is involved in all this."

Joan chuckled. "You listen to my daughter too much. I'm a thief, not a murderer."

"Your daughter has never said either. My brother, though . . ."

Joan laughed and kissed her brother-in-law on the cheek. "I'm glad you're here, Baltazar. But I want you to be careful."

"I will not promise to be careful," Balt admitted honestly. "But I do promise many will suffer."

Laying her head on his shoulder, Joan smiled. "I know, Baltazar. I know."

CHAPTER 21

Vic woke up with Livy tucked in his arms. They were both fully dressed and on top of the covers. It had been a long couple of days, and they'd been exhausted. So he wasn't surprised they'd sort of passed out without having dinner.

It was still early, though, so Vic was ready to go right back to sleep when he caught sight of Kyle at the foot of his bed.

"Kyle?"

"Someone needs to feed me."

"Feed you?"

"Yes. I'm hungry."

"You can get food on your own."

"I could. But I won't. I've got work."

"You're *twelve*."

"I'm well aware of my age. I also know that legally someone has to feed me."

"Where's Cooper?"

"Practicing in the basement."

"Okay, then—"

"And he throws things at me when I interrupt him. Your soft eyes suggest you're weaker and won't physically harm me. So I need you to feed me."

"He won't physically harm you," Livy growled from her spot against Vic's chest, "but I will."

"You won't because of your loyalty to my sister. And she's in Siberia. Not metaphorically, either. Literally . . . in Siberia."

Livy pushed herself up on one elbow, locked those beautiful black eyes on Kyle, and said, "But you're also a shifter, which means you'll heal before she gets back in the country. So *get out of my room!*" she ended on a screech.

Vic watched the boy bolt, and Livy dropped back against his chest.

"You're going to have to learn to be firm with him without breaking any of his bones," Livy said. "That kid can smell weakness and will take full advantage."

"It was kind of weird finding him just standing there . . . staring at us. You think he was plotting to kill me?"

"Kyle? No. You're confusing him with his sister Delilah. You find her watching you from the end of your bed, shoot first and ask questions later. Trust me . . . it'll be the only time Toni will forgive you for killing one of her siblings."

"Good to know."

Livy propped her head up with her chin on her fist and her elbow buried in Vic's chest. "What time is it?"

"Six-thirty or so."

"Okay."

"Why?"

"I have to go in to work."

"You're going to leave me here? Alone? With your cranky uncles and Shen?"

"And Kyle."

Vic shuddered. "That kid asked me to pose naked."

"That kid's got an eye."

"Please tell me you're not okay with him asking me to pose naked."

"Not now, but when he's sixteen—"

"Stop. Just stop." Vic pressed his hands to either side of Livy's face.

"What are you doing?"

"Thinking about how beautiful you look in the morning."

"I'm not making you breakfast."

"Come on," Vic whined. "I'm starving!"

"Too bad. You can, however, take me out to breakfast once I have my shower."

Vic grinned.

"I didn't say you could join me in the shower."

"Do you want breakfast or not?"

Livy sat up and ran her hands through her short hair. "Look at you. Making me give you sex so I can get some food."

Vic kissed the back of her neck and teased, "As long as we understand the parameters of this relationship . . . we'll be just fine."

Livy was late getting to the Sports Center but it was for two very good reasons . . . waffles smothered in honey and great sex.

Besides, she didn't have any appointments this early. Of course, she never booked anything this early. She would never say she was crabby in the morning, but she did notice that her normal responses to situations seemed to annoy others more before noon.

The elevator stopped on her floor, and she walked out. She was heading down the hallway when someone grabbed her from behind. Her ski jacket, zipped in the front, choked her when she was lifted off the ground and carried off like laundry.

Livy hissed and tried to twist out of the grip of whoever had her. Unfortunately, they didn't have her by the back of the neck, where the elasticity of her honey badger skin would make it impossible for her opponent to keep a good grip. Instead, whoever this was had her by her jacket. Her stupid, stupid jacket!

Snarling, Livy tried to dig her pocketknife out of the back of her jeans, but before she had it in her hand, she was shoved through a door and tossed across a room.

Livy hit the wall face-first, which only managed to piss her off more. Crouching down, she unleashed her claws, and spun around to face . . . Dee-Ann.

The hillbilly pointed a damning finger at her. "I want you, little girl, to explain to me—right now—why honey badgers are settin' up house outside my baby cousin's den!"

Livy stood, stared, and finally asked, "What the fuck are you talking about?"

"Why is your clan of honey badger *felons* across the street from Bobby Ray's house?"

"*My* clan of felons? Do you really want to go down that particular country road with me, *Smith*?"

Dee-Ann was coming at her when Cella Malone ran through the door. She jumped between them, her arms pressed against their chests.

"Stop it! Both of you!"

"Move, Malone," Smith snarled.

Livy snorted. "Bring it, Ellie Mae."

"That is enough!" Cella shoved, and the Siberian She-tiger forced them to either sides of the room. "And no more *Beverly Hillbillies* jokes, Livy. Only *I* can do that."

Pointing a finger, Dee-Ann snarled, "I will not have that little weasel puttin' my kin at risk."

"Can I talk to you outside for a minute?" Cella asked Dee-Ann.

"No."

Apparently not liking that particular response, Cella grabbed Dee-Ann by the hair and yanked her out of the office.

"We'll be right back," Cella said, trying to sound cheery.

While they were outside, Livy saw one of her recent team pics behind what she now realized was Cella's desk. It had been blown up so it covered most of the wall. And Livy had to admit that as mundane as this work felt . . . she *was* good at it.

The door opened, and Cella and Dee-Ann walked back into the office. Now Dee-Ann looked contrite.

She nodded at Livy. "I'm real sorry to hear about your daddy."

Livy wasn't surprised the protection organizations had already heard about what she'd found. Any time large numbers of honey badgers moved into a single location, the local shifter populace tried to find out why and how soon they would go away.

"Well," Livy said calmly, "you can take your countrified pity and shove it up your flat, hillbilly—"

"Okay!" Cella cut in. "No need to let this get nasty. We just wish you'd come to us, Livy. You know we would have helped you."

"I guess calling in my honey badger family was unreasonable of me . . . then again, maybe I just can't get it out of my head that if you'd found Whitlan when you'd first locked on to him, my father would be alive rather than a stuffed carcass in some rich bitch's living room. So you'll have to forgive me if you're not the first people I came running to in my time of need."

"Wow," Cella muttered. "Honey badgers *are* mean."

Livy slowly nodded. "Yes . . . we really are."

Vic had taken Livy to the Sports Center after their breakfast, with every intention of going back to the rental house to work with Shen. But then Vic remembered he'd have to deal with Kyle again . . .

Look, Vic would admit it. He didn't have the brains to keep up with that kid. The twelve-year-old managed to overwhelm a full-grown adult with his arrogance and awkward requests.

Deciding to wait a while—at least until he was sure that Shen was up and functioning, so *he* could deal with that kid—Vic went into the Sports Center. He worked his way through all the full-humans who utilized the top levels for exercise and sports training, and followed the scent of shifters to a hidden stairwell that then led him to the floors below.

Although it was the middle of a workday, it was still pretty packed. Shifters of all breeds and species were there to work out, train, or get a glimpse of their favorite shifter sports star.

Vic didn't have a favorite sports star. He hated sports. He worked out to keep himself in shape and to work off excess energy that could lead to his shifting into his animal form and rampaging the streets of New York, but other than that . . .

He did tolerate football, though. Could sit with friends and watch it without complaining if he had to. He enjoyed the rigidity of it. The definite lines and rules. He loathed basketball and baseball, however, and seeing really big guys on skates did nothing but weird him out. Of course, he'd felt the same way when he'd seen full-blood grizzlies on skates in Russia.

Stopping by the Starbucks located in the Sports Center—because there really always was one *everywhere*, even among shifters—and getting himself a large coffee and a few honey buns, Vic went and sat down on an empty bench to eat and people watch.

He thought about stopping by Livy's office, but he didn't want to crowd her. She hated that, and Vic didn't want to become someone she actively avoided—like the pretty woman skating by him . . . once . . . twice . . . three times before she finally rolled herself over and stopped in front of Vic.

"Hi, Blayne."

"Hi, Vic."

"Honey bun," he offered out of the Russian politeness his parents had drilled into him for years while he was growing up. But he was really hoping she'd turn him down.

She did.

"So, what's up?" he asked around another honey bun.

She rolled closer. Blayne really was a beautiful woman. And there were few women who could wear shorts that tiny and still look good. She had long, athletic, muscular legs that said she worked out a lot. Maybe she lived on those skates. Did she wear them all the time? To family events? To bed? Did that meathead hockey player *make* her wear those skates?

"I heard about Livy's father," she whispered. "You know . . . about what *really* happened to him."

That snapped Vic back to the moment and away from Blayne's skate-wearing schedule.

"How did you hear?"

"I heard it from Ronnie Lee who heard it from Sissy Mae who heard it from—"

"Okay," Vic cut in, quickly regretting asking her the simple question.

"You know, my mom was hunted, too," she whispered.

"Oh Blayne. I'm sorry."

She waved off his words. "It was a long time ago, and after a considerable amount of therapy, I've compartmentalized it quite nicely."

"Okay."

Blayne moved in a little closer, looked around, leaned down, and added, "Maybe I should cancel my wedding."

"Well, if you don't want to marry the guy, of course you should cancel your wedding. Don't let family or peer pressure push you into a marriage you don't want."

Blayne snapped up straight, her hands resting on her hips. "Of course I want to marry Bo. Why wouldn't I want to marry Bo? I love him!"

"Then why would you cancel your wedding?"

"Because of what happened to Livy's father."

Vic stared at Blayne, but she didn't say anything else.

"I understand you feeling empathy toward Livy, considering what happened to your mother, but I guess I'm unclear on what Damon Kowalski has to do with your wedding."

"Who?"

Vic took another sip of coffee. Maybe he wasn't alert enough for this conversation.

"Livy's father? Damon Kowalski is Livy's father."

"Oh! Yeah, I didn't know his name."

"Uh-huh. So you want to cancel your giant, double wedding because of a man whose name you didn't even know . . . because of your mom?"

"No. And I don't *want* to cancel my wedding, but I'm wondering if I should."

"Why would you be wondering that?"

"Because Livy's my friend."

"She is?"

"Yes!"

"Okay, okay. No need to get upset." Although he wanted to use *hysterical* instead of *upset*. "I guess the way to look at this is . . . how would *Livy* react if you canceled the wedding for her? Do you think she'd be okay with it? Or do you think she'd throw another locker at you?"

Blayne, after thinking on that for a few seconds, admitted, "Locker."

"Right. So you may not want to cancel your wedding if the only reason is because of Livy's father."

Blayne sat down beside Vic. "What about having her as our photographer?"

"What about it?"

"Do you think it will be too hard for her?"

Probably, but not for the reasons Blayne was thinking. And Vic briefly entertained the idea of using this opportunity to get Livy out of being a dreaded *wedding* photographer—emphasis on the "wedding" part—but then he realized Livy wouldn't want him involving himself in her career.

No. Livy would have to shoot or not shoot Blayne's wedding on her own. All Vic could really do was keep her from throwing lockers at poor Blayne's head.

"Livy is one of the strongest and smartest women I know. And I think you need to let her take the lead on whether she can handle shooting your wedding or not. She's brutally honest, so if she doesn't think she can do it, she'll tell you. And probably recommend someone great who can step in for her. What's important is that you trust Livy to do what's right. Because she will."

Blayne gazed at Vic for what seemed an excessively long time until she slowly began to smile.

"What?" Vic asked. "What did I say?"

"Oh." She shook her head. "Nothing." Blayne stood. "You're right. I need to trust Livy." She skated a half circle around Vic. "Hey, are you coming to our derby bout tomorrow? It's just a local bout to help raise money for the tristate teams."

"I'm not really a sports—"

"Livy will be playing, of course. She's one of our shortest blockers, but also one of our meanest."

"She is? Oh. Yeah. Okay. Sure. I can come."

Blayne's grin was amazingly wide. "Yay!" She skated off, then skated right back, leaned down, and kissed Vic on the cheek. "Thanks for your advice."

"Anytime."

He watched her skate off again, unable to shake the feeling something weird had just happened.

Deciding not to worry about it, Vic ate the last honey bun and finished off his coffee. He was going to go for another walk when he realized that someone was sitting next to him.

Vic turned his head to see Dee-Ann beside him. She glared at him with her dead, soulless dog eyes.

"You got somethin' to tell me, son?"

Livy was going through some pics she'd recently taken of the shifter girls' gymnastics team. Although these girls could never get into the full-human sports now that testing had become so invasive, it looked as if the shifter-version sport was about to go worldwide like hockey. Which, when Livy thought about it, was much fairer to the full-humans.

When the full-humans destroyed a kneecap coming off the pommel horse, their careers usually ended. When a shifter did the same thing, it was usually not from the landing but because they'd vaulted themselves too far up and rammed their knee into a ceiling beam. Yet the shifters still managed to nail the landing and were healed within twenty-four hours. So . . . yeah. Not fair to the full-humans.

"Hey!"

Livy looked up from her pics and at Blayne. "Hey."

"You're coming to the bout tomorrow, right?"

"Am I?" Livy asked. It was decided that Livy would only come to derby bouts that impacted the championships. Last she'd heard, tomorrow's bout was simply a fund-raising thing. Something casual between the teams that Livy's competitive "win or die" nature tended to ruin.

"You've gotta come!"

"Well—"

"Great! I'll tell the team you'll be there!"

Livy let out a breath, wondering how she was not going to kill that girl at some point.

"She's just so damn perky," Livy muttered.

She returned to her work. She was annoyed because she knew she'd taken some pictures recently of the gymnastics team that she really wanted to use, but she couldn't find them on the memory card she had. She spun her chair around and pulled her camera out of her bag. Livy turned it on and using the LCD monitor in the back of her Nikon, she viewed the first picture that came up. It was a black-and-white one of Vic that she'd taken in Massachusetts.

Smiling, she studied the image. It reminded her of how good she could be when she wasn't thinking too much about it. When she was just letting the moment lead her rather than the million things going on in her head.

Livy placed her camera on her desk and hooked it up to her computer. She copied Vic's pictures and enlarged them on her screen. With some miniscule tweaking, she thought at least one of the pics could possibly work for her upcoming show.

Livy dove into the work, forgetting everything around her as she toyed with the images, seeing what she could pull out of them.

She was so lost in her work, she didn't realize that she wasn't alone until she stopped and reached for the can of honey-roasted almonds she kept on her desk. When Livy found nothing but empty space, she looked up and found a bunch of her cousins standing around her office, passing her damn almonds around.

"What's wrong?" she asked.

"We're bored," Jake filled in.

"That sounds like a *you* problem."

"If you want us to play nice at your friend's fancy house, you better give us a way to work off our excess energy."

"Can't you jog like most people?"

"No," they all replied.

Livy sat back in her seat and looked over her cousins. She thought about seeing if there was some game they could go to in the Sports Center, but that wouldn't be enough for them. And the additional liquor they'd have access to just screamed "trouble."

So Livy racked her brain for another option.

* * *

Reece Lee Reed pulled on a pair of basketball shorts and walked out of the bedroom, easing the door closed so that he didn't wake up the bobcat asleep in his bed.

Yawning, he scratched his head and his belly while walking across the Kingston Arms hotel suite he'd been living in since he'd moved from Tennessee to Manhattan. A decision he still hadn't regretted, although his mother did complain. Apparently her sons had deserted her. No mention of her only daughter, but Reece didn't worry about that. He'd learned long ago to let his sister and mother fight it out between themselves. He had other things to do.

Like bobcats!

Chuckling, Reece glanced at his watch. It was already mid-afternoon, but he hadn't gone to bed until late and then he hadn't slept until morning. But it was his day off since he had a big job coming up on the weekend, so if he wanted to waste the day away with a very nice piece of feline ass, he could.

Lord, he loved his life.

Reece passed his couch, his eyes briefly straying to the big flat-screen TV on the other side of it, which was when Livy Kowalski suddenly popped up.

Reece screamed, jumping back.

"Hey," Livy said calmly.

He hated when Livy did this. Curled up on his couch so he couldn't see her until she leaped out at him like one of those undead killer children in those Japanese horror movies.

"Why are you here?" Reece asked.

"You made me a promise a few months ago. And today's the day I need you to deliver."

Reece made lots of promises to lots of people. He was good about keeping them, but he didn't always remember them until someone reminded him. So he gazed at Livy, waiting for her to do just that.

She raised those pitch-black eyebrows of hers and tilted her head to the side.

Reece threw his hands in the air. "Oh Livy, come on!"

"You promised," she coldly reminded him.

"Wasn't I drunk that night?"

"Very drunk. But a promise is a promise. And I really need it."

"You're taking advantage of me."

"It's not my fault you can't hold your liquor and I was the only thing between you and a couple of really pissed-off brother lions. Who told you to drink that tequila anyway?"

Reece shrugged. "I love tequila. It's so dang tasty."

"You promised," she said again.

"Yeah, but—"

"Promised."

"Livy, it's just—"

"Promised."

"I just—"

"Promised."

"Yeah, but—"

"Promised."

That was the thing with Olivia Kowalski. She forgot nothing and wasn't afraid to call in a favor when necessary.

"Is there a reason I need to do this?" Reece asked, wondering why she wanted a favor now.

"Yeah."

No. Livy wasn't subtle. But she wasn't really open, either. Emotion and information didn't pour from her like it did from the other females in his life. If you asked her a pointed question, Livy would often answer with brutal honesty. But if you didn't know the question to ask, she wasn't about to help you.

"All right," Reece finally agreed, wondering once again what had possessed him to become friendly with a dang honey badger. His mother had warned him. Warned him they were the meanest things on the planet. But he thought she was just being . . . herself. He had no idea there was validity to her statements. "Just let me take a quick shower and call the guys."

Reece had barely taken two steps when his bedroom door opened and the Southern bobcat he'd met a few days ago smiled at him. She wore one of Reece's Tennessee Titans T-shirts—something that annoyed Reece greatly because you just didn't take a man's Titans T-shirt—and leaned against the doorjamb, smiling. "Hey there, darlin'," she purred.

Reece cringed at that sexy murmur and moved. Good thing, too, as the sound he found so sexy did nothing but set Livy off. Just as he bolted forward, Livy was already charging across his couch on all fours toward the bobcat. Livy wasn't in her honey badger form, either, she was just on all fours. And yet she still moved like lightning. Before he could reach her, she was off the couch, fangs and claws unleashed. But he did manage—barely—to catch her around the waist, snatching her out of the air seconds before she could embed all those deadly natural weapons into the bobcat's pretty face.

While Reece held on to a thrashing Livy, the bobcat had thankfully moved fast, as well, scrambling onto a side table and then onto the wall. She hung there now by her claws, hissing down at him and Livy.

"Darlin'," Reece said to the bobcat over all the noise, "why don't you let yourself out and, uh, I'll call you later. Promise!"

Livy slammed her booted foot down onto the back of the wolf lying in front of her, raised her weapon, and screamed out, "By this paintball gun . . . I rule alllllll!"

Her cousins raised their weapons in mutual triumph, cheering at the complete and utter destruction of their opponents.

Grinning, Livy looked over at Reece and his Pack, who were still standing but also covered in red paint. And it was his packmates who were glaring at poor Reece for getting them into this. He seemed reluctant to turn around and face them. Not that she blamed him.

"What a good idea this was," Reece's brother Rory snarled at Reece. "I'm so glad I took off work to do this."

"We got beaten by a bunch of mighty midgets," one of the other Packmates grumbled.

"No," Rory corrected. "We got beaten by a bunch of dang honey badgers." Rory slapped the back of Reece's head. "You put us up against goddamn honey badgers!"

Livy glanced back at her cousins and chuckled.

"Could you move your foot?" the wolf beneath her asked.

She did, and walked over to Reece and the others. "Don't blame him," she told Reece's brother. "I made him bring me here."

"He could have said no."

"Then I would have ripped his pretty little face off for not keeping his promise to take me 'and mine'—his words—'paint ballin' with his kin.' Also his words." Livy smiled, which made all the wolves scowl. Then she jerked forward and all of them jerked back.

"Well," she said, walking over to her own "kin," "this was fun. Thanks, guys."

Livy winked at her cousins, then said, "Kowalskis, in honor of our hosts . . ."

Jake, as always, picked up on what Livy was suggesting. But the others instantly caught on as soon as Jake tipped his head back and began to howl.

Even with all the howling now going on, Livy could still hear the wolves behind her quite clearly.

"Good Lord! What are they doing?"

"Make them stop! Make them stop! It's like hell on earth!"

"No wonder the felines complain when we do it . . ."

Livy let her cousins continue as her phone rang.

The ID said "unknown caller," but she answered anyway.

"Hello?"

"It's Vic."

"Well, hi, Vic."

And as soon as she said his name, her cousins instantly stopped howling.

Livy watched them carefully as Vic asked, "Are you coming back to the house soon?"

"Yeah. Everything okay?"

"Things are moving. Might be better if you're home."

Livy couldn't help but smirk a bit. "You worried about little ol' me, you big, strong, take-charge man, you?"

"Huh?"

Livy laughed. "Forget it. I'll be back in a bit."

"Good."

Livy disconnected the call and wondered how she could be so into a guy who had no real grasp of good comedy.

"So that was Vic, huh?" Jake asked, her cousin suddenly close. "Calling to check up on you?"

"Yes. So?"

"Well, I heard from that weird kid, Kyle, that he found you two in bed together. Fully clothed and cuddling."

"Awwww," the rest of her cousins chimed in. "Cuddling!"

Livy thought about saying something, but instead she just went ahead and shot her cousin in the leg. When he screamed from the pain of the paintball ramming into him at close range and dropped to one knee, she shot him in the head and neck until he was on the floor and covered in red paint.

"God," Jocelyn sneered with a sad shake of her head, "you're being so *weak,* Jake. Get up and act like you've got some real honey badger balls!"

CHAPTER 22

Vic waited for Livy on the stoop. Her uncles had left for Florida earlier in the day. And her mother had left about an hour ago with several of her own family, the Yangs. Vic knew this because he had a contact in the hotel the Yangs were staying at, and he was keeping an eye on them. There was always a risk of what Vic liked to call "blowback." And he was determined not to let any of that blowback hurt Livy. No matter what her family did or didn't do.

A cab stopped in front of the house, and Vic smiled as soon as Livy stepped out.

"Hey," he said when she slowly walked up the stairs.

"Hey." She dropped her backpack by the door and sat down next to him.

"How did your day go?" Vic asked.

"It was all right. I left work early to hang with my cousins."

"You can just leave your day job when you want to?"

"I hadn't thought to ask anyone about leaving. I do it all the time. No one says anything as long as I make my photo shoots on time, especially the shoots with Novikov. And as long as I hit my deadlines . . . they leave me alone."

"That's pretty cool. Most day jobs are a lot less . . . flexible."

"Are you trying to make me feel better about this job?"

"Yes."

"Well . . . thank you."

"You're welcome."

Livy rubbed her eyes, yawned.

"Tired?"

"Just a little. Beating the Smith Pack males in paintball can wear a girl out."

"You played paintball with wolves? Livy . . . no."

"My cousins needed a way to work off some excess energy."

"But beating up on wolves?"

"What makes you think we won?"

To effectively reply to that, Vic just stared at her and raised one side of his mouth.

"All right, all right," she said around a laugh.

"You know how emotionally vested the wolves get about dominance. Why don't you just go beat up some puppies, too?"

Vic heard what sounded suspiciously like a giggle.

"Okay! I get it," she said. "I'll send them an 'I'm sorry' basket of Milk-Bones to make it up to them."

"You are so mean."

"I know. It's a genetic flaw."

"Speaking of genetic flaws, where are the cousins you played paintball with?"

"They went out to eat. But I wanted to come home and see you."

Vic placed his hand under Livy's, wincing at the size difference. His hands looked like giant dinner plates next to hers. But when she curled her fingers in between his, clasping their hands together, Vic realized that the size difference didn't matter.

"Do you want to get out of here?" he asked.

"And go where?"

"My house. Just for the night."

Her nose wrinkled a bit when she grimaced. "We shouldn't leave Coop, Cherise, and Kyle alone in the house."

"Because of what Coop and Cherise might do to the kid when they can't take it anymore?"

"Kyle will have to learn to deal with his siblings on his own. I'm just concerned that with my family out doing what they do—"

"Shen's here. He'll watch out for them."

"Why is Shen here? Doesn't he have a home?"

"Somewhere, but hell if I know where it is. But it's not in Manhattan. Or any of the five buroughs. So until we're done with this, he's not going anywhere."

"You think he'll mind?"

"Coop just ordered Mexican for dinner. Shen will not mind staying."

"Big Mexican food fan, is he?"

"He's a big fan of food in general." Tightening his fingers a bit so Livy couldn't pull away, Vic stood, tugging until she got up, as well. "Come on. Let's get out of here. Just for tonight."

"As long as Shen is watching out for them, that's probably a good idea."

Vic led Livy down the street to where he'd parked his SUV. While they walked, he pulled out his cell phone and sent Shen a quick text to let him know what was going on.

He reached his vehicle and opened the door for Livy. Because of its enormous size, she had to step up and then *into* the SUV. But she turned and faced him before sitting down in the seat, her hands resting on the frame.

She gazed at him for a long moment, then asked, "Do you have honey at your house?"

Vic swallowed. "We can stop at a place I know to pick some up. It's open late. Bear owned."

Livy reached out with one hand, stroked her fingers down his jaw. "Good plan."

Vic waited until Livy was in her seat before he closed the

door. He moved around the SUV, trying really hard not to run. It wasn't easy. He wanted to run. And speed. All the way back to his house. That would be tacky, though. He didn't want to be tacky.

Right? He didn't want to be tacky?

Coop was having a pleasant evening. He was sitting on the couch, working on the symphony he'd started to write a few days ago on a whim. Cherise was on one end of the couch, the remote control in her hand, indulging her secret love of reality television. His music had him pretty well sucked in, but it was entertaining to occasionally look up and see people yell at each other for ratings. On the other end of the couch was Kyle. He was in a sketching mood tonight, and Coop was grateful. When Kyle sketched, he was so absorbed by his work that he was quiet for once. Wonderfully, beautifully, amazingly quiet.

It was nice. Three prodigies, sitting around, being casual . . . while creating work that would last hundreds of years. See? They could be normal like everyone else.

The giant panda, Shen, walked into the living room. He had his cell phone in one hand and one of his *many* bamboo stalks in the other.

Staring at his phone he said, "Got a text from Vic. He and Livy are heading to his house for the night. He wants me to keep an eye on you guys while they're gone."

"Great," Coop said, suddenly not liking the flow of what he'd just written. "Thanks." He reached for the eraser he kept next to him and removed the offending notes, started again.

"You know"—Cherise lowered the sound on the dramatic yelling—"I think Livy's really into Vic."

"Really?" Coop asked, still erasing. He hated seeing the remnants of his failures.

"I'm worried, though."

"Why?"

"He's awfully nice. Maybe too nice. You know, for Livy."

"He's not that nice," Kyle tossed in. "He's seen enough of life and death to be able to handle the darker side of Livy's personality and needs. And Livy doesn't need someone who is like her. She doesn't need a honey badger as a mate. She knows, at least subconsciously, that connecting with someone like her would lead to what her parents once had. She fears that. She is, much to her surprise, a one-man woman. She will never be comfortable with the yelling, cheating, and lying that her parents thought of as sport so things never got too boring. For an artist she's surprisingly conventional about relationships."

After staring at each other, Coop and Cherise gazed at their younger brother with wide eyes and opened mouths.

He glanced away from what Coop realized was a sketch of the Arc de Triomphe, which they'd seen on their three-day stopover in Paris before heading back to New York. And it was meticulous and wonderful and . . . perfection. Still . . . Coop wondered if his brother might be missing another possible career.

"Have you thought about studying psychology, Kyle?" he asked.

"I plan to get my PhD in that. To get my PhD in art history just seems so . . . useless. I study art and its history every second of every day. I mean, when you think about it . . . *I'm* art history in the making. But a PhD in psychology would allow me to understand my enemies so I can destroy them and their careers before they get in my way."

Cherise leaned over and whispered in Coop's ear, "If he starts wondering about the taste of human flesh, you do understand we *will* have to stop him before his murder spree begins?"

"I'm more worried," Cooper whispered back, "that he'll become ruling overlord of the universe and we'll have to find some kind of magic sword if we hope to destroy him."

They both shuddered and returned to their work.

But after a few minutes, all three siblings looked up and saw the giant panda standing by the TV, eating his bamboo and staring at them.

"Something wrong?" Cooper asked him.

"Just keeping an eye on you three. Like I promised Vic. And thanks for not going to different rooms. It makes it easier to do my job."

Coop glanced at Cherise and Kyle. Since none of them had any ideas on how to handle this, they again focused on what they were doing. But at least Cherise turned up the TV quite a bit to help drown out the sound of the panda's munching.

That did help. At least a little.

Allison Whitlan walked into her beautiful home. She removed her cashmere coat and placed it in the closet. She removed her Jimmy Choos, sighing at the cold marble in the hallway against her feet. With the shoes hanging from one hand and her Chanel purse in the other, she went to her living room.

She was halfway across when she stopped, the hairs on the back of her neck raised, and goose bumps spreading up her spine and down the backs of her arms. Slowly, she turned and faced the beautiful but powerfully built Asian woman standing by the gift Allison's worthless father had sent her. She'd kept the gift, as she'd kept all his gifts over the years, but only because it was unique and interesting. Her friends, great world travelers, had been fascinated by such a large honey badger. They'd all been under the assumption that the African animal was much smaller in size.

"How the hell did you get in here?" she demanded of the

woman, who was dressed brazenly in a tight red dress, with bold gold jewelry on her neck and arms.

"I need a name from you."

"What?" Allison took a step toward the woman, but the intruder raised her forefinger, swung it back and forth while clicking her tongue against her teeth. At that moment, in that very second, Allison knew she was in grave danger. That this . . . person could and would kill her without a second's thought.

Allison knew it, and it terrified her as nothing ever had before.

"I need a name."

"It's my father you want, isn't it?" Allison shook her head. "You can threaten me if you want, but it won't matter to my father. He won't care. All you see here, all the money I have, is because of my mother and stepfather."

The woman gazed at her with the blackest eyes Allison had ever seen, and after a moment, she pointed at the stuffed honey badger with one perfectly manicured nail.

"Did your father give you this?"

"Yes."

"Did he bring it himself?"

Allison blinked at the question. She was used to these kinds of questions from the police. The FBI. All of them had been at her door more than once over the years. All looking for her father. Her criminal father. The best thing her mother had ever done was leave that man and marry Allison's stepfather. Not only had he been ridiculously wealthy, but he'd actually cared about Allison and her mother. Took care of them. Even now he and her mother were still together, currently on her stepfather's yacht in the Caymans.

"No," Allison replied. "He didn't bring it himself. I haven't seen my father in . . ." she thought a moment. "Ten . . . maybe fifteen years."

"Then who brought this to you?"

Allison hesitated. But the woman suddenly started walking toward her. Slowly. Taking her time crossing the space between them. She was shorter than Allison, even in those fifteen-hundred-dollar shoes she wore. But good God! Those shoulders! She looked like she could take Allison's stainless steel front door down with those shoulders.

The woman reached her hand out, and Allison struggled not to jerk away, feeling a movement—any movement at all—would get her killed.

The woman gently pushed a loose curl behind Allison's ear. "Don't start lying to me now, sweetie."

She had an accent, but she was trying to hide it. Her words were clipped, almost British. But she wasn't from Hong Kong. Allison had lots of friends who were, she traveled there often, and this woman didn't sound like them.

Nor did she seem like anyone Allison had met before. Ever. In fact, now that Allison was close to her, there was something so primal about this woman, so base, that Allison had to struggle not to cry in abject fear.

Instead, she swallowed back her tears and her fears and she answered the woman honestly. "Some delivery company. Out of Florida. There was no note. Or return address."

"Then how did you know it was from your father?"

"The deliveryman told me."

The woman took Allison at her word, maybe because she could actually *smell* Allison's fear. It wouldn't surprise Allison. This woman knew fear, understood it, and thrived on it.

Finally, the woman stepped away from Allison, absently patting her arm. "Very good," she said, turning away from her and heading across the room.

"If you don't mind," she added as she moved away, "I'll be taking this with me."

And, out of the darkness of Allison's living room, Asian men appeared. She hadn't even sensed they were there. Hadn't known that she wasn't alone with this woman. They were Asian, like the woman, and broad. Short, but so powerfully built, Allison had no doubt any of them could have killed her with one blow.

They went over to the stuffed honey badger and picked it up. And she couldn't explain it, but they seemed to do it with . . . respect. With honor. As if carrying the casket of a fallen soldier.

With care, they lifted the carcass up, stopping briefly by the woman. She rested her hand on the back of it, her head momentarily bowed. That was when Allison felt real . . . pain. Grief. Yes. She felt grief from the woman.

Confused, she watched the woman remove her hand and toss her head back. She let out a breath and made a motion. The men walked out, and the woman looked back at Allison.

"We'll be leaving through the front door here and then the lobby. You will not call the police. You will tell no one we were here. Anyone. I don't care who it is. Understand?"

Allison nodded, and the woman walked across the living room, but she stopped one more time when she reached the archway. The woman faced her.

Allison took in a breath, steeling herself for whatever nightmare was about to come next. Threats? Had this woman changed her mind? Would she now kill Allison?

Gazing at her with those cold black eyes, the woman said, "I love your shoes. Are those from the new line?"

Shocked, Allison swallowed, and said, "Next year's fall line. I have a male friend who works with the company."

"Lucky you!" The woman smiled. "I'd kill for that."

Then the woman was gone. The steel door slammed shut.

Allison dropped to her knees, urine running down her legs and into a puddle beneath her, while her entire body shook senselessly for hours.

While Joan's brothers put poor Damon into the back of the van, she called Balt.

"Yes, my beauty."

She grinned. The man would just never give up, would he? She liked that. "She didn't have a name."

"You believe her?"

"I do. She couldn't have lied to me if she'd wanted to."

"We will take from here then, yes?"

"Good luck. See you when you get back." She disconnected the call and got into the front passenger side of the van.

"Where now?" her younger brother asked.

Joan glanced back at the remains of her mate, but she couldn't look at him for long. It was too painful.

Focusing on the streets in front of her, she said, "Crematorium." Her brother stared at her, and she added, "You don't really think he's going to shift back to human *now,* do you?"

"You have a point." Her brother started the van, and waited to pull into traffic. That was when he added, "But if I find out there's any insurance policy out there with *my* name on it . . . me and you? We got problems."

"Don't worry. There's nothing like that out there."

Then to turn that lie into a truth, Joan put a reminder in her phone to cancel the insurance policies she had on her brothers.

John Lindow had come home early from the party, and he was glad he had. There was someone in his office. A room even his bitch of a wife didn't go into. And even if she was brave enough to try, she was out of the country for the next month, spending his money in France. His own fault, though. He didn't have to marry a "model," as she *still* liked to call herself.

With his two bodyguards behind him, John quietly walked up the stairs of his Miami mansion and stopped outside the office.

There was a man working at his computer. A man he didn't know. Because he had an amazing view from this room and bodyguards to protect him, John's desk faced the big windows, so the man's back was to the door.

John held his hand out, and one of his guards handed him a .22 he kept on him for this sort of thing.

He took aim and shot the man in the back. The power of the shot pushed the man forward, and then he fell out of the chair and onto the floor.

John handed the gun back to his guard and walked into the room. He didn't want to kill the man right away. Not until he knew what he was doing here.

Leaning down, John studied his computer screen, ignoring the splatter of blood.

"Ahh. I see." This man wanted to know who was involved in the shipment that went to Allison Whitlan. Frankie Whitlan's daughter. John's company delivered all sorts of things for anyone who could afford their prices. From expensive rugs legally sent from France to elephant tusks illegally sent from Africa, John's company did it all. But the illegal jobs were dealt with differently. There might be a record of a package going to a certain location, but he wasn't stupid enough to actually write "nearly extinct tiger meat inside. Handle with care" on the box.

Knowing the man hadn't found anything he could use, John stood. "Okay, guys, let's—"

John frowned. His guards were gone. He walked out into the hallway, but they weren't there, either. Had they heard a noise? Maybe, but even when that happened, one guard always stayed with John while the other investigated.

A cracking noise behind him had John spinning around. The man he'd shot was standing now, and that noise John had heard was the man cracking his back.

"You know," the man said, "it'll take them hours to get that bullet out of my back."

John didn't understand. The man hadn't been wearing a

bulletproof vest. Or any protection but a long-sleeved T-shirt. A .22 in the back might not kill, but it should still damage. A lot.

The man took a deep breath and let it out. "But I'm not going to get mad." John backed up as the man walked toward him. He turned to run, but he was caught by his neck. John fought hard. He wasn't a weak person. He had bodyguards, but he knew there was only so much they could do. He still knew how to take care of himself. Yet no matter how many times or how hard he hit the man dragging him down the hallway, John couldn't seem to hurt him.

The man took him down the stairs, down the hallway, through the kitchen and mudroom, until they were out the back door. It was late, so the woman who cleaned his house was in her little bungalow. And John knew she'd never come out to investigate. She'd learned a long time ago that was a quick way to see something she didn't want to see. Yet, even understanding that, John still screamed for help. But he knew it wouldn't make any difference.

Dragged past his pool and into his yard, the man finally stopped, and that was when John was suddenly falling . . . into an open grave.

John landed on his two bodyguards. They were alive but out cold.

He looked up and the grave was surrounded by a large group of men. It was dark out, so he couldn't make out any faces, but the light coming from the house told him it was about eight or nine males.

"You clearly don't know who I am," John warned.

"We do not care," the man said with a heavy Eastern European accent.

"I can give you anything you want."

"We want one thing. Name. Who paid for package that went to Allison Whitlan?"

John swallowed. "I don't—"

Dirt began to be shoveled onto him. All but the man with

the accent, working together to cover him. To bury him alive.

"Wait! Wait!"

The men stopped.

"Give us name," the man said. "And we go. Do not give us name, and we stay . . . 'til we are done."

John hesitated. Going against Whitlan was a very quick way to die. But when it took him longer than thirty seconds to reply, the dirt began to fall again.

"I'll tell you!" he screamed. "I'll tell you!"

"Make it quick. I grow bored."

"Bennett. Lyle Bennett. He paid for the package to be delivered to my company and then to be delivered to Allison Whitlan."

"That is very good."

Then the dirt began to rain down on John again. He screamed and begged, and after a few seconds, the dirt stopped.

"Just joke," the man said as he and the other men laughed. "We make promise, we do not break promise. But be careful who you choose to protect. It could land you in early grave."

CHAPTER 23

Livy sat on Vic's kitchen table. He'd put her there himself. But, she noticed, only after he'd put down a giant beach towel first. That was probably because she was naked, and she did appreciate his need to be tidy.

Vic, also naked, sat in a chair. Livy had her legs hanging over the edge of the table, her feet rubbing against his thighs. They both had jars of honey, spooning it out like custard.

They hadn't had sex. Not yet. Vic had just gotten her naked and gotten out the honey. But there was something about this that was way more intimate than just hitting the door and then hitting the bed.

"I heard you went head-to-head with Dee-Ann today."

Livy licked her spoon and thought on that. "Oh . . . yeah. That was today."

"You know, there aren't a lot of people who *forget* when they have to deal with Dee-Ann Smith."

"Well, when I was a kid, my dad brought a pit bull home for protection. He had eyes like hers, so every time I see her, I think, 'Oh Scruffy. I miss you so.' Then I start thinking about Scruffy and the good times we used to have until he was hit by that truck, and I eventually completely forget about Dee-Ann and whatever her issue is that particular day."

Vic laughed and Livy stretched her legs out so she could press them against Vic's chest.

That was when his laughter faded away and his gaze locked on her.

Vic dipped his spoon into the jar he held. Leaning forward, he poured the honey on her thigh. He popped the spoon back into the jar and placed it on the table behind Livy.

Bracing his arms on either side of her, Vic moved down and licked the inside of her thigh.

Vic's rough tongue against her skin had Livy groaning. She set her jar of honey down on the table so she could bury her hand in his hair. Vic growled in response, his tongue moving up higher until he licked her pussy.

Livy planted her foot on the table and spread her thighs wider. She moved Vic closer by tugging on his hair. His arms wrapped around her, and he gripped her ass with his big hands, yanking her in tight.

His face was buried between her thighs and his tongue deep inside her. Her toes curled and her body shook with every sweep of that tongue. And Livy's groans became louder until she was screaming and coming all over the man's face.

No one had ever gotten her off so fast before, but Vic's brutal tongue worked for her in ways some typical shifters' simply couldn't. And forget the full-human males. They were useless.

Vic finished licking the honey off her thigh before he lifted his head and smiled at her.

"Stop looking so proud of yourself," she snapped at him through her panting, "and get up here and fuck me."

* * *

Vic loved it when Livy snarled at him like that. He liked that he could make her lose control. She made him crazy all the time . . . why should he suffer alone?

Digging into Livy's backpack, Vic pulled out the condoms he now kept in there. He rolled one down his cock and was reaching for Livy when she landed in his lap.

Vic gasped at the feel of Livy's tight ass hitting his hard cock. She wrapped her arms around his neck and kissed him.

"You took too long," she teased when she pulled away.

"If I recall your words correctly, 'Nothing gets in here without a condom.' "

"You could have put that thing on in half the time it took you."

"It took me five seconds!"

She nipped his jaw. "Stop arguing with me and get to work."

"No." Vic stood, bringing Livy with him. He walked out of the kitchen, through the dining room, and into the living room. He stretched out on the couch, with Livy on top of him.

"*You* get to work." Vic put his hands behind his head. "And make it good, baby."

"Typical lazy feline . . . and bear," she muttered as she placed her knees on either side of his hips. "Leaving it to the honey badger to do all the work."

"That's because felines and bears are smarter than *everybody*."

Livy smirked at him, just before she dropped down hard on his cock, the wet, tight heat of her pussy trapping him as surely as any cage or handcuffs. Actually, in the past, he'd gotten himself out of a cage and several pairs of handcuffs. But he didn't think he'd ever get out of this. Even worse . . . he didn't want to. Nothing that felt this good should be something anyone tried to get away from.

With her hands pressed against his chest and her gaze on his face, Livy began to rock her hips.

Unable to keep his hands off her, Vic pulled them out from behind his head and gripped Livy's thighs.

"Tighter," she gasped out.

"What?"

"You can hold me tighter." She licked her lips. "I don't break, Vic. I *can't* break."

Vic did tighten his grip and when he did, Livy's pussy jerked in response. Something that his cock loved more than . . . anything. *Ever*.

Livy fucked him harder then. Harder. Faster. Until they were both sweating and straining against each other. Vic couldn't even think straight. He had no idea what he was doing or where the hell he was, which was when he lost complete and utter control.

They both heard the *snap* but Livy felt it, too, her body jerking forward before abruptly stopping.

Horrified, Vic watched as she turned her head and looked behind her.

That's when she asked, "You slapped my ass with your *tail*?"

"It . . . it was an accident," he said, panicking.

"Your tail?" She gawked down at him. "You have a tail when you're human?"

"When I want to. Or when I lack some self-control. But it's not like I have to tuck it into my jeans every morning or anything." Vic shrugged helplessly. "It's basically a hybrid side effect."

"It doesn't look so dangerously thick when you're in your animal form."

Vic closed his eyes. He'd lost her, hadn't he? Fangs and claws coming and going while human were typical among shifters. It was what they knew. What they were used to and comfortably accepted.

But a tail when human? No female wanted to put up with anything *that* weird. Especially a tail that sort of had a mind of its own.

"Okay." Vic opened his eyes to see Livy raising a finger. "One rule, Barinov: that thing goes in my ass . . . and I tear your balls right off. We understand each other?"

Shocked, Vic could only nod.

"Good." She grinned and added, "And can I just say . . . how cool is it that you have a prehensile tail? My tail is just this thing that does nothing but knock off flies and let other animals know when I'm about to go off. And it's only there when I'm badger. But you . . ." She stopped, blinked. "Awww, it's petting my back."

"It is?"

"Don't you know?"

"Well . . ."

"You do have control over that thing, don't you?"

"Absolutely." At least he could, with some effort. Because Vic would like to keep his balls intact. That was important to him.

"So," he asked, "you're really not freaked out by my tail?"

"Why would I be freaked out about something that's part of you? It's not like you were accidentally hit by gamma rays and you suddenly grew one. *That* would be weird. But we were born like this. My mother dropped me two days after I was born. My aunts said I bounced. I didn't even cry. I did, however, punch my mother in the face when she picked me up."

"At two days old?"

"I'm a honey badger. The woman is lucky I didn't take her eye out." She patted his chest. "See? We all have our . . . uniqueness. Yours happens to be an exceptionally cool tail. Who'd have a problem with that?"

* * *

Vic suddenly sat up, his arms wrapping tight around Livy's waist. He kissed her, and the intensity of it nearly had her coming right then. She didn't know what was going on, but she didn't really care. Not at the moment.

Holding her tight, Vic turned them so that Livy was underneath him. He braced his arms on either side of her, his big, long body looming over her. "Bring your legs up," he ordered. "High on my waist."

When she did, he growled and powered into her, his cock buried deep inside her pussy. Livy's back arched. Nothing she could remember had ever felt this good.

He fucked her hard, and Livy loved it. She wasn't intimidated by his true strength. Instead, the harder he fucked her, the more she begged him not to stop. And Livy had never begged anyone for anything. Until now. Until this moment when she came so hard, she screamed against his chest and buried her claws into his hips.

Vic roared, his body rigid beneath her claws. Then he dropped on top of her, his energy completely gone.

It took him a bit, but Vic seemed to suddenly remember she was there.

"Livy? Oh my God! Livy!" He rolled away from her. "Are you okay?"

"I'm perfect," she said on a sigh. "You're perfect. We're both perfect."

"But could you breathe?"

"Badger," she softly reminded him.

"Does that explain everything about you?"

"Pretty much."

After removing the condom and tossing it in the garbage can by the couch, Vic stretched out and pulled Livy onto his chest. He stroked her hair and kissed her forehead.

"Vic?"

"Mhmmm?"

"I'm starving."

"Oh, thank God. I'm so hungry."

"Why didn't you say anything?"

"It seemed tacky to come, roll off you, and go get something to eat. I hate tacky."

"I actually appreciate that. But right now I'm hungry."

"I've got a couple pounds of pasta and some jars of marinara sauce."

"Perfect!" Livy rolled off Vic and sprang to her feet. "Now get up. I need to feed. I'll get the—"

Livy stopped and turned to the man now standing next to her. "Did your tail just slap my ass again?"

"I think it likes when you get a little pushy."

"*It* likes when I get pushy?"

"Or we like. You know, whatever."

Livy shook her head, but took Vic's hand. "Just remember my rule."

"God, Livy, how can I ever forget it?"

CHAPTER 24

Ira stopped by her brother's house around seven-thirty in the morning. She was surprised to find his SUV parked in the driveway. He'd purchased the house located a few blocks from her home several years ago, but he was rarely in it. Like their parents, Vic traveled a lot. Mostly to Eastern European countries where he had lots of connections and knew the languages and dialects so well.

Ira used to worry so much about her brother. When he'd graduated from high school, he'd left Chicago to attend Stonybrook University and be near Ira. It made sense since their parents were always on the move, and they'd grown up watching out for each other. Vic did well in school, but Ira could tell he wasn't really happy. Then, in the middle of his junior year, he joined the marines, which was scary enough. But several years in, he was suddenly recruited by the CIA, doing most of his work in the Eastern European countries he knew so well. It turned out to be the right job for him, but Ira had not liked the idea of her brother being some kind of spy. Vic didn't blend, and he wasn't a natural deceiver. But he was smart and an excellent judge of character. In the end, the job had worked out pretty well for him, but she was glad when he'd gotten out. Even though freelance tracking work was a dangerous game, as well, she worried less about her brother since the only orders he really took were his own.

All he needed now was to get himself a business partner. Someone to watch his back, and she didn't understand why her brother didn't see Shen Li as that person. But that was okay. Vic could be stubborn, like their dad, but Ira took after their mother and would just keep hammering at her brother until he did what she thought was in his best interest.

It perhaps wasn't the best way for a family to function, but it had worked for the Barinovs for many years now.

Since Vic didn't spend much time at home, and wasn't much of a collector of anything but large quantities of honey, Ira kept many of her home business supplies in his garage and just paid her brother a monthly rent for the storage. Of course, typical Vic, he didn't bother to put any of her checks into the bank, so she eventually started transferring money over automatically every month. She loved her brother for saying that paying him wasn't necessary, but Ira never wanted him to feel taken for granted. It was better to keep her "home decorating for the discerning bear" business separate from family.

But before going into the garage, Ira decided to check the house since Vic hadn't been around.

She opened his gate and was just walking through when she heard, "Yoo-hoo! Irina!"

Ira turned and saw that She-tiger walking toward her. She had a tray of honey buns this time and looked so effortlessly perfect that Ira just wanted to bash her damn nose in.

"Hello!"

"Hi, Brittany."

The She-tiger lifted the tray a bit. "I brought honey buns as a little olive branch. I hated how we ended things last time I was here."

"You mean your judgmental overreaction to my brother's alternative lifestyle?"

"When I thought about it, I realized he was just teasing me."

Ira stared at the feline. "You sure about that?"

Bright gold eyes briefly narrowed, but the tigress managed to force a smile anyway. "I think he'll like these. They're honey."

"I can take them."

"No, no." Brittany brushed past Ira and walked toward the house. "I'd like to give them to him myself."

"He's probably asleep."

"Doubtful!"

Ira thought about picking the bitch up by the back of the head and throwing her out onto the street, but no. She wouldn't do that. Her brother was thirty-three. It was time for him to learn how to handle pushy broads like this. Preferably without his sister's protection.

Ira walked to the front door and unlocked it. Just as she stepped inside, the She-tiger pushed past her, heading right toward the kitchen. Sighing, Ira began to follow, but she abruptly stopped, sniffed the air. And she knew what she smelled in this living room . . . honey and sex.

Biting her lip to keep from giggling like a ten-year-old about to rat out her brother, Ira walked briskly through the house until she reached the kitchen. Brittany stood in the doorway, gazing into the room. She frowned in confusion.

Ira, nearly a foot taller than the feline, only had to look over her head to see that the kitchen was a mess. Open jars of honey were everywhere, in the sink was a strainer with some dried-out pasta, and a saucepan half-filled with sauce.

"I've never seen the kitchen look like this."

Neither had Ira, but sex was the great distractor. It distracted people from work, family, friends, and, of course, housecleaning.

Brittany gasped softly. "Irina," she whispered.

Ira stepped into the kitchen, but other than the mess she didn't see anything . . . until she looked down. That was when she saw Vic's big foot sticking out from under the kitchen table.

Biting her lip harder now, Ira crouched down and saw her brother, in all his naked glory, wrapped snake-like around a naked Livy Kowalski.

Now, Ira's first reaction to seeing this was, "My brother and a honey badger?" She couldn't help herself. Honey badgers had one of the worst reputations in the world of shifters *and* the world of full-blood animals. But then when she really thought about it, the whole thing actually made sense. Ira and Vic were hybrids, which meant they had unique issues. Issues that not every breed or species could handle. But from what Ira knew about Livy, the woman could handle anything but bad art and that crazy cousin of hers.

Still . . . Vic was Ira's brother. And as a sibling, she couldn't just walk out and let the lovebirds get up to face the day in their own time. That was what non-siblings did.

"Victor Barinov!" Ira yelled, imitating their mother's accent perfectly. "What you do with this girl? Nasty boy!"

Vic sat up instantly, yelling, "Mama, I'm up, I'm up!" seconds before his head rammed into the hard wood of the kitchen table.

Livy, however, went right for Ira's face. Ira caught the badger's hands first, shuddering a little when those claws that honey badgers used for digging and killing came so dangerously close.

"Oh," Livy said. "Hi, Ira."

"Ira?" Vic rubbed his head, wiped his eyes, yawned, then realized he was naked in front of his sister. "Ira! What the hell are you doing in my bedroom? Get out! Out!"

"You're not in your bedroom, genius. You're in the kitchen. Naked. With Olivia."

Vic, at a loss, roared. Ira roared back, the windows rattling from the combination of the two powerful sounds. They could have kept it up for a while until Livy screamed, *"Cut it out!"*

They both stopped and Livy looked around. "What time is it?" she asked.

Ira looked at her watch. "Almost eight."

"Shit. We should get back." Livy slid out from under the table and stood. Ira, still crouching, turned a bit so she could see Brittany's reaction, because yes, Ira was that petty.

Although Brittany appeared shell-shocked by all this, Livy didn't seem to notice. She did, however, notice the food.

"Cool. Honey buns." She grabbed two off the tray, sniffed them carefully—which did nothing but piss Brittany off—and nodded. "Thanks."

Biting into one of the buns, she walked out.

Vic managed to awkwardly get himself out from under the table, but he grabbed a dish towel and held it over his groin. "Uh . . . hi, Brittany. Um . . . yeah."

Growing increasingly red from embarrassment, her brother tried to get out of the kitchen without having to actually deal with anything. Something Ira couldn't possibly let *happen*.

"Vic, don't you want a honey bun?" she asked her brother, which got Ira a vicious feline glare from her sibling *and* his neighbor.

"Mr. Bennett will see you now."

Dez stood and walked into the office of Lyle Bennett. He was an older man, with gray hair and bright blue eyes. He smiled when she walked in, standing tall behind his big mahogany desk. He held his hand out and Dez shook it.

"Detective."

"Mr. Bennett. I won't keep you."

"No problem. I'm happy to assist our police department in any way I can." He gestured to the plush leather chair on the other side of his desk. "Please. Sit. Tell me how I can help."

Dez sat down, tried not to groan at how wonderful the office chair felt. She briefly wondered if her perpetually picky mate, Mace, would let her fill the house with these things. They were great!

"Mr. Bennett, I'm hoping you can give me some information on Frankie Whitlan."

Frowning, the man's head tilted to the side. "Frankie Whitlan?"

"Yes. The NYPD has been searching for Mr. Whitlan for quite a while now, and I was hoping you might be able to give us some information on him."

"I'm sorry. I don't think I can help you."

"Really? Huh." Dez pulled out the reporter's notebook she kept tucked into the inside pocket of the leather jacket she'd stolen from Mace years ago. Taking her time, she flipped the pad open and sifted through several pages. "Yes. Here. Over the last few years, you've sent Whitlan's daughter, Allison, several gifts through an AME Shipping Company? Isn't that correct?"

Bennett smiled even as the blood drained from his face and his bright blue eyes darkened. "Actually, I haven't. I'm not even sure what you're talking about."

"Really?" She looked at her notes again. Of course, her notes were just some doodles her son had made the night before. Talented little bastard. He did an excellent job of drawing his father's fangs. "Interesting. So you don't know Frankie Whitlan? You've never given any items to Allison Whitlan?"

"I've worked with Allison on a few charity boards that we're both on. I'm sure I've given her a few thank-you gifts over the years. But . . . that's about it."

"Oh. All right then." Dez stood, still smiling, and placed her business card on Bennett's desk. "Well, if you do hear anything or have any information, please feel free to call me. We're just trying to locate him."

"Understood."

Bennett stood and they shook hands. Dez walked out, smiled at his executive assistant as she passed her, and made her way to the elevator. Once back on the city streets, Dez got into the unmarked vehicle double-parked at the corner. Crush was in the driver's seat waiting for her. She closed the door and buckled up, and he pulled into traffic and headed to their favorite diner for breakfast.

Dez hit the speed dial on her phone and waited until Vic's partner, Shen, picked up on the other end. The panda had called in a favor early this morning, Dez's phone waking up her very not-a-morning-person mate. Normally, she didn't take orders that didn't come directly from her captain, but she still felt tracking Frankie Whitlan down was incredibly important. So if Vic and his friend needed her help, she was more than happy to do what she could.

"Hey, Shen."

"How did it go?"

"He's not going to give up any information to cops."

"I didn't think so, but I wanted to try a . . . friendlier option first."

"I was very friendly. So was he. Still, he acted like he had no idea who I was talking about."

"Okay."

"I checked his record, though. He's very clean. Squeaky. Whitlan likes to have a few of those guys around to help him move in different circles. This guy's no gangster. Not even close. Just a rich businessman thinking what he's doing is no worse than cheating on his taxes. My guess is that Bennett is weak. He'll break if you push him just a little. A push I can't legally make without evidence. So you guys will have to take it from here."

"That's fine, Dez. Thanks so much for this."

"No problem. Call if you need us again."

Dez put away her phone, and her partner grumbled, "What do you mean 'if you need *us* again'? Why are you involving me in this?"

"Because I don't feel like driving today. So suck it up, chuckles."

"You've been living with that cat too long. You're getting way rude."

Vic pulled the SUV to the curb, and Livy pushed the door open, about to jump down.

"Hey," Vic said. "Hey, hey."

"What?"

"Kiss good-bye?"

"I'm just going to work."

"Kiss *good-bye*?"

"Are you going to be a needy lover?"

"Yes."

His directness caught her off-guard and Livy laughed. "You're just so—"

"Delicious?"

"Goofy. I was going to say goofy." She put her arm around his neck and pulled Vic in for a kiss. It went on a little long, but she didn't mind. The man really knew how to kiss.

Finally, with some effort, she pulled away. "I have to go."

"But will you miss me?"

Livy shook her head. "I can't. With you. I can't."

She jumped out of the giant SUV and turned to close the door.

"I'll see you tonight at your derby bout."

Livy stopped mid-door-close. "My derby bout? How did you hear about that?"

"Blayne invited me."

"Of course she did." Livy finished closing the door and walked to the Sports Center.

On her way through, she stopped for coffee and a bagel with cream cheese. She carried those into her office, placing them on the desk beside a wooden box she didn't recognize.

"Hi, Livy!"

Livy glanced up, then back at the box. "Hi, Blayne."

"I just stopped by to make sure you're coming to the bout tonight."

"Yeah. I'll be there. But stop trying to hook me and Vic up."

"I wasn't . . . I didn't . . . yeah, okay."

"Thank you."

Blayne walked over to Livy's desk. "What's that box?"

Livy opened the box, looked inside, and said, "I think it's my father."

"Sorry?"

"This can't be all of him, though. I'm guessing Mom has the rest."

She put the top back on the box and turned to see Blayne staring at her with wide, wet eyes.

"Are you about to cry?" Livy asked.

"No. Of course not," she sobbed.

Livy moved toward Blayne and the wolfdog opened her arms for a hug. Livy stepped in close so that she could put her hands on Blayne's waist, but before those long wolfdog arms could wrap around her, Livy pushed Blayne right out of her office and closed the door in the wolfdog's wet face.

She walked back to her desk and stared down at the box for several seconds. Didn't seem like much, did it? After all humans went through to survive on this planet, when it was all said and done, you still ended up in some box on your bitter daughter's desk. Didn't really seem fair.

Picking up the box, she started to put it away in one of her many desk or file drawers, but at the last second, she couldn't do it. After looking around, she finally placed her father by the art award she'd received when she'd lived in France for those two years after high school.

Livy smiled, though, as she settled down to work, because she couldn't help but remember how much her father had always hated the French.

* * *

Vic found Livy's uncle Balt in the kitchen drinking coffee and trying to recover from what looked to be a magnificent hangover.

"How did it go?" he asked, sitting at the table across from the older man.

"We have name," Bart grumbled. "Lyle Bennett."

"Good. I'll start looking—"

"No. We had your giant panda friend track him down. He wanted to try nice way first, so I let him. But that did not work. So now my cousin and his sons are handling it." Balt rubbed his forehead. "My cousin will do good job. He is smart, like me."

"And as modest?"

Balt snorted. "Why be modest when you already know you are amazing?"

Since Vic didn't know how to argue with that logic, he didn't bother to try.

"Where is my little Olivia?" Balt asked.

"I dropped her off at work."

"Good. She needs to work. It will get her mind off things." Balt raised bloodshot eyes. "And you seem to be helping with that, as well, feline."

"Actually I'm bear *and* feline."

"Do not care."

"Yeah," Vic sighed. "Didn't think you did."

"My little Olivia is not like other girls, you know."

"I know."

"She is smart like me. Devious like her mother. And short on patience like her father. But she is good girl. Has big heart. So you do not break that heart because you get bored like most felines."

"I'm really more bear than—"

"Do not care."

"Right. Forgot."

"And just so there are no complaints later, if you two have baby—"

"Baby?"

"It will be honey badger."

Vic paused in his panic over Balt assuming he and Livy would be having children to say, "Well, actually, any children we had would be a mix of—"

"No. There will be no mix. Just badger."

"That might true be with full-humans." A shifter with a full-human mate created shifter babies, and that was one of the many reasons why shifters were very careful about whom they settled down with to create a family. Because a full-human who couldn't handle what their mates truly were definitely couldn't handle the shifter offspring they would eventually have. "But shifters of different species or breeds create hybrids."

"You mate with badger, feline, you will only get badger."

"How is that possible?"

Balt shrugged. "I do not know. Maybe honey badger cells too mean to let others live. But you will need to prepare. Badger children start throwing things in anger before they can walk."

"Balt, Livy and I aren't really at the point where we're considering children. Or anything else along those lines."

"Maybe my little Olivia is not . . . but you are. I see it in your big, dumb cat eyes."

"Well, that was unnecessarily mean."

"So understand what you get into now rather than later, yes? So you do not complain. I hate when felines complain."

"I'm really more bear than—"

"I still do not care, feline."

"I know, I know. I guess I'm just so dumb I keep forgetting."

CHAPTER 25

"Honey, are you okay?" Lyle Bennett's much younger wife asked him once he'd turned off the car and his three kids had jumped out and run into their house.

"I'm fine," he lied. "Just thinking about work."

It had been hard not to panic and start making calls about the police showing up at his office today. But he knew better. They were probably tapping his phones, waiting for him to call, so they could not only trace the call but somehow connect him to Whitlan.

Lyle had never thought the police would show up at his office door asking about Frankie Whitlan, of all people. There had been many layers between Lyle and Frankie since the man had gone on the run, and since Lyle did nothing to attract attention, he never thought anyone would link them together.

In the end, though, it was Lyle's fault. He never should have agreed to make sure those packages from Whitlan made it to Allison. But he had, even though Allison had wanted nothing to do with her father. A man who'd abandoned her before she'd even begun to crawl.

Still, Allison would never talk to the police, so there must have been another way they'd found out. Had Lindow's business finally been busted by the police? Had he turned rat in order to protect himself? Lyle didn't know, and he was afraid to look into it. Afraid the cops would be able to make a case against him based solely on his actions. What did his lawyer call it . . . evidence of a guilty mind?

But Lyle wouldn't tell any of that to his wife. His time as an associate of Whitlan's was done now that the police had showed up at his office door, and he wasn't about to involve her.

"I'll be fine."

"Okay." His wife smiled, and together they got out of the car and headed into their spacious home.

Lyle went to the kitchen, in desperate need of a scotch. He was just pouring it when he heard his wife call out, "Lyle!"

Setting his drink down, Lyle rushed down the hall. He found his wife standing in the laundry room and staring.

"What is it?" he asked, coming up next to her.

"Look at that." She pointed at a hole chewed into the wall. "Rats?" she whispered. "Do we have rats?"

Lyle crouched by the hole. It was huge, bigger than a rat would make. But it could be a raccoon or some other pest.

"Hopefully not, but—"

"Here's another." His gaze followed where his wife pointed. And yes, there was another hole.

"Were these here yesterday?"

"No. Besides, Lilah would have said something." Lilah was their maid, but she was off today. "She was doing laundry all day yesterday."

Lyle stood and decided to walk through the house. As he and his wife looked, they found more holes. In the living room, the kitchen, the playroom, the closets, the bathrooms. Not only low in the wall but in the ceilings.

"What the—"

"Dad!" one of his children screamed out. *"Dad!"*

Terrified his children had stumbled into a rat's nest, Lyle

ran up the stairs, only to crash into his children running down. They didn't even stop. They just charged past him, screaming and moving faster than he'd ever seen.

Lyle, once he'd steadied himself, continued walking up the stairs until he reached the top. That was where he stopped, his mouth dropping open, as a six-foot-long snake slithered from his eldest daughter's room and right into his son's. The snake hissed as it moved by, but then Lyle realized that he was hearing more than one hiss. He was hearing . . . several.

He began backing up as several snakes fell from a hole in the ceiling and plopped onto the floor in a slithering, hissing ball of scales.

He screamed in horror and charged down the stairs, hustling his terrified wife out the door. He got his family into the car and raced down their driveway.

Once away from the house and checked into a nice, local hotel, Lyle used his cell phone to contact the only exterminator in their small upper-class town. The woman who answered the phone promised to have someone out to his house the next day, but Lyle demanded "now" and promised to pay double the usual fee.

Leaving his family in the safety of the hotel, Lyle went back to the house and waited inside his car.

Several men showed up. Short, powerfully built men. The oldest-looking one walked over.

"You have snakes, yes?" An accent. Russian, maybe? Definitely Eastern European.

"Yes. I need you to do whatever you have to and get them out of there. All of them."

"Won't be cheap. Snake removal very expensive."

Immigrants, Lyle thought. Always looking to shake that last buck from people who shouldn't have to worry about getting snakes cleaned out of their homes.

"Yes. Whatever. Just do it."

"But first you pay."

Lyle was no fool. He wasn't about to play this game with these people. "I'll pay when you clean this up."

"We clean this up when you tell us how we find Frankie Whitlan."

Lyle blinked, took a step back. "What?"

"Frankie Whitlan. You contact him yourself? Or he only contacts you?"

Lyle took another step back, but one of the other burly men was now standing behind him. Somehow they'd managed to surround him.

"I don't under—"

"Do you talk to him yourself? Or does he call *you*?"

"I don't know any Frankie Whitlan."

"Don't lie, rich man. You get gifts from Whitlan and have them delivered to Whitlan's pretty little daughter?"

"Look, I don't know who you people are, but—"

"Just tell us. Then we clean your house and we go. No money needed. Just information. *Truthful* information."

"Or," the man behind him said, the younger man's English perfect, if low-class, "the next batch of snakes will be poisonous . . . and in your bed."

Lyle looked at the men surrounding him. They all had dark, *dark* eyes. Eyes that watched him, waited for him to do something stupid.

Protecting Frankie Whitlan wasn't worth all this. It would *never* would be worth this.

"I haven't been in contact with Whitlan for years. Not directly. He doesn't call me, and I don't call him." The men waited, so Lyle continued. "But I help with . . . managing his money in some foreign accounts."

"Who?" the older man pushed. "Who do you talk to about Whitlan's money?"

"Rob . . . Rob Yardley. That's who I work with. Whoever his connections are, they talk right to Whitlan themselves."

"Good, rich man. Very good. Now . . . you go back to hotel and to your pretty wife and lovely children. You stay there for night. By tomorrow . . . everything will be done. Clean like whistle." Several of the men walked into the house; Lyle had left the door open when he'd fled. "And," the older man said, "you will keep mouth shut. You won't warn Yardley or anyone else. And you say nothing to police, yes? Because that would make us very angry. Not something you want, rich man."

As if to punctuate that, one of the men walked out of the house, a snake wrapped around his fist. That was disturbing enough, but then Lyle realized that the head of the snake was gone, the body just limp, and there was blood covering the lower half of the man's face. And the man was . . . chewing.

Lyle felt bile working its way up the back of his throat, his hand slapping over his mouth.

The older man laughed. "Go, rich man. Go to your nice family. You stay out of this, and we won't be back, yes? And that make you happy. Never to see the likes of us again?" He laughed again, slapped Lyle on the back, which almost had Lyle vomiting right there. "Go, and be happy this will be worst of it for you."

Lyle did. He went back to his car, his wife and children at the hotel, and he tried—for the rest of his life—to forget the last thing he'd heard before he'd closed the car door and driven away from the house he was already planning to sell.

The older man yelling out, "Come, all my beautiful sons! It is time for us to *feed*!"

CHAPTER 26

Vic had changed clothes. Not into anything too fancy. Just his black jeans, black boots, black sweater, and his knee-length black leather jacket. He figured that after the bout, he could take Livy out for dinner. Again, nothing too fancy, but nice.

He walked down the stairs and Livy's cousin Jake came in the front door. He caught sight of Vic and stopped. "Where you off to?"

"What makes you think I'm going anywhere?"

"You shaved."

"Really? I shave and that means I'm going out?"

"Yes."

"God, you're just like your cousin."

Jake smiled. "She is me. I am her. Are you taking her out tonight?"

"She has a derby bout. If she's up to it after, I thought—"

"Derby?" Shen suddenly barreled out of the living room. "You're going to a roller derby bout?"

"Yeah."

"Can I come, or do I have to stay here and keep an eye on the Jean-Louis Parkers?"

"Well, since you completely freaked them out the last time I asked you to do that—"

"Why did I freak them out? I didn't do anything."

"You stared at them for three hours straight until they were forced to go to bed."

"You said keep an eye on them . . . that's what I did. It's not my fault they're sensitive jackals."

"I'm not going out tonight," Jake said. "I'll make sure they're fine."

Vic, satisfied with that since he knew how much Livy trusted her cousin, asked, "Any word yet about Lyle Bennett?"

"Yeah." Jake yawned, scratched his neck. "We got a name from him. It sounded vaguely fancy British."

"Do you remember the name?"

The badger thought a moment, then replied, "Yardley. Rob Yardley. Any guy named Rob Yardley shouldn't be too hard to break."

"No," Vic said quickly. "Don't do anything yet."

"You know him?"

"I know of him. He's a gambler."

"That's even better."

"No. It's not. Don't do anything until you hear back from me. Understand?"

Jake studied Vic a moment, nodded. "Okay."

Vic pointed toward the living room. "And you'll watch . . ."

"It's covered. Go. Have a good time."

Vic and Shen walked out of the house. Shen waited until they were halfway down the block before he asked, "Who the hell is Rob Yardley?"

"A gambler who used to be under the protection of Grigori Volkov."

Shen stopped walking. "Grigori? He's under the protection of *Grigori*?"

"Calm down."

"Calm down? Didn't you say that Livy's family thinks a shifter must be involved?"

"It can't be Grigori."

"Why? Because you like him? Because you went to his

daughter's wedding in Moscow? Because your mother calls him her little *konfetka*?"

"My mother calls everyone her little *konfetka*. It just means 'sweetie.'"

"All I'm saying is, I hope you're being smart about this. I know you like Grigori, Vic, but he's still a gangster."

"I'll talk to him tomorrow."

"That doesn't sound like you're being smart."

"What do you want me to do? Let the Kowalskis meet with him? That can only end badly, and you know it. I'll deal with it. Tomorrow."

"Okay," Shen agreed. "But I really hope you know what you're doing."

Livy walked into the locker room to put on her gear and get ready for that evening's bout. A few of her teammates called out greetings, some muttered condolences for her father. And Livy simply nodded to all of it and moved on until she reached her locker.

Thankfully, no one on her team expected more from her. Olivia didn't eat, sleep, and dream roller derby like most of these girls. For her, it was simply a great way to work off aggression legally. At least legally among shifters. She couldn't get away with half the shit she'd done if she were on a full-human derby team.

The love of the sport, though, was the same for both full-humans and shifters. These girls bought their own gear, did all their own team marketing, and paid for all travel out of their own pocket. They didn't get even a tenth of the trappings that the bigger sports teams received, and yet they didn't care. Livy liked that, too. It cut down on the egos considerably when *no one* was signing million-dollar contracts.

Blayne and Gwen walked in and were greeted enthusiastically by the rest of the team. They'd both become team co-captains last year when Pop-A-Cherry, the old team captain, got pregnant. Once the liger's child was older, she'd probably get right back out on the track, but for now, she was working from home. She did still manage the team's website, T-shirt marketing, and fund-raising, though.

Gwen, a tigon and Blayne's best friend, stopped by Livy. "What are you doing here?"

"Blayne wanted me at tonight's bout."

"She did? Why?"

"Because she invited Vic Barinov, whom she seems to have discovered I've been fucking, and wants to get us married and popping out babies as soon as possible."

"And she thinks all that will happen after he sees *you* playing derby?"

Livy looked over at Gwen . . . smirked.

Gwen's eyes crossed. "I really hate when you two start doing this shit." She walked to her locker. "I really, *really* hate it."

And yet Livy enjoyed it all so much.

As promised, Blayne had a ticket waiting for Vic at the box office. And when he mentioned he needed to buy one for a friend, they gave him one more. For free.

Confused, Vic asked, "Don't I have to pay for this extra ticket?"

The fox behind the window shook his head. "There are seats available in that section."

What did that have to do with anything? "Yeah, but . . . don't I still have to pay for it?"

The fox chuckled. "No one wants to sit in that section. Trust me."

Unsure what was going on, Vic walked back to a waiting Shen. He handed him his ticket.

"How much do I owe you?"

"Nothing. They didn't charge me anything."

"That's cool, huh?"

"Yeah. I guess. Unless they're really shitty seats."

"Jeez, Vic. You really need to learn to relax. Shitty seats. Great seats. Who cares?"

Shen was right. Vic was overthinking things.

They entered one of the smaller coliseums, which was packed with shifters of every breed and species, including hybrids.

Considering they'd gotten free tickets, Vic expected their seats to be way up in the rafters. But those seats were already filled with people.

"We're down here," Shen said, pointing.

"Are you sure?"

"I think so."

They walked down the stairs until they reached the row indicated on their ticket stubs. The seats were nice, plush, and they would be close to the action.

Vic, focusing on the arms of the seats so that he could follow the numbers, went down the line, silently counting until he was forced to stop by very long legs that looked like someone had cut off a couple of tree stumps and covered them in denim.

"Excuse me," he said. "I'm in that seat . . ."

His words faded away when he saw who was sitting between him and his seat. Bo Novikov.

Vic locked eyes with the polar bear–lion hybrid and his instincts took complete control. Especially when he saw Novikov's eyes shift from blue to gold and his hair suddenly drop to his shoulders like a big mane of rage.

They both roared at each other. Novikov leaped out of his seat, the pair of them ramming their foreheads together, fangs unleashing to warn of great bloodshed. It was all very primal and something Vic couldn't control when he got around certain hybrids. Namely Bo Novikov.

"That is enough!" a voice yelled over the roaring. Vic was pushed one way and Novikov the other.

"I am *not* going to put up with this bullshit through the

whole bout. Now get some control!" That from Lachlan "Lock" MacRyrie. Vic knew him through Dee-Ann. He was a friendly enough bear . . . until annoyed. And he was clearly annoyed because Vic could see the man's grizzly hump starting to grow. "Barinov, you and your friend sit over here. Novikov . . . sit down. Now."

MacRyrie placed himself between Vic and Novikov.

Once they were all seated, Shen whispered to Vic, "What is it about that guy that ticks you off so much?"

"I have no idea," Vic whispered back. "I don't even know the man. But I get around him and all I want to do is tear his head off and wear it like a hat."

Shen laughed. "I love hybrids. You guys are always so fucked up. And it's always so random!"

Now that everything had calmed down, MacRyrie nodded at Vic. "Hey, Barinov."

"MacRyrie. This is Shen Li."

"Vic's business partner," Shen volunteered.

Vic gritted his teeth.

"This your first bout?" MacRyrie asked.

"Yeah. Blayne invited me."

At the mention of Blayne's name, Novikov looked around MacRyrie and snarled at Vic, baring extremely long fangs. Vic roared back.

"I have no problem killing both of you," MacRyrie snapped. "And keep in mind, I used to kill for a living."

Well aware that MacRyrie used to be in the same Marine unit as Dee-Ann, a unit that hunted the hunters, Vic decided not to push the issue. Thankfully, neither did Novikov.

"So how does this work?" Vic asked MacRyrie.

"The jammer has to pass as many of the opposing team as possible within two minutes. The problem is, the jammer has got to get past the blockers—and they don't want to let her do that."

Vic stretched his neck, trying to loosen the tension there. "I'm going to be so bored."

"You might like it."

"Vic hates sports," Shen explained.

"I don't hate sports. I just don't understand its purpose in my universe."

MacRyrie grinned. "I get that, too. Not everyone enjoys sports of any kind. But if it helps, the players on this derby team all wear tiny shorts and tank tops."

Vic shrugged. "That actually does help."

Two lion males walked to the empty seats in front of Vic's. At first, he was annoyed. Those manes would just disrupt his viewing pleasure. But then he saw the face of one of the lions.

"Hey, Mitch!"

Mitch Shaw turned and smiled. "Vic!" They shook hands. "How ya doin', man?"

"Pretty good."

"What are you doing back here? I thought you were still in Albania?"

"Nah. Doing a local job. This is Shen Li," Vic said, pointing at the panda. "Shen, this is Mitch Shaw. He works for Bobby Ray's security company. I get a lot of work from them."

"This is my brother, Brendon Shaw."

"You're not going to say hi to me?"

The lions' expressions turning to disgust, matching gold gazes moved from Vic and Shen to MacRyrie.

"We are going to be family, after all," MacRyrie added. "Doesn't that mean anything to you two?"

Vic watched the felines fight their desire to rip MacRyrie apart, finally settling on ignoring the man altogether.

Mitch nodded at Vic. "We may have some work coming up for you soon. I'll let you know."

"Great."

With one more glare at MacRyrie, the two cats sat down in their seats.

"What was that about?" Vic asked the grizzly.

"Nothing really." MacRyrie grinned. "I'm just marrying their sister."

The main lights were turned off and AC/DC's "Back in Black" was cranked up. Colored strobe lights moved across the track, and a female announcer who sounded like she needed to lay off the cigarettes said:

"Ladies and gentlemen, cats and dogs, foxes and bears. It's what you've been waiting for . . . what you've been needing . . . what you've been *craving*. Now is the time and this is the hour for you to finally get exactly what you deserve! And tonight it's the ruling champions against the angriest bitches on the block. So welcome, one and all . . . to Buroughs Brawlers Banked Track Derby!

"Let's give a big hand to our first team, the toughest bitches on the East Coast . . . the Jamaica Me Howlers!"

The first team came out on the track, fists pumping, screaming at the crowd, working to get everyone psyched up for the bout. When each team member was introduced, depending on the breed or species, different parts of the auditorium erupted in applause and cheers.

Yet even with those cute, tight outfits on the players, Vic could already tell he was losing interest. He finally pulled out his cell phone and opened up a book on Stalin that his father had told him he might find interesting. "Although," his father had added, "nothing about that fistfight he had with your grandfather over woman."

While Vic read, he stopped listening to the announcements and the music that was playing and the teams. What could he say? He really was not a sports fan. Not even when it involved hot girls. But then suddenly Vic heard booing and hissing. It came out of nowhere and seemed strange since he hadn't heard any of that before. And when he looked up, he saw that Livy was moving across the track.

"And it's the woman you love to hate, the bitch you know to fear . . . it's The Bringer of the *Pain*!"

That was when the booing got even worse.

Horrified, Vic watched Livy, wondering if this was why she didn't play all the games. Because everyone was so mean to her.

The Bringer of the Pain, aka Livy, stopped on the track, looked out over the booing, hissing, *screaming* crowd, and raised both her arms to about chest height, middle fingers extended from each fist. She stuck her tongue out and made some gestures with it that he was not entirely comfortable with her using outside the bedroom, and then turned on her skates and basically told them all to kiss her ass.

But he knew Livy well enough now to know that she wasn't upset. No. She was enjoying herself. She liked being the bad guy of the derby world. The one everyone hated. And without the usual confinements of a relatively polite society, she was able to express her own feelings right back.

Of course, Vic figured out within the first ten minutes of the game why Livy was hated and why she had earned her particular derby name.

Because Olivia Kowalski brought the pain to *everyone*.

The whistle blew and Livy unwrapped herself from the She-lion's head and landed on the track. She shook the blood off her hands.

Livy glanced up in time to see the She-lion bring her head down. The woman's forehead smashed into Livy's face, and blood began to pour from her nose and mouth. The She-lion skated backward, a middle finger raised. If this had happened during the jam, Livy wouldn't have had a problem. As far as she was concerned, anything that happened during the jam was just what happened. But this was done after the whistle, and that pissed Livy off.

She shot after the cat, ready to tear her apart; Livy's claws unleashed, her fangs out.

The two teams charged out onto the track, Livy's team blocking her from reaching the cat, Blayne and Gwen wrapping their arms around her and desperately holding Livy back. The other team simply stood in front of their teammate, ready to protect her from the honey badger that most teams in the league referred to as "that bitch."

The refs, a husband and wife bear team, ordered the track cleared, and a sixty-second break was taken.

Livy was pushed back to the team's infield and forced onto the bench.

Blayne crouched in front of her. "You need to calm down," Blayne slowly explained as if she were talking to a child. "Vic is in the audience."

Livy blinked and wiped blood from her nose. "So?"

"You don't want him to see you doing something that will completely freak him out. When I saw Bo for the first time, I was *positive* the man was a serial killer. It took quite a while to figure out he wasn't. He's just a tough player. Like you. But men are less patient than women. He may not hang around to find out the true you. Is that what you want?"

That was when Livy pushed Blayne to the ground. Not too hard, but hard enough to get her point across.

"What was that for?" Blayne demanded.

"Your face was irritating me."

"Okay." Gwen motioned the wolfdog away. "Enough."

"I was just trying to help!" Blayne snarled before skating off.

Gwen sat down next to Livy and handed her a wet cloth. "Clean your face," she ordered.

"You all right?" Gwen asked when Livy was done.

Livy readjusted her nose until she felt certain all the broken pieces were close enough so that when her nose healed it wouldn't look hideous, then replied, "Yes."

"Good. Now let this go."

"It was *after* the whistle—"

"Let it *go*. Understand?"

"Yes."

"Good." Gwen stood. "You rest, we'll bring you in for the jam when we're ready."

Livy nodded, spit blood to clear out her mouth, and waited.

"I don't understand why they don't use her more," Novikov said about Livy. "They keep holding her back, only using her for some bouts . . . I don't get it."

Halfway through a foot-long hot dog, MacRyrie noted, "We had a honey badger on the hockey team a few years back."

"Yeah?"

"He's doing fifteen to life in Sing Sing after an unfortunate post-game situation that took place in front of full-humans."

"Yeah, but was he good at hockey?"

MacRyrie glanced at Vic before replying to Novikov, "Not as good as you'd think."

"See, but Livy's good," Novikov went on, oblivious. "I wish she could ice-skate." He leaned forward so that he could see Vic. "Does she ice-skate?"

"How should I know?"

"How can you not know? Blayne says you're hot for her."

MacRyrie rolled his eyes. "I think you were supposed to keep that to yourself, brain trust."

"Did Blayne say that?" Vic asked.

"Yes, but I stopped listening as soon as I realized it was about someone else's love life. Someone I don't even really like." Novikov looked at Vic. "Not Livy. She's cool. It's you I don't really like. Don't know why, though. But you do irritate me."

"Shut up."

"Did you," MacRyrie cut in, "stop listening to the conversation because you were busy trying to figure out how to get Livy on our team?"

"Someone has to worry about the welfare of this goddamn team. You and that overrated cook certainly don't."

"Overrated cook? Do you mean your boss?"

"Whoever. I'm the only one doing the work."

While the two males bickered, Vic turned to Shen. "How do they know about me and Livy?"

"Everybody knows about you and Livy. Even the twelve-year-old knows. He said something about creating a sculpture of you two that glorifies the wonders of love as well as a paper on the damaging psychological effects of romance on the creative psyche." Shen ate some popcorn, a needed change from his bamboo, before adding, "That kid's weird. He freaks me out. He is cute, though."

Vic, tired of all the idiots, looked back at the track. Livy was skating out for the next jam. So was the She-lion who had struck her.

"This won't end well," Shen muttered.

Vic had to agree. Especially when the lioness looked back and grinned at Livy. The honey badger's lack of response worried him more than if she'd lunged at the woman.

The whistle blew and the pack took off, Gwen and a jammer from the opposing team waiting to start their part of the game play.

As the two teams jostled for position, Livy moved through the players until she was able to cut in front of the She-lion. Livy didn't ram into her as Vic expected, but she did drag her leg a bit so that the lioness tripped and fell to the ground. The two teams passed by, but Livy skated back and grabbed her opponent by her foot. Then, with strength Vic had been unaware she had, Livy yanked the woman up and spun. Once, twice . . . like the male partner in an ice-dancing team. On the third spin, he noticed that Livy had moved closer to one of the foundation pillars that helped keep the entire Sports Center upright.

And that was probably why Livy used it, angling the She-lion so that the woman's knee cracked against the hard and unforgiving concrete.

The triumphant roar Livy let out when the knee made direct and brutal contact with the pillar managed to silence the entire stadium.

Silence until Bo Novikov stood and applauded. "Now that's what I'm talking about!"

Livy looked up at their section and performed a very princess-like curtsy.

The fact that the She-lion was just a few feet from her, sobbing in pain, was a tad . . . off-putting, though.

The ref skated toward Livy, but she raised a forefinger, waved it. "No need," she said to him. "I'm leaving."

"Oh, come on!" Novikov yelled at the ref. "That was a totally righteous move! You're an idiot!"

MacRyrie sighed. "Now he's arguing with the refs of sports completely unrelated to hockey."

Shen jabbed his elbow into Vic's side.

"What?"

"You better go check on your girlfriend."

"I never said Livy was my girlfriend."

"But you knew who I was talking about."

"He's right," MacRyrie agreed. "That was kind of a giveaway."

Vic briefly closed his eyes. "And to think I could have stayed at home with the weird kid . . ."

Livy made her way down to the locker room and found Vic waiting for her. Probably because she'd stopped several times to sign autographs for the few honey badgers who actually came to these bouts. They were her biggest fans. Okay. They were her *only* fans.

She skated up to him.

"Hi."

Toe tapping, arms crossed over his chest, he seemed unable to look at her. And this was why she hadn't invited him to any of her bouts. Because she kind of knew he wouldn't be okay with the way she played. *Sportsmanship* was not a word she'd been taught as a child. Winning at all costs no matter who one destroys in the process had been her parents' belief system, and it had been the one thing she'd agreed with, of course with the caveat that cheating wasn't allowed unless it was a life-and-death situation. This had made family Monopoly night a little strained when she kept winning despite her parents' stealing money and moving things around on the board when she wasn't looking.

But the way she'd been raised had not been how Victor Barinov, son of Russian shifter diplomats, had been raised.

She decided to let him off the hook.

"Look, Vic—"

Livy's words were cut off when a snarling Vic suddenly picked her up and shoved his tongue in her mouth.

Hitting his chest, Livy forced Vic to set her down on the floor.

Panting, they glared at each other until Livy asked, "This is the feline side of you right now, isn't it?"

Vic cracked his neck and spit out between clenched fangs, "Probably."

Livy reached up and grabbed Vic's leather jacket. "Now we're gettin' kinky!" she cheered and shoved him into the team's locker room.

Blayne waited anxiously until Gwen skated back to the infield.

"Well?" Blayne asked, sorry she'd ever asked Livy to play in tonight's bout. It was such a mistake. She'd just wanted Vic to see her looking sexy in her derby outfit and how well she could play. But she hadn't counted on a cheap shot by a She-lion with a grudge. No. She hadn't counted on that at all.

Gwen stopped in front of Blayne, and the rest of the team surrounded her while they waited for the next jam to be called.

"Well?" Blayne asked again.

"She's fine. Let's just leave it at that."

"What do you mean, she's fine? Fine okay? Or fine as in she's resigned to a life of loneliness without Vic?"

"Uh . . . well . . ." Gwen looked at her feet, bit her lip.

"Gwenie?"

The tigon cleared her throat. "Vic's with her."

"Oh! Good. Are they talking?"

"Talking? No. They're not talking."

"They're not?" Blayne winced. "That's not good."

"I wouldn't say that, either."

Blayne studied her friend. "What are you trying to say?"

"Yeah," one of their teammates asked, "what *are* you trying to say?"

"I'll just say this," Gwen teased, "they were in the bathroom annnnnd . . . skates-up, ladies. Skates-up!"

Blayne knew she was blushing even while the rest of her team laughed and applauded, but she couldn't help it. "In the *bathroom*, dude?"

"Like you haven't gone skates-up in the bathroom with Novikov."

"I didn't say that, either . . ." Laughing, Blayne covered her face and Gwen dropped her elbow on Blayne's shoulder.

"Good work, crazy girl," Gwen whispered. "Another perfect Blayne match."

"Oh, shut up."

CHAPTER 27

About a felony assault, and a good fuck in the Sports Center bathroom while she had her skates on, and Livy was ready to go home. But no one had asked her what she wanted. Instead, her team, the Babes, had preyed on poor, defenseless Vic. He'd worked the feline out of him by fucking her. Once the cat was gone, all that was left was a weak-willed grizzly who couldn't stand up to a few perky broads.

So, where was she now? A bar. Something else she wouldn't mind. A good felony was always nicely topped off with a stiff drink. But this wasn't just a bar . . . it was a karaoke bar in the Village. A group of the wild dogs who lived across the street from the brownstone were in attendance. Not all of them, though. The wild dogs split up their activities so there was always a group with the pups. It seemed nice, but Livy wasn't sure she could deal with that many people in her life, all day, every day. She barely tolerated having to deal with herself, much less a crowd.

"I don't believe it," Vic muttered with a snarl.

Livy looked up from her untouched shot of vodka, her nose twitching as it continued to heal. "What?"

"It's your cousins."

Uh-oh.

"I'll make sure they don't start anything with—"

"That's not what's bothering me. Jake is with them. I told him to stay and protect the Jean-Louis Parkers."

Livy waved that off. "Coop, Cherise, and Kyle are with the wild dogs across the street. Coop wants Kyle to be around other children. Normal children. Or as normal as wild dogs can be . . . which, when you think about it, is a hell of a lot more normal than any of the Jean-Louis Parkers. Coop texted me, and I made him promise to stay with the Packs until we get back tonight."

"The Packs?"

"Some of the Smiths are there. They never leave the wild dogs on their own now that Jess Ward's hillbilly spouse has a spawn."

Vic smiled. "That was so romantic."

"I'm all about true love."

Then she laughed. Although even Livy had to admit it sounded a bit sinister.

"Hey, cousin," Jake said as he sat down in their booth. "And her giant boy toy."

Jake took Livy's vodka and swallowed it in one gulp. He stuck his tongue out, disgusted. "You call that vodka?"

"I tried to tell her," Vic complained.

"What are you two . . . friends now?"

They didn't answer. Vic just pushed his vodka over to Jake. Her cousin took it, drank it, and grinned.

"You really should listen to this man."

"I am Russian," Vic said in a thick accent. "Vodka I know."

"I hate you," Livy admitted, "because you sound really hot when you do that accent."

Vic leaned in and murmured in that damn accent, "I can do it more . . . just for you."

"Stop *it*. We're stuck here 'cause of you."

"Who can turn Blayne down? There were tears."

"With Blayne there's always tears! And it works on every one of you pathetic males."

"You're the one doing her wedding," Vic reminded her.

"For a fuck-load of money, hybrid."

Jake smiled. "You two make a cute couple."

"Shut up," Livy shot back.

Having been told to shut up lots of times by Livy, Jake was more interested in what was happening on the stage.

"What the hell am I listening to?"

"Someone's really bad version of 'The Safety Dance.'" She stared at Jake and said it again. "'The Safety Dance.'"

Jake patted Livy's shoulder and stood. "Now, now. No need to get homicidal. Jake is here to handle everything."

Vic watched Jake make his way to the stage. "What did he mean? What's he going to handle?"

Feeling surprisingly playful, Livy stared at Vic and said with deep meaning, "You don't want to know, baby. You don't want to know."

Jess giggled and pressed her face into Bobby Ray Smith's neck.

"That ain't right, y'all," he said, laughing. "Callin' that sort of thing 'skates-up' is just wrong."

"If your skates are resting on his shoulders . . . that's skates-up," Gwen explained, her hand wrapped around a bottle of Guinness, her butt on Lock's lap. "Although the height difference is so huge between the two, they were really resting on his arms."

Blayne smiled, very happy to be here with her friends and her mate.

"Hey, Gwen." Jess took a bottle of ice-cold Coke from the waitress. "I heard your dad's coming in for the wedding."

"He is."

Jess's face dropped. "I thought you'd be happy about that."

"I am. But he's bringing his sisters. That means my mother and her sisters against my dad's sisters. She-lions versus She-tigers. *That* I do not look forward to."

"My uncles will attempt to keep them busy," Lock reminded her. "I believe they are looking forward to it."

"My father's sisters will chew them up and spit them out. But I'm relatively certain your uncles will enjoy that while it lasts."

Mitch came over to the table. Brendon had gone to be with Ronnie Lee and his baby, which Blayne was starting to secretly worry was possessed with a demon of some kind. Or maybe that was just what happened when one combined feline and canine DNA.

Mitch tried to sit in the booth, but that would mean Bo would have to get out of his way. With Blayne on his lap, Bo didn't seem inclined to bother.

"Could you move?" Mitch asked.

"I could . . . but I won't."

Rolling his eyes, Mitch grabbed a chair from one of the other tables and slammed it down in front of them. "There are honey badgers here," he announced.

"I thought you liked Livy," Blayne said, sipping her sugar-free Mountain Dew.

"Not just Livy. There's a bunch of them now."

Gwen lifted her head a bit. Nodded. "And one of them is heading for the stage."

"But I was enjoying the wild dog version of 'The Safety Dance.' "

Bo shook his head at Blayne. "No, you weren't. Please don't lie."

"I was *trying* to enjoy it. Okay? Happy now?" She crinkled up her nose a bit. "I'm not sure I'm in the mood for a song that a honey badger would sing, though."

"Why not?"

"One time at the Sports Center I saw Livy sitting on the

floor, wearing earbuds. I asked her what she was listening to. Turns out it was the Lords of Acid. Tech music with a lot of singing about fucking, which I'm fine with. But what freaked me out was that she was just sitting there. Like she was meditating. Who listens to dance music that talks about fucking and doesn't move?"

"A honey badger who coldly and brutally crushed the kneecap of a She-lion who pissed her off?" Lock asked.

The male honey badger got on stage. He'd already chosen a song, and it began to play. But when he started to sing without even looking at the words on the screen, Blayne didn't know if she should be charmed or completely and utterly freaked the fuck out.

"'The Piña Colada Song?'" Mitch asked them, flabbergasted. "Honey badgers like 'The Piña Colada Song'?"

"No," Gwen observed, her gaze moving over the crowd. "They *love* it."

Obviously, since they'd all moved to the stage to sing along, some raising lighters in the air, others just their arms. They waved and they sang.

But when Livy got up on the stage with that badger, put her arm around his shoulders, and sang along with him, Blayne was sure about one thing . . .

"The world's about to end!" she announced cheerfully, certain that if the Rapture was coming, she'd done enough good in her life to ensure her passage to Paradise. "Because I'm sure this is a sign of the End of Days."

Mitch stared at Blayne for a good minute before he agreed, "It's 'The Piña Colada Song.' And honey badgers. It just doesn't seem right, does it?"

Livy sat back down beside Vic. "'The Piña Colada Song'?" he asked.

"It's a family favorite. Played at all Kowalski weddings, along with every polka song you can think of."

Vic scratched his head, stared at Livy, until he finally asked, *"Polka?"*

It was enough of a shock that the karaoke machine actually had polka music on it. But it was even more startling to see Livy up on the stage with Jake and Jocelyn, singing along . . . in Polish.

Vic had thought he knew Livy . . . but he didn't know her at all. She was, however, fascinating.

Freaky, yes. But fascinating.

"You need to make this stop."

Vic looked up to see Novikov standing over him.

"Come on," Vic said. "I know the Novikov name. You're Russian like I am, and we have polka, too."

"I'm half-Russian and half-Mongolian, but that's not the point. Blayne likes the polka music. She now wants it at our wedding. So we can dance to it. Dance to polka. Me."

"I'm sure your Cossack ancestors would happily dance to polka music at their weddings. You should feel honored. It's probably a family tradition."

"It is not a family tradition."

Vic snorted. "It is now."

The pair sized each other up until Novikov asked, "Why don't I want to kill you right now?"

"Remember that song the wild dog sang a few minutes ago?"

" 'The Lion Sleeps Tonight'?"

"That's the one. Your lion's asleep."

"Pardon?"

"You had a couple of drinks, right?"

"Yeah."

"The feline part of you is out cold, numbed by the alcohol and lack of danger. I had a couple of vodka shots, so my tiger is out for the night. My grizzly, however, is up and ready to party." Vic grinned. "Wanna dance?"

"Not with a dude."

"See? The polar gives a rational response to my question. If the male lion in you had been awake when I asked that, we'd be tearing each other apart and destroying this quaint bar right now to sadly prove how manly we both are."

Novikov thought on that, shrugged, and replied, "Yeah. Whatever. Is that vodka you were drinking good?"

Vic grinned. "The best. Let's get some."

Livy and Jake helped Vic up the stairs to the Jean-Louis Parker rental home. Blayne, who was sober, ended up driving Vic's SUV back to the house. She and Novikov would then spend the night at the wild dog house across the street.

"He weighs a ton, Livy," Jake complained.

"Put your back into it. We're almost there."

"Move," Novikov said, pushing Livy and Jake away.

"Hello, my hybrid brother!" Vic crowed.

"Christ, Novikov," Jake demanded. "How much vodka did you give him?"

"I don't know. A bottle. Or two." He then picked Vic up in a fireman carry, and Livy rushed up the stairs to unlock the door.

Novikov carried him to their room, dropping Vic onto the bed.

"Can you make it back to the wild dog house?" Livy asked.

"Of course," Bo snapped. "I'm not weak like him. I'm strong. Cossack strong."

Then Novikov walked into a wall, stumbled back, and passed out on the floor by the bed.

Livy stared down at the two snoring, drunk males. "Well . . . I'll go tell Blayne that Novikov is staying here for the night."

"Hey, cousin."

"What?"

"Think we can get some signed jerseys from Novikov?"

Livy faced Jake. "Are you asking because you've suddenly become a hockey fan, or do you just want to sell them for some outrageous sum to very rich European shifters?"

Jake shrugged. "Does it matter?"

Sighing, Livy walked away from her cousin and went to track down Blayne.

CHAPTER 28

Livy felt someone stroke her hair, and she looked up to see a showered, shaved, and expertly dressed Vic crouching beside the bed she'd gone to sleep in the night before, when she'd left him and Novikov snoring in the other bedroom.

"What time is it?" she asked.

"Almost eight. You going in to work?"

"Sure. Where are you going?"

"Have to go meet someone."

"A woman?"

"No. Why?"

"You're all dressed up."

"There are some people you don't meet looking shabby."

Livy snorted. "You're meeting a Russian mobster?"

Vic blinked, his entire body tensing. "How did you know that?"

"You ask me these questions when you *know* I come from a family of unrepentant felons."

He chuckled and kissed her. "I'll call you when I'm done. Novikov's already gone to get in his training. So don't worry about him."

"I wasn't planning to worry about him," she sighed out, snuggling into her pillow. "Be careful."

Vic stopped in the doorway and gazed at her a moment before replying in Polish, "I will."

That was when she realized she'd actually cautioned him in Polish. A language she reserved for talking to her family. And it was like Vic understood the significance of that slip.

Livy, however, refused to dwell on it. Refused.

Vic met Grigori Volkov in a private dining room above the Russian restaurant the mobster owned with his Pack deep in the heart of Brighton Beach.

The Volkov Pack out of Moscow had a rich and violent history. Some American Packs referred to them as the Smiths of Eastern Europe. An insult that had started many a mauling back in the day.

The two men were sitting at a small round table dwarfed by their size, cups of coffee poured for them by a pretty She-wolf waitress.

"It's good to see you again, Victor Barinov," Grigori cheered. Unlike many wolves, the older male was a typically happy canine, but his cheerfulness hid a dangerous side that no one really wanted to face without body armor and an escape route. "It has been long time."

"It has, Grigori. And it's good to see you, too. I hope all is well with you and your Pack."

"Very well. The streets of this city are paved with gold and need. My two favorite things."

Vic smiled, hating himself a little for liking the mobster so much.

"My brothers handle Russia. I handle business here. It all goes well for the Volkovs. But I know you're not here to catch up on old times, dear Victor. So, what has you coming to Grigori?"

"I've been looking into something for someone. And I came across a name that I know was associated with you and your Pack in the past. Don't know about now, but before anyone moves forward—"

"You want to make sure no ugly lines are crossed. You are so thoughtful for man with feline mother."

"A feline mother who turned you down for a date, I believe."

"She did. Big mistake. You could have been *my* son. All this could have been yours."

"Oh, let's admit that your mother never would have let that happen. She'd have seen you and my mother dead first."

"Excellent point. My sweet mother does hate felines more than fleas in heat of summer." He flicked his hand. "But that is past. Tell me this name and we will go from there."

"Rob Yardley."

And Vic felt it. In that moment. In that second. The air went out of the room. The other wolves who played chess and watched TV nearby slowly looked at him.

Immediately, Vic raised his hands. "Not a problem. I'll—"

"Quiet," Grigori snapped. He looked around the room. "Everyone *out*!" The wolves slowly got to their extremely large feet. *"Move as if there is purpose!"* Grigori bellowed.

Within seconds, the room cleared out, leaving the two males alone.

"Listen, Grigori—" Vic began.

"No, Victor. No. I speak to you as friend who came to my little girl's wedding. The friend who saved my life many years back."

"Grigori, come on. We paid each other back for all those things many years ago."

"No. I used to think, how do I pay back man who saved life when he is not part of Pack or family or breed? But now . . . now I can pay you back."

Vic was suddenly very confused. "What are you talking about?"

"Yardley is degenerate gambler."

"You love degenerate gamblers."

"Yes. And he owed me much money. But I sold his debt to another."

Vic leaned back in his chair. "You *sold* his debt? After you broke his legs or arms or something?"

"No." Grigori leaned in, lowered his voice. "I would have not sold his debt because I like people who owe me to pay me back themselves. But I did it anyway. What does that tell you, Victor Barinov?"

"That Stalin himself came back from the dead and paid Yardley's debt? That's the only reason I can think of that might prompt you into doing something you don't want to do."

Grigori looked off. "Zombies do terrify me, but no." He looked back at Vic. "I admit this only to you, my friend. But there is only one man I would ever think of giving in to since the *untimely* death of my father."

Vic blinked at the statement. The death of Grigori's father had been untimely . . . because he'd been murdered in the streets of Moscow. Cut down in full view of passersby with a knife against his throat. A murder that no one had ever been tried for because the one who'd used that blade had been . . .

Vic let out a breath. "Chumakov? Rostislav Chumakov? *He* bought Yardley's debt from you?"

"It sickened me. To give that man anything. But you know why I did it."

To protect his Pack. To protect his children and mate. Because all of them would have been at risk if Grigori had said no.

"You must back away from this, Victor Barinov. I tell you this as my friend. Because if he hears you look for those connected to him, even a rumor . . ."

"I can't."

"Victor—"

"No, no. I mean . . . I have no problem backing away. But those I'm helping—they will never back off, Grigori. They will never back away."

"Are they foolish full-humans? Because what species or breed would not back away from Rostislav Chuma—"

"Honey badgers."

"Oh," Grigori said, his usually cheerful canine eyes suddenly looking very sad for Vic. "Oh, my friend . . . we would be better if this involved zombies."

Vic walked out of the restaurant and over to his SUV. He rested against the vehicle, wondering how he was going to handle this.

And that was where he stayed for a good hour—with absolutely no ideas on what to do next.

So he did what he always did when he didn't know what to do next.

Vic pulled his phone out of his back pocket and hit the speed dial. When he heard the voice on the other side, he sighed out gratefully.

"Papa," he said in Russian, "I need you."

CHAPTER 29

Livy placed the two prints side by side on the work desk at the far side of her office and stepped back. They were both prints of one of the shots she'd taken of Vic, but she'd played with each differently. Now she was trying to decide which to put in her show.

With her arms crossed over her chest and one hand pressed against her mouth, she studied the work with a critical eye now rather than a strictly artistic one. She needed to see the flaws that others would see and fix them. The problem was, she could only see Vic in these prints.

"Livy!" Blayne cheered as she charged into Livy's office. For once, the wolfdog didn't have on her skates, but was dressed in work pants, work boots, and a worn sweatshirt with B&G PLUMBING scrawled across the front.

"Hi, Blayne," Livy said, her attention drawn right back to her prints. "What do you think?" she asked.

"You should go home."

Livy blinked, studied the prints a little harder. "Are they that bad?"

"Is what that bad?"

"The prints." Livy gestured to her work by raising her elbow.

"Oh." Blayne looked at the prints. "Oh my God. They're beautiful."

"Thanks."

"Is that Vic?"

"Yeah."

"Is he naked?"

"Mostly."

"Yowza."

Livy couldn't help but nod. "I know, right?" She turned to Blayne. "Wait. If it's not the pics, why should I go home?"

"Huh? Oh! Yeah. That She-lion from last night?"

"She-lion?"

"The one whose knee you crushed?" Livy shrugged. "At derby last night?" Livy continued to stare. "You were thrown out of the bout early because of it?" Livy stared some more. "Then you went skates-up with Vic in the team locker room?"

"Oh yeah. What about her?"

Blayne scratched her head and said, "Yeah, her Pride's here and looking for you. They want you to handle her medical bills because she had to have surgery on her knee to fix it correctly. I know you won't do that because . . . well, you're *you*. So Cella wants you to go away while she handles them."

"Why?" she asked. "I can tell them to suck up their own goddamn bills myself."

"No!" Blayne cleared her throat. "I mean . . . that's not necessary. Cella will handle it for us."

Livy smirked. "You afraid I'll do something bad, Blayne?"

"Of course not! It's just . . . why make the situation worse? Right?"

"If I go home, I'm not coming back, and you've got that stupid wedding meeting you keep insisting I need to come to, so—"

"Just make yourself scarce. Out of your office. For a little bit. I promise, me or Bo will track you down when it's safe."

"It's safe now," Livy reasoned. "I don't have a problem talking to some bitchy cats."

"Livy!"

Rolling her eyes, Livy grabbed her camera off the desk and her backpack. "No need to get hysterical, Mighty Mutt. I'll take the back stairs down and see if I can get some random shots of the gymnastics team. If you or Bo don't know where that is, ask one of the other hockey players. They *do* know where to find the gymnasts."

Blayne snorted. "Thanks, Livy."

Livy walked out of her office and down the hall to one of the stairwells that could be used during an emergency. It was a quick way to get back up to the street and out of the building without alerting the full-human populace to the presence of people who ranged in sizes from five feet to more than seven-and-a-half and had eyes that reflected nearby street lamps. Very important during night games.

Livy had only made it one flight when she heard female voices coming the other way. She sniffed the air and immediately scented She-lions.

Yeah, Malone might be currently showing that Pride Livy's empty office to prove she wasn't there, but cats were always smarter than that. Whoever was in charge had sent a separate bunch up another way to see if they could track Livy down.

Grinning, she eased open the door she'd stopped in front of and stepped out of the stairwell. She carefully closed the door and waited. The She-lions were loud and so busy shit-talking about what they were planning to do to "that little rat girl"—and the other name for honey badgers was *ratel,* not rat—that Livy didn't actually have to strain her ears to know when they'd passed, nor did she worry too much about their scenting her out.

Yeah. You could always tell the city shifters from the country ones. The country ones knew how to actually hunt.

Livy heard the door close on the floor she'd just escaped from, and she went back into the stairwell. She went down another flight of stairs and opened the door.

But before Livy could step through, she was flying back and down the stairs she'd been tossed on until she hit the wall.

Laughing, she looked up the stairs to tell the cats to fuck off . . . but it wasn't bitter She-lions blocking her on both the stairs leading up and the ones leading down.

There were bears. Big, brooding bears. And she quickly figured out how much trouble she was in when one of the bears walked down the stairs, crouched in front of her, and greeted her in Russian with, "Hello, little badger. You should have left your father dead and stuffed."

Blayne was starting to think that having Cella handle this wasn't any better an idea than having Livy handle it.

She-tiger versus She-lions had begun to get pretty nasty, pretty fast.

So she was grateful when she saw Gwen come through the training rink doors for their three o'clock meeting with Cella's mother, who was now part of the current argument going on.

"What the hell is this?" Gwen asked, dropping her backpack to the floor. Gwen had just come from a job and was also dressed in her work clothes like Blayne.

"The sisters and cousins of the Howler Livy got into it with at last night's bout."

"Why are Cella and her mother arguing with them?"

"Cella offered to handle them."

"And you agreed to that?"

Blayne shrugged. "It seemed like a good idea at the time. It's not like Livy's going to pay for anyone's medical bills."

Gwen rolled her eyes. "Is that what this is about?"

"Pretty much."

"You make everything so complicated," Gwen complained.

"What did I do?"

Her best friend walked away without answering, but she pointed at Bo and Lock, who were eating ice cream and watching the fight with obvious bear-enthusiasm.

"You two . . . go get Livy."

"Can't we watch the fight?" Lock asked.

Gwen stopped, put her hands on her hips, and glared at her mate.

"Okay, okay. It was just a question."

Lock got up and gestured to Bo.

Bo shrugged. "What do I need to go for? He can bring back Livy without me."

"Do you really think the rest of their Pride isn't around here somewhere looking for Livy right now? They're She-lions. That's how they hunt. So get off your ass, Novikov, and find her before the rest of the Pride does. Then escort her back here; you'll be her protection."

Sighing, Bo stood.

"She's two floors down photographing the gymnasts," Blayne told them. And, as Livy had suggested, it had been Bo's hockey teammates who'd told her where to find the gymnasts.

Gwen was near the arguing cats when one of the She-lions shoved Cella. Knowing exactly what that would lead to, Gwen ran between the females, slapping her hands against Cella and holding her back. Then she did what Blayne knew her best friend in the universe would do. Gwen turned just her head one hundred and eighty degrees until it lined up with her spine and told the She-lions behind her to, "Back the fuck off!"

The She-lions roared and scrambled away from Gwen and her "freaky little neck thing." Freaky it might be, but that move had ended several fights over the years and scared off more than a few drunken frat boys, as well, without either Gwen or Blayne having to bloody their claws. So Blayne definitely saw it as a hybrid benefit.

The kick to the gut sent Livy into the wall. Then the bear crouched in front of her again. He helped Livy sit up by wrapping his hand around her throat, and pulling her up while squeezing.

"You," he said now in accented English, "should have left this alone, little badger. You should have taken your father and buried him and forgotten all about it. But you did not. So you leave us no choice."

He threw her into the other wall and stood. Livy, coughing and trying to breathe, saw the bear and two others pull guns. With care, the bears screwed silencers onto their weapons, and pointed. Livy only had time to pull herself into a tight ball and grit her teeth, and endure the pain as the bullets tore into her back, hip, and ass.

Lock, busy staring at a bunch of really sturdy women and girls doing amazing backflips across mats and launching themselves off pommel horses, heard a noise he hadn't heard since he'd been a Marine in a shifter-only unit that used to hunt the hunters of their kind.

Turning, he walked out of the training room, tossing his ice cream cone into a nearby trash can. Bo came up behind him. He still had his ice cream.

"I didn't see Livy in there. So, where are we going now?"

Lock didn't answer; he just followed his ears. He reached the end of the hall and pushed the door open. He stepped into the stairwell and saw Livy's crumpled body in a corner, blood pouring from multiple gunshot wounds. Three grizzlies stood over her with guns drawn. A black bear at the bottom of one set of stairs and another black bear at the top of the other were just watching.

Novikov's ice cream cone hit the ground, and the hybrid's mane dropped to his shoulders as his body began to shake with rage. Lock knew it was rage because his own grizzly hump had grown three times in the last two seconds, his claws easing out of his hands, his fangs out of his gums.

The black bear at the bottom of the stairs looked back, his eyes growing wide at the sight of them.

"Jasha!" he yelled out, his hand reaching for the gun he had under his jacket.

Novikov was down the stairs and had the black bear's hand in his. Then he crushed both gun and hand.

The black bear roared in pain as the other bears spun around, their weapons now pointed at Novikov and Lock.

One of them yelled out something in a language Lock didn't know, and all the bears suddenly focused on the hybrid.

And none of them took a shot.

Instead, the bears began to back away from them. They still had their guns trained on both males, but they didn't fire once, and one had his free hand up, speaking to Novikov. What he was saying, though, Lock had no idea.

But when they smiled and nodded at Novikov, Lock suddenly understood that these bears were hockey fans. Fans who didn't want to hurt Bo "The Marauder" Novikov.

Disgusted, he wondered if these idiots really thought that either Lock or Novikov would ever consider letting them get away with shooting some helpless woman to death in a stairwell.

At least that was what he was thinking until that helpless dead woman slowly and silently pulled herself up into a crouch and unleashed her obscenely long claws.

Taking her time, Livy moved until she was right beneath

one of the other bears. She waited a beat, two . . . and rammed those claws between the bear's legs. His agonized roar of pain rang out as Livy twisted her claw, dragged it out a bit, readjusted, then rammed it back in again.

The uninjured black bear aimed his gun at Livy, but she caught hold of it with her other hand and stood. She yanked at the gun, but he didn't give it up, so she went up on her toes and slashed the shorter bear across the face. He screamed, one of his eyes landing a few feet away.

Livy took the black bear's gun from his now-weakened grip, and Lock grabbed Novikov from behind. He yanked his teammate up the stairs and dropped them both to the ground as shots hit the wall and door where they'd just stood.

In a few seconds, it was all over, and together, he and Novikov stood and walked to the top of the stairs, looking down at all those dead bears and Livy. Who was not dead.

Without her head moving, her gaze lifted to Lock's. He saw the rage in her black eyes. Something he'd never seen from her before. He'd seen her annoyed, but never truly angry. But as blood wept from her many wounds and her body shook, Lock wasn't exactly surprised when Livy unleashed a roar of her own.

Lock pulled out his cell phone. When the call was answered, he said, "Dee-Ann . . . we have a *major* problem."

After arranging his parents' flight to the States, and their hotel room at the Kingston Arms, Vic and Shen went to the Sports Center. Vic had already lost an hour of his life arguing with Livy's uncles, and the last thing he wanted was for her to hear the latest from them.

So it was with the intent of telling her what was going on that he walked into her office, freezing halfway into the room when he saw giant pictures of his naked self on her desk.

"Oh my God."

Shen came in behind him, his cell phone ring of zoo pandas eating bamboo really annoying Vic at the moment.

Looking for the phone in his jacket, Shen laughed and pointed at the big prints. "Is that *you*?" He laughed harder. "I can't wait until your mother sees *that*. This is Shen," he said into the phone.

A few seconds later, Shen walked out of the room and Vic stood there, staring.

"She can't seriously be planning to show these to anyone . . . can she?"

Vic stepped back to rest his ass against Livy's desk, but as he did he saw her camera there.

Frowning, Vic picked it up, disturbed by the rattling sounds coming from inside it. The high-end Nikon had been seriously damaged. The lens appeared torn out, the body of the camera battered. Then he noticed the blood covering the back of it.

Vic lifted his head and saw Shen standing in the doorway, his friend staring at him silently, his phone still in the hand hanging limply at his side.

"Where is she, Shen?" Vic asked. "Where's Livy?"

CHAPTER 30

Shen had insisted on driving, which was probably a good idea. Vic couldn't think straight. He couldn't focus. He could barely breathe.

They arrived at a house on Long Island in the middle of what Vic knew was Malone family territory. The Malone tigers were descended from Irish Travellers and would take over entire streets so that strangers couldn't wander in and get into their business.

Shen parked the truck next to a silver BMW that Vic recognized. It belonged to Livy's uncle Balt. It seemed her family had been informed about what had happened before Vic. Something he was not happy about but not really interested in at the moment.

Vic stepped out of the truck, and he heard a screen door open. He scanned the street and saw Cella Malone standing on the porch. She waved and Vic walked toward her, Shen following behind.

Cella let him into the house, and without a word, led him through the home, to the kitchen, and down into a finished basement.

As he made it down the stairs, Vic stopped. Livy's family

filled the room. The older aunts and uncles sitting on couches and chairs, the younger nieces, nephews, and cousins on the floor.

Vic looked at Cella and she moved forward, stepping around the badgers until she reached a room. She opened the door and Vic walked in.

A black woman, whom Vic scented as a mountain lion, leaned over an unconscious Livy, pulling bullets out of the honey badger with surgical instruments. She didn't wear a mask, but she'd managed to get on latex gloves. Still, it was obvious to Vic she'd gotten right to work as soon as Livy hit the table because the sleeves of her bright white cashmere sweater were haphazardly rolled up and the front covered in blood splatters.

The woman glanced up, and Vic recognized her from the Sports Center. He'd occasionally seen her hanging around Cella Malone's office, but he didn't know her personally.

"I'm almost done," the woman said. "I'll be out in a little bit."

Cella motioned Vic out, and he stepped back into the other room. She closed the door and stood in front of it.

Vic stood there for a bit, but he couldn't take it. He walked up the stairs and out of the house. He rested his arms against the fence that circled the property and took deep breaths, trying to calm down. It wasn't working.

"Vic?"

He looked down to see Blayne and Gwen staring up at him.

Gwen shook her head. "He's about to have a hybrid break."

"We have to calm him down," Blayne said.

"No time for that," a voice barked. Big hands grabbed Vic from behind and pushed him out of the gate and into the street. Vic looked back to see Novikov holding him.

"Can't . . . can't breathe . . ." Vic panted out.

"Breathing's not your problem." Novikov looked around and finally pointed at an old but well-maintained bright red '78 Camaro. "That one."

"What . . . what?"

Novikov took Vic's hands and placed them on the car. "Do it, Barinov. It's the only thing that'll stop you from killing everyone in a five-mile radius. Just do it."

Vic didn't know what Novikov was talking about. He didn't understand anything right now. He just knew he couldn't breathe. He couldn't think. He couldn't do anything because something inside him was breaking loose and . . . and . . . and . . .

Blayne bit her lip and winced as Vic Barinov picked up that Camaro and sent it flipping and rolling down the street.

"Hey!" Dee-Ann said, running out of the house. *"That's my car!"*

Blayne caught Dee-Ann before she could run into the street, and threw them both to the ground seconds before Vic's roar of rage and emotional pain was unleashed. House and car windows exploded up and down the street as car alarms blared.

After Vic had roared himself out, Bo placed his hand on Vic's shoulder and steered him toward the house. "I'll take him back inside."

Dee-Ann finally lifted her head. *"What the holy fuck was that?"*

Gwen, who'd dived to the ground on the other side of Blayne, lifted her head and said, "It's called a hybrid break. They're rare, but they happen."

"And what about my car?"

"If it hadn't been the car," Gwen explained, "it would have been *everyone else*."

Blayne offered, with a smile, "Think of it as a sacrifice for the good of all!"

"Shut up, poodle!"
"Or I can shut up."

Coop stretched out on the couch and turned up the sound on the living room stereo. The strains of Vivaldi filled the entire space around him, and he relaxed into that. But before he could really lose himself in the work of a master, he heard the front door open and suddenly there were wolves standing around the couch, staring down at him.

Muting the sound, Coop sat up. "Hi, Ric."

Ulrich Van Holtz forced a smile at Coop, gave a small nod. "Hi, Cooper. Are Cherise and Kyle around?"

"Cherise is practicing in the basement, and Kyle is sketching in the kitchen. Why?"

Ric glanced over at Reece Lee Reed and his brother Rory Lee. At one time, Coop couldn't tell the difference between one Smith Pack wolf and another. But he'd met quite a few since his family had become friends with the Kuznetsov Pack wild dogs.

The Reeds went off in search of Cherise and Kyle, Coop guessed, while Ric continued to stare down at him. "I'm going to need you guys to pack. I have a car and driver waiting to take you to the airport. The Van Holtz jet will be taking you back to Washington tonight."

"Tonight? Why? What's happened?"

"There's been a problem, and it's for your safety and the safety of your siblings."

Coop got to his feet. "Where's Livy?"

"We can discuss that—"

"Where is Livy?"

"She's been hurt."

"Then I need to see her."

"No. She's been taken to a safe place, and there's nothing you can do for her right now. But your safety is of utmost concern. So we're taking you home. The Van Holtz Pack will watch out for you and your family once you get there. And Rory and Reece will travel with you on the jet."

"How bad is she?"

Ric took a breath before he answered. "Pretty bad."

"I need to let Toni know."

"She's being notified. But we need to get you and your siblings out of here . . . now. Understand?"

Sadly, Coop understood all too well.

Ivan Zubachev watched Antonella Jean-Louis Parker rub her face in exasperation. Ivan didn't know why he enjoyed tormenting the little canine, but he did. Maybe because she looked so adorable when she was frustrated. Ahhh. If he were only twenty years younger, the wolf she'd chosen to be her mate wouldn't have a chance against Ivan Zubachev. He'd have happily stolen her heart from him or any other worthless male dog.

But that wasn't really an option. He had his own mate whom he not only loved, but feared quite a bit. She could be mean when she thought he wasn't paying enough attention to her, but he liked her strength and she did make him laugh.

So that left Ivan with only the tormenting of the little canine. Like he was doing now.

"Are you really arguing this one point with me, Ivan?" she demanded. "Are you really?"

"It is important, little doggie."

"It is *not* important. And stop calling me 'little doggie.'" She looked at her watch. "Oh, come on, Ivan. It's already after—"

"I know what time it is, my tiny puppy."

She started to protest her new nickname, so Ivan quickly reminded her that, "You said I could not call you little doggie. So I did not."

"You're doing this on purpose, aren't you, Ivan? You're making this difficult simply to *be* difficult."

"That is crazy talk, my dear Antonella. Now, about the breeding females you will provide to my players—"

"I will *not* provide females of *any* kind to your players or to you. Ever!"

Ivan held up his forefinger. "Hold. We must discuss."

The little canine rolled her eyes while Ivan pushed his chair back a bit, his team's coach, manager, and three of his sons surrounding him.

"We should go out to eat when we are done here," he said to them in Russian.

"I am hungry," his eldest son replied.

"Maybe steak?" the coach suggested.

"We'll bring the little canine with us . . . and the Smith."

"Does he have to come?"

"She won't come without him," Ivan sighed.

"Too bad."

Thinking he'd tortured Antonella enough, Ivan rolled his chair back to the table. But before he had a chance to speak, the conference room door opened and "the Smith" walked quickly into the room. With a phone gripped in his hand, he crouched by Antonella's side and began to whisper to her. Ivan watched the color drain from Antonella's beautiful face, saw shock in her eyes.

His younger son came into the room and hurried to Ivan's side.

"What happened?"

"There's been an attack on her friend in New York. It was *very* bad." His son leaned in closer and whispered, "It was Russian bears."

Ivan reared back a bit. Everyone knew that Antonella Jean-Louis Parker and her family and friends were under Ivan's protection, even if Antonella Jean-Louis Parker had no idea of that.

"Who?" Ivan demanded. "Who did this?"

His son's lip curled. "Chumakov."

"I'm sorry, Ivan," Antonella said, her voice as shaky as her body. "I have to leave now. I . . . have to go home."

"Yes." Ivan stood. "You do. And it will be my jet that takes you home. And we . . . we will escort you back."

"That's not necessary," she started to argue.

"Oh . . . it is, my little doggie," Ivan growled out, his gaze briefly straying to the American wolf standing straight and tall by Antonella. "It is *absolutely* necessary."

Cella stepped back and her best friend, Jai Davis, MD, stepped out of the room, closing the door behind her.

"Well?" Cella pushed after turning her back away from the honey badger family members waiting to hear about Livy's condition.

"The next twenty-four hours will tell. I don't want her moved yet, but if she suddenly gets worse or doesn't wake up by tomorrow, we're going to have to take her to a hospital."

"The shifter-run one on Old Country Road?"

"Yes. I have privileges there, and I already have a call in to Dr. Ford. He's an arrogant male lion I have thought about beating to death on more than one occasion, but he was a combat doctor for several tours. He would know how to deal with this if it gets bad."

"Good. But we need to be careful who we involve in this. We don't know if Chumakov's men are still around. Whether they know Livy survived or not, and if they do know she survived, if they're waiting to take another—"

Cella's words stopped abruptly when the door behind her and Jai opened, and a naked Livy walked out.

"What time is it?" the badger asked.

"What the fuck are you doing up?" Jai snarled.

"Did you get all the bullets out?" Livy asked in her usual calm tone.

"I believe so—"

"Then I'm fine."

Livy gave a short whistle at one of the badgers on the floor and someone threw her a T-shirt. She pulled it on, then stopped to bend and twist her back. Something cracked into place, and she gave a little head shake. "There we go." Livy looked around. "Where's Vic? I thought I heard his voice."

"Upstairs."

Livy patted Jai on the shoulder. "Nice work, doctor. Thank you."

They watched the honey badger confidently step over and around her relatives as she walked through the basement in only a T-shirt. Cella would admit she was no surgeon, but the predator in her knew when another animal was strong and would be too much trouble to attempt to kill unless you were starving—which was what Cella saw when she watched Livy.

"Cella?" Jai asked.

"Huh?"

"I gave that woman enough pain medication to take out an elephant with a strong constitution. I pretty much put her in a short-term coma so her body could heal."

"Okay."

"So, it was a really great idea," Jai softly pointed out, "bringing a dangerous, unstable species to our home where our daughters live. A species that is apparently impossible to kill. Next time you should just bring in a serial killer. Or an atomic bomb!"

"Drink this."

Vic looked at the cup Novikov held out to him. "What is it?"

"Tea."

"What kind of tea?"

"Earl Grey."

"Just Earl Grey?"

"As opposed to . . . ?"

"Some magic tea for hybrids that will calm me down?"

Novikov looked deep into the cup. "I didn't know there was a magic tea. That's kind of cool."

"I don't know what I'm going to do," Vic said, deciding he was done with the tea conversation. "What if she—"

"Don't. Don't do that to yourself. I almost killed my annoying, asshole cousin because I started what-if-ing about Blayne when she was hurt bad once. But Dr. Davis is really good. Let's just wait and see what she says."

"Okay." Vic lifted his tea. "Thanks for this."

"No problem. Blayne always says hybrids have to stick together. Maybe she's right."

They both looked up at the same time, nodded at Livy, and went back to their conversation.

"My parents are coming tomorrow," Vic said.

"To visit? Or about this?"

"About this *before* anyone went after Livy."

"Have you arranged to have them picked up from the airport?"

"I was going to do it—"

"You can't go now. Give me their information and I'll arrange a car to pick them up."

"Thanks, man, that's really—"

Vic abruptly stopped talking and jerked around. "Olivia?"

She grinned. "Were you really the one who fucked up Smith's car?" Livy asked. "Because she's still in the house snarling about—"

Vic shot off the bench, picked Livy up in his arms, and held her against his chest. He needed to feel her. He needed to feel her skin against his, know that she was warm and safe in his arms.

"Now that we're dealing with awkward emotions," Novikov muttered, "I'm going . . . away."

The back door of the house opened and closed, leaving Vic alone with Livy.

Vic, unable to help himself, held her tighter.

"I'm okay," she whispered, her legs wrapping around his waist, her arms clinging to his neck. "I really am."

"I thought I lost you," he admitted against her neck.

"You know my kind is too mean to go out that easy. We make a man work for it."

"Olivia—"

"Hey." She pulled back, and urged his head up with her hands, forcing him to look her in those dark eyes. "They failed. They tried to kill me, and they failed. So I'm not going to sit around and think about what was supposed to happen or what could have happened or anything else. I don't care about any of that."

"The problem is, I do care. I care about you, Livy. So, pretending this didn't happen and just—"

"We can't pretend this didn't happen, Vic. We won't."

"We?"

Livy glanced over, and Vic saw that the once-empty yard was now filled with Livy's family. They silently stood there, in the brutal cold, watching and waiting. Waiting for Livy.

"So," she said, her lips grazing his cheek, "this isn't about what might have happened. This is about what's going to happen. What we're *going* to make happen."

"Which is?"

"We knew," Balt said, stepping away from his relatives, "that a shifter might be involved in luring my brother to his death. But we were willing to settle for this Whitlan. No use starting war when all we wanted was him. But now? Now we want war."

Vic understood that on many, *many* levels. And he also knew the shifter code that even the honey badgers abided by . . . you never betray your own for a full-human. The ones who'd shot Livy had done just that. Not just the gunmen, but the one who'd sent them into a shifter-protected space and had them shoot down a fellow shifter. Not over a territorial clash. Or lusting after someone's mate. Or even just annoyance with their presence on this planet. No. She'd been gunned down merely for the continued protection of Whitlan and because the man behind those gunmen wanted to prove he was not to be fucked with by anyone.

Bad move, though, when dealing with this particular species. Shooting Livy hadn't made the rest of her family afraid. These were not people who backed off or backed down. These were not people who understood normal, everyday fear.

Instead of making a point, the attack would bring nothing but blood and death and pain.

"We will not stay here," Balt said, his suspicious gaze studying the entire yard. "But I think our safe houses may not be so safe anymore."

Vic silently agreed. Livy's attackers had known exactly where to find her. So it was a safe bet that the Kowalski and Yang safe houses were compromised, as well.

"I can get us a safe place."

"Vic"—Livy's hand pressed against his jaw, turning his face toward her—"you don't have to get into the middle of this."

That was where Livy was wrong. Vic was already in the middle of this. Deep in the middle. There was no way he would walk away now. He couldn't even if he wanted to. Because where Livy went, he would always follow.

Of course, this wasn't the time to tell her all that. She might be up and walking around, but she was still recovering, and he could see the exhaustion on her face. So any talk about what their future together might hold would have to wait.

Unable to say what he really felt, Vic just kissed Livy on the nose and said to Balt, "Let's get out of here."

* * *

"Jesus, Mary, and Joseph, Smith!" Cella snapped. "My brother said he'd take your car to his body shop and fix it. And one of those badgers already handed over an ungodly-sized wad of cash to pay for everything Barinov's roar destroyed, including your car. So enough with the dog whining like you got your paw stuck in a gopher hole."

"I can fix my own car, Malone. It's just, you don't mess with a woman's automobile. Do you have any idea how much work I put into that thing after I won it from Sissy Mae?"

"I don't care."

"Well, thank you very much."

The pair sat on the stone wall that partially surrounded the house Cella had grown up in. The rest of the fence and the gate were chain-link and could hardly handle the combined weight of Cella and Dee-Ann's collective asses.

"What's really going on with you?" Cella finally asked the female who'd somehow managed to become a very good friend. Although that still surprised her. Because Dee-Ann was such a canine sometimes.

"What?"

"It's not just your car that's bothering you. Is it what happened to Livy?"

"Not really."

"As always, such a caring person."

"Look, the whole thing don't sit right with me. I mean, to outright shoot that girl."

"You expected more from Whitlan?"

"Darlin', this is no longer about Whitlan. Those bears tracked Kowalski down at the Sports Center. And they were out-of-town bears, not even from this country, but they found her anyway." Smith turned a bit so she could look right at Cella, and leaned in a bit. "And don't it bother you a little bit that our bosses pulled us off the Whitlan case?"

"They didn't pull us off . . . they just gave us other jobs and lowered the priority of the Whitlan case." Cella winced. Even she couldn't make that sound positive. But still. "Dee-Ann, you can't possibly think that KZS, The Group, and BPC—"

"Are busy protecting Frank Whitlan?" She shook her head. "Nah. That don't sit right with me, either. But something about all this seems . . . expected somehow. By everyone but us and that poor little honey badger."

"Poor little honey badger, my hefty Irish ass. She walked out of the surgery without even a limp. Jai said she took sixteen bullets out of her. *Sixteen!* Who gets up from that?"

"Well, we better start talkin' to her and Barinov, if we want to know what the hell is goin' on."

"Cella?"

Cella looked over her shoulder to see her mother standing on the porch. "What's up, Ma?"

"I was about to order food for all those badgers . . . but they're gone."

Cella twisted around. "What do you mean, gone?"

"I mean, they're gone. We searched the house."

"I just saw them no more than thirty minutes ago, Malone," Smith said. "No way they would have gotten past either of us without our knowing."

"Did you check the yard?" Cella asked her mother.

"We haven't searched it, but I'm sure I'd spot that many people standing in our backyard from the dining room window."

Cella looked at Dee-Ann, and they both jumped from the stone wall and ran around the house to the backyard.

Her parents' house was surrounded by Malone family homes on both sides and in the back. So Cella assumed that the badgers must have just snuck out that way rather than going through the front. She decided to ask the uncle who lived behind her parents first, since she could see him in his backyard taking out the trash. But as Cella ran across the yard, she felt the earth go out from underneath her and used the power of her legs to launch her body across the yard. She landed a good ten feet away and spun around to see that Smith had not been so lucky.

Cella ran back, stopping at the edge of what she realized now was a pit in her parents' backyard. A pit Dee-Ann Smith had fallen into face-first.

Crouching, Cella looked down at the poor She-wolf just getting back to her feet. "Are you okay?"

"Why is there a pit in your backyard, Malone?"

"There wasn't." She gestured with an arm wave. "Look behind you."

Smith did. Then, with her arms thrown up, she exclaimed, "They *burrowed* out of here?" Dee-Ann looked at Cella. *"Burrowed?"*

"Clearly this whole thing doesn't sit right with the honey badgers, either."

"Or Vic. He and that giant panda went through here, too."

"Any suggestions where we go from here?"

Smith held up her finger, and still facing Cella, she jumped up and back. A skill only the She-wolf shifters seemed to have.

Landing on the side of the pit, Smith stood and lifted her nose to the air. She sniffed a few times, then headed over to Jai's house, on the right side of Cella's. Jai and her family were the only people unrelated by blood or marriage to the Malones allowed to live on this street.

When they reached Jai's backyard, they found her, Blayne, Bo, Gwen, and Lock sitting at the patio table drinking big mugs of hot chocolate.

Smith stopped in front of the table. "Where are they?"

"Where's who?" Blayne asked, looking particularly sweet. Something that Cella was certain was only going to piss Dee-Ann off.

Smith took an aggressive step. "Now listen to me, poodle—"

Bo slammed his fist on the table, which was thankfully made of stone rather than wood. *"Tone,"* he snarled at Dee-Ann.

The She-wolf's eyes narrowed, and Cella quickly stepped in front of her while Jai softly excused herself, picked up her mug of hot chocolate, and went back into her house. She stood by the open sliding-glass doors so she could watch the entertainment, but she was a mountain lion. She wasn't about to get into the middle of a predator fight unless she absolutely had to.

"We're all friends here," Cella reminded everyone. "So let's calm the hell down." Cella took a breath. "We just want to know where we can find Livy and Vic. We really need to talk to them." The small group, three of which were hybrids, stared at Cella but didn't say anything. "Are you really not going to tell us?" Cella demanded. "I'm your coach," she reminded Bo and Lock.

"But you're not asking as our coach," Bo said. "Our coach doesn't care because Vic and Livy don't play for her team."

"You guys, we just want to help."

"Then leave them alone," Lock suggested, his shoulders hunched. "I'm sure if at some point the honey badgers need you, we'll all know."

Yeah, but that was kind of what worried Cella. Because by the time they knew anything, it would probably already be too late.

CHAPTER 31

Livy woke up in a strange bed and she knew she'd been placed there, because she would have put herself either under the bed or in one of the kitchen cabinets.

The last thing Livy remembered was sitting next to Vic in his SUV. Her body had been exhausted and she'd felt safe, so she'd gone to sleep. And based on the sunlight peeking through the blinds, she must have slept through the night.

Naked, Livy slipped out of bed. When she stood, she immediately felt how tight her muscles had become. Especially in her right shoulder, where she'd been hit many times as the gunmen had attempted to reach her head. That was the only thing that had saved her life. No clear head shot, which was the surest and quickest way to kill a honey badger.

Starting with her neck and shoulders, Livy proceeded to stretch out all those muscles. Moving down her body until she could easily bend over at the waist and touch her toes.

Livy let out a relieved sigh. It felt good to move. Hell, it felt good to breathe. She was even looking forward to shooting Blayne's wedding. Then again, how could she ever think to complain now? It had been MacRyrie and Novikov who'd saved her life. Their timing had prevented the head shot she'd known was coming; Novikov's fame among the Eastern Europeans had distracted the gunman while Livy got to her feet.

Of course, her behavior *after* she got to her feet might be considered an overreaction by most people, but by honey badger standards, Livy was just being true to herself. She felt a little strange about it, but she didn't feel guilty. She would never feel guilty. She was just grateful she hadn't had to deal with the cleanup. She hated cleaning up.

Still bent over at the waist, Livy wiggled her fingers and attempted to stretch a little farther down.

"Now I understand," a woman's heavily accented voice said from behind Livy, "what my son sees in you."

Livy slowly rolled back up and turned to face the woman standing in the bedroom doorway. The tigress smiled at her, and Livy saw Vic in that smile. "You do not startle easily, I see. That is good."

The She-tiger walked into the room, all the while sizing Livy up. "We were just listening to tales of your troubles. I was sorry to hear what happened to your father. I knew him, you know. We were not friends, and I am not surprised he died so young, but still . . . none of us should die like that."

Vic's mother was impeccably dressed in a designer suit, designer shoes, and with a designer handbag under her arm. Her long black hair with streaks of red, white, and gray was twisted into a perfect chignon. Her makeup was subtle but enhanced her brilliant gold eyes. Although she was in her early sixties, the woman dripped poise and elegance and sex. Raw, feline sex.

But Livy wasn't fooled. This Siberian tigress was a hardened predator.

Now beside Livy, the She-tiger touched her shoulders and gently turned Livy around.

"Tsk-tsk. So many bullets. And yet you still live. But your kind has never been easy to kill."

"Tried a few times, have you?" Livy asked, turning back around since she knew tigers always attacked from behind.

"We all have done things in our past we'd like to forget. I'm sure one day you will try not to remember shooting all those bears in the head and leaving their cooling corpses on the floor of your Sports Center."

"They shot first."

"Yes. Of course they did."

"Is there something you want . . . um . . ."

"I am Semenova Gribkova-Barinov."

"Please tell me you have a nickname."

"My American friends called me Nova. Although I did not think my name would be a challenge for you."

"Only if I have to say it every time I talk to you. So . . . is there something you want, Nova?"

"Just get dressed and come downstairs. We have much to discuss with you and your family."

"I'll be right down."

The She-tiger walked out, and Livy started to grab clothes from a duffel bag one of her cousins had brought from Livy's apartment. God, it felt like forever since she'd been back to that apartment. Was it even still standing, or had Melly returned and destroyed it?

Livy began to put her clothes on, but she hadn't had a shower since the day before and she felt a little . . . icky. So she found the bathroom attached to the bedroom she was in, but froze in the doorway. She'd never seen a bathroom like this before. The floor was marble. The sink marble and stainless steel. There was an enormous built-in tub and a separate shower with glass doors and more showerheads than seemed necessary with temperatures that were managed digitally.

It was a really nice bathroom, if a little extravagant. For her taste anyway.

So Livy ended up taking a longer shower than she planned. Hard not to once she realized she could adjust the temperature of each showerhead individually.

By the time Livy had dried off and dressed and reached

the first floor—from what she could tell, the place was four stories with marble staircases and lots of rooms and bathrooms—the arguing had already started. She could hear her Uncle Balt hissing at someone in Russian, *"Out! We don't want your kind here!"*

Livy walked down the marble-floored hallway, stopping briefly when she spotted Melly leaning against the wall and furiously texting on her battered phone.

"What are you doing here?" Livy asked.

"I keep asking myself the same damn question." Melly glanced up, smirked. "Heard you got your ass shot up pretty good. Hope it hurt."

"Suck my—"

"I said out!" Uncle Bart barked from farther down the hall.

Deciding not to get into a fight with her idiot cousin, Livy continued on until she found everyone in what she guessed was the library, based on all the books.

Vic—poor, poor Vic—was trying to be the peacemaker, trying to soothe her uncle. But she could tell Bart wasn't about to soothed.

"I cannot believe you brought bear here! After what happened to my poor little Olivia!"

Vic, trying so hard to be reasonable, argued, "But this is my father."

And that was the problem. Vic's father and mother weren't exactly friends of the Kowalskis and Yangs. There were several of Livy's relatives doing hard prison time all over the world because of the Barinovs. A smart couple that could sniff out illegal activity by just knowing the right people and spreading money around when necessary. They weren't even law enforcement. They did what they did on the side and made very good money at it. Sometimes working for the wealthy who wanted their stolen items back, and sometimes working for worldwide law enforcement. And the Barinovs were often worse than law enforcement because they had fewer rules to worry about, but much more brawn.

Vic and his father were the same height and the same build, and if Vic aged as well as his father . . . that would be very, *very* nice.

"I don't care he is your father. He is also bear."

"You didn't mind me bringing Shen," Vic reasoned.

"The panda? He is like giant stuffed toy. Adorable and nonthreatening. But this one . . ." Balt sneered at Vic's smiling grizzly father. "You put us all at risk."

"Uncle Balt," Livy said. "Let it go."

"But, my sweet Olivia—"

"Let it *go*."

"Fine!" her uncle snapped, walking over to one of the heavy leather king chairs and dropping into it. "Make same mistake as your father . . . see how well it does for you."

"Well, I've already outlived him."

"Awwww, Livy!" her family admonished.

"I was joking. Joking!"

"Not funny," her mother muttered from behind her.

"You people just have no sense of humor."

"Yes. That must be it."

Livy jerked a bit when she felt her mother's hand on her back. "How are you feeling?" Joan asked.

Confused, Livy asked, "In what sense?"

Her mother let out an exasperated sigh and marched around until she stood right in front of Livy. "Is it too much to ask for you to give me a straight answer? Just once?"

"Well, I don't know what you're asking."

"You were shot, you little idiot! And now I'm asking how you feel? Better? Worse? *Stupider?*"

"Don't yell at me, old woman!"

"Livy." Vic put his arm around Livy's shoulder and steered her away from her glowering mother. "I want you to meet my father. Vladik Barinov. Papa, this is Olivia Kowalski."

"This? This is little Livy? So beautiful!"

Livy held out her hand for a hearty shake, but then she was suddenly swallowed whole, completely smothered in bear as Vic's father picked her off the ground and hugged her in his giant arms.

"Papa," Vic said, trying to pry Livy from Vladik's arms. "Papa. Give her to me."

"I'm just saying hello."

"Mama! Papa won't let Livy go!"

"Such a big baby," Vladik complained, finally allowing his son to remove Livy from his arms.

Once she was again standing on her own feet, Vic smiled at her and said, "Would you like to meet my mother?"

God, not again.

"She's in the kitchen, making coffee."

"I met her. She says I can call her Nova."

"Oh good."

"Yes. Very good." Vladik took Livy's hand. "Come. We must talk." He led Livy to one of the many heavy leather chairs and waited while Livy sat down.

"So," Livy said, looking around at everyone, "who tried to have me killed yesterday?"

Vladik gazed down at her. "It was Rostislav Chumakov."

Livy thought on that a moment before asking, "The *art* patron?" She glanced away. "I can't imagine anyone hating my work *that* much."

Vladik looked at his son, and Vic explained, "Livy's an art photographer, Papa. She's not part of the . . . uh . . ." He cleared his throat. "She's not part of the Kowalski or Yang family businesses."

"Oh good!" Vladik cheered. "Then I will not have to have you arrested like your cousin in the Balkans."

Balt was nearly out of his chair, an angry snarl on his lips, when Livy snarled first. "Sit *down,* Uncle Balt."

Balt dropped back into his chair, but his glare was locked on Vladik.

"There is something else you need to know about Rostislav Chumakov, sweet Olivia."

"You mean other than his being a murdering art patron with apparently a low opinion of brilliant photography?"

"He is bear," Vladik explained.

"Kamchatka grizzly," Nova added as she walked into the room. She lifted her coffee mug, blowing on it to cool the liquid down. "You must have really pissed him off."

"Mama," Vic admonished.

"No, no." Livy cut in. "She's right. I must have really pissed him off." She sighed. "What can I say? It's a skill I have."

Livy stood. "I'm hungry," she announced and walked out of the room.

"Did we upset her?" Vic's father asked.

"No. She's probably just hungry."

"I, too, am hungry," Balt said and followed Livy. The rest of the Kowalskis and Yangs trailed behind him.

"What a lovely family your Olivia has."

"Mama."

His mother snorted. "You always had interesting taste, my handsome son. But this . . ."

"I'm not discussing my love life with you, Mama. Not now. Not ever."

"If I had listened to my mother, my love," Vladik said to Semenova, "I would have killed you with a big rock and buried your body by the river near our village. Are you not glad I never listened to her?"

"Your mother was a petty little cu—"

"Semenova."

Vic's father didn't ask much of his wife, but talking about Vladik's mother was and always would be off-limits. No matter how horrible the woman had been. And God, had that woman been horrible.

"I like her, Mama. I like Livy a lot. But whether you like her or not is not my problem."

"*I* like her," Vladik stated emphatically, causing Nova to roll her eyes. "Not only is she cute, but she can take sixteen bullets to back. Now that is woman!"

Vic looked at his mother. "We need your help, Mama. You and Papa. Will you help us?"

" 'We and us' . . . so soon? My son, some days your bearness overwhelms."

"Mama."

"Of course, I will help my handsome son and the little rat."

"Mama!"

"It's badger, my love," Vladik explained, always a bit oblivious to his wife's pointed attacks. "Honey badger." Vladik pointed at Vic. "You'll need to buy her big coat." When his wife and son just stared at him, "Honey badgers are born of heat. When you bring her to visit in Moscow for the holidays or during the winter bear games, she will need big coat. What did I say that's so confusing?"

Livy appeared at the library door. "Vic?"

"Yes?"

"Whose house is this?"

"Novikov's wedding gift to Blayne. It was purchased under his sport agent's name so she wouldn't find out, but that should keep the bears off our backs for a while. So I think we're pretty safe for a little bit if that's what has you worried."

"But this is Novikov's house, right?"

"Right."

Livy stepped back and yelled down the hallway, "Hands off the paintings and silverware and anything else you thieving felons might like to take! This house is under *my* protection as of this nanosecond!"

Livy's statement was greeted with whining and accusations of "going soft."

"The man saved my life," Livy said over all that grumbling. *"You think I'm going to just let you steal his shit?"*

The grumbling stopped, and Livy looked at Vic. "There's bacon. We're making bacon."

She walked off.

Vic smiled. "Isn't she amazing?" he asked his parents.

His mother sighed and walked out. Vladik put his arm around Vic's shoulders. "The best thing about sweet Olivia being shot is that if she can survive that, we can almost guarantee she can survive your mother."

"You do know, Papa, that doesn't sound nearly as positive as you think it does."

"You've been away from Russia too long, my son. Because to Russian bear . . . that is as positive as we are willing to get."

Vic set up a giant whiteboard in the kitchen while Livy and her family feasted on big piles of bacon. The groceries had been delivered by a nearby shifter-owned store that morning.

They were on Rhode Island. That was where Novikov's mansion was located. And it was an amazing home. There was a heated pool outside, a heated pool inside, and a separate building that housed an NHL-regulation ice rink and another building that housed a banked track for derby training.

Although Novikov wasn't the most outwardly affectionate man, he'd clearly been thinking of his bride-to-be when he'd had this house built, and he wasn't afraid to spend money to make Blayne happy.

So for him to allow Vic to bring Livy's entire felonious family to this house, to risk the gift he'd spent a lot of money on, in order to ensure Livy's safety meant more to her than she could possibly express.

Mostly because she was bad at expressing anything but her disdain.

Once the whiteboard was set up, Vic, his parents, and Livy's family ate bacon from the big platters on the island in the middle of the room and . . . stared.

"Are we actually going to use this whiteboard?" Jake finally asked.

"We need a picture of Chumakov," Shen said as he wrapped bacon around his bamboo stalk. "Then we need arrows pointing to the picture."

"Arrows from where?"

"No idea. I just know that's how it always looked when we worked at the CIA. Lots of boards with a main guy and then arrows pointing to him from other, lesser guys. Except we have no guys."

"Or," Balt suggested, "we can all travel to Russia, track Chumakov down, and kill him like dog in street."

"If we do that," Livy said, "we'll need to be back in time for Blayne's wedding. I'm their photographer."

Everyone turned to stare at Livy until Melly asked, "So you're doing weddings now? Because I'm getting married in September and—"

"I am *not* doing weddings now. I'm doing *a* wedding."

"You'll do a wedding for outsiders," Melly accused, "but you won't do it for family?"

"When you have such perfect timing that you save me from getting shot in the head, then, *yes!*" Livy exploded. *"That's when I'll photograph your goddamn wedding!"*

"You are such a selfish bitch!"

"*I'm* a selfish bitch? And who exactly are you marrying? *That hipster loser with a restraining order against your dumb ass?*"

"You'll never understand our love!"

"Because I don't have a *psychosis*!"

"That is enough! *Both of you!*" Vic's mother yelled before she turned those angry gold eyes on Joan. "Why are you not doing this? This one," she accused, "is your child, is she not? I mean based on eye—"

"Mama!"

"—color."

Livy whispered against Vic's ear, "Nice race-save there, Ruskie."

"Stop it."

"Is anyone listening?" Nova demanded.

Busy staring at and tapping on her phone, Joan lifted her head. "Huh?"

"We need to lure Chumakov here," Vic's father suggested.

"Good idea," Balt agreed. "We lure bear here and club him to death like seal."

"No." And Livy could see Vladik's patience beginning to wane. "We lure Chumakov here so that we can have this Whitlan person taken care of in Russia."

"Wait, wait," Vic cut in. "How do we know Whitlan is in Russia? Chumakov could be hiding him anywhere."

"Trust me," his father said flatly. "If Chumakov has Whitlan, he has him on his territory in Motherland."

"Papa, don't call it that."

"Best place to protect him is there."

"This no longer about Whitlan," Balt snarled. "It was not Whitlan who sent bears to kill my dear, sweet, defenseless niece."

"The defenseless niece who took out five bears in a stairwell after being shot at least sixteen times? That defenseless niece?" Shen asked.

"Quiet, stuffed toy!" Balt snapped. "I want Chumakov!" he yelled at Vladik.

"You cannot have Chumakov, you fool. Not unless you want entire bear nation coming down on you like flames of hell!"

"He is right, Baltazar Kowalski," Nova cut in. "Rostislav Chumakov is very powerful in the BPC. If you kill him without clear evidence, bears will no longer find honey badgers cute and adorable like rat in sewer."

"Especially with new commander of the BPC."

"Who's the new commander?" Vic asked.

"Bayla Ben-Zeev. She used to be Israeli commander. Her father and mother used to hunt Nazis. She is cold, calculating, and very loyal to bears. Other breeds, species are second to her." Nova raised a finger. "However, considering her size . . . she has lovely sense of style. It must not be easy to find things to fit her—she has shoulders like man—but manages to really pull off clothes I would never even think to put on her."

"Is it her accessories?" Joan asked. "Because good accessories can make the She-bear."

Livy glanced at Vic and crossed her eyes in annoyance. "I'm so very sorry to interrupt the fashion-bonding going on between you two, but can we get back to the cold, calculating nature of the BPC commander rather than where she might find shirts that fit her giant man-shoulders?"

"If you kill Chumakov now," Nova explained, "without any proof that he was the one who tried to kill your Livy, they will crush your little rat heads."

"It's *ratel,*" Aunt Teddy snarled.

"But we have proof," Jake said. "We have the bears. If we identify them, maybe we can prove that they work for Chumakov."

"Yeah . . ." Vic began, looking over at Shen, who began to munch harder on his bacon-wrapped bamboo stalk and look down at the floor.

"What?" Vladik asked.

"Well, Dee-Ann handled the cleanup for us."

"So?"

Vic cleared his throat. "She usually gets . . . uh . . . a clan of hyenas to do it for her."

"So?" Vladik asked again. "They must have put the bodies somewhere."

"Yeah . . . that's not actually what this particular hyena

clan does with the bodies that Dee-Ann gives them. But what they do is effective. You know . . . to make the bodies disappear."

"Until," Shen muttered, "those hyenas have to take a shit."

Vladik recoiled in disgust. "Oh . . . son!"

"*I* don't ask the hyenas to do it."

"No. But you associate with Smith Pack," Balt tossed back at him. "Demon dogs of underworld."

"Bottom line is," Jake rationalized—since no one else would bother, "we have no proof."

Joan lowered her phone. "Then Vladik Barinov is right—we should lure Chumakov here and go after Whitlan."

Balt slammed his hands on the island. "You will let this bear get away with what he did to your daughter *and* my brother?"

"Do not question me on this, Baltazar!" Joan snapped in Mandarin.

Balt frowned. "What?"

"Do as I say," she told him in English.

"But—"

"She is *my* worthless daughter!" Joan pointed out.

"Hey!"

"Damon was *my* worthless husband! This is *my* decision, Baltazar Kowalski. Not yours." Joan settled down. Smiled. "So we lure Chumakov here and then have Whitlan dealt with in Russia."

"Okay," Livy agreed, willing to play along even though she didn't trust her mother to let things go with Chumakov that easy. "But A: how do we lure Chumakov here? And B: Who takes care of Whitlan in Russia?"

"I don't know about B," Jake replied, "but I've got an idea for A."

"Which is?"

"Livy, you say he's an art patron. He's also a scumbag

mobster. Something tells me a lost, let's see . . . how about a lost . . . Matisse? Worth millions. That would be something that would get his interest."

"I'm afraid to ask," Vic sighed, "but do you have a lost Matisse?"

"No. We just need a good picture of a lost Matisse."

"A picture?"

"Like, out of a book."

"And what are you going to do with that?"

As one, the Kowalskis all turned and looked at Melly. She didn't notice, though. She was too busy texting someone. The way her fingers were moving, Livy could tell she was arguing with someone. Probably her stalked not-really-a-fiancé.

And Livy knew she was right when Melly suddenly jumped up and yelled at her phone, "I will kidnap myself *again,* before I *ever* let you leave me!"

Melly looked up at her relatives. "What are you all staring at? I'm not talking to any of *you*," she snarled.

Niles "Van" Van Holtz kissed his sleeping mate on the cheek before slipping out of bed. He pulled on sweatpants and left the room, carefully closing the door behind him so as not to disturb his wife.

Yawning, he headed down to his big kitchen, prepared to make breakfast for his family and any of his Pack who wanted to join in, before he headed off to his restaurant to prepare for that evening's dinner service.

He opened the refrigerator and studied the contents. Waffles were his first thought, but wolves always ate waffles. Vacations among his Pack had actually been cancelled in the past when it was discovered the resort they were going to didn't serve waffles for breakfast.

"Maybe French toast." Van did love cinnamon.

Deciding on French toast and sausage, he grabbed several gallons of milk and turned away from the refrigerator.

That's when Van screamed and jumped back because Dee-Ann Smith was standing behind him like the angel of death.

"What the fuck are you doing?" he demanded.

"Sorry. Didn't mean to startle ya."

"Yes, you did."

"Yeah. I did. But I have some questions for ya, and I didn't want you to have a bunch of time to organize your lies."

Van walked around her to place the milk he hadn't dropped on the floor onto the counter. "What are you talking about?"

"You had us back off the Whitlan case . . . why?"

"What?"

"I know you heard me."

Yeah. He had.

Van picked up the gallon of milk he'd dropped on the floor and placed it with the others.

"You knew about Damon Kowalski, didn't you?"

Facing the She-wolf, Van folded his arms over his chest. "Some of us were . . . aware of the turn of events."

"Turn of events? Is that what you call it?"

"That's what it was."

The She-wolf gave a short laugh. "I see. You knew what the honey badgers would do once they found out one of their own had been hunted and stuffed."

"We knew that they had a good chance of drawing out Whitlan, and the ones protecting him. The badgers function with fewer rules than the rest of us."

"So you put Livy up for the slaughter?"

Van dropped his hands. "Oh, come on, Dee-Ann. Do you really think any of us had any idea that they'd attack Livy that way? Right there in the Sports Center?"

"I see. Y'all expected warnings and such."

"I guess we did."

"They took sixteen bullets out of that little girl."

"And I'm very sorry about that."

"It's gonna get nasty now," Dee-Ann needlessly told him. "Those were bears that came after her. Bears that we cleaned up." When Van didn't say anything, Dee-Ann smirked. "You're going to let them deal with it on their own."

"Honey badgers have always functioned separately. They have never wanted to be part of us."

She walked up to him, stood barely three inches from him. Van was slightly taller than his favorite cousin's mate, but Dee-Ann was built like a linebacker for the Seattle Seahawks.

And behind Dee-Ann, Van saw his eldest child and only daughter, Ulva, ease out from the pantry, her claws unleashed.

"Well, you can go on being a politician, Niles Van Holtz, but if they need help from me or Malone, they're gonna get it. Do we understand each other?"

"We always understand each other, Dee-Ann."

"That's good." Dee-Ann held up one finger and said to Van's daughter while still staring at Van, "And you still ain't ready to take me on, little girl."

Shocked Dee-Ann had so easily sensed her, Ulva stopped in her tracks, her claws instantly retracting.

The She-wolf left as silently as she'd come into his home, and his daughter was immediately at his side, her arms around his waist.

"How can I be Alpha of the Pack, Daddy, when that female scares the life from me?"

"You'll be Alpha because you're already smart enough to know who to challenge and who not. And trust me, baby, when I tell you, I don't want you challenging Dee-Ann Smith or her father at any point in your life."

His daughter, as brilliant and beautiful as her full-human mother, nodded. "Okay."

CHAPTER 32

The private jet landed at the small New Jersey airport. Dee-Ann said her good-byes to the pilot and flight attendant and went into the tiny terminal. Malone was supposed to pick her up alone, so Dee-Ann was surprised when she saw Ric with her. In fact, she was kind of grateful.

Dee-Ann went into his open arms and hugged her mate tight.

"How did it go?" he asked, not bothering to complain that she'd gone to see his cousin without a word to him.

"Me and Malone were right." She stepped back. "Can't speak for BPC, but The Group and KZS knew, at the very least, about Damon Kowalski."

"They knew the badgers would bring whoever was protecting Whitlan out in the open." Ric's handsome face turned angry. "And put Livy at risk."

"Don't think your uncle knew it would get that bad that quickly, but—"

Dee-Ann blinked, her words stopping abruptly after a fist slammed into her face.

Of course, the blow didn't hurt her as much as startle her. Too bad the one swinging that fist couldn't say the same.

Toni Jean-Louis Parker, looking exhausted and angry and

surrounded by extremely large bears and Ricky Lee, held her fist and yelped from the pain.

"Good to see you, too, Antonella."

"Don't talk to me, pit bull. I know you did this. I know what you did to Blayne that time, and now you set up poor Olivia!"

"Hey!" Malone cut in. "This isn't Dee-Ann's fault."

"How would you know?"

"I know!"

Ricky Lee raised his hands, attempting to placate, which he was usually good at. "Why don't we all just calm down."

"I don't want to calm down," Toni snapped. "I want her beaten horribly!" She pointed at Dee-Ann. "Get her, Ivan!"

The seven-foot-plus bear stared at Toni. "Get who?"

"Dee-Ann."

"Smith? You want me to beat up Dee-Ann *Smith*?"

"Yes."

The bear glanced at the other bears surrounding him. "Uh . . . we don't believe in beating up women."

"She's barely female."

"Hey!"

"Sorry, Ulrich. I know she's your mate, but—"

"Come on, Ivan." Dee-Ann grinned. "Give us your best shot."

The bear took a step back. "No thank you."

"Wait, wait." Ric stepped in front of Dee-Ann. "Stop goading."

"Didn't realize I was."

"Yes, you did," Malone muttered.

Okay. She did know. But Dee-Ann actually felt horrible. Unlike with Toy Poodle Blayne, Dee-Ann liked Livy. She didn't talk more than was necessary. She tolerated Reece Lee better than most. And she found Blayne as annoying as Dee-Ann did. What was there not to like about the girl? So this whole thing didn't sit right with Dee-Ann at all.

Dee-Ann's time in the military meant that she'd been

shot quite a few times, but never sixteen . . . at one time. One shot hurt enough; she couldn't imagine that many shots over and over, believing the whole time you were about to die. No one should go through that. Especially when all the girl wanted was the man who'd hunted and killed her daddy.

Which meant, at least to Dee-Ann, that a little fight with big ol' bears might make her feel a bit better. At least in the moment.

Ric smiled at her. He could read Dee-Ann without her saying a word.

"Listen, Toni," Ric began, turning to face the jackal, "we'll . . ."

Ric stopped, looked around, and finally asked Ricky Lee, "Where's Antonella?"

Ricky Lee Reed glanced at the suddenly smug-looking bears and shrugged. "Got me."

Vic walked into the bedroom he'd set Livy up in and found her desperately rubbing her back against the bathroom doorway.

"What are you doing?"

"My back is so itchy."

Closing the bedroom door, Vic went to Livy and turned her around. He lifted the sweatshirt she had on.

"Sex? Now?"

Vic chuckled. "I'm looking to see if any of your wounds are infected, silly."

"Oh. Okay."

Carefully studying the multiple wounds that Livy had received, Vic was glad to see that there was no obvious infection. Instead, it looked like the wounds were healing so fast, her body was itching because of that.

"They all look pretty clean. But I think we should put some anti-itch stuff on your back."

"Do we have that?"

"Novikov has first-aid kits in nearly every room of this house and first-aid *trunks* out by the rink and derby track. I can't tell if he's just super-prepared or if Blayne is that clumsy."

"Both."

Vic went into the bathroom and pulled out cotton balls and a bottle of anti-itch gel that should help Livy get through the worst part of her healing process.

He walked back into the bedroom and stopped in his tracks. Livy was naked and facedown on the bed.

"Uh . . . Livy? What are you doing?"

"Making it easy for you to deal with my wounds." She looked at him over her shoulder and grinned. "See how helpful I am?"

"You are such a bad influence."

"I know."

Vic kicked off his Converse sneakers and sat on the bed beside Livy. Determined to get this done before they did anything else, Vic forced himself to focus on each of Livy's wounds. First he applied the gel to her back, then rolled Livy to her side and dealt with the ones on her hip. She watched him while he worked, and Vic had to admit having her eyes on him was beyond distracting. He wanted her so badly, but he didn't want to rush her. Not physically. She might think she was completely okay, but Vic wanted to be sure. Really sure. He didn't want to do anything that might hurt her more.

"I think that's it," he said, pulling his hand back and tossing the used cotton balls away.

"You sure?" Livy asked as she slowly sat up.

"Yeah."

"Good." She placed her hand on either side of his jaw and kissed him. Suddenly, the idea of taking it slow or waiting to make sure she was really okay evaporated from his weak, pathetic mind. He kissed her back and began to lower her to the bed when a knock on the door stopped him.

Livy pulled out of their kiss and snarled, "What?"

Jake opened the door enough just to stick his head in. "Decent?"

"Do you mean morally?"

Livy's cousin rolled his eyes. "Put your clothes back on, ho."

Growling, Livy tugged on her sweatpants and shirt. She stood. "What is it?"

Jake pushed the door open and stepped in, revealing a tired-looking Toni standing behind him.

The two women stared at each other for a long moment until Toni burst out with, "You *bitch*!"

That seemed a surprising reaction to Vic, but Livy turning to him, and accusing, *"You called her?"*

"I did not! But I'm not surprised she found out since Ric Van Holtz had Coop, Kyle, and Cherise sent back to Washington as soon as everything happened."

"Wait a minute." Toni stepped farther into the room. "What was Kyle doing here? He was supposed to be in Italy."

"Do you see what you started?"

Vic reared back at Livy's accusation. "Me? What did I do?"

"He didn't call Toni," Jake cut in. "*I* did."

"And why would you do that?" Livy demanded.

"Because," Toni answered for Jake, "I told him when we were sixteen, if he ever hid anything from me when you got yourself into trouble, I would hunt him down and cut his balls off!"

"And you believed her?" Livy asked her cousin.

"Yes," Jake answered bluntly. "Yes, I did. When it comes to you two"—he waved a finger between the females—"I don't get in the way. A rational man never would."

"I can't believe you didn't call me, Livy!"

"Coop and Cherise were here to watch Kyle, and Coop told me your parents knew everything!"

"I'm not talking about that idiot Kyle. I'm talking about *you*. How could you not tell me about your father? About being shot? *About everything?*"

Livy gave a small shrug. "I didn't want you to worry."

"And *you*!" Toni snapped at Vic. "How could you not tell me what was going on?"

"Why do I keep getting dragged back into this?"

"Just don't think for a second that because of your freakish size—"

"Freakish?"

"—and obscenely thick neck—"

"Well, that's not necessary!"

"—that I won't hunt you down, too, *and cut your balls right off!*"

"Hey, Vic," Jake said calmly, "why don't we see if anyone left us some honey to eat? Downstairs. Far away from here."

Deciding it was best to leave before things got any stranger, Vic got up and walked out of the room. When Vic reached the stairs at the end of the hallway, Jake turned to him.

"Are you serious about my cousin?"

Vic didn't see the point in being vague. "Very."

"Then a little advice. When it comes to those two, just say, 'Hey, why don't I go get us some honey?' Then leave the room."

"But I—"

"No, no. There's no debating this. This is a standard plan I've had in place for years from hard-earned lessons."

"It's just that—"

"No, no. You're still doing that bear thing."

"Bear thing?"

"Going with logic. There's no logic when a jackal and a honey badger are friends. In the wild . . . they eat each other's cubs. In suburban Washington, they watch out for each other's siblings and violently threaten or attack those they feel may have emotionally harmed their best friend. So I'm telling you, 'cause I like you, and because I can tell how you feel about my cousin . . . next time, just smile and say . . . ?"

Vic stared down at him.

"And say . . . ?" Jake prompted again.

Vic sighed and parroted, " 'Hey, why don't I go get us some honey?' "

"Good man." Jake patted his arm. "There might be hope for you yet."

"Please don't cry," Livy begged as the two women held on to each other. "I'm okay. I promise."

"I can't believe you didn't call me!"

"You were in Siberia. Not Brooklyn. *Siberia*."

Toni pulled back, wiping her eyes with the backs of her hands. "You found out about your dad *before* I went to Siberia, though. Didn't you?"

"I didn't tell anyone about that. Not even Vic. I did, however, yell at my mother."

"Please tell me she didn't actually kill the person we put in that grave."

Livy went to the nightstand and grabbed a tissue from the box. "She swears whoever it was, was already dead. I decided not to push her on it."

Gently, Livy wiped her friend's face. "I'll be honest, Toni. I didn't know what to do. I never liked my old man, but . . . to see him like that."

Toni took the tissue, blew her nose. "What did you do?"

"You mean other than getting shot?" Livy shrugged and sat down on the edge of the bed. "I beat up Melly, got thrown into jail, and Vic took me to a bear-only town called Honeyville. Then I jousted."

"You have always wanted to try that."

"I was really good against the cats. The bears kicked my ass, though."

Toni sat down on the bed next to Livy. "Did Vic joust?"

"No. He would have been great, too, but he was too busy yelling at me about how dangerous and stupid it was for me to joust."

"He yelled at you because he's in love with you."

Livy lifted her feet, studied her bare toes. "Did you know Honeyville has over three hundred and seventy types of honey? I think I tried almost all of them."

"So you're going to pretend I didn't just say what I just said?"

"Pretty much."

"Avoidance is still your friend, I see."

"How else do you think I've managed to survive with this family?"

"You'll have to face it eventually," Toni singsonged to her.

"You're gonna have to shut up," Livy singsonged back.

Toni put her arm around Livy, and placed her head on her friend's shoulder. "I'm so very glad you didn't manage to get yourself killed."

"That's the nicest way to blame the victim I've ever heard."

"I'm really good at that. So did Kyle ask Vic to pose naked?"

"Yes. But I can't blame the kid. The man has amazing cheekbones."

Jocelyn pushed open the door to her cousin's bedroom and sighed. "Help me," she ordered Jake and Shen.

Jake responded immediately, but Shen stopped in the doorway and stared. "Is she dead?"

"No," Jocelyn said casually as she crouched down. "Just drunk off her ass."

"Another fight with the boyfriend she stalks?" Jake asked.

"No. He's the stalked fiancé now."

"Maybe we should call an ambulance . . . or something."

"Not necessary." Jocelyn stood. "Just pick her up, Shen."

"Pick her up?"

"Pick her up."

Sighing, Shen reached out and lifted Melly onto his shoulder. She seemed to barely weigh anything, and it was terribly easy. But then Jake said, "If she starts squirming, drop her. She's about to piss on you."

"And if she grunts," Jocelyn added, "throw her. She's about to shit or projectile vomit."

Horrified, Shen practically ran to the room they'd set up for Melly. Easels and paints and the brilliant lighting from the above skylight made the room perfect for an artist. But he had a hard time believing the woman over his shoulder was an artist.

"Stand her up for me," Jocelyn ordered.

Shen did, making sure to turn Melly away from him. Although he realized that might not actually save him.

Jocelyn stared at her cousin for several moments before pulling back her hand and slapping Melly in the face. The first time did nothing, but the second slap had Melly swinging fists and cursing.

"Melly. Melly!"

The honey badger stopped. "Hey, Jocelyn. What's going on?"

"We need you to work for a little while."

"I don't feel like it." Melly searched her dress, which had no pockets. For her phone, Shen guessed. "I don't understand how he can't love me."

Jake looked at Shen and rolled his eyes.

"We'll have to worry about that later, sweetie. Because I really need you to handle this right now."

"Handle what?"

Jocelyn held up a poster of an old Matisse painting that had been stolen from a Belgian art museum nearly ten years ago and never recovered.

"Ohhh," Melly drunkenly sighed. "Matisse. I love Matisse."

"I know you do." Jocelyn nodded her head at Shen, and he released Melly's shoulders. Jocelyn began to walk backward, holding the painting up and Melly stumbled after her. "Only you can do this, Melly. You know that, right?"

"Yep. I know." She waved her hand at Jocelyn. "Pin it. Pin it."

Jocelyn pinned the poster to an easel and Melly stood in front of it. She stood. She stared. She weaved a little.

With a finger to her lips, Jocelyn gestured for the men to leave. Together, the three walked out, Jake silently shutting the door behind them.

Shen started to say something, but Jocelyn shook her head and indicated for them to walk down the stairs. Once they were on another floor, Shen asked, "Are you sure we should leave her alone? She looks about to pass out again."

"She'll be fine," Jocelyn said with absolutely no concern in her voice.

Shen wasn't so sure but . . . he wasn't about to go back and risk getting hit with all manner of disgusting things. He just hoped the family knew what they were doing since a lot of what they were planning hinged on a bipolar honey badger female with an obvious drinking problem.

Toni watched Vic open another jar of honey, put a spoon into it, and hand it to Livy. "The cinnamon-infused."

"Thanks."

"I'm going to go watch TV with Shen."

"Ball game on? Maybe a little hockey?"

"No. *Star Trek: The Next Generation* marathon."

"Of course."

Vic kissed her cheek and walked out, leaving the two females alone in the kitchen. They sat on the island, their feet hanging over the side.

"Honey?" Livy offered.

"I hate honey."

"What kind of demon hates honey?"

"So, how long before you admit to Vic that you love him, too?"

"Why don't you shut the fuck up?"

Toni laughed. "Oh my God. This is the best. I actually have something to torture you with. This is like heaven on earth."

"Shut. Up."

Livy's mother pulled the sliding glass door open and walked into the kitchen. She'd clearly been shopping, her hands filled with bags from stores like Chanel, Coach, and Saks Fifth Avenue. She stopped, though, when she saw Toni sitting next to Livy.

"Oh. Antonella. How nice," her mother practically sneered.

"Chuntao," Toni said, always knowing how much Livy's mother hated when Toni and Jacqueline called her by her given name. She'd worked hard to be Joan Kowalski, and she didn't appreciate being called out by "those artistic snobs." "How are you holding up?"

"Fine. Just fine. Thanks."

Joan cut across the kitchen.

"Love the mink," Toni lied. "It's always nice to wear the fur of a dead animal on your back."

Joan paused by the doorway that led to the hall. "I'm so glad you've come, Antonella dear." She looked over her shoulder and smiled so that the pair could easily see her fangs. "It's so hard these days to find a good friend."

Once Joan was gone, Toni asked Livy, "Your mother really does hate me, doesn't she?"

"I think she hates your mother much more. But you are a close second."

Toni gave a dismissive wave. "Then my job here is done."

Sitting at the dining table, a glass of red wine nearby, Semenova chewed on elk jerky, flipped through a copy of Russian *Vogue,* and watched honey badgers skitter around. They probably didn't see themselves as "skittering," but that was how it seemed to Semenova. They moved quickly, stopped, listened, moved again.

Watching them made her want to go on a hunting-killing spree, but she knew her son wouldn't appreciate that. So she focused on her magazine and her elk jerky instead.

She heard bickering and glanced through the big glass windows that looked out on the backyard. It was that Olivia Kowalski and her mother Chuntao "Joan" Yang.

Semenova knew Joan Yang. Not personally, but anyone in her line of work made it their business to *know* the Yangs and the Kowalskis, as well as all the Mongolian Chinbats, the Russian Popovs, the African Owusu, the Albanian Dushku, the American Phillips . . . good God, the list of honey badger families went on and on.

The honey badgers, however, had always been unique among shifters. They dealt mostly with full-humans and didn't involve themselves in shifter politics. They did, however, involve themselves in full-human politics because it amused them to do so. It amused honey badgers to fuck with people. It amused them to steal, torment, and toy with those who weren't part of their families. They bred many to ensure their strength among the shifter nation, in general, and other honey badger families specifically.

Of all shifters, Semenova always felt that the honey

badgers were the ones who could take over the world . . . they simply never felt like it. Instead, they managed to keep the balance. They kept the world from ending, but they *never* allowed things to become perfect.

Perfection was a curse. Perfection was boredom—and badgers hated boredom.

So they served their purpose in the world, but she still treated badgers as the criminals most of them were. Especially in Eastern Europe and Mongolia, where Semenova and her mate worked long and hard helping law enforcement keep control.

What could Semenova say? She and her Vladik were very good at what they did. Her Vladik was the sweet-talker, negotiating with everyone, from mobsters to pirates to government rulers.

Semenova, however, was . . . what did her son call it? Ah, yes. She was "The Bad Cop." She'd been trained by her mother, who had been Soviet Secret Police. Not because she'd been forced to or recruited, but because she'd enjoyed it. She'd enjoyed it greatly.

Just as Semenova enjoyed what she did . . . greatly.

A sudden banging on the table had Semenova looking up from her magazine. An old Asian She-badger stared down at her. An old She-badger she knew.

"Hello, feline," the badger greeted.

"Ancient rat."

The badger smirked. "*Ratel* . . . but you know that." She pulled out one of the dining chairs and slowly sat down. Every bone creaked as she did. How old was this woman? Semenova had seen at least six birth certificates. Some from China, others from the States. One from Paris. And she looked anywhere from seventy to eighty to ninety.

"Tell me, *ratel,*" Semenova asked with a smile, "how many of your . . . what's the English word? Kin, is it? How many of your kin have I had put away? At least two daughters, a son . . . that third husband of yours."

"I liked him. He was young. Very handsome. Good amount of insurance on him. Tragically died in Qincheng Prison." She pressed a perfectly manicured hand to her chest. "Broke my heart."

Semenova laughed. "It's fun to pretend that either of us has one."

The badger, grinning, reached into her large handbag with the atrocious flower pattern and pulled out a bottle of the best vodka that Russia had ever produced.

She slammed the bottle onto the table. "Let's drink, feline. Drink . . . and chat."

The bottle slid across the table and into Semenova's outstretched hand.

Curious and desiring a taste of home, Semenova opened the bottle and took a deep drink. "Yes, old woman. Let us chat."

Vic glanced away from the TV to see Livy walk into the living room. She sat down on the floor near his legs and stretched a large towel out.

"What are you doing?" he asked.

"Jake stopped by my office and picked up my camera." She placed the damaged equipment on the towel. "I'm going to see if I can fix it."

"You know how to fix cameras?"

"I've restored cameras. Fixed a few minor problems." But never had the inside of a camera been in so many pieces before. She looked at Vic. "If I hadn't already killed those bears . . . I'd totally kill them again. Because this"—she held up her damaged camera body that still made those very disheartening rattling sounds—"is just *wrong*."

Shen leaned forward so he could see around Vic. "Are you crying?"

Tears fell down her cheeks. "Because this is so wrong!"

"But . . . they *shot* you and you didn't cry. You found

your father's body stuffed and in a woman's apartment and you didn't cry. But the bears break your camera and . . . you're weeping."

"I don't understand your point."

"Okay." Shen leaned back into the couch, nodded at Vic. "I'm done."

Livy cleaned up her tears and worked on her camera until an elderly honey badger with a vicious long scar running down one side of her neck slowly made her way past the living room archway, her walking stick tapping against the marble flooring.

"Great-Aunt Li-Li?"

"Don't mind me."

"I don't mind you," Livy replied. "I just didn't know you were still here."

"Well, I am."

"Why are you still here?"

"Livy."

"What?"

"Be nice." Vic leaned in and whispered, "She's old."

"Yes. And that doesn't make her any less mean. So, Aunt Li-Li—" Livy stopped talking, and Vic realized that her great-aunt had disappeared.

"Where did she go?" Shen asked.

Vic shook his head. "Something tells me we probably don't want to know."

"We don't," Livy promised. "You don't get to be one step below matriarch of the Yang family without some . . . let's just call it edge."

"One step below?"

"Until her mother dies, she'll be one step below."

"Her *mother* is still alive?"

"Oh yeah. She's outlived eight husbands, too." Livy glanced at Vic. "Some of them even died naturally."

"You know," Shen said low to Vic, "you *really* need to stop asking her questions about her family."

"You're right, because the answers continue to freak me the heck out."

Livy walked into the room she shared with Vic. He was in bed, reading a *Star Wars* novel.

"Exactly how high is your geek level?" she asked.

"Pretty high. Is that a problem for you?"

"I just like to know what I'm getting into here."

Livy walked over to the garbage can in the room and dropped the towel filled with what was left of her digital camera into it.

"Just giving up?"

"Sometimes you have to." She started toward the bed. "My camera's fucked."

"I'm sorry."

"It could have been worse. They could have done this to my Hasselblad. Then, of course, I would have had to destroy the entire bear nation and all of Russia."

"Why?"

"Because my Hasselblad rig cost more than your SUV when you bought it new."

"For a camera?"

"The *best* camera."

Livy turned away from the bed and toward the bedroom door when she heard a knock. She opened it and smiled up at Vic's father.

"Hello, Vladik."

"Hello, beautiful Olivia," he boomed. The man didn't seem to have any volume control. "Is my son too busy to see his papa?" He leaned down and said in what he probably thought was a whisper but was still more yelling, "You two were not busy, were you? I hate to interrupt."

"Papa."

Vladik walked past Livy, not waiting to see if he was interrupting anything. Just lumbering by as bears liked to do.

"What is the tone?" Vladik asked his son. "I am just glad you found woman. I was a little worried," he said to Livy. "He is very shy, my handsome son, and his mother and sister coddle him."

"Papa, please stop talking."

"I only speak truth. But my little girl"—*Ira's little?*—"she says she likes you, beautiful Olivia. You are small, but very strong. You will make my son good mate."

Vic tossed his book across the bed. "Papa!"

"Again with tone! Why tone?"

Vic rubbed his forehead. "Olivia and I are just—"

"Just? Just what? Why waste time with just?"

"Papa, do you *need* something?"

"We leave."

"Leave?"

"Go."

"When?"

"Now."

"What's wrong?"

"Nothing. We have things to do. We came to check to make sure you were safe and that beautiful Olivia had not been killed. You are safe. Olivia is alive. We now go."

"Are you sure it's safe? Chumakov—"

"Does not worry me. But don't you be foolish. You see what he will do."

"Yeah. All to protect a full-human."

Vladik snorted. "He does not protect Whitlan to protect Whitlan."

"What does that mean?"

"It is about honor for him. He has given Whitlan his protection. If he can't protect Whitlan, his precious honor will suffer. That is all he cares about. Remember that. Now we go. Come say good-bye to your mama."

Vic slid off the bed while Vladik hugged Livy, which was like being briefly suffocated by a giant.

"Take care, beautiful Olivia."

"Should I go down and say good-bye to Nova?"

"No," both males immediately replied.

"I won't be long," Vic added sheepishly.

He walked out with his father, closing the door behind him. Livy yawned, pulled off her clothes, and naked, stretched out stomach-down on the bed. She picked up the book Vic had tossed and read the back cover. She barely made it halfway through before she rolled her eyes and tossed the book back onto Vic's side of the bed.

Vic walked out the front door of Novikov's house. His mother sat sideways in the rental car, her legs hanging out and crossed at the knees, while she freshened up her lipstick.

Coming down the stairs, Vic stopped by Livy's honey badger uncles. "Mind not staring at my mother like that?" he asked, trying desperately to keep in mind they were Livy's blood relatives.

"Your mother is very pretty," Balt remarked, his brothers smiling beside him.

Vic gave a short roar that managed to shake the house windows and moved the car a few feet.

The smiling turned to badger sneering. "That is annoying, hybrid," Balt snarled.

"We have no time for this." Vladik grabbed Balt and Gustav from behind and, ignoring the hissing and claws, tossed them toward the front door, quickly followed by Otto and Kamil. He was reaching for David when that badger held up his hands.

"I can walk, bear. I can walk."

"Come." Vladik moved to the car, remotely releasing the Mercedes-Benz trunk. "Take this."

Vic opened the heavy briefcase, looked in, blinked, gazed at his father. "Seriously?"

"Take it. Use it. You cannot just sit around all day using your tail inappropriately with that She-badger—"

"Papa!"

"—and not do something to help yourselves out of this situation."

"What are you talking about?"

"Victor," his mother called out. "Victor, my dear. Come to Mama."

Vic closed the briefcase and walked around the car to his mother. He crouched down in front of her since he knew she wasn't about to stand.

"Take this," she said, touching the case. "Use it." She lowered her voice to a whisper, "Hide it from badgers. They are nothing but thieves."

"Mama."

"I do not mean your little Olivia. She has no distinct criminal record for at least a decade now. That is good. But her family." She rolled her eyes. "Good luck protecting your wallet."

Before Vic could ask his mother to stop—or just simply repeat "Mama" with tone—she went on. "The thing you must remember is getting this Whitlan person is just part of what you need to do. If you want to protect your badger, you'll need to ensure Chumakov is made impotent."

Vic reared back a bit from his mother. "That doesn't sound right. Are you sure you're using the right word?"

"Do not insult me, Victor Barinov. Ungrateful boy!"

"I'm sorry. I'm sorry."

"Be smart. Take care of this."

"Yes, ma'am."

"Now kiss me so we can go."

"Where are you going?"

"To do what we can from our end."

"Which is what, exactly?"

"Why do you question me so?" his mother bellowed. "It is like you do not trust me!"

"I trust you! I trust you!"

Vic kissed his mother on both cheeks and stood while he

was grabbed by his father in one of his all-encompassing hugs, then kissed twice on both cheeks.

"My brilliant, amazing son!" Vladik boomed. "Do not get yourself killed or my rarely seen rage will be unleashed on the entire world!"

"I know, Papa."

"Good. And you take good care of our little Olivia. Your mother may find her too tiny to be worthy of love—"

"When did I say that?"

"—but I like her. She is good for you and doesn't appear to find your awkward silences off-putting."

"Thanks, Papa."

Vic walked back into the bedroom, a briefcase in his hand. Shen was beside him, but when they saw Livy naked and on top of the comforter, Vic shoved the leering panda out of the room by poor Shen's face.

"Hey!" Shen yelled through the door. "What was that for?"

"What are you doing?" Vic asked Livy.

"Waiting for you."

"How about some clothes?"

"I felt like being naked."

"What do you mean, you felt like being naked?"

"I really don't know how to make that sentence any clearer."

"There are people all over the house."

"My family's seen me naked. And there are no cubs . . . so I'm not sure what the problem is except you're jealous that Shen saw my ass."

"Yes," Vic replied. "I am jealous he saw your ass."

"It is a nice ass!" Shen yelled through the door. "You should feel very proud!"

"Thank you!" Livy called back.

Vic yanked the door open, and Livy heard Shen's big panda feet running away.

"Enjoy that, did you?" he asked, slamming the door.

"I do so like being naked," she teased. "If I could, I'd walk around naked all day long."

Vic chuckled. "And if I could, I'd let you."

Vic placed the case his parents had given him in the closet and stretched out on the bed with his back against the headboard. If Livy noticed the case, she certainly didn't show it.

"Sorry about my father," Vic said. "He has no boundaries. Especially when he likes someone."

"I find his directness refreshing. Like Kyle, without the personality disorder."

"Kyle doesn't have a personality disorder."

"No. He just makes other people have them."

Vic studied the cover of his book and asked, "My father didn't . . ."

"Scare me off?"

"You like your space."

"I like tight spaces, but I don't like to be crowded and I don't like to be backed into corners. I don't feel that way with you. Never have. That's why I was always in your cabinets. Tight space but no crowding. Which, considering the height and width of your immediate family, is extremely amazing. More importantly, there's something you keep forgetting."

"And what's that?"

Livy placed Vic's book aside and crawled into his lap, her thighs on either side of his, her arms resting casually around his neck. "I don't scare. Kyle told me my lack of fear was a sign of my sociopathic nature. I told him that should make him very worried that I would kill him in his sleep. So he stopped saying it."

Vic laughed and stroked Livy's naked back. His fingers traced the healed wounds—now scars, he guessed. Some were indented, reminding him of the holes they'd made. Others were raised, keloids. It reminded Vic how close he'd been to losing Livy.

"You make me want to burrow," Livy told him, her arms moving down to his waist as she snuggled into his chest. "Usually I want to burrow away from people," she murmured. "You're the first I've ever burrowed *toward*."

Vic wound his arms around Livy, making sure to keep her close so that she couldn't see his smile. So that she wouldn't know, not yet.

Because her words meant everything to him. More than he'd ever thought they would.

CHAPTER 33

Livy woke up swinging, her fist ramming into Vic's palm, which he was quick enough to raise so that she didn't hit his face.

"Good morning."

Livy cleared her throat. "Sorry about that. I dreamed I was fighting rampaging squirrels . . . and Blayne."

"Were you winning?"

"I don't want to talk about it." She sat up. "You going out?"

"Back to the City." Vic lowered his head. "I've got important work to do."

"You look adorable when you're trying to be terrifying."

"Are you saying I'm not terrifying-looking?"

"No. I'm saying that I find your terrifying look . . . extremely attractive. Should I be worried about where you're going?"

"No. Just organizing a few things. But there is something you should know."

"What?"

Vic gave a weird, almost guilty smile, which made her nervous. "Well . . ."

"What?"

"It's funny you mentioned Blayne."

Livy scrambled to her knees. "She's here . . . isn't she?"

"She wanted to talk to you about the wedding. Since apparently she still plans for you to be the photographer. But, if it helps, Gwen, Lock, and Novikov are with her."

"You're not lying to me, are you? She is here. Just to torment me."

Vic kissed her on the cheek. "I may avoid telling you things because I don't want you to snap, get your hands on a death ray, and start wiping out whole countries . . . but I would never lie to you."

"How do you know I'd get my hands on a death ray?"

"Kyle said he was designing one, because it needed to be aesthetically attractive, and was going to have Freddy and Troy build it."

"Then I *can* get my hands on a death ray . . . that's good to know."

"And that's what has me worried."

"Are you going into the City alone?"

"Bringing Shen."

"You'll be careful?"

"I will. You promise not to throw another locker at Blayne?"

"No."

"Livy, remember? Novikov and Lock saved your life. And Novikov loves Blayne."

"Why?"

"Livy."

"I'll be nice." She tried to smile to show her sincerity, but Vic leaned away from her.

"Don't . . ." He shook his head. "Don't force it."

"That bad?"

"Yeah. It's that bad."

* * *

Gwen sat down on the couch next to Lock. He'd been quiet since they'd pulled into the driveway, and although he wasn't a chatty bear in general, it wasn't like him to say nothing.

"What's going on with you?" she asked, not bothering to lower her voice since she couldn't be heard over Blayne's excited squealing as she ran out the French doors that led to an enormous backyard.

"Nothing."

"Hate when you lie to me."

Lock shrugged those massive shoulders she sometimes hung off just because she could. "He bought her a house." He glanced over at Novikov, who didn't seem impressed by his own purchase. Then again, Novikov rarely seemed impressed by anything. "Actually, he bought her a mansion. I made you a table."

"The mahogany one you had in the back room of your workshop?"

"You saw it?"

"Saw it. Loved it. Already planned to move it into the new apartment."

"It's not a mansion."

"And you're not Novikov and I'm not Blayne."

Blayne squealed again and charged back into the living room, slamming the doors behind her. Something rammed into the doors from the other side, nearly sending Blayne crashing to the floor.

"Squirrel!" she squealed.

"What?" Novikov asked.

"Squirrel!"

"What did you do to them now?"

"I didn't do anything. They just attacked me!"

Novikov rolled his eyes and began looking around his house again. "Man, these badgers are sloppy. We'll have to bring that cleaning service I like in to go over the place again before we can stay here." Another bang at the door and Novikov glared at Blayne. "Would you stop fooling around with those squirrels?"

"*Me?* I didn't do anything!"

"You sure? You didn't try to pet one?"

Her back still against the door, Blayne admitted, "I just wanted to see if they were friendly."

"Well . . . now you know they're not."

Gwen looked at Lock. "And I am seriously okay with not being them."

Livy walked into the room, and Gwen was happy to see her friend-in-derby, whom she privately called "my personal battering ram" looking healthy and surprisingly happy, considering.

"Hey," Novikov greeted her, a real smile on his face.

"Hey." She nodded at Novikov and then Lock. Livy's way of saying "thanks for saving my life" without actually saying it.

"Livy! Hey!" Blayne cheered from her spot at the door, her body the only thing keeping the squirrels outside.

Livy studied Blayne. "What are you doing?"

"Slight problem with a squirrel. Or squirrels. Probably squirrel*s* at this point."

"Oh yeah." Livy walked up to Blayne, grabbed her wrist, and yanked her from the door. She snatched the doors open and hissed. Panicked squeals and chattering followed, and Livy closed the doors.

"Sorry about that. My uncles got drunk the other night and kind of had a feeding frenzy out there with the squirrels and raccoons."

Horrified, Blayne demanded, "Why would they do such a thing?"

"I wouldn't let them bring snakes here and they were hungry for something that would fight back."

"Thanks," Novikov said. "For not bringing snakes in here."

"You're welcome."

"Really?" Blayne asked her mate.

"What do you want me to say? 'Go on, bring your snakes in'? That sounds poorly planned, in my opinion."

Blayne dismissed her mate with a wave of both hands and suddenly walked toward Livy, arms opened wide. The badger immediately held her hand up, stopping Blayne in her tracks.

"No," Livy told Blayne.

"But—"

"No. No hugging. You can say 'good to see you' from there."

"Oh, come—"

"No." When Blayne stamped her foot in frustration, Livy offered, "I can open those doors and let those squirrels right back in here."

"Fine. But you're being kind of a bitch."

"To be honest, I've never been *kind* of a bitch. I just am."

Blayne glared at Gwen. "And you can stop laughing."

"I could . . . but I won't."

Dee-Ann sat at the kitchen island in the apartment she shared with her mate. And it was her mate who put a cup of coffee in front of her and said, "I'm worried about you."

"Don't know why."

Ric sat down next to her. "Because you're kind of . . . depressed. I've never seen you depressed before. It's completely freaking me out."

"I failed. Hate failure. Just another word for weakness."

"How did you fail? If anything, it sounds like our bosses failed. Miserably."

"You didn't see how *your* friends all looked at me. Like I'd shot Kowalski myself. I've never not been trusted before."

"Dee-Ann."

She revised her statement. "I've never not been trusted before by those I wasn't actively trying to kill. Happy now?"

"Just trying to keep you honest."

The doorbell rang, and Ric kissed Dee-Ann on the forehead before walking out of the kitchen to answer.

"Dee-Ann?" Ric eventually called out.

"What?"

Ric came back into the kitchen. "You have a visitor."

She looked up to see Barinov taking up the entire doorway.

"Hey, Dee-Ann."

"It wasn't me!" she suddenly exploded, surprising everyone in the room, even herself. "I'd never put someone in that kind of danger. All right, maybe Blayne, but Kowalski ain't ever annoyed me as much as that mutt—"

"Dee-Ann. Dee-Ann!" Barinov chuckled. "I'm sorry we bailed the way we did. At the time I was not comfortable trusting . . . anyone."

"You trusted Novikov," she couldn't help reminding him. "And *Blayne*."

"It's a mutt thing."

Ric snorted, and when Dee glared at her mate, he quickly walked toward the refrigerator. "Would you like something to drink, Vic? Orange juice? Honey soda?"

"No thanks. I'm actually here to let Dee know . . . wait. There's honey soda?"

"Y'all!"

"Sorry. Sorry. We found Whitlan."

Ric closed the refrigerator and faced Barinov. "You found him?"

"He's being protected. Heavily."

Dee-Ann shrugged. "Don't care if he's being protected by Satan himself, where is he?"

"Russia."

"Oh, you can't go there," Ric immediately replied.

"Van Holtz—"

"Don't even, Dee-Ann. *You* can't go to Russia."

"Ain't nobody gonna stop me."

"Since the prime minister still so lovingly refers to you as The Murdering Twat, I think we need to come up with another option. And who, exactly, is protecting Whitlan in Russia?" he asked Barinov.

"Rostislav Chumakov."

Ric's mouth dropped open, and he took a step back. "Are you sure?"

"Positive. We have a plan to lure him to New York, but we need someone to deal with Whitlan in Russia. We could use one of our Russian contacts, but considering who Chumakov is . . ."

"He's on the BPC board."

"Plus, he's a powerful mobster. I don't know many shifters willing to take on bears. Especially connected bears like Chumakov."

"I do," Dee-Ann said. "I know someone who'd be more than happy to do this job."

"Dee-Ann," Ric reminded her, "you can't go."

"Not me. But it is someone I'd trust with my life. And all yours." Dee-Ann grinned, and both men backed away from her.

Barinov shuddered. "No offense, but I really wish you wouldn't do that."

Livy looked over the unbelievably meticulous drawing of the wedding venue that Bo Novikov had created.

"This is very . . . precise," she noted.

"I knew you probably couldn't come to see it until the day of the wedding."

"Very true. Did you study architecture in college?"

"Never went to college. Figure if I want to know something, you can always find books to read about the subject."

"I see." No wonder Toni knew how to handle Novikov so

well. He was just another freaking prodigy. Brilliant while emotionally stunted.

"You will be at the wedding, though . . . won't you, Livy?" Blayne asked.

She could have tormented Blayne, like she did most days. But Livy just didn't have the heart. Not when the wedding clearly meant so much to her.

"I wouldn't miss it."

"Russian bears with guns wouldn't keep you away?"

They all looked across the table at Gwen. She shrugged and admitted, "It sounded much funnier in my head. Then when it actually came out of my mouth . . ."

Lock took Gwen's hand. "I think the phrase you're looking for is 'too soon.' "

Livy shrugged. "There's no 'too soon' with the Kowalskis."

"You know what really sucks," Blayne pointed out. "You can't come to the bachelor-bachelorette party we've planned. No strippers."

"Although my mother did beg," Gwen sighed.

"My mother did, too," Lock added. "But only out of intellectual curiosity."

"Yeah, right," Livy snorted. But when the grizzly glared at her, she choked back her laughter. "Just kidding."

"You know what?" Blayne jumped up from her chair and began to pace around the table. "We should move the party here."

"You're unfamiliar with the concept of being in hiding, aren't you?" Livy asked.

"We'll just invite a few friends. That way you don't have to miss anything!"

"That sounds like a great idea!"

Snarling, Livy turned toward her nosy cousin. "No, Jake."

"Come on! Everybody loves a party."

"I was very clear to you about how you're going to treat this house. No parties. No snakes. No stealing."

Novikov tugged on Livy's sweatshirt. "I find detailed lists about what they can and cannot do . . . very helpful. They may not stick to it, but you do have proof that you told them."

"You guys are forgetting something," Blayne stated. "This is *my* house. A wedding gift from my future husband. And if I want a fucking party here, I'm going to have a party."

Lock pointed at Livy. "Your eye is twitching uncontrollably."

"We in the family," Jake said, his hand landing on Livy's shoulder, "call that Livy's tell."

Livy spun and rammed her fist into her cousin's stomach. He didn't drop, but his knees looked ready to buckle and his face blanched.

"Did I tell you *that*?" Livy asked.

"You want me to help *who* get into my country?" Grigori Volkov demanded.

Vic held up his hands. "No, no. I can get him into the country. I need your Pack to lead him to Chumakov's territory through yours."

"Oh! Well then!" Grigori's voice boomed around the room. "Is that all?"

"Grigori—"

"You come to me, bringing your stuffed panda with you—"

Shen looked away from the e-mails on his phone. "Hey! What did I do?"

"—and you dare," Grigori yelled, getting in Vic's face—one of the few men who actually could—"ask me to lead this . . . mangy *sobaka* into the territories of *my* people?"

Vic placed his hands on Grigori's shoulders. "Referring to a fellow wolf as a dog does not help anyone, Grigori Volkov." Vic stepped closer to his friend. "But giving a fellow wolf assistance in this matter . . . would reward *you*, old friend, with a powerful ally."

"More powerful than me?"

"In this country? Yes."

Grigori turned away, and Vic knew the old wolf was turning over the possibilities of an alliance in his head. Like a true Alpha wolf, Grigori only *appeared* to be led by emotion, when in fact, wolves were a cold, calculating species, often loving only to those they considered part of their Pack.

"To help you in your decision-making," Vic said, "I have something for you. From my father."

Vic placed the briefcase his father had given him on the table and opened it.

Grigori glanced at it, quickly looked away, then slowly back. "That is for my Pack?"

"The gold bricks are. The cash is for any last-minute issues that might come up. A sign of goodwill."

"Your parents," Grigori said, smiling, "never fail to surprise me, Victor Barinov."

"Are you in?"

"To help an old friend?" Grigori held his arms open wide and happily bellowed, *"How could I not?"*

CHAPTER 34

Vic drove down the Rhode Island street. His errands had taken longer than he'd wanted, but still . . . things seemed to be working out.

Shen tapped his arm. "Hey, Vic?"

"Huh?"

"Are those cars heading down the road to Novikov's house?"

Vic sighed. "It's my fault really. I left Blayne Thorpe alone in a house full of badgers. It was like I was asking for it."

Sure enough, they pulled into the long, curved driveway in front of Novikov's house and saw all the cars parked there, the doors and windows of Novikov's house wide open, music blasting from inside.

"I'd have to say," Shen remarked, "this is not discreet."

Shaking his head, Vic stepped out of his SUV. He stopped to grab a shopping bag from the backseat and then followed Shen into the house. It wasn't too late, but the party was already going strong, Novikov's house filled with wolves, wild dogs, bears, and felines, as well as the honey badgers who'd already been staying there.

"Do me a favor," Vic said to Shen. "Check on Melly."

"Because she's smelly?" He laughed at his joke.

"Shen—"

"I've got it," he said, heading for the stairs. "I've got it."

Vic walked through the house, greeting those he knew, nodding at those he didn't but who looked like they might come over to talk to him if he didn't nod.

He'd never been a fan of crowds. Small dinner parties were more his speed. Quiet discourse over good food. But this sort of thing just made Vic nervous. He'd been caught in too many out-of-control crowd situations during his time in the military.

And something told him that—for different reasons—Livy felt the same.

"Vic! Vic!"

Vic turned and saw Toni making her way through the crush of bodies. Once she reached him, she placed her hand on his arm, and Vic leaned over so she could say into his ear, "You know where to find her, Vic."

He stared at Toni a moment, then smiled. "Thank you."

"You're welcome."

Vic cut through the crowd and headed into the kitchen.

"Vic!" the badgers cheered, bottles of snake poison–infused vodka spread out on the island along with what he was guessing was snake jerky.

"Hi."

"Vodka?" Balt offered.

"Nyet."

The badgers laughed at his quick use of Russian, not realizing he always fell back on the first language he'd learned when he was particularly stressed out.

Vic walked to the high cabinet where he and Livy had stashed their favorite honeys, out of easy reach of her family. He opened the door and Livy—thankfully fully dressed this time—glared at him until she recognized Vic.

"Where the holy fuck have you been?"

Vic didn't answer; he just put down the bag he carried

and reached in for Livy. He pulled her out of the cabinet, dropped her over his shoulder, retrieved the bag, and escaped out the sliding kitchen doors.

Livy didn't complain that she'd been tossed over a man's shoulder like some sort of deer trophy. She was just glad to be out of that house with so many goddamn people.

What happened to the small party Blayne had talked about? "Just a few friends," she'd said. Lying wolfdog!

Livy loathed crowds unless she had her camera. Her camera gave her a wonderful feeling of apart-ness that nothing else did. She felt safe with a camera in front of her. But her camera was in pieces in a trash can. So she'd ended up feeling completely naked with everyone talking to her, trying to hug her, trying to show affection. Yeah, yeah, they were happy to see her alive. That was great. That did *not* mean they had to touch her.

Toni had tried to help her stay at the party, but eventually her friend came to the same conclusion that Livy had—without a camera, all Livy wanted to do was start killing people. Eventually Toni had distracted everyone by giving Blayne a sugar-filled drink but telling her it was sugar-free. By the time the wolfdog was doing backflips across the living room floor, Livy was able to slip into the cabinet and away from everyone.

Until Vic.

He'd come, and like a knight in shining armor, he'd rescued her from all the annoying singing, dancing, and general enjoyment everyone was feeling, carrying her off into the wooded area around Novikov's house.

She'd never been so grateful before. And yes, that included the time Novikov and MacRyrie saved her life. Getting shot was one thing, but being social and friendly was "a whole 'nother," as her father used to say.

Finally, Vic stopped and placed her by a tree, the full

moon giving their predator eyes enough light to see everything.

"Are you all right?" Vic asked, crouching in front of her.

Livy responded by throwing herself into his arms. "Thank God, you came!"

"How did this happen?"

"It was Blayne's fault," Livy couldn't help but spit out. "Since we were going to miss her stupid bachelor and bachelorette party. As if I'd have gone to that little event in the first place."

"You went to karaoke."

Livy pulled back and relaxed against the tree. "That was your fault."

"True."

She let out a relieved breath, finally feeling free again. "Everything go okay?"

"Everything went fine."

"Good. I'm glad you're back."

Vic sat down across from her. "I brought you something."

She smiled. "Honey?"

"Don't you have enough honey?"

"I kind of ate most of it while I was in the cabinet. Especially after I heard my mother shout, 'Let's do the hustle!' Honestly, is my life not hard enough right now?"

"Apparently not."

"So, what did you bring me then, if not honey? Diamonds? A fancy watch? A small child I can use as slave labor?"

"You don't wear jewelry, so that takes out the diamonds and watches. And you don't seem to like children unless they're prodigies."

"Stupid children bore me."

"So I brought you this instead." He placed a large paper bag with handles next to her. Livy dug into the bag and let out a sigh. She gazed at Vic a moment before saying, "You magnificent bastard."

* * *

Vic watched her pull out the boxes, handling each one with a reverence he'd only seen from holy men at the Russian Orthodox church he'd visited in Moscow when he was trying to track down a contact.

Livy looked at everything for a very long time until she finally said, "You got me a camera."

"The guy at the store said it was the best. Now, before you think, okay, they saw a sucker coming, Grigori recommended the store. And they knew Grigori recommended it, so they wouldn't risk pissing him off."

"Vic . . . I can't take this. It must have cost you a fortune."

"Grigori-friend discount, which apparently translates into fifty percent off. And after seeing the price tag . . . I'm very grateful for that fifty percent." Again, Livy didn't say anything for a very long time. "Is it okay? Because I'd kind of hate to take it back after the discount and all—"

"It's perfect. It's a pro camera. The best Nikon makes. One step above the one that got destroyed."

"Good. I did remember your brand. Just not the model number or anything. If you want, you can put it together now and then go back to the party."

Livy's head came up and she looked at him. "Huh?"

"I know you hate crowds without your camera. Unless, of course," he felt the need to add, "you're jousting bears. Because you're *that* ridiculous. And no, I'm not letting that go."

"Fuck," Livy said as she buried her face in her hands.

"What? What's wrong?"

She looked at him. Actually, it was more of a scowl. She scowled at him.

"I'm in love with you," Livy snapped. "And it's your fucking fault."

"Uh . . . sorry?"

"Oh, shut up."

"Well . . . if it makes you feel better, I'm in love with you, too."

"As a matter of fact, it *doesn't* make me feel better. Do you know why?"

"Not a clue."

"Because love is a trap. Just ask my parents."

"But your parents were divorced."

"Several times, apparently. But no matter how many times they were divorced, they were always together. Why? Because they were madly in love. Like idiots."

"Maybe that's how *they* love. We're different."

"I am tainted by their bloodline."

"You're not tainted. I'm not tainted by my parents."

"And how do you figure that?"

"I can't saunter into a room and make everyone in there want to have sex with me or kill me like my mother. But I can have a conversation in a tone of voice that doesn't travel through several states . . . unlike my father. And although you have a mean streak a mile wide just like your mother, you seem to only use it on Blayne. And like your father, you do seem to like a good fight, but you only seem to enjoy fighting Melly . . . and beehives. And to me that means we can love each other any way we want to. Even like normal people."

"You mean normal people who have a mouthful of fangs and a prehensile tail."

"You like my tail."

"I also like my mouthful of fangs . . . that doesn't make us normal."

"Well," Vic asked, since he was at a complete loss, "do you want to go back inside?"

"No," she snapped, "I want to stay out here by this stupid giant tree and fuck." Livy threw up her hands. "See? Pathetic."

"You're a very hard woman to understand sometimes."

"Don't bullshit me," she accused. "You understand me better than anybody."

"And that irritates the hell out of you, doesn't it?"

"Yes! Because I'll rely on you now. You'll always mean something to me. You'll be important in my life. My *art* is the only thing that should be important. Love is just this fucking distraction. It destroys good art."

"Only if you let it, which you won't because you are self-ish enough not to."

Livy nodded. "That's a good point. And you travel a lot, so I won't come home every day to find you sitting on the couch, waiting for me to be there, so you can annoy me with your attention and affection."

"God forbid."

"Yeah," Livy said, not quite getting the sarcasm.

"But, hey, you never know. We could still get killed. We're not finished yet."

"But we both know that's bullshit. I'm a honey badger. And you're just . . . freaky."

"Thank you."

She sighed as if she'd realized the worst thing imagina-ble. "We're going to be together and in love forever, aren't we?"

"Probably."

"That's so fucking typical of my life," she spat out. "I can never get a break."

"I'm sorry."

"No, you're not."

"No. I'm not." Vic leaned down and pressed his forehead against Livy's. "Can you say it again?"

"I don't want to. No. That's not true. I do want to, but I shouldn't want to."

"Say it anyway. For me."

She reached up and cupped his face in her hands. "I love you."

"I love you, too."

"See? Why do you have to be so mean?"

Laughing, Vic hugged Livy tight. "Sorry. That must be the feline mean streak I got from my mother."

"Probably."

Finally getting past all those people, Shen peeked into the makeshift art studio and found Melly doing what she'd been doing since she'd been given the job to create a perfect Matisse . . . she was sitting and staring.

An arm reached around him and softly closed the door. The arm belonged to Jocelyn.

He started to say something, but Jocelyn shook her head, one finger against her lips. She took his arm and pulled him down the hallway.

"I don't want to doubt you guys, but . . . she's just sitting there, staring. That's all she's been doing."

"She'll start when she's ready."

"We don't have a lot of time."

"There are some things you can't rush."

"Yeah, but—"

"You, understandably, may not have faith in that crazy bitch. But you can have faith in us. We've been doing this sort of thing for a very long time. We know what we're doing."

"I really hope you're right. There's a lot riding on this."

"Trust me, sweetie. That I do know. Livy and Jake are the only cousins I haven't actively tried to kill or dismember." She thought a moment. "Well, definitely haven't tried to kill."

The orgasm eased through Livy slowly, almost languidly, but it was more powerful than anything she'd ever experienced because it was with someone she loved.

When the last wave passed, she dropped onto Vic's chest

and his big arms surrounded her, and held her close while his tail stroked her back and eventually curled around her thigh. She hated him a little for making her feel so safe. But it was just a little hate.

They lay under that tree, not bothering to speak. Something Livy adored about Vic. No postcoital chattiness. She loathed analyzing sex that had happened just seconds before. Thankfully, Vic didn't need to confirm his sexual prowess by grilling her on how it all went. Instead, she knew he was probably thinking about food—as was she. The problem was whether to go back to the house to get food or ignore their growling stomachs until everyone eventually left.

Yet before they could debate the pros and cons of both alternatives, Vic suddenly turned on his side, Livy going with him. He raised his head as he sniffed the air.

"Vic?"

He began to growl. A low, rumbling noise that rolled through Livy; his lips curling and twitching; his body tense and trembling.

"Vic?"

Staring off toward the house, Vic let out a snarl and he suddenly released Livy. He scrambled to his feet and shifted, his body going from big to enormous. Livy was forced to scramble away so she didn't get crushed by his giant ass.

Vic took off toward the house, and Livy grabbed her clothes and ran after him. She came out of the trees just as Vic locked on to his only natural foe—and charged him.

The two hybrid predators collided in midair, Livy immediately forgetting she was still naked as she watched Victor Barinov go ridiculously-sized claw to ridiculously-sized fang with Bo Novikov.

Someone grabbed Livy around the waist and carried her over to stand with the crowd of predators watching the battle.

"Don't worry," Lock said as he placed her down and quickly released her. "This is just play fighting. Now that they've both gotten lai—" Lock stopped, eyed Livy. "Now that they've both had some one-on-one time with their women," he revised.

Bears. So damn polite.

"Play fighting?" Livy asked. "Seriously?"

"I know it doesn't look it. But I think . . . because they can't really do this with anyone else without killing them . . . they're doing it now with each other."

"What is going on with Novikov's fangs?" Livy wanted to know. "Are those tusks?"

"They're not *tusks,*" Blayne argued, pushing past Lock. "They're fangs. Like the mighty saber-toothed cat of yore."

"It is like watching *Jurassic Park,*" Livy's mother muttered.

"And before we start throwing stones," Blayne said, the most-likely-sugar-filled drink in her hand giving her a lot of bravado, "let's talk about that tail good ol' Vic is rocking there."

Livy slowly turned her head to look at Blayne. "What about it?"

"It's a little freaky-lookin', is all I'm saying."

"Uh . . . Blayne?" Lock shook his head as Livy began to shift. "I wouldn't do that if I were you."

"You're right," Blayne said immediately. "That was mean. I'm sorry," she said as she turned to face Livy. "I never should have said that to—*badger!*"

Toni winced when she saw Livy take Blayne down like an African beehive. She grabbed Ricky Lee's arm. "Stop them."

The wolf shook his head. "I ain't gettin' in the middle of that."

Lock MacRyrie rolled his eyes in disgust. "I'll take care

of it." He reached down to grab Livy's honey badger form off Blayne, but he immediately stumbled back, his hands up to protect his eyes. "Okay, I'm out! I'd rather get between the woolly mammoth and the saber-tooth cat."

"Get her off me!" Blayne screamed. "Get her off me!"

Toni went to grab Livy, but Ricky Lee caught and yanked her back. "Have you lost your dang mind?"

"In case you haven't noticed, honey badgers don't play-fight!"

"Move, move," Balt and Livy's uncles said as they pushed through the crowd. "Such weakness," Balt sneered, his eyes red from all the poison-infused vodka he'd been swilling the last hour.

"Be ready," he told his brothers before he reached down and grabbed Livy by the back of the neck. He lifted her up and off Blayne, and Livy's uncles immediately grabbed her legs and held them away from her body while she snapped and hissed at them all.

"Come!" Balt ordered. "Let us take our lovely niece inside and relieve her of having to look at these weak species."

Toni let out a breath once Livy was back in the house, and Gwen helped Blayne to her feet.

"You all right, Bland?" Toni asked.

"It's Blayne!" the wolfdog yelled.

"Oh God!" someone from behind Toni called out. "They're heading for the pool!"

Sure enough, the two behemoths battled their way across the giant yard until they tumbled into the pool. But so much predator landing hard in an Olympic-sized pool with heated water that kept it from freezing . . .

Toni turned away but it didn't help; the first three rows of spectators were drenched by heated water. The only ones who managed to get away in time? The honey badgers.

A group of them stood off to the side, dry, drinking their vodka, and laughing.

And the two males who'd caused this? Now flopping

around like two bear cubs in the water that was left in the pool. No longer bothering to fight because they were enjoying being goofy way too much.

"Well, I'm going inside," Gwen announced, trying to shake off the water. But she stopped when she saw Lock walking by with a hose.

"What are you doing?" she asked her fiancé.

"Filling up the pool," he explained. Lou Crushek—the polar bear—took the hose from him and went on to finish the task. "So we can shift and relax in there. Basically a bear version of a hot tub."

Toni, with a shake of her head, went inside for a dry towel and to get a stiff drink. Hell, why not? She wasn't driving tonight.

In a dry pair of sweatpants and T-shirt, a towel over his wet hair, Vic threw back his head and laughed at Crushek's story about taking down three Volkov Pack wolves during an ill-planned jewelry heist in Queens.

"One of them tried to make a run for it, and he just ran into these thick, bulletproof glass doors. So they didn't break, but he got knocked out cold."

"What's really sad," Vic finally admitted, "I know them. Those were Grigori's less-than-bright nephews."

"How are you friends with wolves?" Lock asked.

"I used to think it was because somehow the bear and feline parts cancelled each other out. But I finally realized it was my mother. The men love my mother."

Vic heard a *click* and looked over his shoulder to see Livy standing by the doorway, snapping pictures of them. She'd put her new camera together and was thoroughly enjoying the evening now that she had something between herself and the crowd at the house.

The one thing he knew not to do, though, was to point out that she was again using her camera. Nothing annoyed Livy more than when someone stated the obvious. Like, "Hot day, huh?" during an August day, or "Hey! That's a camera," when she was holding a camera.

Those were things that irritated her. So Vic returned to his conversation with men mostly built like him, but who didn't feel the need to drag him into playing a sport. According to Novikov, "I'm glad you don't play hockey because you could be better than me and then I'd just have to destroy you so you didn't get in my way."

He'd said that simply, as if it was something they should all understand—and they all did. It was clear Crushek and MacRyrie didn't agree with him, but they understood his logic. Vic, however, kind of agreed. He could be pretty competitive, but he hid it well.

Shen walked in with glasses and the bottle of forty-year-old scotch he'd found.

"Poison free," he promised as he poured each of them a glass.

"You sure?"

"I double-checked with Livy," he said, pointing to where Livy had just been standing. She'd gone off to take more pics of the partygoers. "Apparently we should all be grateful there aren't snakes here. It seems a honey badger party ain't a honey badger party without some black mambas roaming around."

Vic shuddered. "I hate snakes," he complained before sipping his drink.

"Then you better not go to any Kowalski-Yang reunions with Livy, my friend, because that is how they all roll."

"I've been thinking about adding snake to our menu," Van Holtz announced. "Cobra with a nice red wine sauce. Or should one have white wine with snake? Or should the wine vary with the type of snake . . . ?" He shook his head. "I'll have to do more research."

Vic and Novikov exchanged glances across the room until both shuddered and went back to their drinks.

* * *

Livy sat on the stairs, teaching herself how her new camera worked. Toni sat down next to her, handed her a Coke.

"I thought your camera got destroyed."

"It did. Vic bought me this one."

"He *bought* you that? That must have been expensive."

"It was, but he got a deal," she said proudly. She wasn't a fan of receiving stolen items—like the black pearl necklace her father had given her for her sixteenth birthday. Something he'd picked up from a heist a few days before. But Livy always did enjoy a good discount or haggling.

"You really are in love with Vic Barinov, aren't you?" Toni asked her.

"I am. I told him it was his fault and I'd never forgive him."

"He's not your dad, Livy."

"But am I? Am I going to make his life miserable?"

"You've damaged the man's home several times and eaten all his honey. If he's not miserable yet . . ."

"Thanks, friend o' mine."

Toni grinned. "You're welcome. Oh!" She went into the back pocket of her jeans and pulled out an envelope. "I got this in the mail yesterday. It's from Kyle."

Livy pulled the sheet of paper out of the envelope, unfolded it, and sighed. "Wow."

It was of her and Vic, asleep on the bed. Thankfully, they were both dressed as they'd been the morning Kyle had seen them that way.

"I didn't know you could look so serene."

"The serenity that comes with destroyed creativity."

Toni rolled her eyes. "You and Kyle with that ridiculous theory about love and the destruction of creativity." Toni took the camera from Livy's hand and looked through the pictures she'd taken so far, using the display screen on the back of the digital camera. "Look at that," she said, showing

Livy a picture she'd taken of Vic and Novikov chatting outside. They'd both just shifted and hadn't put on clothes yet. She'd shot them from behind . . . yeah, it was a great shot. And she hadn't even futzed with it yet, but she had shot it in black-and-white.

"So can we stop with this bullshit, please?" Toni asked, pushing the camera back at her.

"I guess."

"Aren't there bigger issues you have to worry about?"

"You mean the whole shot-by-bears thing?"

"Nah. You're through that. I'm talking about the illegal thing your cousin's doing upstairs. You guys are just going to piss off Chumakov. Apparently he's not one to back off when shamed. He may come after you again."

"Did you hear that from your new Russian bear friends?"

"Maybe." Toni glanced around. "Where is Zubachev anyway?"

"Flirting inappropriately with my mother in the kitchen."

"I wouldn't worry about that. He's very married."

"But he's near the poison-infused vodka—and my *mother*."

"Shit!" Toni jumped up. "He hasn't signed the contracts yet for the hockey games!"

Livy went back to playing with her new camera. "Some days, it's just too easy to manipulate these people."

CHAPTER 35

It took three solid days and Shen couldn't believe it. He could *not* believe what he was looking at.

He held up the print of that old missing Matisse painting and compared it to the painting Melly Kowalski had created.

It was hard to believe this mess of a woman—and good God, was she a mess—could create such an amazing copy of another artist's work. A great artist's work. She'd even used an old canvas her family kept for such occasions and aged the work.

Shen looked at Vic. "This is amazing."

"I now see why the Kowalskis put up with her. Apparently she can copy any artist or artist's style."

"So she's like a drunk-savant."

"I've never seen anyone drink so much vodka before in my life. She just passes out for a while, and when she wakes up, she's ready to eat and get back to work. It's utterly disturbing."

"So now what?"

"Now we let the Kowalski and Yang connections do what they do best."

"Which is?"

"Sell the Kowalskis' fake bullshit art to ridiculously rich people who are so desperate to have a piece of important art they refuse to know any better."

Shen smiled. "Excellent."

Grekina Renard opened her arms and hugged the giant bear of a Russian whom she'd invited into her art studio.

"I'm so glad to see you, Stepka Chumakov."

"And you, Grekina." He sized her up. "You look beautiful as always."

"Now, now, old friend. I didn't call you here for any of that."

"Then what do you want? My father is expecting me back in Moscow in the next day or two. You can come with me," he sweetly offered. "See your old homeland?"

"I'm only half-Russian. I was raised right here." Grekina dropped down into a comfortable chair. "Remember that offer you made to me a year or so ago?"

"I made lots of offers to you."

Grekina smiled. "I'm talking about the one that would get me money." And before he could run with that, she added, "If I brought you unique . . . art?"

"My father likes art. But he's very choosy."

"What about a Matisse?"

"He has one. Actually, he may have two."

"This one he won't be able to have on display."

"What do you mean?"

"It was stolen a few years back. It really belongs to a local museum."

The Russian suddenly sat up in his chair and paid close attention to what Grekina was saying rather than staring at her tits.

"You sure about this?"

"I have lots of friends in the art world. They tell me things."

"Is it here? In Belgium?"

"No. You'll have to travel for it. It'll be worth it, though. Interested?"

"Maybe." Stepka stood up. Adjusted what had to be a tailor-made suit because the man could not possibly shop at a regular store. "Text me the details, yes?"

"And, Stepka?"

"Yes?"

"My finder's fee?"

"When we find something . . . you'll get paid. Okay?"

"Perfect."

Grekina jumped up and walked to the elevator door of her studio. She lifted it and waved at Stepka before lowering it again. She went to one of the big windows and watched the street until she saw him leave the building and get into a Mercedes-Benz stretch limo.

Once he'd driven off, Grekina pulled the no-name cell phone out of the pocket of her denim shorts and dialed a number.

"Give it a day," she said to the voice that answered on the other end. "I'm positive he's in? How do I know?" Grekina grinned. "He stopped looking at my tits for longer than two seconds. That's how I know."

"Good news and bad news," Jocelyn announced as she walked into the living room. She stopped and stared at her cousins sitting on the floor. Each on laptops, with headphones on.

"What are you guys doing?"

"Killing stuff," Livy said, her gaze focused on her screen.

"Not killing," Vic said as he passed Jocelyn. The big hybrid dropped onto the couch. His hair was wet, and he'd changed out of what he'd worn earlier in the day. He never made much about it, but he'd clearly been enjoying

Novikov's indoor pool. Not that she blamed him. "Massacring. They've been massacring."

"What?"

"They joined a game, created a league, and now they're killing everyone and taking all their shit."

"I now have the most amazing armor," Jake said, grinning. "It's got spikes. If I were a warrior from back in the day, I would totally have spiked armor."

"Anyway," Jocelyn said, totally dismissing this conversation since she didn't understand the appeal of gaming. "Word has come down that Chumakov is sending an art appraiser to evaluate the painting before he'll come to the States." She glanced at Vic. "He's apparently being very cautious at the moment."

"Can you blame him?"

"No."

"So what if he's sending an appraiser?" Jake asked, his fingers pounding on his poor keyboard. Now Jocelyn understood why he had one laptop for his "work" and one for his gaming, considering the abuse the gaming one took. "Who cares?"

"We need to." Jocelyn waited a moment for full dramatic effect, before stating, "He's sending Pierre-Phillipe Anwar from Paris."

Every honey badger eye turned to Jocelyn and she knew why. Although the hybrid didn't.

"Who's Pierre-Phillipe Anwar from Paris?" Vic asked.

"Well, we're screwed!" Jake announced, always more dramatic than the rest of them.

"Pierre-Phillipe? Are you sure?" Livy asked.

"I'm sure."

"Still don't know who that is," Vic said.

"One of the best art appraisers in the world."

Livy scratched her ear. "Jake's right. We are so screwed."

"Is it really that bad?"

"Pierre-Phillipe Anwar works for the biggest and most powerful museums in the world," Jocelyn explained. "He's testified in federal and international cases that have put people away for decades, including a few of our relatives."

"Poor Cousin Bronislaw," Jake sighed, sadly shaking his head.

"But I thought Melly was the best."

"She is. But so is Anwar. If anyone can sniff out her work, it's him."

"Then what do we do?" Vic asked.

"Can we bribe him?" Livy asked.

"We tried with Cousin Bronislaw. That was added to his federal charges."

"Oh."

"So what do you want to do, Livy?"

Never one for rash decisions, Livy was silent as she thought on that. After a bit, she said, "Let's see how it plays out. We're going through a third party anyway. If it blows up, we can clean up and be gone in less than thirty."

"Should we tell Melly what's going on?"

"She's not even here," Jocelyn replied to Jake's question. "She went back to the City with Antonella. To meet up with her 'boyfriend,'" she said with air quotes.

"Thousand bucks says she's in jail by the end of the week," Jake tossed out. Sadly no one took him up on it.

"Did you tell my mother all this?" Livy asked.

"And Uncle Bart." Jocelyn shrugged. "They both said to come to you."

Livy rolled her eyes. "I hope they don't think this is some kind of training. I have no plans to join the family business because of this."

"I don't think that's it," Jocelyn admitted. "Your father, your decisions. That's how it works. Besides, you've become too much of a goody two-claws from hanging around those Jean-Louis Parkers. You're very lucky we still allow you to call yourself a Kowalski."

Livy snorted, returned to her ridiculous gaming. "As if I could be anything else."

Dez stood behind the Kowalski contact handling the selling of the painting. She was fully aware this was illegal. Selling a painting she knew to be a forgery. Helping the Kowalskis lure a man to this country so they could kill another man in a foreign country . . .

She couldn't even pretend this was *kind* of legal. It wasn't. Not a little. Even if she wanted to bust the guy who was going to be evaluating the painting, she couldn't do that, either.

And yet . . . Dez felt no guilt. She should. Before her life had changed to include a husband who could shift into a five-hundred-pound lion and a son who would one day be able to shift into a five-hundred-pound lion, she'd been a very clean cop. Something she'd been proud of.

But with life changes came moral changes sometimes. At least for her. Because protecting her family had become the most important thing. Sometimes the only thing. So if that meant helping a family of honey badgers track down and kill a man who'd been hunting shifters like her husband and son for sport . . . Dez was going to do it.

The art appraiser glanced up at Dez. He had small eyes behind those glasses he wore. Small and beady. And his French accent annoyed her. She didn't know why. When Mace had taken her to Paris for their anniversary last year, she'd loved every minute of it. God, especially the food. She almost went up a pant size eating all that great food. But this guy . . .

Maybe it was just the rude arrogance behind that French accent and those beady eyes that was annoying her. Yeah. She could see that.

"Who is that?" Anwar asked, pointing a long, thin finger at Dez.

"She is my protection," the contact replied.

"I see."

"You don't expect me to walk around New York with a Matisse and not have some protection, do you?"

"If it *is* a Matisse," he sneered.

Dez watched the little man work. It took hours. Seriously. Hours.

Hours of staring, of pulling out small lights and things to test as much as he could. There was some muttering about more intensive tests like X-rays or carbon dating. But he'd need help with that, and no matter how much he was being paid by Chumakov, Anwar wasn't about to risk his reputation with legitimate museums and reputable art dealers by taking a stolen Matisse in to have it flippin' x-rayed.

As they hit hour six, Dez began to panic. How much longer would this take? And what if he didn't think it was a real Matisse? Then what? Dez liked Livy. She wanted her safe. She wanted all shifters safe, even the ones she didn't like . . . her sister-in-law coming to mind.

Finally, the man stood tall and sniffed in such a way that Dez was convinced they were screwed.

He pulled out a cell phone—a different one from that phone he'd been checking all day—speed-dialed someone, and said something in what sounded like Russian. Although Dez didn't know. She spoke English and Brooklyn-English, which involved some Spanish, and mangled Italian and Yiddish. But that was it.

With a nod at the contact, he packed up his crap and walked out without a word.

"Well?" Dez asked the contact.

The pretty girl smiled and gave a thumbs-up.

With a relieved sigh, Dez unclipped her cell phone from the holster attached to her jeans and called Vic. "It fuckin' worked," she said in Brooklyn-English. "I can't believe it, but it fuckin' worked."

* * *

Vic put down his phone and looked at the three badgers and panda he was playing Texas Hold 'Em with at the kitchen table. Livy, Jake, Jocelyn, and Shen. He looked and said nothing.

As one, the four shifters turned and looked out the sliding-glass doors where Melly yelled into her cell phone, *"You will never stop loving me! I will kill you first!"* She burst into tears. "Please don't stop loving me," she sobbed. "Please! *You motherfucker!*"

They faced forward again, shook their heads, and went back to playing their game.

CHAPTER 36

Bayla Ben-Zeev reviewed the finances for each of the department heads who reported to her.

Unlike her predecessor, Balya did not nitpick each and every dime spent. If a fellow grizzly liked to spend BPC money on honey or a nearly eight-foot polar needed to invest in an extra-strong office chair designed for his four hundred and fifty pounds of muscle, she wasn't going to argue. There were always more important things for her people to be doing than worrying about the cost of chairs.

Besides, Bayla occasionally liked this kind of busywork. Adjusting numbers, deciding which department needed more, which could survive with less. This kind of work had always been a nice break from what her real work was, which at first had been protecting the Israeli people. But now, it was protecting her fellow bears.

Both jobs she was exceedingly proud of.

Bayla's office door was thrown open and a large grizzly stormed in.

He threw his arms wide. "Bayla, my love!"

Bayla sighed, already apologizing to her ears for the next few minutes of onslaught.

She leaned back into her chair. "Vladik Barinov. I'm not surprised to see you in my office."

"Really?" He dismissed Bayla's assistant with a wave of his hand.

But the Bronx native black bear wasn't so easily sent away. She looked at Bayla.

"It's all right, Judith. You can go."

The door closed behind the She-bear, and Vladik dropped his mighty bulk into the chair across from Bayla's.

"You are looking good, my dearest one. This New York City life agrees with you."

Bayla ignored the compliment. Instead, she went back to her paperwork and said, "I've been hearing things about your son." She thought a moment. "Victor."

"My wonderful boy! So very handsome! Just like his papa!"

"Unfortunately, Vladik, he's become friendly with a rather unsavory element."

"Honey badgers have right to be pissed, do they not?"

"Do they?"

"Rostislav Chumakov is not a friend, my dear Bayla."

"He gives BPC lots of money."

"Is that why you protect him?"

Bayla looked up from her work. "I protect Chumakov as much as I protect you or any other of our kind. I need proof before I condemn a bear."

"You will have proof."

"Will I?"

"Oh yes. But he must know, Bayla—that retaliation of any kind would be foolish on his part." Vladik grinned. "You know me. I am friendly bear! Everyone loves Vladik! But if he tries to kill my son's lovely little badger again—I will cut him up into little pieces and bake him in pie. My grandmother did that once to a full-human she did not like in a neighboring village." His smile faded. "She fed him to his family—and laughed while they ate him."

His grin returned. "For we are jovial bears, the Barinovs! And we do not like unnecessary strife. What is the point, yes?"

Bayla leaned back in her chair. "I'll make sure everyone's clear on this issue. As you know, I believe in protecting hybrid bears as much as their full-blood brethren. That's important to me."

"Hearing that brings me joy, beautiful Bayla."

"But for this to go any further than just warnings, Vladik—I better have proof he's been protecting Frankie Whitlan."

"Do not worry, my dear—as I said, proof you will have. Most likely more proof than you could ever want."

Livy woke up when someone touched her arm. "Jake?"

"Chumakov's in town."

She nodded and said to her cousin, "You know what to do."

"We're already on it." Her cousin walked out. Livy looked up to see that Vic was awake, his gaze focused on her face.

"Already on what?" he asked.

"Keeping an eye on my mother."

"Your mother? Why?"

She yawned, snuggled back into his chest. "It's something she used to always tell me when I was growing up. Kowalskis never forget . . . but Yangs *never* forgive."

"We promised my father we wouldn't make a move on Chumakov until we had proof. And even then . . . we should still go through the BPC."

"Don't worry. Balt will keep her busy. How, I don't want to know. But we should be fine. At least until Chumakov heads out again."

"Good." Vic rubbed her back. "Besides, I doubt he'll be staying in the States for long. Not once he gets the news . . ."

* * *

After handing over three and a half million American dollars, four of his men packed the Matisse away and took it out a back door of the small Greek grocery store where they'd met the full-human contact who had the painting.

Rostislav Chumakov was so happy with his purchase—three and a half million for a Matisse, stolen or otherwise, was what Americans called a "steal"—he didn't notice anything was wrong when he stepped out of the small store and onto the Manhattan street until his eldest boy stopped walking right in front of him.

Rostislav leaned over a bit and he forced himself to smile. "Bayla Ben-Zeev," he said, walking around his son and over to the She-bear resting her big bear ass against his limo. "You look wonderful as always." He kissed both her cheeks.

"It's good to see you again, Rostislav. What brings you to the States?"

"A little business. I can't stay long."

"That's fine. Probably for the best. I heard you've been making some enemies lately." Ben-Zeev shook her head. "Badgers? You're pissing off badgers now?"

"I didn't know the BPC involved itself in a bear's personal business."

"We don't . . . unless it threatens what we have. When you told me I could use my people for more important work because you had a handle on the Whitlan situation"—she shrugged—"I took you at your word. A bear's word is very important to me, Rostislav."

"And I do have a handle on it. My men will track him down any day now."

She dramatically winced. "You may be too late on that."

"I do not understand."

"It's my understanding they may have found him. Whitlan, that is. In fact, I think things are already on the move."

She pushed away from the limo, pressed her hand against Rostislav's expensive suit. "If I were you, I'd let things play out . . . and just let it go."

"What?"

"Let it go, Rostislav. For your own good and the good of your family. Let it *go*." Bayla stepped away. "Safe trip back, old friend. Safe trip back."

They watched the She-bear walk to the corner, get in her own limo, and drive away.

"I wouldn't worry, Papa," his eldest sneered after Bayla. "I'm sure everything at home is—"

Rostislav focused on his son. "If you say the word 'fine,' I will beat you to death in this street." His boy said nothing else, which was good. "Now get me home," he ordered. Even though Rostislav already knew he was too late.

CHAPTER 37

Boris Krupin was bored. But his boss was a powerful bear who paid his people well. So if Rostislav Chumakov wanted them to protect a full-human, that was what they would do.

Still, Boris was happy when he heard the first wolf howl. Normally, a wolf howl this close to Chumakov territory just pissed Boris off. But tonight it did nothing but excite him. He relished the thought of slapping around some wolves.

Boris looked at his fellow bears and they all nodded, shifted, and went after those infiltrating wolves, leaving behind three bears to keep an eye on the useless full-human.

Frankie Whitlan heard the howling ring out and pulled his .357 Magnum. He went to the window and stared down at the front of the house. He watched several of the guards shift to bear and run off into the night. They were chasing wolves? Really?

These fools were here to protect *him,* not chase after local wolves like the filthy animals they were. These idiots were supposed to be smarter than their non-shifter counterparts. And yet they seemed just as stupid and worthless.

He decided to get them back so they could do their god-damn jobs. Frankie spun away from the window toward the study door but stopped short when cold yellow eyes, like a dog's, stared at him.

"Hi, Frankie," a voice growled from behind a massive beard and thick black hair.

Frankie immediately raised his weapon, but a big hand caught his and held the gun off. Then he saw a flash, and a blade rammed into Frankie's neck, instantly cutting off his ability to scream and breathe.

But that wasn't enough for the man killing him. He twisted the knife, forcing Frankie to the floor.

"That," the beard and black hair growled out as everything went dark for Frankie, "is for making me bring my hillbilly ass all the way to goddamn Russia just to kill you."

Eggie Smith of the Tennessee Smith Pack watched Frankie "The Rat" Whitlan die. The full-human tried not to, but the one real skill Eggie had was knowing how to kill a man. When the breathing and the heart stopped, Eggie knew he could leave.

He'd only do a job like this for his little girl. But she'd only ask him if it was real important. She knew that Eggie didn't like leaving his Darla unless he really had to.

Eggie walked out of a surprisingly tasteful study—considering the tackiness of the rest of the home—and into the hallway. That was where he found three bears waiting for him. They were armed but hadn't pulled their weapons yet. Probably figured they didn't have to for just one wolf.

One of the younger bears said something in Russian and started toward Eggie. But the older bear, a grizzly with lots of silver in his hair, pulled the boy back.

He said something to Eggie but, again, it was in Russian.

"What?"

The older bear's head tipped to the side. Very slowly, in

thickly accented English, the older bear asked, "Who are you, doggie?"

"Name's Eggie Smith. Nice to meet'cha."

Color drained from the older bear's face and he pulled the younger bear back by his T-shirt.

The younger bear didn't like that, arguing the point. But it was all in Russian, and Eggie didn't understand a dang word. So he patiently waited.

Got a little heated after a time, but then the older bear must have said something real pointed because the boy stopped and pointed at Eggie. "Smith?" he asked.

"Da. Smith," the older bear said.

All three bears looked over at Eggie—and Eggie smiled.

The bears jerked away like he'd thrown fire at them and stepped back so Eggie could walk by.

He did, but as Eggie passed he stopped because he felt the need to say, "And y'all should be ashamed of protecting that man. Ashamed," he repeated. When they only stared at him, appearing confused, he added, "Look it up."

Eggie walked out into the woods surrounding the estate and tossed his weapon at the Volkov wolves whom he'd been surprised would let a Smith anywhere near Russia. Apparently these wolves were friends with that Vic Barinov hybrid. Normally, Eggie would only trust his own connections for a job like this, but his baby girl had said Barinov could be trusted, as could the man's connections. So Eggie had taken the risk, and it had paid off.

He nodded at the Alpha Male of the Pack, much appreciatin' the vodka the man had let him taste during their lunch together, and headed toward the waiting car. But before he stepped into the vehicle, he heard vicious hissing.

Eggie watched the honey badgers trot past him and the wolves and head toward Chumakov's territory. While Eggie had been brought in to make sure the job was done and done right—these honey badgers had come from Mongolia. The Volkovs kept jokingly calling them the "Mongol Horde."

But that was basically what they were. If any bears got in their way, they'd crush them. Why they'd been hired or who'd hired them, Eggie didn't know. Nor did he care. His job was done.

He got into the car that would take him to the local airport so that Eggie could get right back where he belonged—the United States of America and his Darla Mae.

CHAPTER 38

Vic walked into the bedroom they'd been sharing since they'd been at Novikov's Rhode Island home and found Livy packing up her duffel bag.

"What's going on?"

"I need to go back. That feline wedding planner is getting way text-bitchy. 'When are you coming back?' " Livy mimicked in a high-pitched voice. " 'Should we hire someone else? For what you're charging, you should be on-call at al-llll times.' "

Vic sat down on the bed next to her bag. "Are you sure?"

"She may not really sound like that, but she was definitely being text-bitchy."

"Not *that*. Are you sure about leaving?"

"I can't hide out here forever."

"But," Vic said, getting to the heart of the matter, "there's a pool. I love that pool."

Livy laughed and put her hand on her shoulder. "I know this will be a sacrifice for you."

"It really will. But for *you*, I'll do it."

Vic watched Livy shove a bag of dirty clothes into her duffel bag then zip it closed. "Livy?"

"Huh?"

"Are you going back to your apartment?"

"I'd rather set myself on fire."

Startled, Vic laughed out, "Why?"

"It'll smell like Melly. Smelly Melly. I can't have her drunken scent surrounding me. I can crash at Toni's place, though, until I get another place that's hopefully snake free."

"Or you could crash at my place," he offered, trying his best to make it sound casual, even though it wasn't. "If you want, I mean."

With a sigh, Livy moved her bag aside and sat down on the bed next to Vic. "But . . ." she said hesitantly, "you don't have a pool."

Sadly, it took Vic a little longer than it should have for him to figure out she was joking. And by then, he was just embarrassed, grabbing Livy and yanking her onto his lap.

Vic kissed her neck and tickled her ribs, loving the way she laughed and tried to wiggle away from him until Livy's mother strode up to the door. The older She-badger had on her mink and held the handle of her bright red travel suitcase, which she rolled behind her.

"I'm leaving," Livy's mother announced.

"Bye, Joan."

Joan sniffed, tossed her hair, and walked off.

"Is she mad?" Vic asked.

"Who knows?"

"Shouldn't you ask?"

"Except I don't really care."

Vic's cell phone vibrated once, letting him know he'd gotten a text or e-mail, and he grabbed it off the nightstand. He opened a picture that had been sent to him and reared back.

"Oh my God."

"What?"

He sighed. "Well . . . Whitlan's dead."

Livy glanced back at him. "What?"

He held up the phone and Livy studied it. "Oh . . . yeah. He sure is."

"I can't believe Eggie Smith did this, though."

"That's not a Smith move. That's all honey badger."

"How do you know that?"

"I know my people. Any other shifter would have gone in, ended Whitlan, moved on. But my people . . . we're a little petty. Very mean."

Vic looked back at the picture, studied it a little more. "Livy? What's that? In the house."

Livy glanced over, shook her head. "It's a hole. They burrowed into Chumakov's house. Who knows what they did once they were inside."

"So, we're *actively* pissing off Chumakov now?"

"My family is, apparently. I'm just trying to get ready for this wedding." Livy stood, picked up her bag. "Come on. Let's get out of here. I'm done with hiding."

It took Chumakov more than two days to get home, including delays and a snowstorm that hit part of Eastern Europe. But when he stepped out of his car and saw Frankie Whitlan hanging upside down and skinless from the front of the house, all his travel exhaustion went away.

It wasn't that Whitlan had meant much to him beyond always providing the best entertainment. He could find anyone to do that. But he'd given Whitlan his protection. The protection of Rostislav Chumakov. That meant something. Or, at least, it used to.

But that girl was still alive, from what he'd heard. Whitlan was dead. And everyone now knew it.

"Hey, Chumakov," one of the bears from a nearby village called out. "Nice decorations!"

The other bears who'd come to see Rostislav Chumakov's shame laughed.

"Papa," his eldest urged. "We should go."

"No. I want to see all of it."

Rostislav walked into his home. There were holes torn into the foundation where the disgusting animals had dug through. Furniture had been pissed on. The lesser artwork he had acquired because he just liked the pieces had been slashed with claws. The expensive pieces had been taken. The electronics taken. His safes had been cracked and every bit of cash, gold, diamonds, everything, were gone. All the weapons he had were gone, and he'd had enough to equip an army. Expensive rugs were removed and expensive flooring destroyed.

Nothing, absolutely nothing, had been untouched. Even his pools, his workout equipment . . . everything.

And there were only three bodies here. Whitlan and two of Chumakov's most loyal men. But the other guards . . . they'd run. Bears had run from rodents.

"They've taken *everything*!" his youngest son yelled as he charged back into the room. "Even the paintings downstairs."

The artwork that Rostislav obtained through the black market, he kept in a special vault room. But the thieves had gotten in there, as well.

His eldest was busy on his phone and announced, "They cleaned out our bank accounts."

"The Moscow banks? That doesn't matter."

"All the accounts, Papa. They cleaned out *all* our accounts."

Of course Rostislav had money that was in no bank. He had gold and silver. He had businesses. He had other homes. But none of that was the point. The fact that he was still rich meant nothing when he could hear the laughter of his neighbors outside. Mocking him.

And that, more than anything, was something Rostislav Chumakov would not stand for. Not now. Not ever.

CHAPTER 39

Livy looked up from the new shots she'd taken a few days earlier and blinked in surprise.

"How long have you been standing there?"

Toni shrugged, smiled. "Not long. Just watching you work."

"Watching me work?" Livy looked down at her proofs and the loupe she'd been using to analyze each pic, which meant she'd been sitting in the same spot for the last two hours. "Okay."

Livy marked one of the proofs. "Are those Russian hockey bears of yours finally gone?"

"I thought you liked Zubachev."

"I liked the deal you signed with him and the Russian teams."

"Isn't that deal great?" Toni asked, grinning. "Everybody loves me right now. Loves, loves, loves me!"

Livy shook her head, chuckled. "Yes. Everybody loves you right now. But don't let that fool you into thinking they won't expect more from you any day now."

"Not a problem. I already have interest from the Swedish, Norwegian, and Mongolian teams."

Livy looked at her friend. "Novikov against a Mongolian hockey horde . . . I am *so* there."

"I know, right!" Toni jerked her thumb behind her. "Look, I'm about to head home for the night. You need anything?"

"Nope."

"And are you okay? About how things worked out?"

"I'm not losing any sleep, if that's what has you worried."

"Considering you sleep through anything . . . that's never been a concern of mine." She winked and stepped away. "I'll see you tomorrow."

"Night."

Livy worked for another thirty minutes or so until she realized she was thirsty. Standing up, she took a long stretch, arms over her head. Grabbing her denim jacket, she pulled it on and walked out of her office. Stopped, walked back, grabbed several dollar bills out of her backpack, then restarted her nightly journey to the soda machine.

With her show just a couple of weeks away, and Blayne's wedding in just a few days, she'd been spending nearly every night late at the Sports Center in order to get all her work done.

Of course, she was ready for Blayne's wedding. All her equipment checked, double-checked, and triple-checked. This might not be her future, but she still took it seriously. And once she made a promise . . .

Livy stopped, looked over her shoulder. She was right by the main ice rink, and she thought she'd heard something behind her.

Livy sniffed the air and tried to see if one of the security guards was wandering around. When she saw nothing, she turned around and abruptly jumped forward, her claws and fangs out.

"Wait! Wait!" The She-bear held up a hand, and the guards about to protect her and attack Livy instantly backed off. "Olivia Kowalski?"

"Yes."

"I'm Bayla Ben-Zeev."

"Good for you." Livy retracted her fangs and claws and walked around her, continuing on to the soda machine. After ordering her guards to stay behind, Ben-Zeev followed.

"I just wanted to give you a warning."

"About?"

"Rostislav Chumakov has disappeared. Deep into the bowels of Moscow. And those, honey badger, are deep bowels."

"That is a disgusting analogy."

Livy stopped in front of the soda machine. She got a Coke, a bottle of water, and a bag of Doritos. Coke and Doritos reminded her of high school, staying up late with Toni, studying for exams.

"Your family may have started something with that bear they will not want to finish."

"Oh?"

"They took all the money he had in his bank accounts, had him declared dead—" Livy snorted at that; she didn't mean to, but that had to be Jake—"stole everything out of his house and destroyed the foundation. It's crumbling as we speak."

"That last part wasn't Kowalskis," Livy admitted. "That was Mongolian badgers. But I'm sure my family asked them to do it."

"I warned Rostislav to let it go, but he won't. Not now. Not after what your family did."

"You wanted proof Rostislav Chumakov was protecting Whitlan. Now you have it."

"Anyone could have tacked Whitlan's body to the front of Chumakov's house. It doesn't mean the man had been living there."

"So the BPC is still protecting Chumakov? Even now?"

Ben-Zeev took a breath, released it. "No, we're not. But

there are bears, friends of Chumakov's, who do *not* believe he had anything to do with Whitlan. That he was set up by honey badgers who just wanted his money. And they *are* willing to protect him. To hide him. So it may take some time for us to track him down, and until we do—you and your family are in danger. He won't stop until he destroys all of you."

"Yes. I'm sure that's true." She smiled at the She-bear. "Thanks for letting me know."

She stepped around Ben-Zeev and walked back toward her office. That was when she saw Vic. The way he was scowling, she knew he was looking for her. Not surprising with her past history involving bears tracking her down at the Sports Center.

"I'm okay," she announced right off the bat.

"What's going on?" he demanded. "There's a small caravan of BPC bears outside the Sports Center."

"Ben-Zeev came here to warn me that Chumakov went underground."

"Because your family fucked with him?"

Livy laughed, took Vic's hand. "I didn't know they were going to, but I'm not exactly sorry."

"I feel like I should put you into protective custody or something."

"No more hiding." She tugged his arm until he came down and she could easily kiss him on the cheek. Then she whispered, "Honestly, I wouldn't worry much."

"He's a vindictive prick."

She smiled, nuzzled his jaw. "Vic, you still don't get it . . . I come from a *family* of vindictive pricks."

Kiril wanted to run away. He wanted to get out of here. But something told him he should not be noticed. Not by these men.

There were lots of big men in Moscow. He was used to them. But there was something about these three men . . . Then they began talking. Talking about killing. First a girl and her boyfriend, then the girl's mother, and uncles.

Kiril was horrified. He knew gangsters came to the *banya* for a good steam. Some *banyas* were just for them. But those criminals never talked business in front of outsiders. Never. Yet these men . . .

Did they know Kiril was in the room? Did they have any idea? Or did they just plan to kill him, too? He didn't know, and he was too terrified to make a run for it. It was like dealing with a dangerous dog. Any sudden moves would have the vicious animal focusing on you. He didn't want that. He just wanted to go home.

Eventually, the two younger men stood—holy God, the size of them. The sheer size of them!—and the older one stayed behind, pouring water over his head. He was no youngster, but his muscles, his body in general, was still very fit. He bore scars. Some looked like old knife marks, a few gunshots, but some seemed to be claw marks.

Kiril knew he should get up now, but this older man was scarier than the younger ones. So much scarier.

While he kept his head down, pouring water over it, the older man didn't notice the wooden bench beside him. Like the one Kiril sat upon, it was hollow, the entire thing tacked to the wall. But a piece of wood at the bottom was moving and suddenly it opened.

Fascinated and horrified, Kiril watched a small woman work her way out. She was old. And Asian. Chinese maybe? A long scar on one side of her neck. Without a sound, she eased her way out of the tiny space she'd been in. How she'd fit in there, he didn't know. Kiril was sure there was a vent behind that bench, but how did she get through it? She was not slim. Just a wide-shouldered old lady.

She got to her feet, and Kiril saw the walking stick she

held. Using her other hand, she grasped the head of the stick and pulled out a thin, stainless steel dagger. She stepped up to the older man, and when he lifted his head, suddenly realizing someone was standing next to him, she proceeded to stab him in the throat.

It wasn't wild stabbing, either. But very precise, deep jabs all across his neck.

Gasping for air and wrapping his hands around his throat to stop the bleeding, the man stood, stumbled, and fell to the ground. The old woman walked over to him, flipping him onto his back. Not an easy feat considering his size, but she seemed to have no trouble. She straddled his chest and then sat on it. She watched him for a bit.

"You never understood, did you?" she said in perfect Russian. "Kowalskis never forget . . . but Yangs *never* forgive." She tossed white hair that had slipped out of her simple bun from her eyes. "If you'd like, though," she taunted, "you can pretend this last bit is mercy. But," she said as she raised her arm, "we'll both know it really isn't."

Then she stabbed the man in both eyes and finished him off by slashing the blade across his throat.

She panted a bit while waiting for him to die. When he did, she stood, slid the blade back into the walking stick, and slowly made her way back across the room. She crouched down by that opening in the bench—and that was when she looked up at Kiril.

She held one very old finger to her lips. Then winked at him. She slipped back into that impossibly tiny space, somehow managed to put the wood panel back, and was gone.

Kiril still didn't run. He still didn't leave. He realized later that his not going had saved his life. Because when the two younger men came back in, screaming and wailing over what he now realized was their father's body, they quickly dismissed him as the culprit because he appeared so terrified. Finally, one of them grabbed the other, more hysterical one, and they ran out of the room.

And, after throwing up, Kiril finally went outside and told the staff that they needed to contact the police. Now.

CHAPTER 40

Livy checked the lighting while she waited for the bride and groom. Toni stood watching and drinking a can of Sprite. Leave it to Toni. The fanciest wedding either of them would ever be invited to, and Jean-Louis Parker breaks out the can of soda.

"Sooooo," Toni sang, "I got an excited text today from Michael, telling me how wonderful your show is going to be. He is so excited about the last batch of prints you gave him."

"Why is he talking to you about this and not me?"

"Because you frighten him."

"I don't know why."

"He said something about the way you stare at him."

"I stare at him like I stare at everyone."

"Yes. And you frighten many with that stare. I promised him he would only have to deal with me from now on."

Livy picked up her camera. "I have an agent."

"Not as an agent. More like a go-between once deals are done. But your agent thinks it's a good idea. He's sure this upcoming show is going to catapult you to the next level, but he's afraid your lack of social skills will destroy any goodwill your art creates."

Livy thought on that a moment. "He's probably right."

"The ceremony was beautiful, wasn't it?"

"Oh God," Livy sighed. "Are you going to insist on marrying that hillbilly now?"

"Why? So Ricky Lee's sister and Sissy Mae can argue with Kyle about how my wedding should look while Oriana tells me my ass is too fat for the dress I choose? I think the answer is no."

"Good. Because we both know I'd spend all my time with Coop tormenting you."

"I know."

"Oh, by the way . . . I went to the ATM this morning to grab fifty bucks out of my account. Just in case I needed the extra cash for anything. And I found some additional money there."

"How much additional?"

"Two-point-eight million dollars."

Livy turned just in time to avoid the spray of Sprite that came at her.

"What?"

"Keep your voice down."

"Why is there that much money in your account, Livy?"

"At first I thought it was Jake fucking around, but then I figured out it was from my mother."

"Your mother gave you money? *Your* mother?"

"I'm guessing it's from my father's life insurance policies."

"So? Your mother never gives you money. She expects you to steal it like everyone else in your family."

"That She-bear from BPC told me that someone had cleaned out Chumakov's bank accounts. Chances are that was my mother with the help of Jake. So it's easy for her to hand over the cash she got from the insurance, plus it's a really smart way for her to get Aunt Teddy off her back. I'm his only daughter, so the Kowalskis can't really complain that they didn't get a cut."

"What are you going to do with all that money?"

Livy shrugged. "I don't know. Maybe I'll just stick it in my savings and hope that the banks don't crash again."

"You know . . . you'd think you'd show a little enthusiasm now that you have so much cash."

"It's nice to know it's there, especially if I ever lose my health insurance. But with lots of money comes lots of problems."

"Are you going to tell Vic?"

"Not right away. Maybe in a few months."

"Why so long?"

Livy held up her new camera rig. "He paid a fortune for this to replace the old one that got damaged. So I'm not about to turn around now and tell him that I could have bought sixty of these if I'd felt the need and still had lots of money left over. The money's there if we need it, but I'm not going to make him feel he has to keep up with me when I did nothing to actually earn it."

"Insurance money is to help your family after you've gone."

"I told that old bastard I didn't need his goddamn money. And his exact words back were, 'Then you will get nothing, you little bitch!' "

"You and your father had an . . . interesting relationship."

"The word you're looking for is *dysfunctional*. We had a dysfunctional relationship."

"And you plan to keep it dysfunctional even after he's dead?"

"That has been my plan all along."

Vic smirked when he saw Novikov look at his watch . . . again.

It had never been part of Vic's plan to attend the weddings of Novikov and MacRyrie to the lovely Blayne and Gwen. Livy would be working, and he would have only come as her escort. But then Blayne had begged—literally, *begged*—for him and Shen to be Bo's groomsmen. Apparently half the hockey team was standing up for MacRyrie, but other than two foxes who received a stern lecture about what they could and couldn't do at the wedding from Novikov, followed by a printed-out, multi-page description of those things; and super-hockey-fan Lou Crushek, there was no one else to be his groomsmen. So Vic and Shen had agreed. Especially when Livy again reminded Vic about Novikov saving her life.

The service went well, though. Blayne cried, Gwen didn't. The bridesmaids were made up of derby girls, wild dogs, wolves, and felines. When the two couples were announced to be husbands and wives, the wild dogs howled . . . badly.

And there, during it all, had been Livy. Dressed in black slacks, black sweater, and comfortable but sleek-looking black boots, she'd moved around that ceremony barely noticed. He loved watching her work. Her focus was always so intense. But when she worked, she didn't stand for anyone annoying her. Especially wedding planners. She'd already threatened Cella Malone's mother to "back up off me, old woman."

Novikov glanced at his watch one more time before jumping to his feet and storming over to the door of the dressing room the brides were using. He banged on it, nearly taking it off the hinges. "You are late!" he yelled through the door.

"I will not be forced into a schedule by you!" Blayne shot back.

"Not forced! You *agreed* to this schedule! *Agreed!*"

"If you don't back away from that door, Bold Novikov, I'm going to mule-kick it!"

Shen leaned over and whispered, "You owe me fifty bucks. I told you he wouldn't last ten minutes."

"I'd feel bad for Blayne," Vic whispered back, "if I didn't know for a fact she knew *exactly* what she was getting into."

"You have five more minutes!" Novikov bellowed. "And then I'm comin' in!"

"And what?"

"And I'll bring your father with me!"

"You *bastard*!"

It took another twenty minutes for the ladies to finish changing into their reception dresses. Gwen just looked bored by it all, never smiling unless she was looking at MacRyrie. It was clear she was doing this for his family and his family alone; the MacRyries were a respectable family of grizzlies.

But Blayne . . . Blayne was in her element. As far as she was concerned, this was a big party and she wanted *everyone* to have a good time. All those bears, felines, and canines together should lead to lots of fights and snarling, but Blayne had already managed to keep all the factions tolerant enough. The music and liquor would also help, of course. And Vic was sure that Blayne and Mitch Shaw would be able to get a good number of people out on the dance floor.

Vic was there to give Novikov a reprieve now and again from the crowds and all the loud music. They'd go outside the majestic reception hall that had been rented and stand around, talking about Russia and the great steakhouses Vic knew about. They ended up making plans to take a group trip there. A vacation. Something Novikov had started doing more because of Blayne.

If they actually went, Vic hoped they could also stop in Poland so Livy could spend some time with her Kowalski kin.

Vic didn't know if any of that would be fun, but it would be worth a try.

Blayne suddenly skated through the dancing, partying crowd, pulling a reluctant Livy with her.

"I'm ordering you to take a break," Blayne said as she shoved Livy into Vic's lap. "You've been working for hours!"

"That's what you paid me to do, Blayne. To work. At your wedding."

"You've taken a ton of pictures. Just take a break."

"Malone's mother is gonna bitch about that."

"I'll deal with her. You just"—she wiggled a little—"relax with Vic." She giggled and skated away, having removed her fifteen-hundred-dollar shoes and replaced them with sparkly white quad skates.

"You know," Livy said, placing her camera on the table, "I think she actually believes she got us together."

"Let her believe it. What do we care?"

"I hate seeing her so happy. She just gets perkier."

"You could shift and attack her again."

Livy laughed. "I don't know what it is, dude, but my badger self just wants to *maul* her." She cleared her throat. "But this is her wedding day. I will not maul her on her wedding day."

"That is very big of you."

"It is, isn't it?"

She put her arms around his neck, relaxed her head on his shoulder. "I love my camera," she softly sang.

"I'm glad it's working for you."

"Me, too. Oh. By the way . . . Melly's back in jail."

"The boyfriend again?"

"No. His wife. There was a fistfight."

"There's a *wife*?"

"I never told you that?"

"No!"

"He's married. And Melly fucked her parole by hitting his wife in the face. A few times. She'll be going in for another six months, probably."

"Maybe you guys should consider getting her some help."

Livy lifted her head, looked him in the eyes. "Help for what?"

Vic shook his head. "Nothing."

"By the way, my mother says you're a bad influence on me."

"Me? What did I do?"

"Nothing. But because I didn't track down Chumakov and rip his balls off when he was in town to pick up Melly's painting, she thinks I've gone soft."

Livy suddenly snapped her head around to glower at the tigress standing a few feet away, impatiently tapping one foot and glaring at Livy. *"I'm on break!"* Livy bellowed.

"For as much as we're paying you, skank, you could at least get off your ass and do your goddamn job!"

"*You* aren't paying me shit. And if you come at me one more time, *I'm going to rip the eyes out of your fucking head!"*

Blayne suddenly skated up to Cella's wedding planning mother and took her arm. "Come on, Barb!"

"But, Blayne, she's taking advantage of you!"

"There's a problem with the chocolate room! And you know what will happen if the wild dogs don't get their chocolate! I need you!"

"Fine!" She pointed a finger at Livy. "You've got ten minutes, and then you better get out there and do your goddamn job!"

Livy gave the older woman two middle fingers and added, "Eat me!"

After Blayne and the wedding planner moved away, Livy focused on Vic again and calmly asked, "What was I talking about?"

"How you're going soft."

"Right. So I just thought I should warn you that you have my mother very concerned."

"Should I say something to her?"

"No. I like that she's tormented. Let her marinate in that for a while. Maybe until her *death*."

"Okay, then. Although, you know going soft is a risk when you fall in love."

"Really? I've always thought of love as rage-inducing."

Vic laughed, kissed Livy's forehead. "Of course you do."

"It's a good thing, though, you're very calm."

"It is?"

"Sure. It would be bad if both of us were easily angered."

"Especially because you'd take me in a fight."

"Exactly. And then you'd feel nothing but shame."

Vic wrapped his arms around Livy, held her tight. "For you, Livy . . . I'd endure the shame."

"That's good," she said, nuzzling his jaw. "Because we both know my family will always be there to induce it."

"Aw, Livy . . . so will mine. But we'll be able to suffer the shame together."

"Always you with the romance, Barinov," she joked. "Always you with the romance."

Read on for a preview of Shelly Laurenston's newest Call of Crows novel, *The Unyielding*, available next April!

PROLOGUE

"Up. Now."

Harvold immediately woke at his mother's words. She already held the baby. His sister who could barely walk. And she roused his younger brother with the same words.

She led him and his brother to the secret exit at the back of the house. It was there in case of raids. But it was the middle of winter. Who would raid now?

"Go," she ordered, pushing his sister into his arms. "Go and don't look back."

"But—"

"Do not ask questions!" It was her biggest complaint about him. He asked too many questions. He needed to know "too much."

But he was nearly thirteen years. He was almost a man. It was time he received answers.

"Just go." She suddenly hugged him, tight, his sister trapped between them.

It was a fierce, terrified hug. Then she hugged his brother the same.

"Go, Harvold. Protect your brother and sister. And *don't* look back."

The latch was unhitched and he and his brother snuck out

of the house and ran through the forest and up the hill, their sister in his arms.

But Harvold stopped. He would look back. He always did.

"Harvold!" his brother whispered.

Harvold ignored the desperate plea and instead found a place for his siblings to safely hide. A large boulder would do the trick and he planted them there.

The hiding place was perfect. Big enough to keep them out of sight, but located so that he had a perfect view of the village.

After handing their sister to his younger brother, Harvold eased around the boulder and looked down on the village that had been the home of him, his father, his father's father, and back and back for generations.

Those he'd known all his life were forced into the center of the village square, their elder men and warriors shoved to the ground by men he'd never seen before. Large men. Harvold had never seen men such a size before. The women and children were kept from leaving, the entire village encircled by these large, terrifying men.

One of those terrifying men stepped forward, glaring down at Eindride the Patient. He had long hair and a big beard so that all Harvold could see, even from this safe distance, was those fierce eyes.

"Tell me," the large man growled, his words, although low, carried on the crisp winter wind so that it was like Harvold stood next to them. "Where is it?"

"I told you before . . . we don't know what you're talking about!"

The big man crouched in front of Eindride, one arm resting on his knee. "Do you know who I am?" he asked.

Eindride glared up at the man, because even crouching, he still towered. "You are Holfi Rundstöm."

Harvold's brother gasped at the name and Harvold quickly covered the boy's mouth with his hand.

Even though his brother was only nine, he'd heard of the Rundstöms. All of them had. Their reputation went back for generations and they were feared for good reason.

"Yes," Rundstöm replied. "I am Holfi Rundstöm." Then the big man stood, lifted his blade and brought it down at a brutal angle. Not on Eindride, but across the neck of his oldest daughter.

Poor Eindride cried out in rage. He had seven daughters and he adored them all.

Rundstöm must have known this. Harvold guessed it was no accident he'd killed Eindride's eldest.

Then Rundstöm grabbed the next eldest of Eindride's girls and pressed his blood-covered blade against her throat.

"I will ask one more time, old man," Rundstöm growled. "Tell me where—owwwww!"

The hammer seemed to come out of nowhere, ramming into Rundstöm's giant head and forcing him to release Eindride's daughter and stumble back several feet.

Yet it shocked Harvold that Rundstöm didn't fall to the ground dead. Because that was not a normal warhammer, it's head a thousand times bigger than anything Harvold had seen before from any blacksmith. Who had that much iron to work with and put into a single weapon?

Rundstöm's men, who appeared unarmed, grabbed nearby weapons from the blacksmith's stall and from anything available. Like a chopping axe.

"You dare come here, Holfi Rundstöm?" a bare-chested man demanded as he walked from the woods. He wore fur pants and boots but no shirt. The image of the large hammer he wielded branded on his chest, a gold torc around his thick neck. "This town is under my god's protection."

"Fuck your god," Rundstöm growled back. "Fuck you."

Another hammer was tossed to the leader and he swung it a few times as he walked. The head on the weapon was so large, Harvold had no idea how he managed not beating himself in the face with it.

As those with hammers approached, Rundstöm and his men jerked their shoulders back, big black wings exploding from their flesh. Like the wings of Odin's ravens Huginn and Muninn, except much larger.

"It's true," Harvold couldn't help but whisper over the panicked screams of his neighbors. "It's all true."

"What is?" his brother asked. "What's happening?"

Harvold motioned to his brother to stay in place, while he continued to watch.

He'd heard the old women of his village talking about this, but few had believed them. The stories of warriors chosen by one god to represent him or her in this world. To do their bidding. His parents worshipped any god they needed at any time, but these men, they only had one god they listened to, whose orders they followed, whose power they worshipped.

Those with the hammers must belong to Thor. And the men with the wings . . . their god had to be Odin.

Harvold felt his very bones grow cold. Odin. So feared, his parents rarely called on him for anything except during a time of war. And something told Harvold that the men Odin chose to wear his wings would be no better. Reason and talk would mean nothing to those who worshipped at the blood-soaked feet of Odin.

"Hold your weapons, ridiculous men," a woman called out. She wore long robes, a hood covering her face. There were others with her, all women based on the way they moved. They came from the east. They had no weapons of their own from what he could see, but they also showed no fear, striding toward the male warriors.

"Holde's Maids," the hammer wielder snarled. "What are you heinous bitches doing here?"

"Hold your tongue, Slayer, or I'll tear it from your mouth with my teeth."

"He's right, Alvilda," Rundstöm cut in. "Why *are* you here?"

The hooded woman stopped and stared beyond the men, toward the lake of the village. "Perhaps that is a question we should all ask," she said, waving her hand toward the water.

From the cold depths of the lake they appeared, naked and beautiful. Men and women, swords at the ready.

A woman led them, her hair in thick braids down her back. She gazed at the different groups, wide blue eyes slowly blinking. Even though she was naked and soaking wet, snow under her feet, she didn't seem the least bit cold.

"What's going on?" the naked woman asked.

The two male leaders began to speak but the hooded woman cut them off with a quick swipe of both her arms. "Why are you here, Eerika?" she asked.

"We heard you and the Ravens were planning an attack on our god's temple, not too far from here."

"Why would we ever bother attacking your god's fish-covered temple?"

From the north, bursting off the nearby mountain, came another group. This one all women. They cut through the snow easily by using long sticks attached to their feet and pushing with long poles held in their hands.

They each jumped from the high mountain ledge, some of them easily flipping in mid-air, before landing near the growing groups.

And from the northern woods charged a pack of white wolves. They growled and snarled and bit at each other until they stopped near the groups and turned from animal to human. Easily, with no more than a thought.

The six groups stared at each other for several long moments.

"I don't understand," Holfi Rundstöm said to them. "Why are we all here? At the same time?"

"We've been lured here, idiot," the Holde's Maid snapped from behind her hood.

"By who?"

"The Silent aren't here," another of the winged warriors suggested.

Holfi sneered. "They wouldn't dare."

"And Loki's Wolves aren't part of the Nine," one of the Maid's said.

"But we should be," a man who'd been a wolf laughingly suggested.

"But you *aren't*."

The leader of the Maid's raised her hands to silence everyone and practically yelled, "Then *why* are we here?"

Harvold was wondering the same thing when another woman—a very *different* woman—silently landed on the boulder he and his siblings hid behind.

He looked up at her, knowing instantly she had not been born in these lands. Her skin was brown, as if she'd been in the sun for a thousand years, her eyes almost black. She still had the brand of her master on her arm. Harvold remembered her. She'd been hung from a tree by her master for trying to escape. She'd been a slave. She still had the scars from where her master had beaten her before. He'd left her still-bleeding corpse hanging from the tree near his hall when it had suddenly disappeared.

Most of the adults assumed a necromancer had taken her for his dark works. But if a necromancer had brought her back, he'd have brought back a corpse that would have continued to rot for however long it roamed the land.

But the corpse that now stood over him and his siblings . . . she was young, healthy, and well-armed.

She was *alive*.

She glanced down at Harvold, studying him closer. She was sizing him up, seeing if he was a threat to her.

Much to Harvold's relief, she finally raised her finger and pressed it to her lips. "Shhhh."

Harvold shrunk back and nodded.

Smiling, she raised her bow, nocked an arrow, and aimed. After a few seconds, she let the arrow fly. It struck Rundstöm through the neck, the bigger man looking shocked before he fell to the ground.

More arrows flew from the trees and mountains surrounding Harvold's village, tearing into warrior and villager alike. Once that stopped, the woman on the boulder dropped her head back and unleashed a war cry that tore across the land.

"*Crows!*" one of the gods' warriors screamed out in warning and the slave women seemed to appear from everywhere. Women who had not been born of these lands, some still wearing the brands of their masters on their arms or faces, bursting from trees, leaping from the mountain ledges, or just dropping down into the middle of the village.

Women with large black wings and a rune branded on their upper backs.

Harvold recognized that rune. It represented Skuld; one of the fates his grandmother had been talking about lately.

"Treat your slaves well, my young Harvold," his grandmother would often say, "for if they die poorly at your hand, Skuld may send them back to tear you apart."

He thought she spoke of something rising from the grave. Something decayed and desolate, to reap revenge before being swallowed back into the hole it had sprung from.

But he'd been wrong.

These thriving, angry foreign women attacked without hesitation. Some lashing out with long, thin blades, impaling necks, inside thighs, and spines. Others wielded swords and shields, using crushing blows to decapitate, dismember. Battling anyone who would take their challenge.

Many of the villagers were struck down as they tried to escape, unable to avoid the battle that had exploded around them.

It was a brutal thing, no one spared. Until all that remained were the winged women, and even they had suffered heavy casualties. But those who still breathed had no pity. They walked among the bodies, killing those—whether gods' warriors or innocent villager—they felt might still survive by slashing throats with their thin weapons.

One large, very brown winged woman, grabbed one of Odin's warriors by the back of his throat, lifting him so he sat up a bit. He'd lost one of his wings and a leg during the battle, but still he breathed.

"Why?" he asked the woman. "Why have you done this?"

"Did you think the Crows would ever forget what you and the others did? That you killed our sisters? You cut them down while they slept. All of you attacking at once."

"That was—"

"Ten winters ago. Yes. And we did not forget, Raven." She leaned in. "We *never* forget."

She rammed her thin, but strong edged weapon into the warrior's eye, forcing it in deep, and yelling over his screams, "*And now you can be like your god!*"

When the warrior's screams died off, the slave women raised their blood-covered weapons and roared in triumph.

Harvold didn't realize he was crying until he was forced to wipe his face. The entire village gone . . . even his parents.

His brother was resting on the boulder with him, also watching. Also crying. Harvold didn't make him look away. No point in protecting him anymore. But then Harvold remembered their sister.

"Where is she?" he asked, looking at where she should have been, but wasn't.

The brothers scrambled from the rock and turned, both halting in surprise.

Men stood behind them. Men with wings. Not the black wings of Odin's warriors but large white wings.

They gazed down at Harvold's sister as she reached up to them with her fat arms.

"No!" his brother snapped, Harvold covering the boy's mouth with his hand to silence him.

As one, the men looked at them. They had large eyes that didn't move. Instead, just their heads moved and they blinked at Harvold.

Harvold pushed his brother forward, and he scrambled to pick their sister up. He returned quick to Harvold's side, their sister tight in his arms.

After another minute of staring, the men walked around them in two lines before taking to the skies and launching an attack on the remaining slave women.

"*Protectors!*" one of the slave women screamed. "*Prepare yourselves, sisters!*"

Harvold decided not to watch that. He'd seen more than enough this day.

Pushing his brother ahead of him, their sister still in his arms, they headed toward their grandmother's hut hidden deep in the woods where they would hopefully be safe.

As they walked, his brother finally asked, "Why do you think they killed each other like that, Harvold? Why are they still killing?"

Harvold shrugged his shoulders and replied, "Guess they didn't get on . . ."